Christmas Revels II

FOUR REGENCY NOVELLAS

Kate Parker

Louisa Cornell

Anna D. Allen

Hannah Meredith

SSP

Singing Spring Press

CHRISTMAS REVELS II : FOUR REGENCY NOVELLAS

ISBN: 978-1-942470-00-7 (Print)
ISBN: 978-1-942470-01-4 (E-book)

Published by Singing Spring Press

Table of Contents

The Vicar's Christmas

by

Anna D. Allen

The Vicar's Christmas

SIR WILLIAM TRENT DIED on a rainy Thursday afternoon at the advanced age of seventy-two. His had been a protracted, declining illness that gradually took away the soundness of his mind. Margaret, his eldest daughter, tended his bedside in dignified sorrow, as did his physician—likewise in dignified sorrow—as Sir William had been a great patron of his therapeutic but ineffective services.

And as with so many other gentlemen, Sir William's holdings went to his closest male relative, in this case a cousin's grandson, believed to be named George. Or maybe it was Frederick. *Perhaps Edward?* Whatever the moniker, his parents had christened him after some Hanoverian prince, and neither Margaret nor her father could remember the name of the boy—a boy now grown with his own children, but, in the mind of Margaret, forever a child in need of having his nose wiped or his posterior cleaned.

The funeral occurred the following afternoon. It should have continued to rain, but the weather, never one to accommodate mere mortals, shone bright and sunny, albeit exceptionally cold and frosty for a

November day. Margaret was the chief mourner. In fact, she was the only mourner. The villagers of Edgecombe, while paying their sincerest respects—after all, they had liked the old gentleman—could not properly be called mourners as *he was not a local* and his family had come to the village *only* twenty years earlier. *Hardly enough time to get to know him at all.* Lord and Lady Latham politely declined to attend, as—they felt—they would take precedence over the chief mourner if their noble presence graced the occasion, and that just would not do.

Nor did Sir William's other daughter, Jane—the younger of his two surviving offspring—attend her father's final rites as her husband deemed the distance to the neighboring county much too far to travel on such short notice, especially since the hunting at his box in Berkshire was so much more... *more* than the hunting at Edgecombe Hall in Wiltshire. Besides, they would be returning home to London any day now. His lady wife, in keeping with her perpetual habit, conceded to her husband's better judgment, despite her grief, and conveyed her regrets by post.

Of course, the Reverend Mr. Henry Ogden, the vicar of St. Winifred's, officiated. Had he not presided, one could have called him a mourner. Over the past five years since arriving in the village, he and the deceased had become friends, despite their age difference. Reverend Ogden viewed the gentleman as a colleague, owing to his vast library, skills at chess, and exceptional—but slowly dwindling—mind.

And so, Sir William Trent departed this life, in sure and certain hope of resurrection to eternal life, while leaving mere mortals to deal with the more mundane matters he left behind.

More than a fortnight later, on yet another frosty morning, Reverend Henry Ogden sat in his study, surrounded by his books, his papers, his writings, his research, and only God knew what else. It was very much the abode of a bachelor. A good fire blazed on the hearth, and all Henry needed was a hot cup of tea to be happy as he sorted through the morning post.

Unfortunately, the letters included a response from the Prince Regent's librarian, a Mr. Clarke, denying Henry's request to visit Buckingham House in order to view His Majesty's drawings by Holbein in the Royal Library. Instead, much to Henry's frustration, Mr. Clarke referred him to the most recent edition of Chamberlaine's fully-illustrated monograph on the subject—a much-studied copy currently lay on the floor by Henry's fireside chair. But the engravings rendered by modern artists failed to match the genuine article. Though beautiful, the flawless engravings lacked all the imperfections that made a work unique and lovely.

Henry considered writing a letter of thanks by way of reply to the librarian in the hope that one day in the near future, the librarian might reconsider the request. *But no.* He decided some other route of access could yield better results—surely one of his cousins knew someone who knew someone who could arrange it.

The morning would be better suited to preparing this week's sermon. Perhaps his congregation needed reminding of the Tenth Commandment—"Thou shalt not covet Thy Majesty's 16th Century silverpoint drawings by German artists, even when Thy Majesty is mad and locked away in Windsor." Henry suspected it sounded better in the original Hebrew. And really, Henry didn't covet the works. He merely wanted to get a good look at them. For several hours. Perhaps followed by a cup of tea. And an invitation to come again at his leisure.

A violent tapping at his window startled the vicar out of his thoughts. On the opposite side of the glass stood a grinning Jack Carden, the stable boy from Edgecombe Hall, all rosy cheeked with ringlets and the vapor of his breath creating a very false cherub-like appearance. He waved a note clutched firmly between the hand and thumb of his mitten. Had it been summer, Henry would have just opened the window and taken the note—no doubt with Jack crawling through in the process to land in a jumble on the carpet. But with these cold days settling in and thoughts of summer far away, Henry was not about to open the window. He probably should not have even drawn the curtains but he couldn't resist the sun pouring into the dark room.

"Go around," Henry said and motioned the boy toward the back of the house. Holbein, Mr. Clarke, His Majesty the mad king, and even God would all have to wait for the more pressing matters of village life.

Henry met the boy inside the hall by the back door and took the note.

"You should hear Miss Trent!" Jack exclaimed with much too much eagerness. "If she weren't a lady, she'd be swearing like a groomsman."

"Ah. None of that, now," Henry calmly scolded, then

pointed toward the kitchen. "Have Mrs. Brown give you something hot to warm yourself. There may be a reply." Between the boy and Henry's housekeeper, the vicar knew the whole village would know of the goings on at Edgecombe Hall within the hour.

As Jack scampered off to the kitchen—Mrs. Brown shouting for the boy to walk and refrain from behaving like a little heathen—Henry broke the seal on the note.

It was a summons from Miss Margaret Trent. Or more precisely, from Mr. Jonah Henderson, the late Sir William's London solicitor's junior partner who had called on Miss Trent that morning. He reported the lady was quite hysterical—how Henry hated that word, especially as he doubted Miss Trent had ever been anywhere near exhibiting such symptoms in her entire life—and that she needed Reverend Ogden to come immediately to offer comfort and consolation in her time of bereavement.

A solicitor, especially one up from London, never boded well. And this note reeked of mendacity. While anyone and everyone in the village could more than happily lecture on what exactly Miss Trent *needed*, comfort and consolation in her time of bereavement were definitely *not* among them. If anything, the gossips said she demonstrated an unusual lack of emotion upon her father's death. Never one to put store by gossips, Henry knew Miss Trent to be dignified, proud even, and that she would never allow for a public display of her feelings to all and sundry. Tears were a private matter reserved for intimates.

Margaret Trent, in Henry's view, was probably the

most self-reliant of all his parishioners and therein—he suspected—lay the reason for her continued spinsterhood. She managed quite well on her own, and whatever the situation unfolding today at the hall, Henry sincerely doubted Miss Trent *needed* him for anything.

He took out his pocket watch and clicked it open. Quarter to eleven. *Blast and blazes!* He would have to do without his eleven o'clock tea. Worse—well, maybe not worse—the farrier had told him not to ride his horse until after Christmas due to a recent bout of lameness. Walking from the vicarage to the church was easy enough, but all the way to Edgecombe Hall, a distance of at least two miles, in this cold, would be miserable. *Still. Needs must.* If Jack could manage it as cheerfully as he did, so too could Henry. And the lad could keep him company on the way.

Henry informed Mrs. Brown that he had been called to Edgecombe Hall about a matter and did not know when he would return home. He checked himself in the mirror; despite his dark, spiky hair and the ever-growing number of faint lines around his eyes, he would do. He bundled up against the cold, wrapped a muffler around his head, pulled on his gloves and hat, and, seeing Jack was finished with *his* cup of tea and biscuit, headed out into the gray frosty world with the boy tagging along beside him.

Within no time, Henry found it difficult to keep up with Jack. And he realized why the boy seemed impervious to the cold. He ran, he skipped, he jumped, he trotted, he prattled on down the road, full of energy and exhausting to behold. Henry half-expected him to start doing cartwheels and somersaults. And somewhere in the midst of it all, Henry managed to learn nothing further about Miss Trent's supposed summons, except that the entire household was in a *tizzy*—Jack's word—over the arrival of the gentlemen—*two* gentlemen—from London this morning to see the mistress.

Henry also realized very quickly that he had dressed inappropriately for the weather. The brilliant sun and stunning blue sky belied the reality of the embracing icy grip Henry found himself struggling against. Despite the lack of wind, the cold stung his face, like a frozen fire burning his bare flesh. Frigid pain gnawed his fingers within his gloves, and he tucked his fists under his arms in a vain attempt to keep them warm. His toes fell asleep—he supposed that was numbness—and he tried to move them, wiggling them around in his shoes, only he couldn't feel if the toes actually moved.

By the time Henry reached the hall and Jack had run off to the kitchen via the servants' entrance, the vicar was half frozen and breathing hard. He simply wanted to thaw out before a fire and then slip off to bed with a warming pan, even though it was not yet midday. Never had he ever experienced such a raw winter.

To his great relief, the door opened and he found himself inside, the butler, Mr. Harvey, and the footman assisting him with his overcoat.

"Where on earth is your horse?" *That* was Miss Trent, dressed in black but draped in a great, indigo Indian shawl. "Don't tell me you walked here. In this weather. Surely not!" He had failed to see her arrival in the entry hall, but she was there, unwrapping his muffler and freeing him from his gloves. Only, once finished with the task, she grasped one hand and then the other, rubbing each vigorously in turn, her pale chiseled features just inches from his frosted face. Her blue eyes focused on her task, while his focused on the great mounds of dark hair, flecked with rare strands of silver, piled atop her head in a becoming but unfashionable style.

As a vicar, Henry was accustomed to unexpected behavior when entering a home, especially one where death lingered. From tearful embraces to angry dismissals, he had experienced many varying receptions. So he would not have been surprised by the bereaved clutching his arm or grabbing his hand. However, the fact that Miss Trent did the grabbing and clutching today surprised Henry to no end. Only then did he realize he shivered uncontrollably.

Clasping his hand, Miss Trent led him to the library, Sir William's library, still strewn with the late gentleman's papers and piles of books. It looked much like Henry's own study, albeit with a vastly greater number of books, perhaps ten times as many, arranged haphazardly on shelves. She led him past the library table overflowing with stacks of books, around the settee loaded with an equal number of books, and finally to the fireside chair, book free.

There, in the blessed warmth before the fire, Henry stood, shivering and holding his hands before the flames as he waited for Miss Trent to take the seat opposite him. Only, she did not take it. Instead, she turned him to face her and began unbuttoning his jacket.

"Miss Trent!"

With a fierce glance at him—they were nearly the same height and met almost eye to eye—she said, "Your fingers are too cold to do it," and continued working the buttons. Once she finished that, he reluctantly allowed her to tug his jacket off, leaving him standing there in his shirtsleeves, much to his discomfort. Really, it was most inappropriate, especially before a lady.

She carefully laid the jacket over the arm of the settee and gathered up a blanket there. She wrapped it around the vicar's shoulders, motioned to the waiting chair, and then busied herself in the corner of the room. Henry heard glass clinking against glass, and she soon handed him a brandy.

"It'll thin the blood and keep it flowing and warm your toes while it's at it," she said all in one breath. Arms akimbo—and appearing very tired, Henry noted—she looked him over, exhaled deeply as if frustrated, and sat down on the nearby footstool. At last, Henry sat down. No sooner did his bottom touch the seat cushion than she was up again. Henry endeavored to rise as well, only to be met with a stern "Stay!" from Miss Trent. It was the sort of command one did not ignore, and despite his uneasiness over the idea of sitting before a standing lady, Henry obeyed the mistress of Edgecombe Hall.

But his anxiety quickly worsened. Miss Trent reached over to the opposite chair and picked up the lap rug lying there in her father's chair. She shook it out and then spread it over him. She knelt to tuck it about him before sitting back down on the footstool.

She cocked her head to one side and asked, "Where

is your horse?" as if he were a child who had mislaid his shoes near a mud puddle while playing outside on a glorious summer day.

"He's gone lame."

"Then you should have sent Jack for the carriage."

"You worry about me, but not the boy?"

"We can barely keep him inside as it is, and if he got into trouble, it would be from eating too many sweets at Mr. Forbes's shop, whereas you...," Henry half expected her to shake her forefinger at him, "...spend all the winter indoors beside the fire with your books about you." He had to admit, she was right about that, and he wondered how she had gained such insight into his private life.

At that moment, Mr. Harvey, the footman, and Sir William's very burly valet, James, entered the library. Between them they carried a large porcelain basin and two cans of water. Henry's discomfort now turned to mortification as he realized what they were about. Miss Trent moved out of the way, and as expected, they set the basin at his feet.

"No, no," he assured them, "this is quite unnecessary."

"You have no say in the matter," Miss Trent countered as the footman poured steaming water into the basin. James the valet added additional water from his can—presumably filled with cold water. They set their cans down, and Henry feared Miss Trent would take over now. But to his relief, James the valet took over, removed Henry's shoes and stockings, and the vicar placed his now bare feet in the basin of hot water, to the agony of his toes, which seemed to scream in protest over being defrosted as sensation returned to them and they remembered their pain.

The servants left, leaving the library door appropriately opened, and finally, Miss Trent took up her position in the chair opposite his own. She gave him a look, not unkind but quite serious, and calmly said, "If you ever come again on foot in such weather, you will suffer the same indignities all over again."

He felt duly chastened. Despite his embarrassment over everything, he knew she was right. He should have taken more care.

"Understood, Miss Trent." What a sight he must be, he thought, sitting there, his feet soaking in a basin of water, blankets tucked about him, as if he were already in his dotage. A grim vision of his future passed before his mind's eye—the shivering old man hunched over before a fire. Next, he'd probably call for his pipe and then call for his bowl. What he really wanted was a cup of tea, but instead, he took a sip of the brandy. It burned all the way down to his stomach and gave no satisfaction.

"So," Henry asked, "you sent for me?"

Miss Trent's face transformed from confident mistress of the house to an expression of pain and confusion, with her brow creasing in consternation. She lowered her eyes and turned her face away from him toward the fire. When she looked at him again, she attempted a weak smile.

"As a wiser soul admitted," she said, "I know little Latin and less Greek." Henry recognized the quote from Shakespeare. She took a deep breath. "You have always been honest in your dealings with me. My father trusted you and respected your opinions."

"How may I be of service to you, Miss Trent?" He spoke calmly, trying to assure her simply with the tone of his voice.

"I need an advocate... or in the very least, someone who can confirm whether or not what they tell me is true. Because I don't understand any of it."

"'They?' You mean Mr. Jonah Henderson and...?"

"Mr. Martin Wells." She ground out the name, her previous commanding disposition instantly returning. "My brother-in-law's solicitor."

"They're here now?"

"Heaven help me! They are in the drawing room, and if I survive the day without throttling one of them, it will be a miracle worthy of the Apostles."

Henry knew she was not serious, but whatever the news they brought her could not be so bad as to warrant such a reaction. Miss Trent did have a reputation for being difficult—although he had never found her so— and perhaps that explained the current situation.

"You will see soon enough," she continued. Realization suddenly covered her face, and she stood. "Oh, I'm so sorry. I forgot." She reached for the bell. "I'll have Mrs. Jenkins bring you...."

At that moment, before Miss Trent's hand touched the bell pull, two immaculately dressed gentlemen appeared in the doorway and entered the library without invitation.

"At last," the taller of the two said with an exasperated sigh when he spotted the vicar.

Henry attempted to rise, but Miss Trent held out her

hand to stop him and said, "They do not deserve the courtesy."

"I beg your pardon!" the short, round solicitor exclaimed, bristling with indignation, while the taller one stood with his mouth wide open.

The vicar spoke in a calmer voice. "Miss Trent. Please."

"Very well then." She turned to Henry and did not hide her disdain as she said, "Reverend Ogden, I present to you Mr. Jonah Henderson, junior partner to my father's solicitor, and Mr. Martin Wells, solicitor to my *illustrious* brother-in-law."

"I must protest!" the short, round one—Mr. Martin Wells—said. "I resent you speaking of my client in such a tone. And Mr. Henderson and I take precedence over a clergyman."

"With all due respect," Miss Trent said with a tilt of her head, the smile blatantly false, "the grandson of an earl, the nephew of an earl, the grand-nephew of a duchess, the cousin of a viscount and several viscountesses, as well as the godson of the Bishop of Rochester takes precedence over two mere *gentlemen*."

Henderson and Wells now looked at Henry with more regard than before, especially given the vicar's present state of undress, and seemed notably impressed. His paternal relations *were* remarkable, Henry had to admit. However, his mother was the daughter of a shopkeeper. But what surprised Henry so much was the fact that Miss Trent clearly knew his familial background. He could not recall ever discussing it with her or even with her father. He didn't know whether to be frightened or amazed by her, this Valkyrie standing before him. And like any warrior under attack, she did not back down but stood her ground.

"Tell Reverend Ogden what you told me," she ordered the two men and folded her arms over her chest. Henry half wished they might defy her; if his treatment by her that morning gave any indication of her wherewithal, she'd probably grab their ears and drag them from the house like naughty schoolboys.

Mr. Henderson, the tall one, junior partner *et al.*, cleared his throat and said, "Trent Abbey and all of Sir William's land there and the revenues earned from that land is, of course, entailed and goes to his heir, Augustus Trent."

"Ah, that's it. After the Duke of Cumberland." Miss Trent turned to Henry. "We knew it was after some Hanoverian prince. Just couldn't remember which one." She scrunched up her nose and shook her head. "Disgraceful, if you ask me."

How could she be so glib? "Does this mean you're left with nothing, Miss Trent?" Henry asked, fearing what would become of her.

"Oh no," Mr. Wells assured him, "quite the opposite."

"So you claim," Miss Trent said.

"You and your sister...," Mr. Wells began.

"Mrs. Knowles," Mr. Henderson provided.

"...are well provided for," Mr. Wells continued. "Three thousand a year for you and two thousand a year for Mrs. Knowles."

The figures impressed Henry, and he smiled. "Oh, that is quite nice, Miss Trent. You will want for nothing."

"Wait," she calmly said, "there's much more." She waved her hand at the two solicitors and said, "Pray, continue." It was only then that Henry realized the gentlemen spoke without notes or even a copy of the will. And why, he wondered, did Mr. Wells relate this, when he represented Mr. Knowles, not the late Sir William.

"Edgecombe Hall, of course," Mr. Wells said, "was Lady Trent's property, which your father had for his lifetime along with any income. With his passing, the estate is now jointly the property of Miss Trent and Mrs. Knowles."

This revelation left Henry speechless. Despite Sir William's estate being entailed, Miss Trent was an heiress, a lady not only financially secure but with landed property—extensive lands. This great house now belonged to her, along with the land and the monies earned from it—albeit shared with her sister. He could not understand how she could be so upset over the matter. True, she gained her fortune at the loss of her father, but she should at least be satisfied her parents had provided for her so extremely well. Perhaps some truth lay behind the rumors about Miss Trent, that she was an ungrateful, difficult, peevish, termagant who could frighten a harpy into Hades.

"Miss Trent," he said at last, his voice full of astonishment, "you are an heiress. A wealthy lady. More than amply provided for by your parents."

"Yes." She smiled again, but Henry could tell it was forced. "It does *sound* that way, doesn't it? But for some reason I can't quite fathom, that is simply *not* the case."

Henry glanced from her to the gentlemen—both of

whom suddenly reminded him of cornered rabbits—and he asked, "How so?"

"Gentlemen, please explain to Reverend Ogden what you are forcing me to do."

"Miss Trent," Mr. Wells said with an adamant shake of his head, "no one is forcing you to do anything."

"No? Then why am I being driven from my home?"

"I beg your pardon?" Henry asked. Surely he misheard her.

"Ah," she said, this time with traces of a genuine smile, "you begin to see the problem."

She is too fond of her own way. Lady Latham had said as much about Margaret once at an assembly. Not in Margaret's presence, of course, but Margaret heard the words clear enough from across the room during a pause in the music. She always remembered those words, and now she saw these men, in her home, and she knew they thought much the same, even Reverend Ogden, although she knew him to be too considerate to actually ever say such a thing. He simply had that look about him, that questioning look of *how could she not be pleased with such an inheritance?* Because she was difficult, a virago, a harridan, an old maid with too much time to think and in need of a man to set her straight. *That* was what they all thought. She was that most unacceptable of creatures: a female who spoke her mind.

The knowledge that she would never want for anything—anything material that is; she would always want for her family—was a comfort and a relief. Of course, she had always known Edgecombe Hall would pass to her and Jane. She had also always known she would have an income as well, her share larger than her sister's since their father had settled a portion on Jane at the time of her marriage to Frederick Knowles. But to have it all confirmed had been a relief.

Only, these two glorified clerks had appeared on her doorstep that morning, and now nothing was truly settled. It was all wrong. And she couldn't understand how this could happen. To lose her home after everything they'd been through.

"You must be mistaken, Miss Trent," the vicar said, "No one can drive you from Edgecombe Hall. It's yours by law."

Poor Reverend Ogden. She had undoubtedly humiliated him this morning, and he would probably never forgive her. But he had jeopardized his own wellbeing by coming here on foot in such dangerous weather. Jack could run off to the village and back without the least bit of concern for the frigid temperatures. The boy was used to it and had sense enough to know when to come in. But Reverend Ogden was a man of books and learning, made for sitting indoors, not for enduring such harsh conditions, as his buckled shoes, knee breeches, and plain overcoat confirmed. No, he was not a man who could easily deal with physical discomfort.

However, with all his learning and high education, he might find a way out of this mess for her.

Mr. Wells, as usual, spoke for the two solicitors. "Miss Trent is only partially correct, Reverend Ogden. She owns only half of the property. The other half belongs to her sister, Mrs. Knowles." Margaret found it so interesting that Mr. Wells, solicitor for Mr. Knowles, did all the explaining; it told her exactly who pulled the strings in this calamity.

"Be that as it may," Reverend Ogden said, "It doesn't require Miss Trent leave her home. It simply means the earnings from the estate will be divided between the sisters."

Margaret sat down opposite the vicar, pulled her shawl tight about her, and couldn't help but smile. *Yes*, his understanding of the situation matched her own.

"See," she said, "just as I told you, gentlemen." There was so much more to come, she knew, but whatever else they might say about her, they could not say she was irrational. Even the learned vicar educated at Oxford concluded as she did. All the rest of it had to be some nefarious scheme concocted by the two solicitors and Mr. Knowles.

"No, you don't understand." Mr. Wells said.

"What's to understand?" Margaret asked, knowing full well what came next. They had been telling her all morning, as if she were a simpleton.

"Miss Trent." Mr. Wells used a tone normally reserved for small children. "As we've tried to explain, the house and all its contents are to be sold."

A horrified look passed over the vicar's face.

"That's outrageous!" he said.

"Oh, good," Margaret said, "I'm not the only one who thinks so. It's bad enough the house is to be sold, but all the contents as well? It's unreasonable."

"But Miss Trent." Mr. Henderson spoke for a change,

finally finding his voice; unfortunately, he sang the same tune as Mr. Wells. "You won't have any place to put the contents once the house is sold."

Margaret felt the blood in her veins turn to ice and pierce her stomach. "I beg your pardon?"

"It's just that," Mr. Henderson continued, "a lady, such as yourself...." *What exactly did he mean by that?* "You won't need all these furnishings and trappings. You'll live quietly, modestly, in a small abode, with no need for entertaining. All of this..." He waved his hand about the room. "...will be a burden to you."

Ice turned to fire. Margaret felt the anger boiling up inside her, and just as it prepared to spew forth, another angry voice lashed out, calm and contained, but with a dangerous, controlled edge.

"How dare you decide what Miss Trent needs or doesn't need." Reverend Ogden rose from his chair, one bare foot still in the basin, the other dripping on the Aubusson carpet. There he stood in his shirt sleeves, barelegged from the knees down—Margaret suddenly wished she had been less concerned about his wellbeing and had left him properly dressed so he didn't look quite so ridiculous right now. But, *oh*, what a relief she felt. For once, she was not the one who had to shout and raise a fuss about a matter.

He didn't stop there. "And someone had better explain why the estate or anything else for that matter must be sold. There is absolutely no reason for Miss Trent to be turned out of her home."

The two solicitors both spoke at once.

"But she's not being turned out." That was Mr.

Henderson.

"Because Mr. Knowles has no need of this property." That was Mr. Wells. And at last, someone revealed the truth behind the whole matter.

Margaret stood up, pointed her forefinger at Mr. Wells, and demanded, "What was that?!"

Mr. Wells took a fearful step backward and said, "Mr. Knowles has no need of another property, especially one so far from Town, and he feels everyone would be better served...."

"But the property belongs to *Mrs.* Knowles," Reverend Ogden pointed out.

"Well, yes, but...."

"Oh, I see." Margaret moved toward Mr. Wells, who took another step backwards. "It is bad enough that the black man is deemed property by some..."

"There is no need to bring your radical politics into this," Mr. Henderson spat out, his voice full of disdain.

"...but that my sister should be nothing more than that man's property...."

"You misunderstand, Miss Trent." Mr. Wells held his hands up to her in a futile effort to placate her. "According to the law...."

"They have made the law a tyrant! And my property, by some twist of that law, is Mr. Knowles's property as well, it seems."

"No. No. Not at all." Mr. Henderson jumped in. "Your property belongs to you."

Margaret turned on him. "Then tell me, sir, how is it Mr. Knowles can force me to sell *my* property?"

Neither solicitor spoke.

"He can't." That was Reverend Ogden. "But he can take you to court and the courts would order everything sold in order to obtain an equitable division."

Margaret turned and looked at him. His words took all the fire out of her. She knew he spoke the truth. And she knew Mr. Knowles could do worse. He could take the matter to the courts and have her declared unfit. He could easily pay two physicians to sign the necessary papers. Then, as her nearest male relative, Mr. Knowles would have control of the entire estate, not just Jane's portion. Margaret would be left with nothing, assuming she managed to stay out of Bedlam.

She looked about the room, her father's library with all his books. The core of the collection belonged to her mother's family, but for the last ten years, Sir William had devoted his free time to reading and collecting. Each shipment brought such joy when it arrived. She and her father had opened those crates from London with such anticipation, whether it was a case of newly published volumes or forgotten tomes hunted down in ancient manors. Now, all of it would be divided up and sold, just because *Mr. Knowles* didn't see a need for any of it. Margaret knew exactly what her brother-in-law needed—other than a swift kick in the head. He needed money for his horses and his stables and his hunting parties. Her father's labor and their family's sacrifices would pay for Mr. Knowles's amusements.

It made Margaret sick. There wasn't even a good reason for it all, just the whim of Mr. Knowles. And despite the inevitability of it, she saw no reason to be pleasant about it.

She sank down into the chair. Reverend Ogden followed suit and began drying off his feet with a towel the valet had left behind. Margaret turned to the solicitors.

"So," she said, "how exactly do we go about dispersing the remnants of our lives? Am I to be allowed to keep my possessions, or are those to be sold off as well, with Mr. Knowles receiving half the money?"

"Miss Trent," Mr. Henderson said this time, "there's no need for that."

"No?"

"Of course not." Mr. Wells sounded too confident of the situation. "You will keep your possessions."

"And who, pray tell, is to decide what is mine? Will you be going through my drawers and marking down what is mine and what belongs to the estate?"

Mr. Wells looked uncomfortable and hesitated before speaking. "I'm sure what is yours and what belongs to the estate will be obvious when it comes to it."

"Such as the pair of portraits by Gainsborough?" Margaret asked, "They could fetch as much as six guineas for the pair. And I wouldn't want to deprive Mr. Knowles of his three pounds three shillings."

"Perhaps something could be arranged and you could...."

"What? Pay Mr. Knowles for portraits of *my parents*? How magnanimous of him." Margaret was pleased with herself for not shouting at the two men. "Quite the quagmire, isn't it? Perhaps it would be best if Mr. Knowles tended to his own house and left mine alone."

Mr. Wells glared at her. "I'm afraid that's not

possible, Miss Trent."

Reverend Ogden finished putting on his shoes and stood up.

"Gentlemen," he said, taking his jacket and putting it on, "before any decisions can be made, an inventory must be compiled and everything must be appraised. This will take time, of course. And I would like to offer my assistance toward that endeavor."

In an instant, with the shock of those words, Margaret's fine opinion of the vicar plummeted, and she struggled to contain her composure. Despite her bravado, doing battle with the two solicitors distressed her greatly, and now, for the vicar to betray her as well cut deep. For some reason, though, she held her tongue as the anger built up inside her.

"This library alone could bring in a tidy sum," Reverend Ogden continued, "only none of us is qualified to appraise these books, and if we act too hastily, a small fortune could be lost."

Margaret wanted to scream. This man, this man of God, was dividing up her father's books and speaking of them as monetary assets, not as true treasures containing the thoughts and ideas of human minds for thousands of years, voices from the past speaking to the generations yet to come. Reverend Ogden owned a small library, she now recalled, and she quickly concluded he contemplated expanding that collection at her expense.

"What do you recommend?" Mr. Wells asked the vicar.

"I have a number of friends in Oxford and London." Reverend Ogden moved over to the short, round solicitor and laid his hand on his shoulder, all the while speaking softly, in a conspiratorial manner. "Librarians, book dealers, scholars, antiquarians. I could write to them and invite them to come and examine the collection. You'll be doing me a favor as well, as it will be an excellent excuse for my friends to visit me. And I can commence on an inventory as soon as possible. We'd simply fill in the assessments at a later date."

His cheerfulness at the prospect sent the blood in Margaret's head pounding in her temples and roaring in her ears, while she saw the scheme brighten Mr. Wells's face. He reached for the vicar's hand and shook it, thanking him profusely with a look of victory. Margaret could take no more. She rose and rang the bell. The butler, Harvey, appeared in the doorway without the slightest delay—he was probably listening in the hall.

"Mr. Henderson and Mr. Wells are leaving." Margaret glared at the two men but addressed the butler. "They can wait *outside* as their carriage is brought around."

Mr. Henderson gave a gasp while Mr. Wells looked as if he'd been struck, but neither said a word.

"Gentlemen," Margaret continued, "there is a posting inn just three miles down the road. I'm certain you will find it most agreeable. Good day."

They turned to follow Harvey from the room; however, Mr. Wells turned back one last time.

"Oh, I forgot," he said, "Mr. Knowles will be coming here for Christmas."

"I beg your pardon?" Horror filled her mind at the prospect of Frederick Knowles coming to this house.

Mr. Wells smirked, far too pleased with himself.

"Along with his family. Good day, Miss Trent."

And at last, the solicitors departed. But Margaret felt no sense of relief.

The moment the door closed and Harvey returned to his duties elsewhere in the house, Margaret turned on the vicar. She spoke softly, her voice keen and sharp, even to her own ears.

"I do believe I could scratch your eyes out and feel nothing but deep satisfaction." Only, she couldn't remain calm any longer. "My father's library! Now *my* library! To be torn apart and sold piece by piece to the highest bidder! You of all people know what this library meant to my father!"

"I'm sorry, Miss Trent, but it was all I could think of at the moment."

"All you could think of?" She nearly shouted the words, unable to comprehend his meaning.

"To stall."

That Margaret never expected, two small words that explained so much, and it stunned her into silence. She suddenly felt very ashamed of her previous thoughts regarding the vicar. She exhaled deeply and felt a weight lifted from her, although now she realized she trembled uncontrollably and felt quite weak, her arms heavy, as if she could no longer hold herself upright. And she wanted just to sink down to the floor, she felt so unsteady.

"Something is terribly wrong here. This isn't right," Reverend Ogden continued, pensively gazing into the fire, his hand perched upon the mantel, "You are correct; the law is being perverted, but there must be some way around all this, some way that doesn't involve the loss of your home. I just... I just need time to think."

"Oh." She reached for the back of the chair to support herself. "I see."

"The truth is, I'm afraid an inventory will be done of the estate regardless of what happens," he said, looking at her, "but I can guarantee none of my friends will venture from their homes until spring is well underway. So that, at least, will give us time."

"Us?"

"Of course. You needn't suffer through this alone. And regardless of the outcome, you do have friends." He gave her a small smile, his hazel eyes full of kindness. Margaret had liked him since his arrival in the village five years ago. Although, he looked less the vicar and more like a curate. Vicars, in Margaret's experience, were white-haired with large bellies, while curates always seemed a tad on the thin side, as if they were never fed quite enough. Reverend Ogden, while possessing a well-cut figure and a fine leg, always looked like he wanted another serving of pudding. He was not young, a couple years older than she, probably nearing forty, and no one would call him handsome in a classical sense. He never wore a wig, as some clergymen still did, but nonetheless kept his dark hair cropped short, causing the top to spike up in an endearing sort of way, as if the strands refused to lie flat and insisted on standing at attention. And the first traces of balding had already begun, giving him a high forehead. But he had such a pleasant face. And his smiles, the way they crinkled around his eyes, always brightened Margaret's moods, or at least, they always *had*, until now.

"Miss Trent, are you all right?" He reached out to her, and Margaret accepted his strong hand to steady her as she moved to sit down.

"I'm so very sorry, Reverend Ogden," she said once seated, without looking at him, "I misjudged you. I thought you had betrayed my trust."

"An entirely understandable conclusion," he said, "but you are unwell. Please, tell me, what can I do?"

"Would you ring the bell, please?"

Within moments of Reverend Ogden ringing the bell, Harvey appeared in the doorway. But before the vicar could say anything, Margaret spoke as if nothing were amiss.

"Reverend Ogden has missed his morning tea," she said, "Could you ask Cook to prepare something? Cake, sandwiches, biscuits, whatever she can manage along with a pot of strong tea."

"Right away, Miss."

As soon as Harvey departed, Margaret looked up to see Reverend Ogden staring at her, a surprised—but pleased—look on his face. She motioned for him to sit down again, and as she did, she noticed her hand shaking. And she realized the vicar, from the opposite chair, noticed it as well, his eyes full of concern.

"It has been a trying morning." She clutched her hand to her chest in an effort to calm her nerves. "I so hate getting angry. It takes so much out of me." Not that she had much left in her these days. The constant care and attention her father had needed over the last year had worn her out, physically and emotionally, to the point she seemed to grieve more for him before his death than after. All the pain of watching him suffer, waiting for the inevitable…, although, in truth, he seemed to have departed some time ago, as if his spirit slipped away one day, perhaps last spring while sitting beside the open window and had simply left his wracked body behind.

But all the little things added up, leaving Margaret with nothing but exhaustion. She felt completely spent and wrung out like a wet rag.

"That's to be expected, especially after all you've endured. To lose your father and now this."

Margaret shook her head. She had enough to deal with without thinking about all she'd endured in the last year. True, she deserved a long, peaceful rest, preferably some place warm, but that was not the course chosen for her.

"I don't understand," she said, changing the subject, "how someone, a virtual stranger who has never set foot on this land, can claim half my inheritance and take all of it from me."

"Technically, and legally, that's not what is happening," Reverend Ogden pointed out. "Mr. Knowles is your sister's husband and entitled to certain rights, as much as you might object. But for all intents and purposes, he is stealing your parents' estate, selling it off, and giving you half, all the while claiming this is fair and just. He is taking your comfort and security, because, even from a financial point of view, the money you could earn in a lifetime from the estate would be more than it's worth in one lump sum."

"Divided by two."

"And, of course, it is your home."

"I doubt the law takes that into consideration." Margaret felt despondent. Even with Reverend Ogden's help, even with his stalling tactics, she couldn't see a way to stay in her home.

For a long moment, Reverend Ogden sat quiet, looking preoccupied. And then he took a deep breath and asked, "Did you notice that, other than the matter of your father's entailed property, Mr. Henderson explained very little concerning the dispersal of the estate?"

"Yes, I did notice that." Margaret perked up a bit. "Mr. Wells provided all the explanations."

"And he represents Mr. Knowles, not your father." Reverend Ogden shook his head.

"Nor does Mr. Henderson, when you consider it. He's a junior partner to Mr. Goodwin, and it is Mr. Goodwin who has been my father's solicitor for the last fifteen years."

"Then how is it a *junior* partner came and not the senior partner?" Reverend Ogden leaned forward toward her. "For an estate this size and a gentleman of your father's standing, Mr. Goodwin should have come himself."

Margaret smirked in a most unladylike fashion. "Perhaps my reputation precedes me."

He did not react to her comment. Instead, his mind seemed hard at work. "Did they provide you with any explanation for Mr. Goodwin's absence? Perhaps he is ill or detained by some matter and will arrive later?"

"No. Nothing."

"And did you notice they *told* you everything? It is customary to *read* such matters with the documents there in hand. But they didn't have a copy of any paperwork. Not your father's will, not the entailment, not the terms of your mother's settlement, if one ever existed. Perhaps she even had a will of her own. It's all very curious."

"Suggesting something nefarious to you as well?" Margaret asked. Even without his answer, Margaret began to feel something growing in her, a sense of hope and the realization she was not alone in all this.

Reverend Ogden slowly nodded. "I have friends at Gray's Inn. I'll make inquires with them regarding Mr. Goodwin and his junior partner, as well as Mr. Wells. Everything may be perfectly legitimate, but I have sincere doubts. And regardless, it's best to be certain."

Harvey returned at last, carrying a tray with a dish of cake, plates, silverware, and serviettes and set it on the table beside Margaret while the footman removed the basin and cans of water. A maid soon followed with a tray of sandwiches, which she handed to Harvey. Then, at last, the tea arrived.

"Shall I pour, Miss Trent?" the butler asked.

"No. Thank you, Harvey. We can manage."

Harvey and the other servants left, and Margaret poured a cup of tea for Reverend Ogden—milk and sugar.

"You remember," he said with a smile as he accepted the cup and saucer.

"Yes. You take milk and sugar." Margaret poured a cup for herself, milk first. "Lady Latham prefers coffee and claret—not together, of course. Lord Latham likes brandy and a pipe, although I'm not supposed to know the latter but how could I not, given you can smell his tobacco all over the house? Mrs. Wainwright takes tea, milk only, while Mr. Wainwright...."

"Do you know the preference of everyone in Edgecombe?"

"No, of course not." Margaret added sugar to her tea. "Just anyone who has come to the house."

"Ah." Reverend Ogden watched her for a moment. "You take sugar?"

Remembering her words earlier about enslaved men, Margaret realized what she had done and that the vicar had caught her. And she felt ashamed, thinking of the slaves in the West Indies who had produced this sugar and the horrific conditions of their lives.

"There. You have me, sir." She set her spoon down on the saucer. "I am a hypocrite. I haven't the courage of my convictions."

"Nor I, it seems." He took a careful sip of his hot tea. "But I don't think that means we are bad people. I just find it difficult to comprehend that the life of an unknown man or woman on the other side of the world could possibly be made better by me denying myself a spoonful of sugar with my tea."

"Yes. That's it exactly." Margaret could barely contain herself as she realized someone else thought as she did. "And what if by this action we unintentionally cause more harm than good?"

The vicar smiled, his face filled with amusement, as if he found her words humorous. "You've been reading your father's philosophy books."

"No, I assure you, I have not." Margaret took a sip of her tea, suddenly feeling strangely shy, but she could not end the subject there. "I think Mr. Wilberforce has a better chance of making a difference in these matters than any small thing you or I might do."

"Most likely." He had that pensive look again, gazing off into the flames. "But we can still make a difference in the lives of people we encounter, even with small things."

He turned his eyes—those hazel eyes filled with kindness and concern—toward her again, and Margaret wondered how she had never noticed before how attractive he was.

"Such as coming to my aid this morning?" she asked.

He raised his cup to her. "Such as remembering my morning tea."

Henry returned to the vicarage in time for dinner so as not to upset Mrs. Brown, although he would have preferred to accept Miss Trent's invitation to dine with her that evening. He did accept the offer to use her father's horse until such time as Henry's horse recovered, especially since Miss Trent made it clear he had no choice in the matter. As a result, the ride home, while frigid, passed briskly without the frost setting too heavily in Henry's bones. That, however, did not stop Mrs. Brown from fussing over him, almost, but not quite, as fervently as Miss Trent had.

After dinner, Henry sat down at his desk to write his promised letters by candlelight in his study. He still found the day's events amazing, and Miss Trent had surprised him, which in and of itself was totally unexpected. Capable, confident Miss Trent—whom he'd always believed to be the most self-reliant, independent individual he'd ever encountered—needed help. His help. For five years, before that even, since the death of her mother, she had run Edgecombe Hall. And over the last two years, that had included not merely the household, but the estate as well, since illness prevented her father from dealing with most matters. So it was hard to believe she needed anything, let alone the help of a vicar.

But there was something more. When he saw how her hand trembled, it struck him to the core, and for the first time, he felt a deep sympathy for her. He realized in that instant how truly frightened she was, despite all her bluster and boldness. There was a vulnerability underneath, a frailty hidden within. While he did not doubt her explanation that her anger left her in an anxious state, those two solicitors had beset her that morning with no one to defend her. She had no choice but to stand up for herself, in this matter as well as others. And for doing so, her neighbors dismissed her as difficult.

Henry had no delusions about himself. He spent most of his time worrying about when his tea might arrive while ensconced in his study with his books. On pleasant days, he wandered the lanes and paths of the countryside and found that exhilaration enough. His thoughts rarely strayed beyond 16th Century portraiture or Biblical texts. He was no champion. After all, ladies did not swoon before vicars with thinning hair. But in his small way, he would do whatever he could to help Miss Trent. And right now, that meant writing letters to ask favors from old but equally dull friends.

The following morning, this time going on horseback

rather than on foot, Henry went to Edgecombe Hall. Miss Trent, again in black and wrapped in that indigo India shawl, met him with tea and biscuits before the fire in Sir William's library. There, he reported his undertakings thus far. He had written his friends in Oxford and London who possessed the skills to evaluate the collection of books—Miss Trent frowned and looked away from him while he spoke—but he assured her that, like him, they preferred to spend their winters huddled in their studies with their books and papers to await warmer days. He had even gone so far as to request they make excuses to delay any journey to Edgecombe for as long as possible.

Furthermore, he had made enquiries with his friends at Gray's Inn. Although they were barristers and not solicitors, everyone in the world of law in London knew everyone, either directly or by reputation. They would relay any facts and all the gossip concerning Misters Goodwin, Henderson, and Wells, and even Mr. Knowles. If something foul was afoot, they would uncover it, as they were good, diligent men who would not delay. This, more than anything since Henry's arrival that morning, appeared to brighten Miss Trent's mood. He omitted that they might send a bill along with any information, but he had already decided he would cover the costs if it came to that.

He also imparted to her his plan for doing the inventory. He had contrived the most tedious, drawn out process he could imagine. He hoped it would be equally confusing. First, they would record every item in the house with a description. Then, once they finished with that, they would transcribe the information, by room and in alphabetical order, into leather-bound quarto ledgers. This process would have the effect of doing the inventory twice. Furthermore, Henry knew such ledgers were not available in Edgecombe and would have to be ordered; he suggested a stationer he rarely frequented in London as they were notoriously slow in fulfilling orders.

Miss Trent burst out with a very brief laugh. "It'll take a year!"

"Precisely." He grinned, unable to contain his pleasure with his own plan.

Then, she feigned seriousness, conceding to Henry's genius. "But it is *most* efficient."

"We should start in here." He glanced around at the stacks of books, the thought of foraging through them filling him with delight, but also sorrow, as little could be done to save them from the auctioneer's gavel. "It will take the longest. As much as I'd like to delay, we do need to show some degree of progress when Mr. Knowles comes for Christmas."

"Oh, don't remind me." She sounded thoroughly distressed by the prospect, not merely annoyed by its inconvenience.

"In all my years here, I've never met him." Henry recalled meeting Jane Knowles twice, and on both occasions, she gave the distinct impression of having recently taken a dose of laudanum, as she displayed that otherworldly gaze so common in users. "Is he really that bad?"

"In truth, I have little experience with him." Miss Trent nibbled on a biscuit then continued. "Jane accompanied our mother to Cheltenham for the waters during her final illness. They met Mr. Knowles, and he beguiled them both."

"Beguiled?"

"So it would seem." She shrugged. "I saw little to commend him except an extraordinarily handsome face and a penchant for purchasing the most exquisite hothouse flowers. But before I even met the gentleman, Jane was betrothed to him. And despite my serious concerns, she did not hesitate to marry a man with one dead wife and fourteen living children."

"Good Heavens!" Henry nearly choked on his tea. "Will they *all* be coming for Christmas?"

"I certainly hope not. There's nowhere to put them all." She sipped her tea. "Several of the elder children are married, so perhaps they will not come, and Jane has no children of her own." Miss Trent took another biscuit. "You will come for Christmas, of course?"

"You may rely on my support." Henry gave her a military-like nod.

"And Christmas Eve, too, before Midnight Service?"

"I am at your service whenever you have need."

"Won't your other parishioners need you?"

Henry inhaled deeply and tried not to sigh too loudly. "In truth, aside from the usual weddings, christenings, occasional baptisms, and all-too-frequent funerals no matter how rare they might be, most of your neighbors only call upon me in order to gossip about their fellow neighbors. If I am not at home, they will simply chatter away with Mrs. Brown, and she reports all I miss on my return."

His disclosure seemed to dishearten her. She

lowered her eyes and stared into her cup of tea. He wondered what he'd said to sadden her. But then she looked up, saw him watching her, and smiled.

"Then," she said, "as you suggested, we should start in here. But first, before we—I should say *you*—begin the inventory, I would suggest we organize and sort everything properly." She motioned to the books lying around the room, the stacks of papers on the desk, and the disordered shelves.

"Excellent suggestion. That will require even more time."

"True, but before all this happened, I was actually trying to organize the books and papers in here. My father never did have a coherent system. He just stuck the books wherever he might find a spot. I was attempting to sort them by subject."

"Then we just continue with that."

"Would you mind...?" She hesitated. "That is, could you work on sorting the books? You are, no doubt, better suited to sort the Latin and Greek. There are even some Hebrew texts. I'd prefer it if I went through my father's papers."

"Of course."

"It's not that I think there's anything untoward, but my father's private papers should remain as private as possible."

"I understand."

"But *all* these papers and letters and ledgers weren't my father's." She motioned to the various piles of papers throughout the room. "Much of this was here when we arrived. All that's left of lives lived long ago. And I find I...

I enjoy sorting through my family's history." She looked embarrassed. "That must seem strange."

"Not at all. I am fixated on the 16th Century."

"And I on the Restoration."

"Really? How scandalous."

"You have no idea." Her face lit up, and she positively beamed.

"Do tell."

She leaned forward and spoke with a slightly lowered voice, as if revealing great secrets. "I discovered a box of letters written from Court by my grandmother's grandmother's sister. The letters suggest she was a mistress to Charles II."

"Along with everyone else." Henry grinned.

Then he heard the disappointment in her voice. "But the corresponding letters—the ones written by my great-great-grandmother—are missing."

"Half a conversation." So very sad, he thought.

"She—my distant aunt—married Lord Weston. The fourth or fifth one, I'm not sure, and I imagine if the other letters survived, they're at Weston Hall."

"How very tantalizing."

Miss Trent sat back in the chair, bolt upright, and her tone returned to that of mistress of the house. "I am going to remove the letters to my chambers, and if you would be so kind, you will conveniently fail to include them in the inventory. I know that's theft, but God will forgive me."

Henry nodded in conspiratorial assent. "Anything else you'd like to secret away to your chamber?"

"A handwritten copy of *The Canterbury Tales*, some

books printed by Caxton, a box containing dueling pistols."

Unbelievable, Henry thought. The room, despite its dust and disorder, was a scholar's dream waiting to be explored.

"What?" he joked, "No First Folio?"

Miss Trent raised her eyebrows and gave the smallest nod. "Perhaps. Who could tell in all this chaos? I'll leave all but the letters here for now so you can examine them at your leisure."

At his leisure. The idea filled him with joy. "I'm sure that will delay the inventory even further."

"Oh dear." Miss Trent matched his sarcasm, but Henry recognized it hid her concern.

Over the rest of the week, Henry came every day, if only for a few hours. Each time, Miss Trent welcomed him with a pot of tea by the fire, and after a brief respite, they would get to work. Often, they worked for long stretches in comfortable silence, Miss Trent at one of the tables, Henry shelving and reshelving volumes, gradually—but slowly—bringing some semblance of order to the collection, until one of them would say *Oh, how fascinating*, to be met with *You found something?* Their heads would come together over some dusty script, all other thoughts forgotten as they absorbed themselves in the past, until an hour or two elapsed, and they would remember the time and ring for tea.

Henry came to enjoy being in Sir William's library, and he felt as at home there as he did in his own study.

On Sunday, despite his entirely facetious idea from earlier that week, Henry gave his sermon on the Tenth

Commandment. He had to admit—only to himself, not to the congregation—that throughout the days of sorting Sir William's library, Henry did find himself coveting some books in the collection. He loved the leather-bound volumes he held in his hands, the spines still creaking when opened, the editions so tight and clean. Some pages weren't even slit, forcing Henry to choose whether to mar the books by unlocking the secrets hidden between uncut leaves or allow them to remain untouched and unread, in pristine condition forever. Miss Trent laughed at him and permitted him to do as he wished. And so he chose to delay satisfaction until this whole sordid mess was resolved once and for all.

He also found himself *coveting* Sir William's daughter—although that wasn't the same thing; *that*, he supposed, was another sin altogether. It wasn't covetousness he felt there. He wished to discover the depths hidden within her tightly closed covers. But was it a sin, he wondered, watching her pore over some ancient missive or crumbling ledger.

She wore spectacles to read, and often, she used a magnifying glass to examine the archaic script. He'd catch himself staring at her, those dark tresses swept up atop her head, the delicate down-like hair at the nape of her neck. Strange, he thought seeing her bent over a book, how he longed to caress that pale neck now when he had never noticed her before, not really. She had only been his friend's daughter, a presence in the house and in the congregation, but little more. He had never spoken with her beyond polite pleasantries. Yet now, he found her lovely, though deeply vulnerable and afraid, and he had never noticed those qualities before. Others dismissed her as nothing but a shrew issuing orders, but he saw the results of her commanding presence—an efficiently run household and a prospering estate.

He did not want to see her leave Edgecombe. His first thoughts were for Sir William's wishes for his daughter. But he also recognized how good the Trent family was to the parish—providing funds for the church when it needed a new roof, but also helping with the poorer neighbors. Their tenants lived more comfortably than even Lord Latham's tenants. Henry always assumed that was Sir William's doing, but he now recognized Miss Trent's influence.

And now, spending these hours and days with her, Henry found he had more selfish reasons for wanting her to stay. She was a spinster, he was a bachelor, there was nothing inappropriate there. And it wasn't lust he felt for her but.... But no. She had enough problems to deal with just now without the unwanted attentions of a country vicar.

The following week, Henry continued his daily visits to Edgecombe Hall, ostensibly to compile the inventory. But instead, his chats with Miss Trent as he warmed himself before the fire and partook of tea and biscuits lasted longer and longer, the chaos of the library temporarily forgotten. Then the need to do something productive would come over them. However, rather than commencing on the task at hand, Miss Trent developed a propensity for requiring Henry's assistance elsewhere in the house. Invariably, it required climbing a ladder. Why Mr. Harvey or the footman couldn't manage, Henry didn't know, but he was more than happy to help Miss Trent in these menial tasks. One day it was hanging curtains, the next day it was hanging pictures. These included several 16th Century portraits, which, although not by the hand of Holbein, were very much in keeping with that artist's style. Henry couldn't understand why these had not already been hung. Miss Trent explained that while her father loved art with a great passion and enjoyed purchasing paintings, he possessed a peculiar aversion to actually hanging them on the walls. Until his death, all the pictures on the walls in the house had been hung before the family's arrival. Now, Miss Trent concluded, she could hang pictures to her heart's delight without fear of upsetting her father.

Eventually, Henry returned to his work in the library. At some point during his absence or while he turned his back, all the scraps of paper, letters, and ledgers Miss Trent found so engrossing disappeared from the library, presumably to some hidey-hole in her chamber. Henry assumed—worried—that she would leave him to work alone, only, much to his delight, she didn't. Instead, she remained in the library. Sometimes, she assisted him in the sorting. Together, they uncovered no less than three—each with subtle differences—Folios along with a dozen quartos of Shakespeare's plays, several 15th Century volumes printed by Caxton, an early, handwritten manuscript of *The Canterbury Tales*, and an unknown number of medieval illuminated manuscripts.

But usually, Miss Trent sat before the fire and sewed, mending various pieces or doing embroidery. And of course, there were the curtains she soon had Henry hanging up.

Henry realized that in all his visits to Sir William, he had never spent so much time with Miss Trent, and as they talked, he learned how little he knew of the Trent family, despite all the years of conversation with his late friend. He knew Sir William as a scholar, a player of chess, a grower of fruit trees, the father of two daughters, and the holder of Trent Abbey and Edgecombe Hall. Henry never imagined Sir William was once a soldier who took his family to Minorca and then India. He never knew that Sir William, in fact, fathered six sons and three daughters, only to return to England with his wife and just two of their children, India taking the others.

He discovered the family was not native to Edgecombe but had inherited the hall by way of Lady Trent's grandmother just twenty years earlier. They had arrived diminished and full of sorrow over their many losses, only to discover the hall nothing more than a large, ill-managed farm—not the great estate it now was. Miss Trent had been only seventeen, still awkward but also viewed as foreign by the villagers of Edgecombe with her Indian birth and all that dark hair. Few issued invitations.

Henry imagined the young girl she had been then. It would have been a shock to Miss Trent coming from the heat of India to the chill of England, even in the reception the family received, never hostile, always civil, but never truly welcoming. She must have been lonely and directed all her energy, love, and attention on the family home and estate.

Now, Miss Trent might be a respected member of the community, but still villagers gossiped and readily gave their two cents on the topic. A cold, domineering woman with chiseled features and a face like marble—*but marble warms to the touch*, and Henry now knew Miss Trent, in many ways, was a casualty of the quest for empire, so men like him could have his cup of tea. And his sugar.

Over the days, Miss Trent recounted to him how her father had labored to transform the farm into an estate—*he knew as much about farming as a fish knows of history*—and how hard Lady Trent and her daughters had worked, pinching pennies, scraping by, selling butter and eggs, making jams, eating potatoes and beans and coarse bread, the only meat small game—*if I never eat rabbit or squirrel again, even as a curry, it will be too soon*—with Sir William selling most game to the butcher. Every farthing went back into the estate, to expand and invest and enlarge and improve the land. He learned innovations in farming and modernized, with even his daughters digging potatoes in the fields, until at last he turned an unproductive farm into a great estate.

And then Sir William's nephew died, leaving no sons, and the old soldier inherited Trent Abbey with all its land and income. Without a son of his own to inherit the Abbey after him one day, he focused his attention on Edgecombe Hall. He invested wisely, expanded their home, and finally, after a lifetime of so much work and sacrifice, lived comfortably, until illness took his wife and, eventually, himself.

Between all their conversations, Henry managed to finish reorganizing the library, with Miss Trent's assistance, and order returned to the great room. As a result, Henry began the process of cataloguing the collection. He used odds bits of torn paper, written in his worst hand, with a poorly cut pen—and poorly dipped without benefit of blotting paper—so ink smudged the page, making it virtually illegible, even to Henry. He commenced with lesser works—modern novels and popular sermons—but made a point to include a few of the more valuable texts as a means of incentive to show Mr. Knowles the tedious endeavor was well worth the painstaking effort.

Henry always left before dinnertime, as he did not wish to disrupt Mrs. Brown's plans. But with each departure, he wished for nothing more than to stay, another minute, another hour, just to be with Miss Trent.

Then, in the third week of their idyll, Mr. Frederick Knowles and his family came to stay for Christmas.

The 23rd day of December arrived and Margaret's *guests* had yet to appear. A curt note had come several days previously and stated Mr. Knowles should be expected on the 21st. He did not have the courtesy to indicate exactly how many she should expect to be with him. She presumed that along with Mr. Knowles there would be her sister, at least ten of the children, along with several servants, plus the coachmen. The nursery—never used in Margaret's time at Edgecombe—was made ready, even though the youngest Knowles children were already too old for the nursery. All the rooms except her father's were prepared. Extra beds were found in the attics so that the servants could double or even triple up.

The cleaning, airing, ordering, arranging, and planning exhausted Margaret, and Reverend Ogden's steady presence provided her only comfort.

Now, with Mr. Knowles due to arrive at any moment, Margaret needed Reverend Ogden to keep her calm even more. She couldn't understand it. She could maintain a stony face in the most difficult of circumstances, never betraying a single emotion. But when it came to Mr. Knowles and his actions, she lost all control of herself, sounding like a madwoman, even to her own ears. And she had no doubt Mr. Knowles would take advantage of that, if given the slightest opportunity. She supposed, however, that having no say in someone taking half the estate was ample grounds for going mad.

The house was at sixes and sevens when the first carriage arrived just after noon. To Margaret's horror, that carriage disgorged the two solicitors, *Jonah and the Wells*, as she now called them. Thankfully, Reverend Ogden, hard at work on his very messy inventory, emerged from the library. He gracefully intercepted the two men in the hall so Margaret didn't have to deal with them, and escorted them to the drawing room while Margaret fretted over where to put them. Obviously, they would have to share a room. Preferably in the stables.

Shortly after the arrival of the two solicitors, three carriages drove up with eleven of the fourteen children, along with their various attendants, as well as Mr. Knowles's valet and Jane's maid, and all their luggage. But there was no sign yet of Mr. Knowles or Jane.

For some time after that, pandemonium ensued, with Margaret attempting to sort out all the children, from the nineteen-year-old to the eight-year-olds, with another pair of twins in the midst there somewhere. Or perhaps it was two sets of twins. Reverend Ogden, much to Margaret's gratitude, appeared on the scene, and with that voice accustomed to lecturing and sermonizing, herded the six youngest children up to the nursery with their two attendants—Margaret wasn't quite sure what to call them—leaving Margaret to manage the rest.

The two eldest girls would share a room, while the other girl would share with their governess. The two boys could share as well, but then there was their tutor, whom Margaret failed to anticipate. She couldn't very well put him in one of the servants' rooms. So he had a room of his own, as would Mr. Knowles, while his valet could double up with the servants. That would leave Jane and her maid. Given the arrival of Jonah and the Wells, Margaret had no choice but to put Jane in their mother's room. She'd worry about the lady's maid once Jane arrived. *But Lord, where was she going to put all the coachmen?* She dreaded telling the groomsmen and Jack to expect more men sharing their bunks.

It was late afternoon before the last carriage arrived, loaded down with an inordinate number of trunks. The door opened, and out sprang Mr. Knowles, handsome as ever, and well he knew it—blond and broad with a matching height, like some Nordic god come to pillage fair England. The mere sight of him turned Margaret's stomach.

"Mrs. Knowles has been unwell." Mr. Knowles shouted this means of greeting as he turned to help his wife out.

"I just need to lie down, Frederick, and I will be fine." But Margaret could see from the first sight of her sister clutching Mr. Knowles for support that she was far from fine. She looked like a madwoman, haggard and listless. Jane's head lolled to one side and rested on her husband's shoulder. She appeared thin, her eyes sunken with dark circles about them, and she seemed green about the gills, as if she would be sick at any moment. Her husband assisted her inside, but once Margaret took over with Jane leaning heavily on her, he ignored the pair struggling through the hall toward the stairs. Margaret could feel Jane shaking, not from the cold but from whatever illness this was.

"My wife seems to have brought her entire wardrobe," Margaret heard Mr. Knowles say with distaste as servants began unloading the trunks and bringing them inside.

"Which room do you have me in, Margaret?" Jane whispered so only her sister could hear.

"Mother's."

"No, please." Jane clutched at Margaret's dress. "Put me in your room, with you. I don't want to be alone."

Without another thought, Margaret decided to do as Jane asked. As they slowly ascended the stairs, Margaret heard Reverend Ogden emerge from the library below and introduce himself to Mr. Knowles in the hall, their voices echoing in the grand space.

"Ah yes. The priest." Mr. Knowles sounded unimpressed. "I understand you're doing the inventory. Really, why trouble yourself? The whole lot should just be sold. A shilling a book and be done with it. It's doing no one any good here."

"Oh, rest assured, Mr. Knowles, it's well worth the effort. The British Library recently purchased a 15th Century edition of *The Canterbury Tales* for nine guineas."

"Nine guineas? Are they mad? That's half a year's wages! No book, however pretty the pictures, is worth nine guineas."

"Your solicitor can verify that sale, I'm sure."

"No, no, I believe you. It's simply incredulous, that's all. The lengths to which some people will go."

"I happen to be acquainted with some of them. I've written to them about coming to appraise the collection, but so far, I've only heard from one, and he cannot possibly come until spring."

Margaret, reaching the landing and guiding Jane down the corridor, could no longer hear Mr. Knowles or Reverend Ogden's voices as they moved into the library.

She was so thankful for Reverend Ogden, who had kept her sane for the last three weeks. The truth was she was terrified. She was losing her home, the only real home she'd ever known. Her childhood had been one of encampments and temporary billets and shacks in the middle of nowhere, with no one for companionship beyond her mother and her siblings—all dead now save for Jane—and the ever-constant shadow that her father could be killed at any moment. Even the family was considered fair game in the eyes of many belligerents, and they had been in danger numerous times. Now, to lose the only peace and security she'd ever known... she had no idea what to do. The law was stacked against her. And if Mr. Knowles decided he wanted everything, including her income, she knew the Crown would side with him. They would find some excuse and claim it was all for her own good.

Margaret maneuvered Jane into her own chamber and then quickly told Mrs. Jenkins to bring Jane's trunks there. Margaret helped Jane remove her coat and gloves, Jane's hand trembling, and then led Jane to the chair beside the fire.

"Where's your laudanum?" Margaret asked, opening the first small trunk brought into the room.

"No." For the first time, Jane lifted her head and stared directly at Margaret. "I don't need it."

"Where did you pack it?" Margaret flipped through folded small clothes and wondered why Jane brought so much for such a short visit.

"I didn't bring any."

Margaret stopped and looked at her sister. "Your physician ordered you to take laudanum."

"It's no better than poison." Jane attempted a weak smile. "Just tea. That's all I need right now. And maybe some biscuits."

This wasn't *Mrs.* Knowles speaking. For seven years, Jane had been a shadow of her former self—meek, mild, demure, silent. The girl who climbed trees and bathed in muddy ponds had disappeared once married to Mr. Knowles. But this woman sitting in Margaret's room.... Margaret recognized her and knew her. It was her little sister.

"Some sandwiches, too?" Margaret asked.

"That would be lovely," Jane replied, leaning her head back and closing her eyes.

Once all of Jane's trunks were brought to Margaret's room and the tea tray arrived, Margaret closed the door and sat down.

"When did you stop taking laudanum?" she asked.

"When Papa died and Frederick wouldn't let me come," she replied, opening her eyes and attempting to sit up straight, "but I had been considering it for a long time."

"Oh?" Margaret handed Jane a cup of tea.

"Since last spring. At a dinner given by Lord and Lady Ashton. A navy captain escorted me in to dinner. We talked, even through the turn—much to the annoyance of Lady Ashton who sat opposite him. After dinner, he sought me out and questioned me about my use of laudanum. He knew all the signs, apparently, and he recommended I consult a physician he knew."

"How fortuitous."

"Frederick doesn't know. Only the doctor who has been tending me knows. The worst is over, he tells me, but I feel horrible. Hopefully, it's the three days in a closed carriage with Frederick and not the lack of laudanum making me so ill now."

Margaret suspected Jane was right but couldn't very well say so. Instead, she said, "Have a biscuit."

Jane did not come down for dinner. Margaret arranged to have a tray taken to her. She knew Jane would enjoy tonight's offering—an assortment of dishes from their childhood in India, recipes passed from their *ayah* to their mother, who in turn, taught them to Cook, who did a remarkable job, especially considering the lack of so many exotic ingredients.

As Margaret came down and neared the library, she overheard Mr. Knowles and Reverend Ogden, still in there, despite the time. The vicar was usually long gone by now, as he did not like to upset Mrs. Brown's plans when it came to dinner.

"I hope Miss Trent will provide some entertainment for us while we are here," Mr. Knowles could be heard saying.

"Miss Trent has far too much to worry about right now to plan for entertainments," Reverend Ogden replied.

"Well, soon enough, she'll have nothing to worry about."

Margaret reached the doorway and saw the two men standing before the fire, Mr. Knowles with a glass of her father's brandy.

"Dinner is about to be served," she said.

"Already? Damnable country hours." Mr. Knowles did not appear to notice the vicar's reaction to his profanity, nor Margaret's reaction, for that matter. "And I haven't even changed yet." He turned to Reverend Ogden with a smile and asked, "Will you join us?"

The vicar graciously declined, as Margaret knew he would, but she wished he had accepted. She had no desire to be left alone with Mr. Knowles and his brood, and she felt stronger, more courageous, more like her real self with Reverend Ogden present, not the person she was supposed to be, not the person everyone thought she was, but the real Margaret.

Dinner was delayed an hour while Mr. Knowles changed. Margaret considered going ahead without him, as she would in any other situation with such a tardy guest, but decided to wait instead. Then, when he finally arrived, Margaret saw to it that she took her father's place at the head of the table while no setting or chair was placed opposite in her mother's place, all so Mr. Knowles could not assume either position. Only two of the Knowles daughters were deemed old enough to sit at table with the family—in their father's view—and so there were only six at dinner. But what a lot they were—Mr. Knowles, Jonah and the Wells, and the two girls, whom Margaret thought were a set of twins but really couldn't tell as all the children seemed to look exactly alike to her. The girls spoke only of the latest fashions. Jonah and the Wells seemed to be living in mortal fear of someone—Margaret suspected it was she. Mr. Knowles acted as if all were right with the world and he was God in His heaven, despite not sitting at the head of the table. Until, that is, dinner arrived.

Margaret had wanted to serve an all-Indian meal, but Cook's good sense prevailed, with a compromise of an assortment of Indian curries with rice and a traditional pork roast with all the trimmings, along with a fish course, followed by mincemeat pie, apple dumplings, and rice pudding for dessert with fruit and cheese. *Something for everyone*, Cook declared. And, as usual in the household, everything was placed on the table at the same time.

Mr. Knowles was not impressed, and the others, knowing who buttered their bread, followed his lead. The curries were too spicy—while Margaret found them a tad on a mild side. The pork was underdone in Mr. Knowles's view, *and where was the apple sauce*? None of the desserts were sweet enough. And the quality of the cheese—from the estate—would ruin any hostess in London.

Had these insults come all at once, Margaret would have stood up and marched out. Instead, they came in dribs and drabs, like water dripping on a stone.

At last, it became too much for Margaret when Mr. Knowles declared Cook, *and probably the rest of the servants*, were taking advantage of Margaret. *And assuredly, your father, too, for all these years.*

Margaret heard the rushing of blood in her ears. She had no idea what she said in reply, but Mr. Knowles continued to talk, Jonah and the Wells concurring, with the girls commenting on the wonders of London; they emphasized the quality of their dressmaker and how they could use a chaperone for outings.

And then she heard Mr. Knowles say, "You have no need of a service of china for twelve, let alone one for thirty-six."

"The price it would bring could secure your living for a year," the Wells added with far too much enthusiasm.

The rage building in her, Margaret suddenly thought of Reverend Ogden. In her mind's eye, she saw him at his table, Mrs. Brown's dinner laid out before him. He ate with his fork in one hand and a small volume in his other. What had he said he was currently reading? Margaret tried to remember.

"You have no children, no family," Mr. Knowles continued. "So you clearly have no need of such a large house."

Despite her half-eaten dinner before her, Margaret abruptly rose, the men at the table immediately doing likewise.

"Milton," Margaret said to no one in particular.

"I beg your pardon?" Jonah asked.

Margaret turned her gaze on him. "*Paradise Lost.* Reverend Ogden is reading *Paradise Lost.*" A story of pride, wickedness, and deception, all leading to the fall of man. And woman.

She saw the looks pass amongst the five of them. They thought her mad, she imagined. But enough was enough. Without another word, she turned and exited the room. She retired for the night to her own chamber, to spend the evening with Jane and enjoy the rest of her dinner there.

Christmas Eve dawned bitterly cold with a heavy frost dusting everything. Ominous, dark gray clouds lingered just over the horizon and, by late morning, prepared to move in toward Edgecombe. Still dressed in his banyan, Henry sat at his desk and put the finishing touches on his sermon for Midnight Service. Then there was his sermon for tomorrow's Christmas Day service. Though largely finished, it still needed a final reading. But in truth, with the frigid winds and bitter frost, he had no desire to venture out anywhere today except to Edgecombe Hall.

He had hated leaving Miss Trent alone with that man and those shysters. But he saw the look on her face when Mr. Knowles invited him to stay for dinner. The invitation usurped her position in the household, and Henry could not accept, no matter how much he wished to say yes, even risking the wrath of Mrs. Brown. But today, he would find some way to stay, inviting himself if he had to.

Henry heard the bell at the door. He expected the post. Within a moment, Mrs. Brown entered with no mere letter but a small parcel. She informed him it had come *by messenger* from London, not by post. *The poor man*, Henry thought, *at Christmastide, all the way from London, and in such horrid weather.*

He didn't recognize the seal but broke it immediately. Inside, he found a letter addressed to him, along with a packet of documents. He read the letter carefully. Then read it again. He glanced over the documents, quickly realizing what they contained, and then he reread the letter yet again, all the while his anger growing with each word—and his hope.

Henry needed to see Miss Trent as soon as possible. But not in his banyan. He called for his horse—Sir William's horse—and quickly dressed.

He informed Mrs. Brown that he was going to Edgecombe Hall and didn't know if he would be home for dinner.

"But the weather," she said, "it's going to blow up something fierce out there."

"No no. Perfectly sound. Have no fear. I consulted the Almanac and we're to have an uneventful Christmas."

Mrs. Brown shook her head and stated she would give the curate Henry's sermon when he failed to arrive for Midnight Service. His assurances to the contrary failed to assuage her concern.

And out he went, into the burning cold that seeps

deep into the flesh, and rode to Edgecombe Hall. He made quick time, and soon enough, he found himself again standing in the great hall with Mr. Harvey taking his coat. He heard children's laughter and the pounding of running footsteps somewhere up above in the house—the nursery, he imagined—followed by a bellicose voice— Mr. Knowles—shouting for order from the stairs. Mr. Knowles glanced down, and his face brightened when he saw the vicar.

"Reverend Ogden," he said, descending the stairs, "what brings you here today of all days? Shouldn't you be busy preparing for tonight? And tomorrow, for that matter."

"All well in hand." Henry endeavored to be cheerful, not wanting Mr. Knowles to suspect anything amiss. He knew it was always best to wrap a lie in the truth. "I have a few hours to spare and hoped Miss Trent would be willing to discuss a matter over a cup of tea."

"Oh? What matter?"

"Matthew 16:18." Henry beamed with feigned delight, as if he'd just discovered the Ark of the Covenant in his cellar. Mr. Knowles's face, however, dropped with confusion.

"I don't know that one," he said.

"'...Thou art Peter, and upon this rock I will build my church....'"

"Oh." He sounded so very disappointed.

"You see," Henry continued with great enthusiasm, "it's unclear what Christ meant by '*this* rock.' The traditional view is he referred to Peter. *But*, according to Mr. Dyson's *Sermons*, Christ referred *not* to Peter but to *what Peter said."*

"Fascinating." But Mr. Knowles clearly felt anything but.

"Puts it all in a whole new light, doesn't it?" Henry hoped Miss Trent would appear soon. He could only keep this up for so long. Not the ramble concerning interpretations of Bible verses. He could do that in his sleep—and frequently did. It was the cheerfulness before this man that waned fast. "So Miss Trent and I were wondering what it said in the original Greek...."

"Oh, there you are Margaret," Mr. Knowles said, motioning to Miss Trent as she came across the hall from the back of the house, "Reverend Ogden is here to see you." He turned to the vicar and said, "Really, most interesting, Reverend, but please excuse me as I must check on... the horses."

As soon as the man was out of sight, Henry said in a low voice so only Miss Trent could hear, "Never fails."

"What never fails?" She motioned him toward the library.

"If you want to be rid of someone, just start quoting the Bible. Works every time."

Miss Trent stopped in the library doorway and shook her head. "I don't think that's what God intended."

"Probably not." Henry continued on over to the fire to warm himself.

"And you were lying."

"True, but I wasn't bearing false witness. In fact, one *could* call it 'spreading the good news.'"

Miss Trent took her usual seat and with a dubious look on her face asked, "How exactly did you become a vicar?"

Henry laughed, noting the mischievous twinkle in her eyes.

"I didn't expect you until dinnertime," she said.

"I wouldn't leave you in your time of need." He stepped away from the fire and wandered over to a bookshelf as he spoke. "And we have things to discuss." He pulled out a heavy leather-bound volume in Greek. He motioned to the book. "To maintain the illusion, in case we are interrupted."

"I don't understand." Miss Trent suddenly looked worried.

"Have no fear." Flipping through the book, Henry strolled nonchalantly over to the door and pushed it to—but did not close it. He found the chapter he wanted—Matthew 16—and holding the place with his forefinger, returned to Miss Trent. He sat down in his seat before the fire, leaned slightly forward, and spoke quietly.

"They've been lying to us."

"Jonah and the Wells?"

"No doubt with Mr. Knowles's backing. You are female. I am a clergyman. What could either of us know of the nuances of the law? Or so they thought." Henry laid the Greek Bible open on his lap and withdrew from his breast pocket the incriminating papers. He held the bundle out to her. "This packet arrived today from your father's solicitor, Mr. Goodwin." She took it eagerly and rapidly began unfolding the pages. "You will want to read his letter first. The rest are copies of the originals in his possession. He said to expect him within the week. He sends his profound apologies. A matter in Bristol has occupied his time for the last three months and he had not learned of your father's death until a friend of mine made inquiries with him. I may be a younger son of a younger son, but I do not lack for connections."

He gave her a moment to glance over the pages before continuing.

"Your father was not *beguiled*," he said.

"Beguiled?" She looked up from the pages.

"Your word. You said Mr. Knowles *beguiled* Jane and Lady Trent but not you. Nor, it now appears, you father, either." Henry pointed to the documents in Miss Trent's hands. "Suffice it to say Mr. Knowles can only sell the estate with Jane's permission and your cooperation."

"Yes, we know that already. And if I don't cooperate, he will take me to court where any manner of horrors would ensue."

Henry shook his head. "But Jane *can't* give her permission to sell because the estate is held in trust."

"Meaning?"

"The trustee decides how much or how little Jane gets at any given time."

"And Mr. Knowles has no say in the matter?" The faint glimmer of hope began to form at the edges of Miss Trent's eyes.

"None whatsoever."

"And who, pray tell, is this trustee?"

"You are."

Miss Trent gasped at the shock of the words. And then promptly burst into tears. For a moment, Henry was stunned. This was not the Miss Trent he knew. He fumbled for his handkerchief, laid the Greek Bible aside, and in a trice, he was on his knees before the weeping woman.

"I'm so sorry," he said, pressing the handkerchief into her hand, "I should have prepared you better." And without warning, she threw her arms around him and buried her face against his shoulder. Quite naturally and without giving it a single thought, he wrapped his arms around her, pressed his cheek against her dark head, and simply held her close. She felt strangely small in his arms, warm too, and he thought he could spend a lifetime like this. Much too soon, though, her sobs subsided. She clung to him for a moment more, and then, to his regret, she pulled away. She did not look at him but dabbed her eyes with his handkerchief.

"How mortifying," she said.

"Nonsense." He covered her free hand with his. "You've barely had time to grieve for your father, and then all this, the possibility of losing everything. It's more than anyone could endure alone. You see to everyone's needs; it was time someone saw to yours."

She raised her head and looked at him for a long moment, her blue eyes red and puffy.

"Would you mind ringing for tea?" she asked.

"Not at all."

He stood up, but rather than doing what Miss Trent asked, he first quickly gathered up the papers and documents which had fallen to the floor in her moment of distress. She watched him as he carefully folded them and then tucked them behind the cushion in her chair.

"I don't think anyone should see these until we decide what to do."

Miss Trent nodded.

He rang the bell. Mr. Harvey soon appeared, and Henry requested tea be brought as Miss Trent was feeling unwell.

"And biscuits," she quietly added as Mr. Harvey left.

Henry sat down, and silence ensued until Mr. Harvey returned with the tea tray. He set it, as always, on the side table by Miss Trent, and departed, leaving the door slightly ajar as he had originally found it.

When Henry moved to pour the tea, Miss Trent quietly reassured him, "I can manage." As she handed him his cup of tea, she said, "Please, if you will, tell me the particulars."

After a cautionary sip of the hot tea, Henry continued with the matter at hand.

"Upon your father's death, you took care of various matters, including a letter to his solicitor, correct?"

"Yes, I wrote to Mr. Goodwin."

"I assumed that Mr. Henderson's arrival was a response to that. Mr. Goodwin has since ascertained that Mr. Henderson intercepted that letter. He never informed Mr. Goodwin.

"In fact, he seems to have been working with Mr. Wells for some time, and both are in the pay of Mr. Knowles. Mr. Henderson knew you were the trustee. Together, they conspired to convince you that you had no choice in the matter on the grounds that the courts would force the division of the estate in order to satisfy all interested parties. Plus the courts are notorious for taking decades to decide a case, and who would want to endure that?"

"They thought they would hand me the papers to sign," Miss Trent said. "Being, in their eyes, a mere female with nary a thought in her head, they assumed I'd never know the difference."

"Precisely."

"This is what comes of keeping females ignorant."

"What I can't understand," Henry said, "is why your father didn't tell you any of this."

"He probably meant to, but you know how he was. His mind was going for so long." Miss Trent shrugged. "And it's possible Mr. Goodwin arranged it all and just had my father sign the papers, even though he was no longer of sound mind."

"One thing, though. It appears the one thousand pounds Sir William gave at the time of your sister's marriage will be forever in Mr. Knowles's control. And he may claim a right to a portion of Jane's share of the income from the estate—that is, a portion of whatever the trustee gives to Jane. But he cannot force the selling of anything. You have complete control... of everything."

"Thank you. Thank you so much for this."

Henry shook his head. "All I did was write a few letters. Mr. Goodwin uncovered it all. I expect *Jonah and the Wells* will find themselves in serious trouble with those in their profession. As for Mr. Knowles...."

"I will need to discuss this with Jane first."

"Of course. However you decide to handle this, you have my full support."

"Thank you, Reverend Ogden."

Henry sat back to enjoy his tea, and he recalled his earlier conversation with Mr. Knowles. "Did you know his family is in the sugar trade?"

"Whose family?"

"Mr. Knowles. That's where his money comes from. Sugar."

"How interesting." She fell silent, gazing off into the fire, her mind obviously elsewhere. Then, Henry thought he saw the faintest trace of a smile hiding behind her lips. "Clearly," she said without looking at him, "my brother-in-law *not* getting half the estate is not going to make a difference in the lives of slaves in the West Indies, but there is something so...." Her voice trailed away, but Henry understood entirely.

"...Satisfying," he completed for her.

The smile revealed itself. "Exactly." She looked shyly down into her cooling cup of tea. And she whispered, "You have been a Godsend." Before he could respond, she grew self-conscious and picked up the plate of biscuits.

Just as Miss Trent held them out to him, the library door swung open to reveal Mr. Knowles standing there. Without missing a beat, she said, "And until you explained it, I couldn't understand how the prodigal son—a Jewish man—would find himself among the swine."

Henry easily followed her. "It shows how far he'd gone, in distance but also spiritually, from his people," he said, "He has become both spiritually and literally unclean."

"And still, his father welcomes him home."

"As does the heavenly Fa.... Oh, Mr. Knowles."

"Care to join us?" Margaret asked, "We were just discussing...."

"No. Thank you. I was looking for Mr. Wells."

"Oh, I last saw him at breakfast." Margaret's eyes glanced up toward the ceiling, as if she tried to recall something. "Have you tried the stables? I believe he wanted to look over the horses and carriages."

"Thank you," was all he said as he turned on his heel.

"You're right," Miss Trent said in a low voice filled with amusement, "No faster way to be rid of him."

Miss Trent finished her tea and then went off to find Jane, with Henry left to his own devices in the library. He did not mind. He enjoyed her trust, and he felt so at home, here, in this room. And with her.

Henry had known Miss Trent for five years. Her father had been his closest friend in Edgecombe. He'd sat with her many times, sometimes as a guest in their home, other times—more rare—at gatherings in other homes or at village events. They'd exchanged polite conversation, never anything too taxing, and always so very superficial. Only now did he seem to know her at all. And he found, much to his surprise, he loved her.

They thought to deceive her. They planned to take everything from her and leave her with *what? Money?* True, Margaret knew she would have had financial security, but at the cost of losing her home. They wanted to take away something infinitely more valuable than money—her home, her land, and twenty years of loving memories with it. And they would have succeeded if not for Reverend Ogden.

She was uncertain how to proceed and whether she should confront Mr. Knowles or wait until Mr. Goodwin arrived to deal with the matter. First, though, she had to speak to Jane about it.

However, finding Jane resting in bed with a migraine, Margaret knew her sister was in no state to discuss things now. Little wonder, she thought. The younger children were being boisterous again upstairs in the nursery, despite their father's reprimand. They needed some diversion, Margaret knew. The older boys, Harvey told her, were out admiring the horses in the stables, no doubt dividing the spoils. *But no*, that was harsh; Margaret knew better than to blame the children for their father's avarice. Where the girls were, Margaret had no idea; probably ensconced in some corner bored to tears.

Margaret returned to the library to find Reverend Ogden waiting for her. Of late, she had noticed his eyes lit up every time he looked at her, and it filled her heart with joy. But she dismissed it as nothing more than her imagination playing tricks on her. She had put aside such dreams long ago.

She ordered something more substantial than biscuits be brought to the library for them. She also ordered a light repast be laid out on the sideboard in the dining room for everyone else to partake of as they came and went throughout the afternoon. Then she settled down before the fire with Reverend Ogden to enjoy another cup of tea—the pot now refreshed—and the cakes and sandwiches newly arrived.

Only, Harvey soon appeared at the door again, the sound of the children echoing through the house behind him.

"Miss Trent," he said, "where would you like the greenery put up?"

"Greenery?"

"Apparently, the Knowles boys, with the help of the groomsmen, took it upon themselves to gather greenery."

"I thought they were all in the stables."

"They were. But they decided to go on an expedition into the wood." Harvey glanced at Reverend Ogden. "Seeing how it is Christmas Eve."

Christmas! Oh, gracious. In the midst of everything, she had forgotten the day. She looked at Reverend Ogden, as if pleading for help, and said, "Well, the drawing room, of course. And the hall. And the dining room. And if there is enough, the banisters."

"Do any of those Knowles girls play?" Reverend Ogden asked Margaret.

"Of course. Jane would never neglect their education in that regard."

He stood up and motioned toward the doorway. "Then perhaps we should adjourn to the drawing room to oversee the decorating and perhaps see how well those girls play."

Strangely, despite everything, Margaret thought it a splendid idea and suggested the younger children come down from the nursery to participate.

Hours later, as the world turned dark, she found herself in the drawing room with the vicar and the Knowles children, along with their governess and their tutor. The girls took turns playing at the pianoforte— Margaret could barely remember their names, and besides, they all looked alike—while the boys did an excellent job of dealing with too many directions for where to hang the boughs of holly and pine branches. Reverend Ogden and the two eight-year-olds sat roasting chestnuts in the fire. And between rounds of bickering back and forth over what song should be played next, they sang carols, as if they were all one, big, happy family. Margaret hadn't had this much fun in years.

After a while, Reverend Ogden joined her on the settee.

"I had no idea you were so good with children," she said.

"So, there are some things you don't know about me?"

She smiled. "I suppose so."

"I taught at Eton for a year."

"Eton?" She didn't expect that. "Why only a year?"

He leaned forward and whispered, "I discovered I didn't like other people's children, which surprised me, because I like all my nieces and nephews despite their very dissimilar characters." He glanced around at the children. "Although, I must say, Mrs. Knowles has done a wonderful job with those in her charge."

"Ah, of course. You come from a large family." It was more statement than question.

"Yes."

"And your cousin is the Earl of Wexbury."

"Yes. How do you know so much about me?"

She raised her eyebrows. "I'm not the only one villagers gossip about."

"Oh."

"So, tell me, how far down the line are you?"

"Very far. At least three dozen of my male relatives would have to die in order for me to become the earl. And, as unfashionable as it is, I do like my family."

"So you have had to make your own way in the world."

He cocked his head to one side and, for a moment, hesitated. "In a manner of speaking, but it has great advantages, being a younger son of a younger son."

"Such as?"

"No speeches in the House of Lords. No London seasons. No need for the latest fashions. No vapid females pursuing me. No forced marriages. No pressure for an heir." He laughed as he said it.

The mantel clock chimed.

"Gracious. Is that the time?" Margaret asked. Both she and the vicar stood up. She told the children to go dress for dinner and reminded them all, even the two eight-year-olds, they would eat at table with the adults that night. They all hurried off, leaving Margaret alone with the vicar.

"Stay for dinner." The words rushed out of Margaret's mouth. "I need your calm presence and voice of reason."

"Of course. Anything you wish."

There were seventeen for dinner. Margaret considered inviting the Knowles' governess and tutor, simply to use more of her china, but after consideration realized—aside from the fact that it was most unusual to have a governess and tutor join the family at dinner— they might prefer a quiet moment away from their charges.

And Jane came down to join them. She still looked unwell, but she seemed to be holding steady, and Margaret even caught her smiling.

With such a large party, Margaret believed there would be safety in numbers. She failed to take into calculation Mr. Knowles's superior vanity. It began with the arrival of the roasted goose—two in fact, one after the other—with all the trimmings. Her brother-in-law immediately lamented the idea of eating the same meal two days in a row. When Margaret, confused, inquired *Whatever can you mean?* he pointed out *Goose for Christmas Eve* and *Christmas Day?* Margaret informed him they would dine on beef for Christmas Day. Reverend Ogden applauded that choice, *Oh, Brava. Excellent,* but Mr. Knowles stated *We always have goose.* To which Margaret promptly replied *We always have beef.* Chastened, Mr. Knowles shrugged and mumbled something about people who grow up in a foreign country.

The tension increased even further when Margaret handed the carving knife and fork to Reverend Ogden. She gave him the honor of carving as thanks for all his help and support during Sir William's illness and since his death. Margaret ignored Mr. Knowles's scowl. Given all he planned to do to steal her home from her, Margaret was not about to let him carve the goose on Christmas Eve.

As soon as everyone was plated, Jane quietly eased some of that tension by inadvertently changing the subject to the topic of the weather and the state of the roads. Her question, completely unrelated to the topic, seemed innocuous enough. And normally, it would have been. However, she asked, "Reverend, do you think there will be a Midnight Service with all this snow?"

"Snow?"

This excited the children. And distressed Reverend Ogden. There had been some flurries while it had still been light outside, but this time of year, the sun set so early that it had been dark for several hours now. Unsure whether it had continued after the sun had set, Margaret asked Harvey for a report on any accumulation.

He returned with grim news. "At least half a foot and coming down hard. You can barely see the stables. And it's colder than ever, miss."

The children erupted in happy chatter, and while Reverend Ogden was quite dismayed, Margaret, inwardly, was glad.

"That decides it, then," she quietly said to him, "You'll have to stay the night."

"But Midnight Service?"

"Your curate will just have to give it. But I doubt anyone will venture out in this. Besides, you're still riding my father's horse, and I will certainly not allow her out in this."

After dinner, Margaret hoped to discuss things with Jane, but her sister pled a headache and went to bed. Reverend Ogden, two of the Knowles boys, the footman, and the groomsmen went out to check the condition of the roads. All returned with the same report. It was much too dangerous to travel, particularly given the poor visibility.

Margaret asked Mrs. Jenkins to prepare a room for

Reverend Ogden and then went to join the others in the drawing room. Mr. Knowles had barely said a word since the disagreement over the goose, and now, he sat drinking coffee with Jonah and the Wells. He looked too pleased with himself, like a housecat biding his time before pouncing. But at least Margaret knew his game. And tonight, she would enjoy herself.

The children, down to the youngest, knew all the latest dances, and soon, they rolled up the carpet and formed a country dance. They even recruited their governess and tutor to join in, with Margaret's approval. And soon, both she and Reverend Ogden were dancing as well.

If it had been up to the girls—and perhaps Margaret, too—they would have all danced until dawn. But the hour grew late. One of the eight-year-olds lay curled up asleep on the settee, the other having disappeared earlier. Their older brother snored in a nearby chair. Their father, along with Jonah and the Wells, had already stumbled off to bed. And at last, the governess forced her charges to retire for the night, with everyone else following suit. Margaret, assisting with the youngest, said goodnight to Reverend Ogden and went upstairs in a gaggle of skirts.

On the landing, she passed Mrs. Jenkins and reminded her to make sure Reverend Ogden got to the right room. Then Margaret continued on up to the nursery. While the attendants saw to the children, Margaret inquired as to the location of the missing eight-year-old. She often climbed into bed with one of her older sisters, the one attendant told Margaret and suggested just leaving her. With a night candle in hand, Margaret went downstairs, did her final rounds, and retired to her chamber, where she discovered the previously missing eight-year-old snuggled up in bed alongside Jane.

Margaret stood for a long time and stared at the pair bathed in candlelight. For all intents and purposes, they were mother and child. The girl had been barely a year old when Jane married Mr. Knowles and so had never known any other mother. Margaret had never considered that before. She always thought of the children as Mr. Knowles's, not Jane's. But today, she had seen Jane's influence in them.

Margaret didn't have the heart to wake them. There was enough room for her, but she didn't want to sleep three to a bed. So she quickly readied for bed, slipped into her night rail and dressing gown, took her hair down, and went in search of another bed.

Only, once in the corridor, she realized she didn't know which room might be empty. Mrs. Jenkins had put Reverend Ogden in one of them, and Margaret had no idea which. She couldn't very well go knocking on doors in the middle of the night, in her night clothes, no less. Someone might see. Oh, it was all so very vexing, and she should have been more attentive in the sorting of rooms.

She decided to do what she'd done so many times before when her father was ill; she went to the library to sleep on the settee. The door, at least, had a lock.

But as she descended the stairs, she could see the door to the library was shut with a warm light spilling out around the edges. *Mr. Knowles conspiring with Jonah and the Wells, no doubt.* Enough was enough. It was time to give her brother-in-law a piece of her mind and put him in his place once and for all.

She flung the door open... only to discover Reverend Ogden standing there before the fire, in his shirtsleeves and waistcoat, with a small volume in his hand. He jumped at the sudden intrusion and gasped. Margaret did likewise, realizing she stood there in her dressing gown, barefoot, with her long hair bound only with a pink ribbon over her shoulder. Then he smiled with obvious relief, and Margaret almost giggled.

"I'm so sorry," she said, "I gave you a terrible start."

"You weren't expecting me?"

"I thought Mr. Knowles and those shysters were up to no good."

"Ah. No. It seems there was no room at the inn."

"I beg your pardon?"

"All the bedchambers are full, except your mother and father's rooms, and that would be inappropriate, especially as the wound is so fresh. And I am not Christ-like enough to sleep in the stables. I told Mrs. Jenkins I could manage quite well here."

"This is intolerable. The tutor has a room to himself. Jonah and the Wells should be in the stables and you should be in a proper bed."

"Truly, Miss Trent, I do not mind in the least. I find this room most agreeable."

Mrs. Jenkins should have informed her of the situation, but Margaret knew she could not blame the servants. They'd gone from a household of two to a household of... *what was it now*, nineteen, plus half a dozen more servants? *Gracious*, there were half a dozen extra coachmen alone sleeping out in the stables right now. And Mrs. Jenkins and Harvey had to manage them all, while Cook fed them all. No wonder Mr. Knowles decided to spend Christmas at Edgecombe Hall; he wouldn't have to pay the expense of all those mouths to feed.

No, this was Margaret's fault. She should have paid more attention and been more diligent in the care of her guests, rather than dancing the night away like some newly-out debutante at her first ball.

"Come by the fire." Reverend Ogden held his hand out to her from the hearthside. "It's very cold tonight. And there is a draft from the door."

Margaret looked at him. He stood in his stocking feet beneath black knee-breeches and a black waistcoat, with his neck-cloth still immaculately but simply tied. He must be frightfully cold, she thought, without even a dressing gown. Then she noticed, other than the blanket and lap rug always kept in the library, there were no additional blankets or linens, not even a pillow for him.

She glanced around and discovered, aside from the lack of linens, there was no basin, no hot water, not even a chamber pot shoved under a chair.

"I will return momentarily," she said and headed toward the kitchen. With her father's illness, she had developed the habit of having someone readily available at all hours, and now, with so many people in the household, she had returned to that practice, temporarily. So tonight, she found the valet, James, and the maid, Mariah, playing cards in the kitchen. They immediately jumped up when Margaret walked in.

"It's not for money, miss," James said.

"I'm just keeping him company, miss," Mariah said at the same time.

"Calm yourselves. I know Mrs. Jenkins would never tolerate anything untoward. Due to a lack of beds, Reverend Ogden is spending the night in the library. James, please bring down the screen from Lady Trent's chamber. It will afford him some additional privacy. Then assist Mariah. He needs hot water, a basin, soap, towels, bed linens, a pillow...," Margaret hesitated, her voice dropping, "and a chamber pot... most of which you can take from my father's dressing room."

They hurried off to follow Margaret's orders, and she soon followed them upstairs, to her father's chamber, where she found a razor, recently purchased but never used, as well as a banyan her father never wore. She gathered a few blankets and returned to the library.

James had finished setting up the screen and Mariah carried in a pitcher of hot water, while Reverend Ogden looked uncomfortable at all the fuss being made over him.

"Should I make up a bed, miss?" Mariah asked.

"Oh, no," the vicar protested, "I can manage on my own."

Margaret told the servants that would be all, and they retired back to the kitchen.

Several heartbeats later, Reverend Ogden said, "I believe I have thoroughly compromised you, Miss Trent." He was looking at her most peculiarly.

Margaret knew perfectly well how she looked—in her dressing gown with hair unbound—with him standing there in his shirtsleeves and shoeless. She could already hear the gossip if word got out. But *this* was not what she imagined *compromise* would be like in the least, and if it were, it was sadly disappointing and greatly overrated.

"Hardly," Margaret said, certain she blushed but hoping he wouldn't notice in the firelight, "but I won't tell if you won't."

Reverend Ogden motioned to the folded bed linens on the settee. "This wasn't necessary. You don't have to take care of everyone. Certainly, not me."

"No. I don't." She wanted to say more, that she wanted to, that his wellbeing concerned her immensely, but couldn't. It would sound too much like a declaration. Instead, she pointed over her shoulder and said, "There is a key to this door on my father's desk."

She moved to retrieve it from where it lay next to the box containing her father's dueling pistols. She held the iron key out to the vicar, but he did not attempt to take it.

Instead, he asked, as if delaying her departure, "So why were you coming to the library? Just to catch Mr. Knowles in an act of villainy?"

"One of the eight-year-olds climbed into bed with Jane, and I didn't have the heart to move her."

His face lit up. "So that's where Georgiana wandered off to."

He surprised Margaret. After only two days around the children he already knew their names. The twins, no less. "You can tell them apart?"

"Yes. Can't you?"

"Not a bit." She laughed. And then they fell into an

awkward silence.

"So," he asked after a moment, "you came to sleep *here*?"

Margaret moved closer to the heat of the fire. "My father often fell asleep in his chair, and it seemed kinder just to leave him. I'd sleep on the settee and when he would stir, I'd ring for James to carry him to bed."

Reverend Ogden said nothing, just nodded his head. It was such strange behavior. He seemed to be looking for things to say, to fill the space and silence between them. That had never been a problem before. Since that day when Jonah and the Wells came to the house, Margaret found she and the vicar could talk so easily and just as easily sit in silence together. But not tonight.

Reverend Ogden motioned to her father's chess board set up for a game. "Do you play?"

Margaret held back a laugh. "I can move the pieces. I wouldn't call it playing."

He merely smiled. And still, he said nothing. At last, they'd seemed to run out of mundane conversation, and Margaret decided to end it.

"Well, goodnight." And she turned to walk away. But the vicar reached for her hand and prevented her from going.

"Please stay." He gently cradled her hand between his. "Otherwise you'll end up in the stables. And there's room for both of us here. You can have the settee, I'll take the floor."

Margaret slowly shook her head. "I don't think...."

"The truth is...." He hesitated. "I find you amazing. And so very beautiful."

"Reverend Ogden!" She had been accused of being many things but beautiful had never been one of them. Her face was too angular, her mouth too wide, and all that dark hair just gave her a foreign look.

"I think you should call me Henry and I should call you Margaret."

"You do?" Now, this was truly baffling. Oh, she very much wanted to call him Henry, but it was so inappropriate, and Reverend Ogden was always most appropriate with her... except for now, because all of this was truly scandalous—*What must James and Mariah think?* But Margaret wished, somehow, it were fitting and proper for them to be alone like this, bathed in firelight, dressed just so.

"And I think we should be married."

Lord in Heaven! She never expected *that*. "You do?" she managed to whisper.

"Yes."

She slowly pulled her hand away from his and turned aside. She had no idea what to say, and the silence was so heavy, until at last, she smiled and jokingly said, "Why Henry, this is so sudden," as if she were some debutante in a conservatory.

"I'm serious."

Margaret nodded. "I know."

"And if you fear I'm just some fortune hunter, you should know I have four thousand a year, on top of my living."

"Four thousand?" That shocked Margaret more than the proposal did. "But you live in the vicarage. You're a younger son of a younger son, *forced to make his own way in the world."*

"True, but the income is from my mother's family."

"Wasn't she the daughter of a shopkeeper?"

"Her brother, though, was a very successful banker and he died without children. His fortune passed to me and my siblings."

"Oh."

"Does that change things?" He sounded worried.

"Not at all," she assured him.

Silence fell over them again as Margaret contemplated everything Reverend Og—Henry had said. It was only natural, she supposed, that a vicar would need a wife, and she had often wondered why he was not married. Too set in his ways, seemed the logical reason, but she was well-accustomed to dealing with men set in their ways.

But then he took her hand again and said, "I know I'm not the man a lady dreams about. I'm no champion. My best days are behind me. My knee already aches every time it rains. I'm losing my hair."

"Who isn't?" she quietly added.

"I like my quiet, comfortable life, dull as it may be, with tea being the high point of the day. But I have come to realize I want you in that life with me. Not merely because I so enjoy your company but because... because, I love you."

How she managed to sleep that night after such a declaration, Margaret would never know, but she did sleep. She woke to sunlight spilling into the library to the accompaniment of the voices of children playing outside.

A dripping sound spoke to her of melting snow and clearing roads. Curled up on the settee, a wretched pain in her back, she realized hope filled her for the first time in a long time. *And why not?* It was Christmas morning, after all.

She looked over at Henry lying on the floor. He was staring at her, his mouth forming a small smile. He held his hand out to her, and before she even thought about it, Margaret took it, as if it were the most natural thing in the world.

"Good morning, my darling," he said.

"I haven't given you my answer yet," she said.

"Oh?" Thankfully, the light did not fade from his face. "After spending the night in the same room with me? Very compromising, if you ask me."

"Well, no one has seen us."

But Margaret spoke too soon.

The door opened, as Margaret realized they'd forgotten to lock the door. And there stood Jane.

"Oh my!" she said, as both Margaret and Henry scrambled to get up.

"Rest assured," Henry said in his shirtsleeves and knee breeches, one stocking down around his ankle, "nothing happened."

"We fell asleep," was the only lame response Margaret could manage as she attempted to put on her dressing gown.

Jane cocked her head to one side and scowled. "How... *unfortunate.*"

That was the Jane Margaret knew, and she was suddenly filled with elation. Her sister had returned to her former self, and she looked bright and cheerful, as befitted one on Christmas morning, fully recovered from her *illness*.

"I beg your pardon?" Henry asked, clearly taken aback by Jane's unorthodox response. But Margaret now knew everything really was going to be all right, one way or another, regardless of what happened next. She moved quickly toward her sister, all smiles.

"I must hurry and dress," Margaret said without stopping as she headed out of the library.

"You will marry her, won't you?" Jane asked the vicar.

"I've already asked but she hasn't given her reply."

"Margaret! For shame. Never keep a vicar waiting." And then Margaret heard Jane add to Henry, "You know, there's a key to this door," before closing the library door and hurrying after her sister.

At last, while she dressed, Margaret had a chance to talk to Jane and tell her everything she'd learned about the estate and the trust. Jane sat perfectly still and silent through the explanation, her face immobile, never betraying a single thought. When Margaret finished—with both her quick coiffure and the story of how Mr. Knowles planned to steal their inheritance—Jane still remained silent for a long moment before taking a deep breath.

At last, she spoke. "I will not be returning with him to London, Margaret. I want to stay here with you. And the children, as well."

Margaret breathed a sigh of relief and suddenly understood. "Thus all the luggage."

"Yes. I came knowing I wouldn't return."

"How long have you been planning this?"

Jane looked down at her hands in her lap. "I've wanted to escape from Frederick for years but never thought it possible. I was stuck with the choice I had made. Until I met Captain…." She looked up then, a bright light in her eyes. *Oh, dear.* What an impossibility that was, Margaret thought.

"I had to deal with the laudanum first," Jane continued, "That was so very difficult, and it was only when Papa died and Frederick said we wouldn't attend the funeral…. It was the final straw. I'd had enough. That's when I decided to see the doctor. And then Frederick said we were coming here for Christmas, and it was like Divine Providence paving the way for me."

"I think it's time we spoke to Mr. Knowles."

The two sisters went downstairs hand in hand. Before they ever reached the library, they heard male voices quietly talking. There they found Henry, cleaned and dressed, standing with Mr. Knowles and Jonah and the Wells.

"Henry," Margaret said, still holding Jane's hand, "I think it time we discussed the situation."

"Of course, my dear," Henry replied, clearly understanding what she meant. "Do you wish to do the honors or shall I?"

"Let me. Given the distress they've caused, I think it's my turn to cause some distress." Henry smiled while the other three men exchanged worried looks.

"Gentlemen," Margaret continued, "we know your scheme. We know you are trying to steal our estate."

"How dare you suggest...?" Mr. Knowles began, his face turning red.

"And we know I am the trustee."

The color drained from the faces of Jonah and the Wells, while Mr. Knowles stood there with his mouth hanging open.

Margaret turned on the two solicitors. "Mr. Goodwin is on his way here."

The two men glanced at one another, wide-eyed with fear.

Jonah spoke first. "Mr. Wells came to me. It was his idea."

"My idea?" the Wells shouted at him, "Mr. Knowles came to me with it. And you had no problem going along with it."

"Only because...."

"Oh, shut up!" Mr. Knowles yelled over them. "Don't say another word!"

The two solicitors glared at him.

"This is your fault," the Wells said, "but I certainly won't take the fall with you."

"Nor I," Jonah said.

And without another word, both men hurried from the room, each trying to get ahead of the other, and headed upstairs.

Feeling very pleased with herself, Margaret looked over at the vicar. "Henry, you haven't had your morning tea. Forgive me for being so lax."

A moment later, the two solicitors came stumbling down the stairs, their luggage in tow, and ran out of the house.

"It appears your collaborators have abandoned you, Mr. Knowles," Margaret said.

"I hope they remember their carriage is in the carriage house," Henry added.

"It's only three miles to the posting inn," Margaret said, "I'm sure they'll remember sometime before they get there."

Mr. Knowles, who had been so very quiet, at last spoke. "This is all very well, Miss Trent, but I can still take you to court."

"On what grounds?" Jane suddenly demanded of her husband. "You do not have the authority to act on my behalf in this matter. My father gave that authority to Margaret."

Mr. Knowles glared at his wife. He glanced from her to Henry and then to Margaret.

"Very well. We're leaving. Now." He marched toward Jane. "We can stay at an inn, but I will not spend another moment in this house."

"I'm not going anywhere with you," Jane said, "not today or ever again. Neither are the children."

"What did you say?" Mr. Knowles's tone filled Margaret with fear, but Jane did not back down, standing up to her husband with a courage she had not seen since their childhood.

"You will simply tell people that 'Mrs. Knowles has retired to the countryside for her health on the advice of her physician and has taken the children with her.'"

"You are my wife." He slowly growled out the words. "I won't allow you to leave me."

And then Jane played her trump card, which

Margaret never expected.

"Will Lady Ashton like having her name dragged through the mud?" she asked.

"How dare you speak of her!"

"More importantly, will Lord Ashton?" Jane continued, "How will his lordship react when he learns you've been bedding his wife for the past two years?"

"You will stay silent!" Mr. Knowles roared at her. He grabbed her upper arm, roughly, causing Jane to cry out, and pulled her into the hall.

In that instant, Margaret seized the first thing at hand—a heavy book—while out of the corner of her eye, she saw Henry moving as well. But she reached Mr. Knowles first, hitting him about the head with the book. He let go of Jane and turned on Margaret, rage covering his face. And then Margaret smacked him again, across the face this time, with the book. He stumbled backward, not so much with the force of the blow but by the shock and sheer audacity of it. Blood poured from his nose.

"My nose!" he screamed, "You broke my nose." And he raised his hand to strike Margaret. "You little...."

An ominous click filled the hall, instantly stopping Mr. Knowles in mid-motion.

Henry stood there with one of Sir William's pistols, cocked and leveled at Mr. Knowles. Both Margaret and Jane moved away, giving ample room for the target.

"I may be a man of God," Henry said in a steady, eerily calm voice, "but I am a man, and I will not feel the slightest qualm killing you. God will forgive me."

Mr. Knowles lowered his hand, slowly, and backed away. He looked at Jane.

Completely and utterly defeated, Mr. Knowles stumbled out of the house without another word. Henry, at last, with a great sigh, lowered the pistol.

"He'll end up with Jonah and the Wells at the inn," Margaret said. "What a merry Christmas that shall be."

"I'll go make sure Harvey sets a watch on them to make sure they don't cause any mischief should they come back," Jane said and left them alone in the hall.

Margaret turned to Henry. She was all smiles.

"You could have killed him."

"Not likely," he said, putting the pistol down on the hall table, "I forgot to load the ball."

Margaret laughed. "Well, you're still my champion."

But Henry looked quite serious. "When he touched you like that…. It was all I could do to keep from…." He stared at her, his hazel eyes dark.

Without warning, he pulled her to him and kissed her. No pure, chaste kiss, but raw and hungry, as if he couldn't get enough of her. Margaret clung to him, only his strength keeping her upright. At last, she freed her lips from his and rested her forehead against his shoulder.

"Yes," she whispered.

"Yes?"

"Yes, I do love you."

"Oh, thank God."

Margaret pulled away, just enough to look him in the face.

"But you promised me dull," she said, "and this morning has been hardly that. You haven't even had your tea."

"Dull, did I? Well, if it's dull you want...." With his hand on her lower back, he guided her back into the library. "In regard to those letters you hid away...."

"From my grandmother's grandmother's sister at Weston Hall?"

"My cousin's husband's sister is Lord Weston's daughter-in-law."

"Really? You *do* know Lord Weston owns a Holbein drawing?"

"Stop teasing."

"I'm quite serious. A portrait reputed to be Anne Boleyn."

"No!"

"Yes! If we left now, we could be there tomorrow in time for dinner."

Henry shook his head. "I'm afraid that wouldn't do. You and me travelling together? We'd have to stay at an inn."

"Oh dear."

"Anything could happen."

"The only solution I can see," Margaret said, as if the idea only just came to her, "is a change in the status of our relationship."

"Well, if you think so, then we must do what we must do."

"For my grandmother's grandmother's sister."

"For Holbein. And then anything can happen."

They laughed, but then Margaret grew serious.

"There's just one problem," she said. "You have an appointment this morning."

He looked at her quizzically.

"It's Christmas."

His face brightened with the realization. He had a congregation waiting for him.

"And a happy Christmas it is, too," he said.

And he kissed her.

About Anna

Anna D. Allen is essentially half-Finnish and half-Southern, which means she has no sense of humor and will shoot you for wearing white shoes after Labor Day... unless you are attending a wedding and happen to be the bride. She holds a Bachelor of Science and a Master of Arts in Language and Literature. She is a recipient of the Writers of the Future award and a member of Science Fiction and Fantasy Writers of America, but she also has a great passion for Regency Romances. It is generally acknowledged that she spends way too much time with the dead and her mind got lost somewhere in the 19th Century. Case in point, her website:

http://beket1.wix.com/annadallen

Rumor has it her novel, *Miss Pritchard's Happy, Wanton Christmas (and the Consequences Thereof)*, will be completed any day now, but she doesn't believe it. Her available works include two collections: *Mrs. Hewitt's Barbeque: Seven Eclectic Tales of Food, Humor, and Love* and *Lake People and Other Speculative Tales*; the novel *Charles Waverly and the Deadly African Safari*; the Regency Romance Novelette "A Christmas Wager," as well as some boring scholarly stuff about dead people. Claims that she writes steamier stories under another

name are met with feigned shock followed by mad
laughter.

A Christmas Equation

by

Hannah Meredith

Chapter One

Brackenheath
Yorkshire, England
1811

BENJAMIN RADCLIFFE, VISCOUNT KITTREDGE, should have suspected something was amiss when he looked out the carriage window and saw a large collection of coaches huddled around the stable block— many more than would be expected for a shooting party. But just as the notion crossed his mind, his setter bitch, Meg, launched herself across the seat, landed heavily in his lap, and began barking a greeting to the approaching house.

"Quiet, Meg! Down!" Ben put one hand up to deflect the feathery tail flogging his face and the other hand down to protect his most sensitive parts, which seemed to be the target for the sharp-nailed, dancing feet of a dog weighing over three stone. With his elbows, he pushed the enthusiastic animal back to the carriage floor.

Any previous thought about the inappropriate number of assembled coaches was replaced with his concern that Meg might be too young and untried to use this week. He'd shot over her a number of times and had been pleased with her steadiness, but she remained an unknown quantity in a group setting. Brutus, awakened by Meg's rambunctious behavior, simply raised his head and then dropped it back onto his paws.

"You need to learn deportment from your father," Ben said, rubbing one of Meg's silky ears. She still quivered with excitement and pressed her head hard against his leg, but she quieted. Regardless of how his dogs behaved, if the weather didn't break, hunting would be more chore than joy. Cold rain and mist had followed him the entire day. He'd been glad to have the dogs in the carriage with him. They took the chill off better than putting hot, wrapped bricks on the floor.

Of course, the weather in mid-December was always chancy. He'd thought it odd Lord Dutton had arranged a shooting party so late in the season, but felt it imperative he attend. While Roger, Ben's late brother, had held the title, he'd allowed centuries-old alliances to languish, and now Ben felt he needed to repair these friendships. Dutton's invitation seemed like an ideal opportunity to begin the shoring-up process. Ben also readily admitted he needed a break from his present chores.

The carriage shuddered to a stop in front of a gray stone facade Ben vaguely remembered from youthful visits here with his father. An alert footman noticed the carriage's arrival and hurried out into the rain to lower the steps.

"Stay," Ben said to the dogs and slipped out the door before an inquisitive nose could insert itself in the opening. He dashed up the stairs and into the hall.

The butler looked confused by his arrival. The feeling that something was not quite right again walked along Ben's spine.

"Viscount Kittredge," he said, handing the butler his hat. "I'm here for the shooting."

The man frowned at Ben. Had he sounded like an imposter when he gave his title? Even if he still felt like one, Ben didn't think it showed. Dog hair? He looked down at his greatcoat, and yes, it was festooned with long, red and white hairs. Gads! Brushing at it now would simply spread the problem to the house. Ben stoically ignored his clothing's decoration, pulled himself up to the top of his considerable height, and frowned back.

The butler wilted under his scrutiny. "If you'd be pleased to wait a moment, my lord, I'll get Lord Dutton."

The man scuttled away, leaving Ben to cool his heels in the foyer. A collection of antique firearms arranged in a fan shape adorned one of the walls, and a number of impressive stag heads glared down at him. At odds with the masculine decor, feminine laughter drifted from an upstairs room. Good heavens, was Dutton old enough to have marriageable daughters? The present Lord Dutton had been a young man when Ben had visited here as a boy, so this was a possibility. Ben hoped *that* hadn't been the reason for his invitation. Ever since he'd inherited the title and all it encompassed, the most unexpected matchmakers had appeared.

Dutton, bluff and hearty, hurried into the hallway. The slim young man of Ben's memory hadn't grown any taller, but he certainly had widened. Ben had long noted that people seemed to age in one of two ways. Some became craggier, as if the winds of time had scoured all the topsoil away to leave only the granite beneath. Others seemed to have encountered rains and slowly melted into rounded hillocks.

Dutton was decidedly a smiling, genial hillock. "Kittredge. This is a surprise, but I'm delighted to see you."

A surprise? Something was definitely amiss, and it had nothing to do with being covered in dog hair. "I'm here to hunt pheasants. Am I in error?" Ben shook Dutton's extended hand.

"You're a month late for the shooting party. It was set for *November* sixteenth. But you're more than welcome now. You find me suffering through the early arrival of part of Lady Dutton's family, who are coming for Christmas. The contingent that has so far descended on us contains a huge number of truly silly women. You'll be my excuse to get out of the house. Please say you'll stay a few days. The birds are plentiful this year."

Dear Lord! He was a month late in arriving. Ben felt the blood rush to his face. He was sure he glowed like a ripe apple in the sun. His damnable complexion immediately showed his chagrin.

Ben quickly searched his limited repertoire of socially acceptable responses to this embarrassing situation. Scowling and uttering some curse words had always worked in the army but weren't appropriate now. "I'm mortified that I missed the correct day and then showed up at this inappropriate time. My secretary put this date on my calendar..." Of course. It was Peters. Ben had inherited his brother's incompetent secretary along with all the other disasters. Ben had hoped for some consistency during the transition period, but it was becoming more and more apparent that Peters would have to go.

He realized he was glowering at Lord Dutton and carefully revised his expression. "I can't apologize enough for my untimely arrival. Your offer of hospitality is most kind, but I wouldn't want to intrude on a family gathering. I'll take my leave and look forward to hunting here at some other date."

Ben smiled graciously and shifted his weight to begin his retreat. Dutton reached out and gripped his arm with surprising strength. A core of granite remained inside the hillock.

"Nonsense, Kittredge," the smaller man said. "It would be ridiculous to immediately turn around when you have just arrived. Staying for a few days only makes sense. And, as I said, you'd be doing me a favor. While more gentlemen will be arriving later in the week, I'm now sorely outnumbered by the ladies and need some antidote for the constant discussion of ribbons and ruffles."

Put that way, staying seemed the proper thing to do. He was already here; he might as well remain.

Ben also silently acknowledged that the idea of leaving had brought a sharp stab of disappointment. He loathed seeing the anticipated, convivial evenings of cards and strong drink disappear. Lord knew he needed the break. Trying to repair the damage to the estates his brother Roger's inattention had caused was driving him berserk. Roger had been a fine man, but he'd definitely not been a manager.

Ben hadn't realized how lackadaisical his brother's administration had been until he'd inherited and discovered disaster—rent receipts stuffed into cubbyholes, tenants' requests for repairs languishing beneath stacks of sporting magazines, and land stewards' estimates of crop yields used as book marks. The list of incompetence was endless. Ben had bent his formidable organizational skills to the task and had yet to make order out of the chaos. The effort was both irritating and exhausting.

He deserved this brief holiday and would gladly take it. "I'd be pleased to stay and get in some shooting," Ben said. "I brought a couple of my gun dogs with me."

Dutton brightened. "Some of those fine, red-speckled setters your father used to breed?"

"The same." Ben pasted a smile on his face and waited for the inevitable comment on how much the spotted dogs resembled the Radcliffe family, which had been plagued with an overabundance of freckles for generations. When no quip came, his smile widened.

"While the staff readies your room, come to my study," Dutton said. "One of my wife's relatives brought me some excellent whiskey from a new Scottish distillery, and it's just the thing to take the chill off."

Ben nodded and followed Dutton down the hall. With fine Scotch whiskey available, the next few days were looking up.

Sarah Clendenin stopped abruptly as she entered the open foyer from the side hallway. Two stories below, a large man twisted from side to side as he carefully examined the bottom of his greatcoat. She couldn't see what attracted his attention, but she thought she knew the man. Then, she *definitely* knew the man. Her breath caught in her throat, and the soft wool of Lady Harley's Kashmir shawl slipped from her nerveless fingers to pool silently on the floor.

Lord Dutton hurried into the foyer, and Sarah dropped back into the gloom of the hallway. While she could no longer see the two men, she could still hear their conversation. Lord Dutton called the man Kittredge—and that couldn't be right. Viscount Kittredge was Roger now, but there was no question the man in the foyer was Ben. All the Radcliffe men were tall with reddish hair, but only Ben had reached truly gigantic proportions and sported bright, fox red hair. Even though it had been seven years since she'd last seen him, the man that Ben would eventually become had been set in the bones even then. She was not mistaken.

For years, she'd been a keen observer of Benjamin Radcliffe.

After her mother died, her father had sent Sarah to live with her mother's widowed sister, Aunt Tess. His reasoning, which he proclaimed loudly and often whenever they were in company, was that Sarah needed a woman's nurturing touch. As a child, Sarah had suspected she was being exiled in favor of her brother Harold, the long awaited heir her father doted on. When she was older, she was sure this was the case.

Aunt Tess did her duty to the best of her ability. She was not naturally motherly, having never had children of her own, but she made sure that Sarah was well-fed and well-dressed, that she followed a strict regimen, and that her mind was improved by a series of governesses. These ladies changed with regularity, their departure prompted by the isolation of the location and Aunt Tess's exacting requirements.

The result was that Sarah received a wildly eclectic education—and was a very lonely little girl. She felt that she'd been abandoned. The silence of her aunt's house pressed down on her like a giant hand, and she fled to the spacious grounds around the estate. The sounds of children's laughter drew her to the closest tenant houses, but as soon as she'd formed a tentative friendship, her aunt arrived to have a word with the children's parents and all contact ceased.

When her legs became long and coltish, she moved further afield and discovered the magic of the moors. The wind, the sun, the mist, the small animals that would bolt from beneath the heather and surprise her into laughter—these became the constants of her existence.

And it was there she met the boy.

She'd seen the dog first, casting from one side of a small dale to the other. Head up, sniffing the air, with his red and white tail flashing behind him like a flag. She made a chirping sound, which brought the animal to a halt. Then he was suddenly bounding toward her, and she wondered if she should be afraid. The dog was big, for all its comical, flopping ears and speckled coloring. He stopped right in front of her, however, plopped onto his hindquarters, and observed her with wise and ancient eyes. She'd just reached out a hand to pet his broad forehead when a whistle pierced the air and the dog dashed away.

She'd felt bereft, as if her aunt had somehow explained to the dog—as she had to her tenants—that Sarah should not be frolicking with the help.

And then the dog had reappeared, this time followed by a tall, lanky boy. The similarity between the dog and master was so pronounced that unbidden, her lips turned up into a wide smile. His hair was the same bright red as the color on the dog, and his face was as spotted. She was later to think she could find every constellation in the night sky scattered among the freckles that dotted his face.

The boy returned her smile. He stopped a few feet away and gave her a formal bow. She responded with a curtsey, after which they both broke into peals of laughter at their ridiculous behavior, since they were meeting in a veritable wilderness.

"I'm Benjamin Radcliffe," he said. "And this is Hannibal."

She'd looked up and up—what an amazingly tall boy—and responded, "I'm pleased to meet you. I'm Sarah Talbot."

And just that easily, her loneliness vanished. They became wandering companions of the moors for the next eight years. Even the long months when Ben was at school saw the arrival of his letters, the promise of another reunion.

Aunt Tess died suddenly when Sarah was fifteen and she'd returned to the stiff bosom of her family. Her father had immediately forbidden their correspondence. *The third son of a viscount,* he'd said incredulously. *You are meant for someone of greater consequence than he.*

Sarah had last seen Ben seven years ago, but there was no mistaking who he was. She would have recognized him anywhere. Just as he would instantly recognize her—and call her by her former name. And then the entire, elaborate lie she now would unravel.

Chapter Two

SARAH STRETCHED HER NECK and rolled her shoulders. A sharp pain radiated down her back from holding the same, awkward position for—she glanced at the mantel clock—Heavens, it was over an hour now. She had to lean to one side to align the crack in the door so she could see down the hallway. She felt ridiculous, skulking behind the partially closed door of the ladies' parlor, but she had been unable to arrive at any other plan to approach Ben unseen.

She'd been at her post since sunrise, knowing the Ben of old arose with the sun and assuming he still did. His tardiness had put that supposition to the lie, however, and she now feared he would walk to the dining room in the company of others. Then what would she do? If she leaped out and accosted him like a spider from its web, everyone would think she'd run mad.

Well, maybe she had.

She'd felt unbalanced ever since seeing Ben in the foyer. She'd pleaded a megrim to avoid going to dinner last night. Lady Harley undoubted suspected there was nothing really wrong with her, but without asking for the reason for the ruse, her employer had allowed her the pretext. Sarah couldn't continue to be ill the entire time Ben was in residence, however, and she couldn't meet him in company until she'd talked with him. Hence, the need to waylay him for a private tête-à-tête.

Sarah had hoped the Ben would just stay the night and then leave, but Lady Harley reported that he would be residing at Brackenheath for some time. Actually, Lady Harley had quite a bit to say about Ben, and when she'd returned to her room last night, the older woman had gleefully described the new addition to the family party.

"One of the biggest men I've ever seen," she'd reported. "With some of the brightest red hair. Because of his size, Cousin Ann's two silly chits acted like an ogre had entered the dining room, or they did until they discovered he was an unmarried viscount. Then they were on him like a pack of terriers circling a tethered bear. Even Cousin Lavinia joined in the hunt, and she's nearly forty if she's a day. I must admit it was highly entertaining. I'm sorry you missed it."

Sarah was glad she hadn't seen Ben being harried by unmarried ladies. He'd always been the kindest of men, and she was sure he hadn't put the predatory females in their places. Just as he'd done when she was a child, Ben would seriously consider their inane questions and then answer with a blazing smile. Sarah had always loved the way the edges of his hazel eyes, green flecked with pure gold, crinkled when he smiled.

She very much wanted to see those eyes again—but only when they were alone. Dear Lord, why would he not walk down that hall—now—and let her warn him before he could do her any damage?

And then, suddenly, he was there, moving toward her place of concealment with the same long-legged stride he'd had as a boy. His pace was so rapid, he'd nearly passed her before she darted into the hallway.

"Benjamin," she said, grasping him by the arm.

He came to an abrupt stop and turned toward her with a quizzical look. His brow almost immediately smoothed, and the slightly crooked smile she knew so well appeared. "Sarah Talbot? I cannot believe it. Sarah."

She put a finger to her lips to quiet him and pulled him toward the door behind her. He followed without protesting, although his face showed confusion. Once he'd cleared the portal, she pushed the door closed. Now her behavior had passed from the bizarre to the inappropriate. She was running mad indeed.

"Sarah, is there a problem? Are you in trouble?" He whispered. Bless Ben for always being a quick study and realizing the closed door indicated the need for secrecy and not an assignation.

"No, I'm not in trouble. Or at least I won't be, as long as we meet as strangers. I'm Sarah Clendenin now, and I would prefer that no one knows anything else about me. It's to avoid trouble that I had to meet with you privately." She hoped this vague explanation sufficed. She didn't want to go into all the real reasons and ramifications with Ben Radcliffe.

He pushed his hand through his hair in a movement achingly familiar. Even all those years ago, he'd done that when he was thinking. She looked up into his face and thought he'd not changed—but had somehow changed completely. The lanky boy had filled out and, if possible, seemed to have added a few more inches to his height. She was a tall woman, but he towered over her, straight and sturdy as an oak. His face had broadened, and the smile lines that had always appeared at the corners of his eyes had become permanent indentations. The pattern of his freckles seemed muddled, however, or at least it didn't completely correspond to the one she remembered.

But the look of kindness and compassion she knew so well remained. He reached forward and ran his hands along the sides of her arms. "Oh, Sarie, if you don't want me to know you, then you *are* in trouble."

His touch and the use of her childhood name brought tears to her eyes. She blinked them back and put on an artificial smile. "I have no problem. Truly. To avoid embarrassment, I wanted to alert you to my changed position. I'm not a regular guest here. I'm Lady Harley's companion."

His hands immediately dropped away. Sarah hoped it was a shocked reaction rather than rejection. She knew how far she'd fallen. She didn't need any reminders.

"Since when is the Earl of Farlough's daughter some old woman's companion?" He growled out the question. "This isn't right. How did this happen?"

It had happened because she'd been young and stupid and headstrong. It had happened because she'd made one wrong turn on the road of her life and had forever lost the way. It should have been easy to say this, but the words refused to leave her mouth.

No one wanted to admit failure to someone she'd always admired—and Sarah had definitely admired Ben.

For eight years of her youth, he was the only bright spot in her life. She'd been devastated when she'd been forced to return home and her father had refused to allow any contact between them. For months thereafter, she'd lain awake and wished Ben had kissed her the last time they'd been together. Of course, they hadn't known that time *was* the last, but it would have been fitting for Ben to have bestowed her first kiss. Instead, he had only held her hand.

She wished he would take her hand now, but he just stood there, looking at her with confusion. And she could not explain.

"Suffice it to say that I made mistakes and my being Lady Harley's companion is the result. But it is the best result that I could ever hope for, so please, please, don't tell anyone that my father is an earl. Lady Harley would have too many questions that I don't want to answer and this could endanger the security I've finally found. I'll be safe if you pretend not to know me when we meet at breakfast. It will be simple. Say you'll do this for me." She hoped her request sounded cool and composed, but she feared she more closely resembled a whining infant.

"I'll do this and more." Ben's face held utter conviction.

"Good. Then go on to the dining room, and I'll follow shortly."

He nodded and, after checking the hallway to make sure it was free of other diners, immediately left. It was only after he was gone that she realized she'd never asked him what had transpired to make him Lord Kittredge. It was odd how so much of his life had rolled on without her.

Ben hoped he appeared interested in Mr. Burwell's monologue. To call it a conversation would have strained the definition. Evidently tasked by his wife to tout the charms of their two daughters, Burwell was fulfilling his obligation with enthusiasm. According to their doting father, Miss Burwell and Miss Some-sort-of-flower Burwell were perfect examples of feminine grace. Ben thought them both quite silly chits, but it would have been nice to get Flower's actual name. Unfortunately, her father always referred to her as "my youngest." Maybe Burwell couldn't remember her name either.

The one name that kept echoing in Ben's head was Sarah. She was the last person he'd expected to meet here at the Duttons'. And so changed. The wild sprite he remembered had become a subdued woman with fear in her eyes. Dear Lord, how had that happened?

He'd last seen her in the spring of his first year at Cambridge. He'd just been introduced to the beauty of pure mathematics and was nearly giddy with the excitement of discovery. As a third son, he'd worried for years about what he would be and who he'd become. Then in a few short months, the reason for his life had finally arrived. The joy of making numbers and symbols confirm abstract concepts overwhelmed him. He lusted after theorems and proofs. He looked into the future and saw himself as a new Robert Recorde, the man who had invented the equal sign. He felt he stood on the shore of an unexplored country.

He'd babbled to Sarah about his discoveries for

hours. She'd held his hand and looked adoringly into his eyes. Even at nineteen, he was no fool, and he recognized the fifteen-year-old Sarah thought he was all that was wonderful. And he'd returned the emotion. He'd imagined they would eventually marry—just not at that moment. Then, the world of mathematics lay before him, and he was intent on conquering it.

Even when her aunt's death had forced Sarah to return to her family home and her arse of a father declared they could no longer write to each other, he'd imagined everything would still come out right in the end. He envisioned himself going to the Earl of Farlough with a shiny new first in Mathematics. He would, of course, have had papers published to much acclaim—and then the earl would see his worth, and he and Sarah would marry. The line graph of his life was clear in his mind.

But that wasn't what happened.

In less than a year, over dinner at a middling inn near Cambridge, his middle brother Joseph had casually mentioned he'd heard the Earl of Farlough's funny little daughter had married. Ben could still remember the knife blade of disbelief and loss that had sliced through him. The occasion had been to commemorate Joseph's leaving to join his regiment in the Peninsula—and it was, indeed, the last time he ever saw his brother—but what he most recalled about that night was the shock of losing Sarah.

Of course, since he'd never mentioned his intentions to her, why would he think she could read his mind and know what he had planned? For that matter, why would she want to marry him anyway? Dear Lord, even at twenty he continued to grow like a well-watered weed. Every inch of skin that saw the sun was freckled and his hair... well, to refer to it as ginger was a kindness. He was no woman's dream of a dashing gentleman. Why would Sarah Talbot be any different?

For the first time in his life, Ben got drunk. When he sobered up the next morning, he logically examined the situation. He concluded that he must have imagined anything more than a friendship between them—one based on mutual loneliness and proximity. As Sarah had matured, she'd found someone more attractive, at least as a potential marriage partner. He saw that his sense of betrayal was illogical. This rationale, however, did not make the feeling go away.

He'd thrown himself into his studies. In the ensuing years, he'd been too busy, too driven, to think about Sarah Talbot. Time had also changed his perspective. He could see that he was not without fault. He'd been willing to place her on a shelf while he pursued his own interests, imagining that she would somehow stay there, unchanged, waiting for him.

And now, suddenly, she had reappeared, requesting that he pretend not to know her. His questing mind wanted to know why. He felt there was some mystery he needed to unravel.

Motion at the door caused Burwell's paean to falter. Lady Harley sailed through, riding on the unfashionably wide skirts of her youth. She was immediately followed by Sarah, who was dressed for no particular decade, although plainly for service.

Ben and Burwell both stood, but once Lady Harley

had made her breakfast selection from the sideboard, she seated herself next to Burwell, with her companion to her right. Although Sarah was not directly across from him, Ben could still observe her from the corner of his eye.

All the remembered light seemed to have gone out of Sarah, as if her drab attire had drained her energy and left only a shadow. Even her honey-colored hair no longer rioted around her face in a myriad of uncontrollable curls. Every lock remained tightly confined within a stupid, linen widow's cap.

When he'd seen her earlier, Ben's surprise had kept him from noticing these transformations—transformations he found disturbing. For now, he would play the part she'd assigned him, but they would definitely meet privately again and he'd discover her secrets.

"Has that roll done something to anger you?" Lady Harley's voice held laughter, but her sharp-eyed appraisal indicated her curiosity. Ben realized he'd shredded a roll in the brief time Lady Harley and her companion had been seated. There was no disguising the carnage strewn across his plate. He felt his color rise.

"My food has given no offense," he said with a self-deprecating smile. "You have just caught me, embarrassingly, woolgathering."

"Well, since you are mentally present now, I'd like to introduce my dear friend and companion, Mrs. Clendenin. Her late husband was the famous Scottish poet, Hamish Clendenin." The well-padded, older woman gave him an expectant look—and then winked.

Winked? Ben had no idea where that had come from

or what it was supposed to mean. As for Sarah's famous husband—Ben had never heard of him. Not that he was particularly conversant with poets, Scottish or otherwise. He *had* met George Gordon, Lord Byron, however, and hadn't much liked the man, who was too dramatic by half. Some part of his mind matched Sarah with a similarly flamboyant man. Ben found this image irritating.

"I'm pleased to meet you," Ben said, hoping the words didn't sound artificial.

Before Sarah could respond, Mrs. Burwell and her two daughters came into the room. They fluttered about like injured butterflies, causing colorful chaos. When they finally landed at the table, the two young women were seated on either side of him.

"Mother told us about your heroic service to our country on the Peninsula," Miss Burwell said. "How brave you must be."

Dear Lord, even her eyelashes were frantically fluttering. Her younger sister simply stared at him, wide-eyed and adoring. Ben had no idea how to respond. While he'd been on the Peninsula, he had hardly been heroic. Perhaps if he described the tediousness of the job he did in the war effort, the Burwell sisters would manage to fly away.

"My late husband was very fond of the black and tan setters we have in Scotland," Lady Harley said, apropos to nothing, but conveniently changing the conversational topic. "I understand you raise the spotted English variety." Although he still hadn't figured out what the wink meant, Ben decided he liked Lady Harley very much.

"Yes, my grandfather began breeding these English setters, and I think we've done much to improve this type of hunting dog." Here was a topic Ben was comfortable with.

"Fine animals," Mr. Burwell said at the same time as his wife gave a huff and said, "Lord Kittredge, watch your language. There are young ladies present."

Ben quickly reviewed the last few words that had fallen from his mouth. He was fairly confident that he hadn't cursed, an unfortunate habit he had brought back from the Peninsula and was trying to overcome. Mrs. Burwell must have been offended by the word "breeding," although he could think of no other way of expressing what one did with animals—be they dogs or horses or swine—to increase their number. Not for the first time, he found himself lost in the labyrinth of polite conversation.

Lady Harley—bless both of her chins—again saved the day. "Mrs. Clendenin has expressed an interest in seeing your animals," she said. "Perhaps after breakfast you can take her to the kennels."

Sarah gave a quick, surprised glance at her employer that indicated she had done nothing of the kind. Ben wondered if Lady Harley knew more about Sarah's past than Sarah suspected. Not that he cared, as long as it allowed him some time alone with Sarah.

"I'd be delighted if you would like to walk out with me," he said.

"That would be lovely." Sarah's tones were somewhat strangled, but she'd said the right words.

Now all Ben had to do was get through this

breakfast. "Do you like dogs?" he asked Miss Flower-something Burwell.

This seemed to reanimate the two sisters, who evidently had a passion for pugs. Ben thought them ugly, yapping little critters, but he smiled and nodded and actually ate his next roll without crumbling it.

Chapter Three

BEN SUSPECTED HE SHOULD not have donned his greatcoat until Sarah appeared. He was getting deuced hot, the condition undoubtedly exacerbated by his pacing the perimeter of the foyer. How long could it take a woman to put on a bonnet and pelisse? If she didn't appear shortly, he'd scandalize the household by going in search of her. He hoped she wasn't hiding from him.

Sarah was keeping secrets from her employer, secrets that Ben, too, was interested in discovering, and he wouldn't let her avoid his questions until he received the answers he needed. Something bad had happened to Sarah in the intervening years, and Ben wanted—no, needed—to know what it was.

He had the confidence, perhaps irrationally, that he could fix whatever disaster had befallen her. After plowing through the mess his brother had left, he was getting quite good at smoothing out life's wrinkles.

He heard her approach before he saw her—light footsteps moving faster than a lady's ought. This hint of her old animation lifted his heart. Unfortunately, the emotion muted when she actually appeared. She wore unrelenting gray and had jammed an unattractive bonnet shaped like a coal scuttle over her widow's cap.

Was she still in mourning for her late husband? Had grief at the loss of her famous poet overwhelmed her? Ben didn't much like the idea if this were true. He also didn't much like the kind of person this selfish reaction made him.

"Shall we go?" He offered her his arm, and they exited the house into a blustery day. The rain had cleared and left clouds like mare's tails streaking a vivid blue sky. They walked in silence, his boots on the gravel of the walkway loud and obscuring the sound of her passage.

When they were out of earshot of the house, he stopped and pulled her to face him. "Why must we act as if we're strangers? If you want me to continue the pretense, I need answers." The words came out as more of a demand than he had intended.

She looked stricken. "Not here. We can be seen from the house. Please keep walking."

He responded more to the expression on her face than to her words and continued strolling toward the kennels. He was searching for something light and innocuous to say when Sarah broke the silence.

"How did you end up with the title? I'd like to know what happened, if it is not too painful, since the circumstances would have to involve a great deal of loss."

So... she was determined to be first inquisitor. Ben would answer her with all honesty, in the hope that he would set the tone for *her* further answers. Yes, he'd give her honesty, but perhaps honesty without all of his thoughts attached. He was still trying to come to terms with his change in fortune.

He decided to start his explanation close to the time they'd shared. "The week I took my first in mathematics—"

"—As expected."

He smiled at her confidence. "Yes, as expected. Anyway, that very week we received news that Joseph had been killed in a skirmish in some small, nameless village in Portugal."

"Oh, Ben, I'm so sorry." She gave his supporting arm a squeeze. "I know you were closest to him."

"Yes. The news came as a shock." There was an understatement. Joseph's death had caused a seismic shift in his outlook. He was unsure how much truth he now wanted to impart. He knew he'd gone a little mad. He kept hearing Joseph tease him about his being the general of numbers when it was manlier to command actual men. Ben came to see his affinity for mathematics as a weakness, his passion for precision as an unworthy quest. What he had taken such pride in now seemed unimportant and childish.

And so he'd done a truly childish thing. He'd dashed out and joined the army. This fact could not be hidden.

"I bought a commission," he said. "It no longer seemed honorable to stay cocooned in academia. I think I had some ridiculous idea of doing my patriotic duty, maybe of exacting retribution. I envisioned myself accomplishing heroic deeds."

He gave a self-deprecating chuckle. "The General Staff was delighted to have a mathematician in their midst. They immediately made me a Commissary Officer. I spent nearly a year in London in charge of the procurement and delivery of food and fodder. Hardly the heroic service I'd imagined."

There was no need to mention that he'd felt like a tethered bear his entire time in Town. He'd been ordered to show up in various ballrooms along with the other junior officers, the better to show the populace the military had everything under control. There he was expected to dance, not his best talent, and forced to overhear comments that indicated he should not be ignored as a potential spouse since he was currently the heir-apparent of a viscount. For him, it was an uncomfortable and irritating time.

"I was finally sent to the Peninsula, but even there I fought bags of flour and melting butter rather than the French."

Sarah gave his arm another hug. "I think you're being too hard on yourself. You were doing a needed job. Hungry soldiers are more easily overcome. Your work saved lives."

Ben patted Sarah's hand that held his arm. A smile curved his lips. She'd always been loyal, and that hadn't changed. "You don't need to try to make me feel better. I'm not a boy anymore. Everyone has disappointments, and this was simply one of mine."

She stopped their progress as they neared the kennels. "But how did Roger die? He wasn't that old."

"Only six years older than me, so definitely not all that old. His death was one of those inexplicable things that sometimes happen. Roger got a new pair of boots, custom made to his specifications by his standard boot maker. For whatever the reason, they rubbed a blister on his right heel. He was at a house party at the time and couldn't be bothered to see a doctor, even when his entire leg became hot and sore. He died three days after he returned home, leaving a hysterical wife and no heir."

He knew his voice indicated his disgust, but this was just another example of Roger's lackadaisical attitude, only this time it had killed him. And left Ben as the sixth Viscount Kittredge, a position he had never wanted but couldn't reject. One hastily scrawled letter from an unfamiliar solicitor had rearranged his life. He would never follow his chosen path and fulfill his youthful dreams; he would never change the face of mathematics.

"Word didn't reach me on the Peninsula for months. And even then, I kept hoping I would get word that Roger's wife, Amelia, found herself in a family way. But that didn't happen. I ignored the summons for as long as I could, but the letters from Roger's man of business became more and more frantic, so I finally had no choice but to sell out and come home."

When Ben had realized the extent of the chaos with the family's affairs, he'd felt guilty for his procrastination. But his arriving home more rapidly would not have changed much.

"You'll make a wonderful viscount," Sarah said, "but I know it is not what you wanted to do with your life."

He could only nod his agreement. To put his frustration into words wouldn't make any difference. He was now the person Fate had decided he would be. The glories of pure math had become bookkeeping, and the complexity of supplying an army had devolved into determining which tenant most needed a new roof. He was constantly busy, but also restless and bored.

This was his life, however, and he would live it to the best of his ability. He shook off his malaise as they entered the kennel and were greeted by the enthusiastic barks of Meg and Brutus.

"Oh, is that Hannibal?" Sarah asked as she hurried toward Brutus.

"No, Hannibal has long been buried in the orchard at Broadlea Hall. It's one of the ironies of life that we are so much longer lived than our most loyal companions. That's Brutus, he is one of Hannibal's get, and the crazy one flopped over on her back hoping for a stomach rub is Meg, who's Brutus's offspring."

"We can't have her hoping in vain." Sarah knelt down and ruffled the fluffy hair on Meg's belly. The dog began to wiggle in delight, forcing an uninhibited laugh from Sarah. Lord, it was a delightful and familiar sound. Ben suspected that this new, more subdued Sarah laughed seldom. The thought saddened him.

"We're as private as we can get," Ben said, "and I guarantee that neither dog will disclose your secrets. Would you please tell me what is going on?"

Sarah smiled slightly at Ben's put-upon tone. He had always been impatient for answers and would persist until he got them. She would have been happier not discussing her past, but he deserved at least an edited version.

"You asked me what the Earl of Farlough's daughter was doing working as a companion." She watched her hand ruffle the dog's silky fur rather than look at Ben.

"This is what happens when the earl disowns his daughter and her family doesn't recognize her anymore."

She felt his hand on her shoulder. "Sarah, this is ridiculous. What could you have possibly done to be disowned? You can't get away with giving me only a portion of the story."

But a portion of the story was all she wanted to disclose. She sifted through the facts to determine just how much stupidity she was willing to admit to.

"After Aunt Tess died, my father brought me home, as you know. I guess he had nothing else to do with me. It wasn't a particularly warm homecoming. I was generally ignored except for making an appearance occasionally at meals, where he would find fault with my appearance and decorum."

She couldn't explain the agony of those painful meals. Her clothing was either dowdy or too suggestive. Her curling hair looked like a rat's nest. She alternated between having no conversation and being overly forward. Whatever she did, the earl was dissatisfied.

The only person who felt his wrath more keenly was Mrs. Hutchins, a self-effacing woman hired to make Sarah ready for her first season. Unfortunately, Mrs. Hutchins' humility was only extended to the earl, and she used his criticism as an excuse to make Sarah's life onerous and uncomfortable. Her younger brother was the only bright spot in an otherwise somber household. And then she got to know his tutor, a man who knew how to smile and compliment and generally make himself attractive to a lonely girl.

"I was seventeen," she said, "and became enamored

with my brother's tutor. We ran off and married against my father's wishes." What waiting disaster was couched in those few words.

Ben took his hand from her shoulder and said brusquely, "This was the famous poet, I assume."

Oddly, she was hurt by his tone. She'd wanted sympathy from him, although why should he have felt sympathetic? She had announced that she'd married a man she loved—a man acclaimed as a famous poet, at that. There was no reason for Ben to be sorry for her. She'd had years to realize her elopement was the greatest of follies. On first hearing it, Ben wouldn't guess she'd made a regrettable mistake.

She straightened to her feet, absently noting the bottom of her gray skirts was covered with red and white hairs. Meg whined and thumped her tail in a bid for more attention. "My marriage was a scandal. I'm surprised you didn't hear of it. Needless to say, my father was furious and completely cut me off."

Ben shook his head ruefully. "That sounds like something your idiot father would do. But that still doesn't explain why you've had to take the position of companion. Did your husband leave you without funds?"

Without funds was a benign way of describing her financial position on Hamish's death. All by itself, the bill presented by the local publican was staggering. Hamish had evidently spent many nights at The White Hart, being famous, and hadn't found it convenient to pay for his libations. And since he must look the part, bills quickly arrived for boots and clothing, a new saddle—the list of merchants expecting payment became immense.

But she couldn't complain about this. She would appear as pathetically needy as the dog at her feet. "Fame doesn't bring wealth, and poets are notoriously poor. Since my family wanted nothing to do with me, and Hamish was dead, being Lady Harley's companion has been a real boon. But I doubt she would want me if she knew I'd created a scandal by defying my father and eloping—and there's no way I could avoid telling her if she learned who my father is. And so, for now I'm well-settled and happy—"

Ben reached out and pulled her to him so the rest of the words were lost in the expanse of his chest. "Not so happy, I think," he said above her head.

And he was right—and warm. She relaxed into his light embrace, and for at least this tiny space of time, she felt cherished. She had given up the right to these feelings because of the debacle that was her marriage, however, and this further saddened her. No longer could she accept the affection of a good man who had a place to maintain in society. If she were associated with Ben in any way, she would only cause gossip to attach itself to him.

She could not, would not, allow her actions to taint Ben. Her desire to enjoy the old connection they felt toward each other was a weakness. And she could not be weak. She straightened her spine and pushed away from his hold.

"Thank you, Ben," she said, and then, knowing all explanations would be excuses, she fled.

Chapter Four

BY DINNER THAT EVENING, Sarah had relived the feeling of leaning on Ben's chest a dozen times. Regrettably, she couldn't get it out of her mind. She hadn't realized how much she'd yearned for a tender, human touch. Oh, Hamish had held her—at least at the beginning. But they had not been married long before she realized he grasped her to exert his control rather than to offer his support. Odd, how totally different the two embraces felt.

Ben had wrapped her in comfort and, for that one brief moment, had made her feel cherished. But it shouldn't—no, couldn't—happen again. The attraction she'd felt for Ben had to be kept in the past. In no way should he be associated with a sordid scandal, especially now he held the title. Sarah had given up all the possibility of a relationship with someone like Ben on the night she left with Hamish for Gretna Green.

What a foolish, foolish girl she had been. But loneliness and dissatisfaction could make people behave irrationally. Hamish had seemed so suave, so dashing. He was someone outside of her usual experience, and he'd utterly charmed her. She felt she'd found the one person who truly loved her. Yes, foolish indeed.

"Mrs. Clendenin, Lady Harley is ready to go down." The voice of Mary, her employer's maid, came through the door.

"Thank you, Mary. I'm ready." Sarah took one last look at herself in the mirror to make sure she appeared forgettable. Her mode of dress was one of the ways she used to remind herself of who she now was. She'd become Lady Harley's companion shortly after Hamish's death and had arrived with a limited wardrobe, all of which had been dyed black. When her mourning period was over, her employer had kindly offered to buy her new clothes, and Sarah had purchased three gray dresses—two for day and one for evening.

Lady Harley had suggested she choose other muted colors if Sarah insisted on half-mourning, but Sarah chose only gray. She really didn't care about appearing to mourn Hamish, since she did not, but gray seemed the best color to wear to be unnoticed. She'd now had more than a year to perfect her ability to blend into the background.

She pulled up her left glove where it tended to droop above the elbow and joined Lady Harley to go down to dinner. Sarah had no problem disappearing when she was around Lady Harley. Tonight, the lady was resplendent in a deep garnet gown with half the pearls of the South Pacific looped around her neck. Lady Harley often wore these pearls. *The better to hide the extra skin, dear girl,* her employer had commented more than once. Sarah smiled at the thought. She was most fortunate to have found this position.

"I see that secret smile," Lady Harley said as they approached the stairs. "Does this mean your trip to the kennels this morning was enjoyable?"

Sarah nearly missed the first step. Goodness, had someone seen Ben holding her and reported it to Lady Harley? "Lord Kittredge's dogs are lovely animals," she said. "Red and white with speckles and charming dispositions."

Lady Harley chuckled. "Rather describes their owner, doesn't it? Red, white, speckled, and charming."

"Well, yes, I guess it does." Sarah couldn't think of anything else to say.

"I thought you'd noticed," Lady Harley slyly said, tapping Sarah on the arm with her fan. Fortunately, they'd reach the bottom of the steps, so Sarah didn't have to worry about stumbling. Where did Lady Harley get the idea that Sarah was interested in Ben?

There had been a time when she was, but that was just another of her childish fantasies. That she couldn't get the memory of being held in his arms out of her mind was of no importance. She'd already made one drastic error in judgment when it came to men, and she was not going to make another.

So, naturally, the first person she saw upon entering the drawing room was Ben. He was in earnest conversation with Lord Dutton but looked up as if he knew she was there. A brief smile flickered across his face, a smile she felt to her toes. *Just a remembered attraction*, she told herself. But she felt unaccountably disheartened when he returned to his conversation with Lord Dutton.

"I see we've added some more men to our number," Lady Harley said, abruptly shifting Sarah's focus from Benjamin Radcliffe to the room at large. There were indeed four more men present, all of whom were known to Lady Harley, who immediately began to give Sarah a brief background on each. The first two were Lord Stanhope, the husband of another of Lady Dutton's cousins, and their son, Mr. Chalmers. The latter could barely be considered a grown man, but this didn't seem to keep the Burwell girls from fluttering in his direction. The third was a rather antique gentleman identified as the Earl of Huntsford, and the fourth was a neighboring squire, Mr. Bigelow.

Lady Harley moved toward the fourth man she'd identified, pulling Sarah in her wake. "I suspect Bigelow's here to balance Cousin Lavinia," she said quietly, "but that doesn't mean you can't enjoy his company as well. No title, of course, but solid and wealthy gentry."

Sarah's employer gave her a knowing look and a wink. Good heavens, was Lady Harley matchmaking? That seemed to be the case when she introduced Sarah as her dear friend rather than her companion, and painted the fame of Hamish Clendenin with a trowel rather than a brush. Squire Bigelow looked suitably impressed, and Lady Harley's timing was impeccable, since they were standing next to Bigelow when Lady Dutton announced that, being primarily family, they should all go in to dinner together.

As expected, the squire offered an arm to both Lady Harley and Sarah and then seated them on either side of himself. The Chalmers boy sat on Sarah's other side. A poisonous look from Cousin Lavinia made Sarah realize she was now flanked by two of the newly added and eligible men. That Sarah was indifferent to both men did not change the seating arrangements.

Throughout dinner, Mr. Chalmers affected a sophistication that only highlighted his youth. He compared unfavorably to the young Ben who still lived vividly in Sarah's mind. Looking down the table at the assured, mature Ben, there was no comparison at all.

Squire Bigelow proved a more enjoyable dinner companion than the callow Chalmers. Long-faced and graying, the squire possessed a no-nonsense manner and a dry sense of humor. Before she knew it, Sarah had forgotten the need to fade into the background and was involved in a lively discussion of how long to hang game birds.

"Well, however long the staff here ages meat, we had a good hunt today and have provided you all with a fine Christmas meal of pheasant," Bigelow said.

"You'll not be staying for the holidays?" Sarah had assumed he was now a permanent part of the house party.

"No, I'm needed at home. My two daughters and their families are coming to visit for Christmastide. I've five grandchildren now. Their existence continues to surprise me." His somewhat comical face took on an odd expression. "Oh, I don't mean I'm surprised my daughters have children... I'm sorry. I sound indelicate. I guess my point is that I don't feel old enough to have grandchildren, but the years do creep up on us."

Sarah smiled at the squire's assumption that she

would be embarrassed by his reference to his daughter's having children. It had been many years since she'd believed that babies appeared under leaves in the garden. She was not about to suggest that his old-fashioned courtliness rather than the lines around his eyes better indicated his age, so she asked him about his grandchildren.

As expected, this was one of the squire's favorite topics. Sarah was laughing at his vivid tale of finding a missing four-year-old by following jam covered handprints when she realized others at the table were looking at her. Good Heavens! What was she thinking? There were still a number of people yet to arrive, and any one of them could know her father. His estate was only an easy two-day journey from where she now sat.

She should have kept her mouth shut and her eyes down. She was acting as if she were a guest rather than a servant. Talking with Ben this morning had left her unsettled and made her forget her place.

She hunched her shoulders and applied herself to eating. When the courses changed and she was again speaking with the Chalmers boy, it became easy to answer in monosyllables and slowly fade into the wallpaper. Sarah sat alone and isolated in the crowd. It was the place she'd made for herself. One she should be used to occupying. But this evening, it seemed both foreign and uncomfortable.

Ben waited impatiently for the gentlemen to finish their port and rejoin the ladies. Unfortunately, the bottle kept making its rounds as those from the hunting party recounted *ad nauseam* the flushing of every bird and the taking of every shot. He was sure he normally enjoyed this recap of a successful hunt, particularly when his dogs were constantly being lauded. Tonight, however, he wanted this protracted conviviality to end.

The need to talk to Sarah had beat through him all day. Well, the need to hold her again was probably more compelling, but he had little hope of accomplishing that. The feeling of her soft breasts pressed against his chest had accompanied him as he tramped through forest and field. His mind had wandered, and he'd never taken so many poor shots. Fortunately, the rest of the party had bagged a good number of pheasants, or, disillusioned, wise Brutus might have sat down and refused to flush another bird. Filled with the energy and optimism of youth, Meg, of course, would have soldiered on.

Both dogs had done very well. The seasoned Brutus could hold a point all day. Meg had done the same, but she quivered in her position, muscles tense to leap forward immediately on release. Ben was proud that she had not broken point and rushed in too soon.

At this moment, however, as Burwell used his hands to show the erratic flight of a bird he'd missed, Ben most sympathized with Meg. He felt as if he were being held in check and quivering to reach his quarry—in this case, the elusive Mrs. Clendenin.

He'd surreptitiously watched her during dinner. She'd initially seemed to come alive talking to Squire Bigelow. Whatever had they been discussing? He'd noted each of her smiles and nods and felt a burning in his gut that might have been jealousy. And then she seemed to shut down, to return to the ghost of herself she most often exhibited.

He needed to find out if the man had given her some offense. If so, he would handle it. The shooting party was going out again tomorrow, and if Bigelow were guilty of anything, it would be easy to accidently push him into a thicket. Dutton's farm manager had not been diligent about clearing thorn bushes out of the ditches, and Lord knew, men Ben's size were sometimes clumsy.

Actually, the idea of doing bodily harm to the squire had occurred to him when Bigelow had made Sarah smile. Her smiles were something seldom bestowed, and Ben wanted to be the only recipient.

Dear Lord. How long could these men keep talking? He shifted in his chair. Would throwing his empty glass across the room make the men leave the dining room? He was definitely losing his mind—or at least he couldn't control where it wandered.

"I think it's time we joined the ladies."

Ben was standing before the meaning of Dutton's pronouncement even registered on most of the room's occupants. By the time it did, he was halfway to the door. With difficulty, he slowed his headlong escape and let a few of those sitting closer to the door exit before him. He didn't want to appear a complete fool.

But in the handful of heartbeats that passed before he entered the drawing room, he realized he *was* a fool. Sarah Talbot had occupied the bulk of his thoughts throughout the day. Some of these thoughts had been blatantly sexual images that involved Sarah, naked, on a wide bed. He'd had to be quite creative to conjure those images, since he had never seen Sarah unclothed. Good heavens, he had never even kissed her.

But most of his thoughts were more tender and caring. In these, his memories of the carefree child Sarah had been mixed together with the woman she had become, and this revived the old certainty that they would marry and have a happy life. This conclusion was as clear to him as an algebraic proof. The equation was unassailably logical and balanced.

He realized this equation was fully rendered only from his perspective. It illustrated *his* feelings and *his* certainties. He had no idea what numbers and variables Sarah would add. He felt he could combat her ridiculous idea that being disowned by her idiot father was in some way a scandal they could not overcome. The true unknown was how to make Sarah see him as a viable choice as a husband after she'd been married to the love of her life. That damned famous poet. That was the part of the equation he might never get to balance.

Sarah was sitting in a stiff chair by the wall, behind and to the left of Lady Harley, close enough to be of assistance to her employer, but not part of the conversation group. Ben marched straight across the room and stopped in front of her. He held out his hand. "Mrs. Clendenin, would you care to stroll around the room with me?"

She looked at his hand in incomprehension. "Stroll?"

"Yes. It's where you take my arm and we perambulate the room, stopping to talk to various groups as we pass. It's something courting couples often do."

"Courting couples?" Her face now registered horror

rather than confusion.

Ben felt the corners of his mouth turn up. His hand did not waver. "Sarah, you're going to have to come up with more conversation than one and two word questions."

"Lord Kittredge, please go away. Is that enough conversation for you?"

"No." Then he laughed. "Now you're reducing me to single words. You will have to walk with me if we are to have a real conversation, since you have seated yourself in a chair without neighbors. I guess I could go fetch another chair, but that would make us even more conspicuous than we already are."

That brought her head up like a hound scenting the wind. When she realized others were observing them, the color left her face. "Ben," she said softly, "do not do this."

He should have felt guilty about distressing her, but he was tired of seeing her trying to hide. She'd seemed to come alive for a brief period during dinner, and he hated to see her retreat again. She'd smiled at Squire Bigelow, and by Heavens, she was going to smile at him. "Walk with me," he said.

To his relief, she capitulated, placing her hand in his and rising. He repositioned himself, tucked her hand into the crook of his arm, and started toward a group that included the irritating squire. "Bigelow didn't say anything to offend you during dinner, did he? You seemed to suddenly become withdrawn."

Sarah's eyes flicked up to observe his face and then returned to contemplating the fine Aubusson carpeting they traversed. "No, he did nothing to give offense."

Ben was rather sad to relinquish the vision of the older man floundering around in a hedgerow and getting constantly pricked by thorns, but fair was fair. "Good, then I won't have to arrange a dawn meeting."

She stopped abruptly. "What are you talking about?"

"Well, defending his lady's honor is something a man does when he's courting."

"We are *not* courting."

He could tell her teeth were clenched as she said that, and her color was now high. She looked altogether magnificent. Well, except for the ugly, dull dress and the ridiculous widow's cap, but neither was part of the essential Sarah.

"If you say so, then we are not courting." He patted the hand that rested on his arm and smiled down at her. Perhaps she was not courting, but she couldn't speak for him. They were at least strolling, and he suspected he would have to make many, little changes to the equation to reach the final balanced form.

Chapter Five

IN THE PAST THREE DAYS, Ben had discovered a number of nefarious abilities he hadn't realized he possessed. He'd always thought of himself as a straightforward type person. But an indirect approach, if not outright mendacity, seemed to be more effective for him right now. When Lady Dutton asked him about his holiday plans, he'd been suitably downcast about having to celebrate alone and had managed to garner an invitation to stay on for the Dutton's Christmas house party. His show of reluctance at intruding on a family gathering was worthy of Drury Lane.

Of course, it *was* true he would have been alone, but he'd manufactured his distress about the condition. He'd long ago resigned himself to spending the holidays by himself and had planned to get a lot of uninterrupted work done during that time. To ensure this privacy, he'd released the entire staff at Broadlea Hall for the week between Christmas and the New Year.

In preparation for the staff's early departure, he'd already chosen what he hoped were appropriate gifts for those on the estate and had the housekeeper put them away. He'd now dispatched a letter telling his secretary,

Peters, to distribute them. Since Peters' gift was among the others, the man should remember to give them out. Of course, Ben would not be surprised if he returned to discover the grooms had been given calico material and the maids razor strops.

Any errors could be straightened out when he returned to Broadlea Hall—hopefully having secured Sarah's agreement to be his wife.

It was for the purpose of courting Sarah—*courting* sounding better than *wearing her down*—that he had lengthened his stay with the Duttons. Everyone but Sarah seemed to realize this was what he was doing, but the object of his attention remained stubbornly oblivious. Or, at least, she pretended to do so.

To aid in his pursuit, he'd also found a latent talent for blackmail. He could get Sarah to agree to his presence by threatening to behave in a way that would draw attention to her. He wasn't particularly proud of this ability, but it was working. It was amazing the lengths a man in love would go to.

In love? Well, that was likely an exaggeration, but whoever heard of the term *in like*, even if it was the correct term? He liked Sarah and thought with a longer acquaintance, *like* could become more. At least on his side. He suspected his affection would never be fully returned. And while he didn't like the situation, he could live with it.

His latest attempt at benign blackmail had been used to convince Sarah she should accompany him while he ran the dogs. Having been used for hunting for three straight days, neither Brutus nor Meg needed additional exercise, but pretending this was the case had been the wedge to pry Sarah away from Lady Harley's side, a place she often sought to escape his presence. At breakfast, it had been a simple task to mention his desire to take the dogs out and to invite Sarah to join him. This suggestion had gotten Lady Harley's enthusiastic support. Sarah wasn't able to withstand their combined pressure. Now, he was waiting for her to appear in heavy outer clothing to begin their walk.

When Sarah came to the top of the stairs, he was disappointed to see she had again donned the same shapeless gray pelisse and coalscuttle bonnet she always wore. If they married—no, *when* they married—the first thing he was going to do was immediately throw everything gray into the rubbish heap. She could stay naked—now that thought brought a smile to his lips— until she owned an entire collection of jewel-toned dresses. He would also make quick work of eliminating that bloody widow's cap.

Sarah evidently, and fortunately, misinterpreted the reason for his smile. "I'm only going for the dogs," she said.

"I love when you're in a romantic mood," he said as he whisked her out the door and into another crisp but sunny day. She gave him a quelling frown that simply made him laugh.

A kennel worker waited for them with both dogs on leads. Ben collected Brutus and Meg, and they set off in the direction of the home farm. Sarah ignored him in favor of stroking and talking to the dogs. Walking through the dry, yellowed grass, they came to a large grazing area and followed the fence until they reached a gate to enter the field.

"There was a time when you would have suggested we climb over the fence rather than hike all this way," he said.

"There was a time when I was a hoyden. But we all eventually grow up."

Ignoring what he suspected was a barbed comment directed at him, Ben leaned down, released the dogs, and gave them the signal to begin casting the field. With a wistful expression, Sarah watched them search the pasture, heads high to catch the scent. "They're lovely," she whispered.

"Lovely, yes. But also useful. When we enjoy our Christmas Day feast, we'll have Brutus and Meg to thank for finding, flushing, and then retrieving the birds. The numbers shot would have been much smaller without their help."

The two dogs suddenly froze, both facing the same clump of brush. "Brutus and Meg are telling us they've located pheasants. If we were hunting, they'd hold that pose until we got within range to take a shot when the birds flushed, but since today is for fun, I'll let them put the birds to flight immediately." Then Ben gave one sharp whistle, and the dogs leaped forward, sending three pheasants furiously flapping skyward.

Sarah laughed at the birds' explosive flight. The sound was more precious for being seldom heard. Ben's chest tightened until it seemed hard to breathe. "I wish you would laugh more often," he said.

She stopped and turned her face up to him so their

eyes met under the brim of her concealing hat. "Some of us don't have so much to laugh about."

This comment, following the one about growing up, seemed to indicate Ben hadn't and brought a flash of anger. "And some of us don't laugh because we just enjoy wallowing in self-pity and acting like a martyr."

Her eyes snapped with an answering heat. "Some of us have had to make accommodations to a life that hasn't turned out as we expected."

"You think my life is the one I wanted?" How could she have so misjudged his desires and character? The thought that she knew so little of him was a living pain. "I'd planned for a career in mathematics. I looked forward to years of intellectual exploration. I yearned for this life. And then, I lost both of my brothers in rapid succession, and what I wanted no longer held any importance.

"I wouldn't wish being the last sprig on an aristocratic family tree on my worst enemy. I definitely didn't want the responsibility of trying to rescue estates that have been poorly managed for years. But this was the life I've been handed, and I'm trying to make the best of it."

"You don't understand." She turned away, effectively hiding her expression behind that damned hat brim.

Without thought, he grasped her by both shoulders and spun her to face him. "What don't I understand? I know you've lost the great love of your life. And I know that a life with me would be a second choice. I'm neither a poet nor famous. But I am offering you a *real* life, not the shadow existence you now have." His voice had risen, and he noticed both dogs were returning to see if there was a problem. "I'm offering you a life where you don't have to wear ugly gray bonnets and old-lady caps."

He released her arms and began jerking on her bonnet ribbons. She tried to stop him, but he brushed her hands away. In a trice, he'd jerked the bonnet from her head and snatched off her disgusting cap. Stuffing the cap inside the bonnet, he held the items high above his head. Sarah reached her hands up and jumped to retrieve them. She was tall for a woman, but she had no hope of retrieving what he held aloft.

"Give me back my bonnet!"

He laughed, suddenly feeling carefree, as if he were indeed guilty of failing to mature. "I don't think so." Then he shouted, "Meg. Catch." and launched Sarah's bonnet into the air. The hat made a poor projectile and tumbled earthward. Before it reached the ground, however, a flash of red and white grabbed it and streaked away.

"Oh, my bonnet—"

"—was exceedingly unattractive," Ben finished. He tilted her face up toward him with one finger under her chin. Her hair, loosened when he jerked off the cap, was already dancing in the breeze that teased the bright loops the color of honey, a mix of blond and brown and tan. How he loved her hair, alive and uncontained. This was how she was meant to be. "Don't you see that I would buy you a dozen pretty bonnets, if you would just give me the chance? I understand that I'll never be your grand passion. I can live with that, especially since I think we both will still be able to find contentment, and perhaps joy."

Then he slowly lowered his head toward hers. His intent had to be clear. If she objected, he would release her. She had only to say no. But she said nothing. She did not turn her face away. He slowly settled his lips on hers, and it was like coming home.

Ben was kissing her. All those years ago, she'd wanted him to kiss her and had wondered what it would be like, but her imaginings paled in comparison to the actual occurrence. She'd assumed she would feel safe in his arms, and while this was definitely the case, this safety was overwhelmed by a tingling rush of excitement.

His lips were both firm and soft at the same time, coaxing rather than commanding. There seemed to be a smile in his kiss, and she responded joyously, as if she had been flushed from her hiding place and had taken to the air. Now freed from the tangle of her life, she could soar.

Her hands slipped across his hard chest and up to his broad shoulders. She was no longer a green girl and wished the muscles that bunched beneath her touch were not separated from her questing touch by gloves and coat. She longed to feel the heat of him.

His hands found the sides of her face and tilted it slightly as he ran his tongue along her bottom lip, teasing and asking for more. She relaxed her mouth and let his tongue slide in to play with her own. Another revelation. Sharing rather than domination.

She leaned into him and relished the solid strength of his long, firm body. Even through their heavy clothing, she could feel the evidence of his desire pressed against her stomach. Heat curled within, and her breasts felt heavy. She experienced a surge of desire that had been dormant for years.

He broke the kiss. She had wanted it to continue until the sun set or perhaps fell from the sky. Kissing Ben was one of the best things that had ever happened to her. Ben straightened to his full height and settled her tightly against his chest. She could hear his rapid heartbeat, a rhythm that matched her own. "I had hoped but never expected..." His voice held a trace of awe.

"Neither did I." She now realized that what she'd felt for Hamish was like the flickering of a glow-worm compared to the lightning bolt she'd experienced with Ben. "Maybe this is just a response to a memory of the friends we once were." She feared this was the case and had to verbalize the possibility.

Ben chuckled, sending little gusts of air around her ear and making her shiver. "I don't think that was remembered friendship. But it bodes well for a life together. I want to marry you. My purpose must have been plain. All you have to do is say yes."

How could he make the impossibility of marrying him sound like a simple task? She pushed back from him. She needed space between them to marshal her arguments. "Ben, I've already explained that my father disowned me after my elopement. Most of the ton thinks my behavior was scandalous, and I don't want to bring that scandal to your door. It would have been difficult enough to marry you if you'd been a third son. But now that you're Viscount Kittredge, it's impossible."

"Not impossible—"

"Yes, it is." She cut him off before he could come up with arguments that would not hold up in the face of reality. "You've said you didn't want the title and all of the responsibilities that came with it, but you're working hard to do whatever is expected of you. Well, one of the things that is now expected is for you to marry and produce heirs. Heirs who are in no way tainted by a mother with questionable character. The woman you marry needs to be someone with an unsullied reputation, someone of whom you can be proud. And that is not me. My previous behavior irrevocably blotted my copybook."

"Sarah, it's not as if you ran off and became the man's mistress. You married. You may have married unwisely, but you *did* marry. You behaved morally. Other than alienating your father, you have done nothing to be ashamed of. The only scandal is your father's behavior, and that's his problem, not yours. He undoubtedly wanted you to make a grand alliance, but you chose instead to marry the man you loved. I know I will be a poor second, but I will cherish you and hope that you can come to care for me too."

The earnestness in Ben's face made her want to cry. She hated to expose all of her folly, but she couldn't let him think she was rejecting him because she thought him unworthy. "Oh, yes, I ran off with a man I imagined was my one great passion. Hamish Clendenin had a way with words, and I foolishly thought he meant them. He told me I was his inspiration, his muse, and I naively believed him. We ran away to Gretna Green, and I was deliriously happy—for a week.

"Then Father refused to give Hamish my dowry, and

his attitude changed. I became an impediment to his artistic impulses. I was a chain that bound him to the mundane. Within a few months of discovering he simply had a wife instead of a *rich* wife, my husband was looking elsewhere for his inspiration." She had thought she was long past disillusionment, but her voice sounded bitter.

"We moved to the small village in Scotland where he had grown up. It's cheaper to live in such a place, and he only had the income from two small volumes of verse. I was not the financial windfall he'd expected. And I was a complete failure at housekeeping and cooking, both of which I was now supposed to do. Hamish no longer even pretended any interest in me.

"But we were irrevocably bound together. That was the horror of the situation, which continued for four miserable years. And then he died, drowned in a shallow stream, drunk as a fiddler and on his way to a midnight assignation with the blacksmith's wife. And I felt nothing but relief." She should have felt guilty that she viewed her husband's death as a deliverance, but she could not find it in herself to feel differently. She was sure Ben could see this character flaw without her having to point it out.

"How could he not treasure you?" Ben seemed honestly perplexed.

"Hamish cared for no one but himself. He married me for the lifestyle he thought he'd enjoy if I were his wife, and when that was not forthcoming, I was of no use to him. Are you familiar with 'The Lass with the Azure Eyes'? It's his most famous poem."

Ben shook his head. "I know nothing about contemporary poetry."

"I personally suspect you have not missed much." Yes, the bitterness was still there. "This poem was written less than six months after we married and is considered a great love poem."

"But—"

"My eyes aren't blue. They're plain brown."

"I always thought of them as amber, glowing with the memory of forests from millions of years ago."

She gave a sharp laugh. "Please, don't *you* begin to sound poetic. I've had enough verse to last my entire life. The point I'm making is that I ran away with a ne'er-do-well. I thought he was my everything—and he was nothing. I was the worst kind of fool. And so, I've learned that I can't trust myself. I'm afraid to once again make an irrevocable mistake.

"You say you want to marry me, that you care for me, and that we could make a good life together. And I want this to be true. But what if it's not? What if this would be an even greater mistake than the one I've already made? You accuse me of living a half-life, a shadow-life, and while this may be true, it's also a safe life. There is no one who can hurt me. If we were to marry and things didn't work out, the pain would kill me."

Tears pooled at the corners of her eyes, and she wiped them away. She already felt the searing pain of what might have been. Perhaps she cried for her own cowardice, but she could not take the chance. "I'm cold," she said, knowing it was the truth. She may have just rejected her one chance to feel warm again. "Can we go back?"

She'd steeled herself for more argument, but it never

came. Without a word to her, Ben whistled in the dogs. Meg still happily carried up her bonnet, now somewhat lopsided. The ribbons, which had trailed in the grass, were covered with burrs. The dog dropped the hat at Ben's feet with what looked to be pride.

Ben picked up the ruined bonnet and turned it over in his hands. "I'm sorry about this," he said.

And then she could no longer stand there in that field where she was surrounded by lost possibilities. She spun around and hurried back toward the house. She thought Ben would call to her, or follow her, but when she'd reached the lane, she looked back to see him standing mute where she'd left him, still holding her bonnet, the two dogs ranged on either side like an odd portrait of a sporting gentleman at his leisure.

Chapter Six

SARAH ENTERED THE HOUSE through a side door and managed to make it to her room without encountering any of the houseful of people. One look in the mirror reinforced just how lucky she had been. Without her bonnet or cap, the wind had reduced her hair to its naturally wildly curling state, and it spiraled around her head in Medusa-like confusion. Her eyes were red-rimmed and puffy. Simply put, she was a mess.

What didn't show in the mirror was her heart, which felt as if it was being squeezed into a tiny ball. How it hurt to reject a dream! She had entered young womanhood with one fervent wish—that she would eventually become Mrs. Benjamin Radcliffe. Sweet words and a handsome face had diverted her from this goal. But now, after she thought she had eliminated the possibility of it ever happening, the dream had been offered to her.

And she could not grasp it.

There could be no Mrs. Benjamin Radcliffe. Now there was only Lady Kittredge, and that was someone Sarah Clendenin could never become. Sarah's motives for rejecting Ben were altruistic and honorable but...

But the most compelling reason was neither

altruistic nor honorable. The simple fact was—she was afraid. It was easier to hide from life than become vulnerable again. At least this was what she kept telling herself. But if it were true, why did it hurt so badly? She collapsed onto a chair and bent over to breathe through her mouth. The pain that lanced through her was decidedly physical.

"Well, did Lord Kittredge ask you to marry him? I suspected that was his plan and thought having you seated next to Squire Bigelow might spur him on. Nothing motivates a man like a potential rival." Lady Harley burst into Sarah's room, the skirts of her old-fashioned dress billowing about her like a ship in full sail. When she saw Sarah, both her body and her words abruptly stopped.

"Oh, my dear girl, has the cad done something to hurt you?" Lady Harley was again in motion, scudding about the room on waves of crinoline. "I certainly hope he didn't make a proposition instead of a proposal. I've not the influence I had in my youth before I married my Scottish lord, but I still have friends who move in society. I'll blacken his name throughout the ton. I'll make his presence anathema. I'll—"

"He asked me to marry him."

Sarah's comment took the wind out of Lady Harley's sails. Becalmed, she drifted into the chair opposite Sarah.

"I beg your pardon? What are you saying?" The older lady frowned in confusion.

"Lord Kittredge asked me to marry him."

"So why are you overset?"

"I refused him." Sarah's voice broke on the last word

and she was suddenly crying again. She covered her face with her hands but could not get control of herself. Ridiculous! Sarah Talbot Clendenin did not sob like a milkmaid. When her father had disowned her, she'd reacted with anger, not weeping. When she'd discovered that Hamish cared nothing for her, she'd shed a few tears and then picked herself up and carried on. When he'd died and she'd learned of her precarious financial position, she'd remained dry-eyed and resolutely tried to make the best of things. But this turn in her life cut her to the bone.

"Why ever did you do such a stupid thing? The man is wealthy and titled and is completely taken with you." Lady Harley's question rang like an accusation.

Sarah ineffectively wiped at her eyes with her fingers. An embroidered handkerchief appeared in her line of vision and then dropped into her lap.

"Dry your eyes and answer the question."

If only there were an easy answer. Sarah needed to protect her position, so there was only so much she was going to tell her employer. "I suppose I knew I couldn't marry him because he *was* wealthy and titled. Such a man doesn't marry a woman like me."

"And what type of woman would that be? One from the highest levels of society? One who is estranged from her family only because her father is an idiot? One who was married to a bounder but is now fortunately rid of him?"

Sarah jerked upright in surprise. "You knew?"

Lady Harley raised one eyebrow; otherwise, her face was perfectly calm. "Of course I knew. Do you think I'm such a nincompoop that I would ask someone unknown into my house. My man of business investigated you. As it turns out, I knew both your parents when I was young. Your father didn't have much to recommend him even then, and he's grown more irritating with the passing years. No one could figure out why your mother married him. He's always had an overblown sense of his own importance."

"Well, if you know my circumstances, you know I'm scandalous—and I would not hurt Lord Kittredge by tying him to someone who would never have the respect of his peers."

"Oh, my. That reasoning certainly sounds self-sacrificing." Sarah was surprised at the sarcastic tone lacing Lady Harley's voice. It was becoming rapidly apparent that she didn't know her employer as well as she thought she did. "No wonder you're crying. Not only are you rejecting a man I suspect you desperately want, you're lying to yourself about it."

Was she? Sarah didn't think the concerns she'd expressed were faulty. And she wasn't going to reveal that her fear of being hurt by a man again was also part of her motivation. She'd never considered herself a coward, so it was hard to admit. But Lady Harley was correct in her assumption that Sarah was rejecting someone she wanted. This was what had made her decision so painful.

Lady Harley sighed and settled back in her chair. Without animation, she suddenly looked old. "Your decisions are, of course, your own—just as the regrets will all be yours. I live with regrets, we all do, and I think this will be one of yours. But I won't let you hide from the man for the rest of the holidays. If you wish to stay in my employ, you will come with me to dinner this evening and will enter into whatever activities are planned for the rest of our stay here. You can be as silent and self-effacing as you like, but you will be present. I'll give you time alone until dinner."

She paused and shook her head. "If you choose to never marry again, then you will have to put up with the dictates of an employer, either me or someone like me. I think doing so is preferable to being on the street, which is probably your only other alternative. All choices have consequences, and this is what you've chosen."

Lady Harley hoisted her bulk out of the chair and sailed out of the room in the manner she'd entered—leaving Sarah to feel even more bereft. She had only pieces of memories of her mother, who had died when her brother Harold was born, but for some reason, she thought her mother would have aged into someone more like Lady Harley rather than like her Aunt Tess. Lady Harley was blunt and exacting but ultimately caring. Sarah recognized that even the scolds her employer often gave were motivated by concern.

And much of what Lady Harley had said was true. Sarah already felt regret. She wondered if she'd been given time alone to reflect on this and perhaps change her mind. She really couldn't see that happening, but her mind had already begun to teem with different possibilities and scenarios.

Ben was surprised to see Sarah among the

assembled throng waiting in the drawing room for the call to dinner. He'd thought she might again retreat to the privacy of her room. He hoped her presence indicated she was rethinking her quick rejection of his marriage proposal.

He still could not fathom how her husband could have found her wanting in any way. He now blamed that man for making the light dim in her eyes and causing her to question herself. He'd been offended on her behalf and had stayed in the field, trying to walk off his anger, for nearly an hour after Sarah had left. Part of his annoyance was that the self-absorbed idiot Sarah had married was beyond his reach.

He was also frustrated that he couldn't think of any way to help her regain her confidence other than expressing his care and concern, both of which she'd rejected. But Ben was tenacious and believed there was a solution to every problem. He just had to find the right equation and then bring its disparate parts into equilibrium.

The full complement of guests was now in residence, the group filling the drawing room with noise and laughter. Good manners required him to stop and converse with those he passed, slowing his progress toward where Sarah stood. Dinner was called before he had moved much in her direction, and any possibility of their talking was lost. Their relative positons also insured that they would not be seated next to one another. But from a distance, she seemed to be livelier and more like the Sarah Talbot her remembered.

And then he realized the difference. She no longer

wore the stupid widow's cap. Perhaps she had but one, and Meg had lost it somewhere in the field. If this were the case, he and the dog had done a good deed this morning.

Dinner stretched interminably even though his dinner partners were interesting conversationalists. They simply were not the one lady he wished to talk to. He also felt the period allotted for the men to enjoy their port lasted longer than necessary. When he was finally released, he made his way to Sarah's side without deviation.

Lady Harley evidently recognized his obvious pursuit. She raised one eyebrow and then smiled with what he hoped was encouragement. Sarah, however, looked apprehensive.

"What would you do if I dropped to one knee and asked for your hand in the midst of this company?" he asked, not sure if he were teasing her or if he spoke in earnest.

"Ben, do not even think of it." That she'd used his given name in public indicated her concern.

"No, I'll not, although I must admit that the impulse to do so is strong. Have you considered my offer of earlier today?"

He waited for her inevitable rejection—had steeled himself to show no reaction when she carefully explained she wanted nothing more to do with him. He was, therefore, surprised when she said, "I've given it a great deal of thought."

When she said no more, he prompted, "And..."

Sarah looked to the left and right, as if assessing if

they could be overheard. Ben didn't think anyone was paying attention to their conversation with the exception of Lady Harley, who was too far away to hear what was said. She did, however, seem to be observing them with pointed glances.

"And I've determined that I would like to have a private conversation with you," Sarah said. She again did a quick survey of those around them. "I've found that I sometimes have trouble falling asleep and often go to the library to find a book after the house has quieted."

"You do this often, then?" Ben hoped the smile that was building inside didn't show in his voice.

"Perhaps not as often as I would like, but I feel that tonight I may be in need of a book after everyone is abed."

"I'm assuming the quietness of the house is important."

"Oh, yes," she said. "That is the best time to read. But now I must attend Lady Harley. If you'll excuse me?"

She scuttled away, leaving Ben to come to terms with what she had just said. To arrange for the two of them to meet after everyone else had retired was scandalous—especially for the oh-so-very careful Mrs. Clendenin. She had to know that he'd be there. And the Dutton library was a good choice. It was bound to be deserted. The Duttons didn't appear to be a family of readers.

The question, of course, was whether this was to be an assignation or if she intended to hand him his heart chopped into tiny pieces and was being kind enough to do so in private. He fervently hoped it was the former, but feared it was the latter. He yawned hugely, pretending to hide his face behind his hand. Perhaps the rest of the company would decide it was time to go to bed. Either way, he would soon retire. He needed to figure out what would be appropriate to wear to what was either a tryst or an execution.

Chapter Seven

BEN SAT IN THE LIBRARY and listened to the house go silent around him. He was leaving nothing to chance. Rather than wander down from his room in the dark, he'd summoned the closest footman and made it clear that he expected to read here for some time. The servants had obliged by building up a good-sized fire and supplying fresh candles before they retired. The room was pleasantly warm. The soft candlelight was welcoming. He'd set the scene for seduction as well as he knew how.

Because seduction was what he intended, regardless of what Sarah had planned. He'd already given her the logical reasons they should marry. Now he needed to convince her that this *something*—which had, perhaps, hovered at the edge of his consciousness for years and had most definitely appeared when they'd kissed—was well worth the pursuit.

Of course, his early arrival had dictated that he wore the same clothes he'd dressed in for dinner. When Sarah had suggested they meet here, he'd envisioned himself clad in a decadent silk banyan—and nothing else. He might be a stodgy mathematician, but he did have an active imagination. Unfortunately, he did not own a silk banyan.

He got up and needlessly poked at the fire. He had to grip the edge of the mantel to keep from pacing. He could explain the most complicated equation so anyone could understand it. He could organize complex shipping schedules so a product was where it needed to be at the exact moment it was required. He'd mastered clarity of instruction, but he was much less sure about how to talk a woman into bed. Oh, he'd known plenty of women in the Biblical sense. Celibacy had never seemed a virtue. But he'd never sexually enticed anyone. His encounters just seemed to happen. And so, now when he needed this expertise, he was left floundering in uncertainty.

Sarah's unlamented, late husband had undoubtedly seduced her, but he was a poet—and verse didn't flow in Ben's veins. Even if the man were the complete bounder he seemed to be, Ben feared he would suffer by comparison. He didn't even know what Sarah's late husband had looked like. He was quite sure, however, that the man had been handsome and dashing. Not some six-and-a-half-foot tall, eighteen-stone behemoth with fiery hair and freckles. Women fell in love with suave, handsome men. They hired the large ones to clear stumps from a field.

But that mysterious connection between him and Sarah had to count for something.

He glared at the mantel clock for perhaps the hundredth time. What if she didn't come? What if after her somewhat brazen suggestion, she changed her mind? Lady Harley could have come up with some late night demand. Sarah might have seen someone in the hall and had to return to her room. There were myriad, legitimate reasons that would see Ben watching the fire burn out alone.

Then, before even turning, he knew she was there.

Sarah stood in the doorway, limned by the glow of the single candle she held before her. She wore a pale green dressing gown with a simple, white nightrail showing at the neck. Her feet were beguilingly bare. And her hair—sweet heavens, her hair was loose, spiraling around her shoulders and down her back. Looking at all that curling glory, no mathematician could have conceived of parallel lines. Errant strands caught the firelight and glimmered like golden arcs.

Something within him shuddered and stilled. Sarah had dressed for an assignation of lovers and not an assassination of hope.

"You came," he said, needing to state the logical axiom, the self-evident truth on which the rest of the night would be based.

"Yes." She gave him an alluring smile that caught his breath in his throat.

He crossed the room and took the candle from her, placing it on a table near the door. Then he gently drew her to the sofa facing the fireplace and sat down next to her. He needed to proceed but was hesitant about how to begin. Then she solved his quandary by leaning over and kissing him.

He was flooded with the same joy that came when he solved an elegant proof. The sharp understanding of how disparate pieces united into a whole. The discovery of the balance within an equation. The realization of where he fit into the universe was staggering—and he could do nothing but kiss her back.

Lips melded. Tongues quested. Time slowed. Ben had no idea what had caused Sarah to change her mind, but he wanted to take full advantage of it. He needed to show her he cared for her deeply and hoped his words and actions would ensnare her affections. But he doubted his ability. The man she had loved enough to marry had seduced her with words, and Ben was not good with them.

And so, he told her with the only poetry he had in his soul that the line of her ear was an elaborate geometrical construct. The slope of her cheek put an exquisite gradient to shame. The column of her neck—well, he could think of no comparison as he kissed his way down to the edge of her nightgown.

Sarah murmured as he slipped the small buttons free. She ruffled the hairs on the back of his neck. Her lips left butterfly kisses on his eyelids. If they spoke different languages, it made no difference. They understood each other.

When he bared her luscious breasts, he knew Pythagoras had never measured the angles of such alluring curves. They put the lie to all known geometries. When he pulled each peaked tip into his mouth, all proofs became obsolete. He found more meaning in loving Sarah than his studies had ever given him.

As he lowered her to the carpet, he realized Fate had been kind. Even though his love of pure mathematics had been strangled by responsibility and duty, he'd now found a new love that would give fulfillment to the life he was destined to lead. When he covered her, every angle, every curve, every plane, was in total alignment, and Benjamin Radcliffe, Viscount Kittredge, knew wholeness for the first time.

Sarah had spent the day overcoming the fear that she would again make a disastrous mistake. To others this trepidation probably appeared illogical, a chimera that haunted her imagination but held no terror in the real world. Even Lady Harley seemed to suggest that Sarah's hesitancy would only lead to regret. And so, she had girded herself for battle and fought her fears until they became smaller and battered, even if they would not completely disappear.

She'd arrived at dinner determined to ask Ben to meet her alone, but it had taken all of her willpower to force the words from her mouth. Once said, however, she felt a surprising confidence. This glow continued until the decisive hour arrived. Then she'd walked to the library on shaking legs. Her heartbeat echoed in her ears, obscuring all other sound.

She knew the risk she was running when she pushed open the door. The last time she'd done something this rash had led to disaster. But this time, the circumstances were much different because the man was different. Ben would protect her and cherish her. She knew this without a doubt.

She'd not anticipated discovering contentment, however. As they lay entwined on the soft Persian carpet in front of the fire, the sudden rush of tenderness and caring was unexpected. She was unimpressed that the angle of her shoulder blade made a Scalene triangle. She was indifferent to the perfect parallelogram hidden in the fold at the back of her knee. But she relished that Ben thought each piece endearing and beautiful.

She lacked the precise words to describe the wonder of Ben's physique, so she didn't even try. Instead, she spoke with her hands, running them over the planes and contours of his body. She could only touch with awe the powerful muscles that bunched in his arms, the strength evident in the cording across his abdomen, the quiet vulnerability she saw in the indentations above his hipbones. He was so big, a force of nature, yet she felt she should take care of him and see that he came to no harm. She realized she loved this man, and maybe always had. How had she not known?

The question unconsciously tumbled out as she lay replete with her head on his chest.

"How could you have known?" Ben asked. "You were only a girl when we were last together. I was nineteen and thought myself a man grown, and I had no idea how I felt. I think then, the four years difference in our ages kept us from seeing what was between us. But I know I love you now. Thankfully, we're finally in the same timeframe."

"I'm so lucky I found you to love," she said, pulling the warmth of his regard around her as a cloak against the cold days to come.

"And you'll marry me?"

A shaft of pain lanced through her. She ached to marry Ben, but to do so would all be to her advantage.

Ben would be stuck with a sullied wife who could prove an embarrassment. She had overcome her own fear of being hurt, but she was still afraid of hurting Ben. "No, it would never work."

"No?" He shot to a sitting position, dislodging Sarah, who tumbled to the floor in an ungainly heap. "After this, how can you say no?" He threw out a hand to indicate the strewn clothes, the warm glowing room, their own nakedness.

She opened her mouth to present all her well-considered arguments against their marriage but was interrupted by the banging of the door. Lady Harley strode into the room, her voluminous robes fluttering around her, enlarging her already substantial size until she looked to be a descending horde.

Ben scooped Sarah up and held her tightly against his chest. He draped something—his waistcoat perhaps—ineffectually around them.

"I assume you're leaving at first light to obtain a special license," Lady Harley said, the words echoing around the room like the voice of doom.

"Most assuredly," Ben answered without pause.

"Good!" Lady Harley reversed direction and flowed out of the room. "A wise person would have locked the door," she said upon exiting.

Sarah didn't know whether to laugh or cry. The ridiculousness of the the situation lent itself to hysterical laughter. But the outcome for Ben made her want to weep.

"What if I continue to say no?" she asked. "You can't be forced to marry someone who is unwilling—and if I'm the one doing the rejecting, little scandal should fall on you. I'm sure you're not the first gentleman to be caught in this situation."

Ben's laugh was surprisingly carefree. "No, I'm quite sure this is not a unique occurrence. But you can't continue to say no, or my reputation will suffer irreparable harm. Now that I hold the title, it is necessary that I marry, and what lady of good standing would want to marry a man who had been rejected by a lady he'd compromised? The gossips would turn me into an ogre of the worst sort, since you must have concrete reasons for rejecting my suit. Parents will hide their daughters if I'm anywhere nearby. So you'll just have to say yes, and we will be married as quickly as possible."

For a man facing a forced marriage, Ben certainly seemed cheerful. Suspicion flashed through her mind. "Did you arrange for us to be found by Lady Harley?"

"Good Heavens, no! I want you to choose to marry me, not be pressured into doing so. I thought when you asked me to meet you here and you arrived *en dishabille* and we..." he paused as if trying to discover a benign phrase for what they'd just done, "got to know one another very well... I thought this was your way of saying yes. If that was not your intention, then why did you arrange this tryst?"

Sarah now had to search for the right words. "I knew I would regret never having loved you, even if we never could marry. I had a long talk with myself today and realized that you are the only man I've ever loved. The only man I *will* ever love. And I decided it would be criminal to avoid an encounter that could be one of the most meaningful of my life. I wanted to know joy, if only for a little while."

Ben pulled her to him and kissed her on the forehead. When she brushed against him, she realized they were both still quite naked. She had been so lost in their discussion that she hadn't noticed. How odd. Even when she was first married and had been in the throes of misplaced lust, she'd always been self-conscious about her nakedness. But now, she didn't feel uncomfortable at all.

"You must see that we are both meant to know joy from now on. All you have to do is agree and I'll be on a horse at dawn to get the license. We could be married before the new year. Just say yes."

And she did. The word fell from her mouth without thought, and once it was said, she saw the rightness of it. "Yes," she repeated, enjoying the sound of the future.

Ben dipped his head and covered her mouth with his. The intensity of his kiss was shattering. She gasped when he suddenly drew away.

"How long have you been here at the Duttons?"

"Wha..." She felt completely disoriented.

"Have you been here four weeks?" He sounded urgent.

"Yes. We've been here close to seven now. We arrived at the beginning of November. It's such a long journey from Scotland, and the roads can be chancy in the winter. We'll stay here until after Twelfth Night and then go to another cousin's estate in Staffordshire until March. Why do you need to know Lady Harley's travel itinerary?" His behavior seemed bizarre.

"Hallelujah!" This time Ben gave her a loud, smacking kiss, much like that bestowed by an exuberant child. "This means we can be married before Christmas. I won't have to go all the way to London for a special license. Since you're now legally a member of this parish, I can get a Bishop's License in York, and we can be married here without banns."

He held up three fingers and counted off. "A day to York. A day to track down the Archbishop and get the license. A day back. We can be married on the twenty-fourth."

Ben's broad grin was contagious. She felt her facial muscles tightening to answer it. How long had it been since she'd had something to grin about? It seemed a lifetime ago that she'd felt this happy. "You're not much of a mathematician if you have to count on your fingers," she quipped.

He laughed. "But I did get the essential equation right." He then got to his feet.

"Where are you going?"

"To lock the door, of course. I don't have to leave for York for hours yet."

Sarah followed him into laughter. She didn't know if it was caused by her imagining what was soon to come or if it was from enjoying the sight of Ben walking about as God had made him. If Lady Harley had been here, she would have proclaimed him a brawn man. And most importantly, he was Sarah's brawn man.

Yes, against all odds, their Christmas equation was adding up perfectly.

Chapter Eight

FOR THE THIRD STRAIGHT MORNING, Sarah awoke with a smile on her face. Her dreams had all been pleasant, and she was filled with happy anticipation. Ben would be returning late this afternoon, and they would be married the next day.

Except for decorating the chapel and having the final fitting of her wedding dress, all was in readiness. She was amazed at how the entire house party had enthusiastically joined in the preparations.

Of course, much of this was due to Lady Harley. Her soon-to-be-former employer had been a wonder—as well as a wonderful liar. In Lady Harley's version of events, Ben had talked with her on the afternoon of the twentieth and declared his intentions. Together, they had planned for him to come to Lady Harley's rooms that night, at which time he'd gone on bended knee and asked for Sarah's hand.

The Burwell girls, as well as a clutch of later arriving unmarried ladies, were all swept away by this romantic Banbury tale. Even Mrs. Burwell had offered her help in arranging the wedding, although more than once Sarah had overhead her complaining to her two daughters that they should have tried harder to get the viscount's attention. Lavinia Herbert, of all people, saying she was closest to Sarah in size, had insisted on lending her a dress.

"No one should marry in gray," Lavinia had proclaimed, and then draped a gorgeous teal gown across the bed.

Sarah knew she shouldn't accept the loan of anything so expensive, but she could not resist. It had been so long since she had worn anything so sumptuous, and she wanted to make Ben proud. The dress required more alteration than expected, however, and Sarah now doubted that the dress could be anything other than a gift. But she was a happy recipient. When she put it on, she felt beautiful.

Lord and Lady Dutton had offered to host the ceremony in the seldom-used chapel at Brackenheath. It turned out to be a charming, intimate space with impressive, medieval stained glass windows. If the sun were shining as brightly tomorrow morning as the brilliant arc slicing around the drapes indicated it was this morning, the entire chapel would glow with color.

On that happy thought, Sarah slid out from under her warm cocoon of covers into the frigid room. It must be earlier than she thought, since the fire had yet to be rebuilt. She padded across the room, pulled back the heavy drapery, and discovered a changed world.

Ice covered everything—the brown grass, the naked trees, the steep roofs of the surrounding buildings. Ice had even crept up to encompass the lower half of the insides of the windowpanes. The sun shone brightly, sparkling off the now reflective surfaces and making the mundane scene into a fairy world. It was beautiful, but deadly.

Her heart leaped into her throat. Ben would be returning from York on treacherous roads. What if his horse fell, injuring itself, or Ben, or both? Being married on a specific day wasn't nearly as important as Ben's safety. She wished there were some way to get a message to him telling him to stay in York until the roads cleared.

She turned from the window and began a rapid toilet at her dressing table. The temperature of the room was not conducive to lingering partially clothed. She donned her heaviest day dress, wrapped a muted paisley shawl around her shoulders, and went to find a room with a blazing fire.

At noon, when his traveling companion's horse slipped and came up lame, Ben realized they would not make it back to Brackenheath that day, and perhaps not even the next. The damned weather had taken a drastic turn for the worse, and treacherous ice covered every surface. If he'd been leaving from York, he would have found arriving at Brackenheath before dark challenging—especially since sunset came disgustingly early on the day after the winter solstice —but trying to cover double the distance was impossible.

Now he and Sarah's brother, Harold Talbot, Lord Wately, were reduced to walking their mounts along the verge. At least the stiff grass provided better footing than the rutted roadway. Up ahead, he could see the small village that boasted what Harold called a passable inn.

There, they could see about getting another mount for Harold and try to warm up. Ben seemed to have lost much of the feeling in his toes some time ago.

Going out of his way to see Sarah's father had initially seemed like a good idea. He'd made it to York in surprisingly good time and, miracle of miracles, had found the Archbishop in residence. For the requisite fee, he quickly had a Bishop's License in hand. This left him with an extra day before he needed to return to Brackenheath.

He suspected a reconciliation with her father might be the best of all possible Christmas gifts for Sarah, so Ben had pressed on to the Earl of Farlough's country seat, which was located a half-day's journey further to the south. Ben hoped the man would be there for the holidays. He'd ridden up the drive of the massive Palladian estate in the middle of the afternoon of the twenty-second, pleased to discover the earl was indeed in residence.

What followed was not particularly pleasant.

Farlough, whippet thin and graying, met him genially. The name Viscount Kittredge obviously meant nothing to him. After the normal discussion of the weather—unseasonably warm at that point—and the state of the economy—the effect of the American embargo on grain prices was negligible—Ben said, "I've come to invite you to the wedding of your daughter, Lady Sarah Talbot Clendenin. She has graciously consented to be my wife, and we are to be married at Brackenheath on the twenty-fourth."

The earl abruptly stood up behind his desk and

glowered at Ben. "I have no daughter, so if you came here looking for money, you are out of luck."

Ben had risen with the earl. He could hardly be cowed by a man he overtopped by nearly a foot. And since it seemed the possibility of a rapprochement was unlikely, he did not need to temper his words. "You'll notice that I did not apply to you for her hand, since Sarah has made it clear to me that you relinquished that position years ago. I came here as a courtesy. I certainly don't want any money, since *my* estates aren't in need of funds."

Ben made no effort to keep the disgust from his voice. "I think it is a sad state of affairs when a gentleman thinks more of money than he does his own flesh and blood. I have to conclude it's *your* estates that are in financial distress. If this is the case, then I am putting you on notice that you need not apply to me for aid. Since you have no daughter, then you can never be a father-by-marriage to me."

Ben turned and strode to the door, gratified that Farlough stood gaping like a fish. But he was disappointed for Sarah's sake. The man might be an ass, but his indifference still had the power to wound the woman he loved.

He wanted to escape the estate quickly but was forced to linger for his horse to be brought around from the stables. When the animal arrived, it was being led by another rider who was obviously not a stableman.

The horseman gave Ben a cheeky smile he remembered gracing Sarah's face when she was a girl. His hair was lighter but had the same tendency to become riotous curls. Ben was, therefore, unsurprised when the young man said, "I'm Harold Talbot, Viscount Wately, Sarah's brother. If the wedding invitation extends to me, I've packed a set of good clothes and am ready to depart."

With a broad grim, Ben shook the rider's hand. "You are more than welcome to attend." Fortune had smiled on him. Ben suspected Harold would be the better gift.

When they stopped at an inn that night, this proved to be the case. Harold was a charming young man who looked forward to becoming reacquainted with his sister. He also produced a lovely sapphire ring.

"It was our mother's," Harold said. "I thought it would mean more to Sarah than it does to me, since she has memories of Mother, whereas I, unfortunately, have none." As if embarrassed, he traced circles on the tabletop with his finger as they sat in the private dining room of the inn. "Please don't feel that you have to use it. I realize you may have a family ring you'd prefer."

"No, this is perfect." Ben was touched by Harold's thoughtfulness. He'd planned to use his own signet ring for the ceremony. It would have been huge on Sarah's finger and, therefore, actually unwearable. He'd planned on having her choose something the next time they were in Town. Having her mother's ring was much more meaningful, and if it needed resizing, the change would probably not be all that drastic.

Ben rolled the ring between his fingers, pleased that all of the pieces were falling into place. He and Sarah would have a beautiful and memorable wedding in two days' time.

And then he'd awakened to an ice covered world and all his plans had gone awry.

He and Harold had covered only half of the distance anticipated. At least they would have shelter tonight and could hire new horses to continue their journey on the morrow. But that would be the twenty-fourth. He would miss his own wedding! Lord, he hoped Sarah would know his delay was due to the roads.

They limped into a surprisingly empty inn yard. Ben had been concerned that the facilities might have been overflowing with other stranded travelers. Instead, it turned out they were the only people who had even ventured out.

"Ye can't be planning on leaving tomorrow." The rotund innkeeper looked skeptical. "I doubt the roads will have improved."

"It has to be tomorrow," Ben said, blowing on his fingers to get them supple enough for him to sign the register. "We're already late for a wedding."

"Must be a good friend's wedding to get ye out in this."

"It's my own."

The cherubic man gave a quick laugh. "Well, that explains it. I'll make sure you have our sturdiest horses. And for now, would a hot bath be in order?"

Harold, continuing to divest himself of outerwear until he had nearly halved his previous size, looked up enthusiastically. "A hot bath, please, and a bottle of brandy. After an application of both, I might be able to feel my extremities."

"The same for me," Ben said. "And if you could

somehow create a thaw, I would be eternally grateful."

Sarah watched the fire slowly die and felt the chill creep up her legs. She should be abed, but she superstitiously believed that as long as she sat in the chair, she had not yet given up on Ben's arrival. Realistically, she knew if he had not come by dark, he had stopped along the way. It was now hours after sunset. But some hope still persisted.

She didn't want him trying to negotiate the icy roads in the dark, but she also wanted him here, so she could know he was safe. And, of course, she secretly wanted to be sure that he was indeed coming.

She had that irritating Mrs. Burwell to thank for putting that last doubt in her mind. The older lady had suggested that Ben might have decided he'd been too hasty in his decision to wed and was using the weather as an excuse to avoid the ceremony. Sarah wondered if Mrs. Burwell said things like this to be malicious or if she were just uncaringly oblivious. It really made no difference, for the thoughts kept sleep away.

Avoiding the ceremony could *not* be the reason Ben hadn't arrived at the appointed time. He would never be so cruel. But she had been so terribly wrong in her assessment of Hamish Clendenin. Why did she think she now had a better understanding of others' character? The doubts chased around her head and held her in the chair. She would not go to bed. She would not give up.

Her wedding dress hung in all its splendor on the outside of the wardrobe. It glowed an odd, pale blue in the low light of the room. She would wear it tomorrow, and Ben would think her beautiful. She had to keep that thought in her mind.

She got up and retrieved the heaviest quilt from her bed. She wrapped it around her and returned to the chair. She would not give up on Ben, ever.

Chapter Nine

BY TEN THE MORNING OF THE TWENTY-FOURTH, Ben had not arrived.

The vicar had, however. He'd trudged up the slippery path from the village only to be told that the groom wasn't present. Sarah had wanted to die of embarrassment; the clergyman had been kind and understanding. But if he had nodded sagely and said something about the inclement weather one more time, the false smile on her face would have cracked and she would have screamed.

And then, to Sarah's surprise, the day progressed as country house parties did on a normal Christmas Eve Day. In spite of the biting cold, most of the younger people ventured out into the surrounding woods and returned with greens to drape about the public rooms. Sarah had not counted herself as one of the young, since she felt immensely old and drained, but Lady Harley wouldn't allow her to hide in her room and had pressed her into helping with the decorating.

As if it were preplanned, no one mentioned the aborted wedding. This, of course, didn't keep Sarah from noting the ladies present seemed to be overly solicitousness and the gentlemen well-practiced at not meeting her eyes. She went about the day in a sort of numbed anticipation, her ear trained to catch the sound of approaching hoof beats or the sound of Ben's voice in the foyer.

The effort left her exhausted, but she soldiered on. When she dressed for dinner, she avoided looking at the accusing teal dress hanging on the wardrobe door and repeated her mantra of assurances. She had not again misjudged a man's affections. She had not been left at the altar like an ugly cliché. Ben would arrive as soon as he could.

She took confidence from this litany and did not put the dress away.

She even joined the group making its way to the village for the midnight service. She let the hope and the promise that was the coming of the Christ Child wash over her and fill in the dark hollows of doubt. Even buoyed by the joys of the season, however, sleep was again a long time coming.

"Sarah, wake up! He's here."

Lady Harley's voice penetrated the nightmare in which Sarah had wandered into a bog on the moors and had to struggle up from beneath the deep muck that tried to bury her.

She forced herself to a sitting position. "Ben's here?" Joy banished the last tendrils of the disturbing dream from all thought.

A smiling Lady Harley came into focus. "He arrived in the small hours of the morning, after everyone had returned from the midnight service and the house was abed. Since then, he's been a virtual whirlwind and has already arranged for the vicar to come at ten. When you hadn't yet appeared at breakfast, he suggested I gently get you into motion. So here I am, with hot chocolate and rolls and a bath on the way."

Sarah pushed her spiraling hair out of her face. That it had escaped from its braid was evidence of a restless night. "Goodness, what time is it?" Her voice came out reedy and breathless. The excitement of Ben's arrival left her feeling weak. She had not been wrong in her estimation of the man. An amazing future opened before her.

"It's nearly nine."

That would hardly be late on a regular morning, but, Heavens, she was supposed to be married in an hour! Sarah swung her legs over the side of the bed.

"Don't get up yet," Lady Harley said, pushing her back against the pillows. "First, break your fast while your bath is positioned and filled."

As if her words had been a command, an army of footmen arrived, carrying the tub and buckets of water. They all grinned but carefully avoided looking at Sarah where she huddled in the bed.

The hot chocolate tasted wonderfully, but she found herself too excited to eat, although she dutifully nibbled at the rolls to placate Lady Harley, who was issuing orders like a general preparing for battle. When the door finally closed, leaving only Sarah, Lady Harley, and two maids, it became apparent that a battle was indeed joined.

The fire had been built up to roaring. The scented

water was the perfect temperature. On any other occasion, Sarah would have lingered, but she was encouraged to bathe quickly. Warm towels were offered, and she was dry and sliding into her undergarments in record time.

Lady Harley's maid brushed Sarah's hair until it crackled, then arranged it on top of her head with elaborate silver combs, allowing curling strands to escape near her face.

"These aren't my combs." Sarah reached up to touch their sparkling surface nestled in her hair.

"They are now," Lady Harley said. "Think of them as a wedding gift."

"Oh, I could never—"

"I will hear no argument. They are a gift. I never had a daughter, and so I never had the joy of seeing her wed. Being involved in your happy day has been your Christmas gift to me." Lady Harley spoke brusquely, but her eyes were suspiciously misty.

Sarah dropped her hands and simply said, "Thank you."

When she was completely dressed, she stopped in front of a large, standing mirror and observed a woman who wasn't Sarah Talbot Clendenin. Instead, there stood an enchanted lady from a medieval tale. The teal dress floated around her like water from a deep lake; the combs in her hair sparkled like stars.

"Oh," she said, putting her hand against the mirror's surface. She could think of no other words to express her delight.

"I suspect your young man will have the same

reaction." Lady Harley dabbed at her eyes but gave Sarah a broad smile.

And then, the hour was upon them, and they hurried to the chapel. Lord Dutton had offered to escort Sarah down the aisle, but he wasn't waiting for her as anticipated. The small vestibule was empty except for a tall, slender young man with blond hair who rocked back and forth on his feet as he examined one of the narrow, stained glass windows.

He turned at the sound of their entrance, and her breath caught in her throat. It couldn't be! But the young man's face was too much like a masculine version of her own for her to doubt. Harold. Here for her wedding. It was a wonder and a gift she had never expected. Her baby brother magically grown into a man.

She made an odd, inarticulate sound and held out both hands, as if Harold were still the boy who would rush to her and hug her around the waist. The grown up version of her brother didn't behave much differently. He rapidly crossed the stone-flagged floor and pulled her into a fierce embrace. His hands now wrapped her shoulders instead of her waist, but the strength of his affection had not changed.

He loosened his arms and pulled back, his face split by a joyous grin. Sarah suspected her face held a matching expression. "How did you come to be here?" she asked.

"Through a lot of ice and cold."

She must have frowned, because he laughed and she realized he was teasing her. "Harold…"

"I guess the explanation you're looking for is that

your intended, Lord Kittredge, showed up at father's house to inform him of your marriage. I overhead the discussion and decided to accompany him. The ride here gave me an excellent opportunity to get to know my soon-to-be brother-by-marriage—and I must say, I applaud your choice."

"And father?" She had no idea why she even asked. Perhaps Ben had given her hope that all aspects of her life could be changed.

Harold shook his head. "Our father continues to be blinded by the brilliance of his own importance. As his heir, he has had to coexist with me, but the rest of humanity seldom meets his lofty expectations." He shrugged. "Some people are not worth the effort, and sadly, our father falls into that category. And so I try not to give him much thought—and this will be easier now that I've again found my wonderful sister."

He folded her into another quick hug. Placing a smacking kiss on her forehead, he said, "But for right now, I believe my job is to walk you down the aisle, that is unless you've changed your mind."

"That will never happen." Sarah realized that she spoke the complete truth.

Harold winged out his arm. "Then let us begin."

Smiling, Sarah placed her hand through the crook of Harold's elbow and they entered the chapel. To her surprise, every pew in the small church was occupied. Some gentlemen even stood in the back. She had a quick impression that someone had decorated with Christmas greens in here as well and saw that the sun, streaming through the ancient stained glass windows, did indeed fill the space with color. But her eyes immediately went to Ben.

He caught her look and smiled broadly. She could do nothing but smile in return. He was the most wonderful thing she'd ever seen, and he would soon be hers. As if fallen from the medieval scene depicted in the window, her beloved towered over the vicar like a stalwart knight from ages past.

When she passed the last pew, she saw who else was waiting at the altar, and uninhibited laughter leaped from her mouth.

Ben could not believe the vision walking toward him was to be his wife. Sarah glowed in a gown of warm greenish-blue, and sparkling silver flashes winked from her hair. Ben knew he loved her, but it was at that moment he realized he was marrying an enchantress, a goddess risen from the sea to captivate not only him, but also the entire congregation. He wished he had the ability to write a poem to her beauty. Lacking that accomplishment, he could only cherish her and hope she recognized his devotion.

She walked proudly next to Harold. Such delight transfused her face that Ben was glad he'd made the effort to ride to the Talbot estate. Even if he'd been unable to convince her fool of a father to accompany him, the gift of her brother's presence was worth arriving a day late. What was such a delay compared to the rest of their lives?

Her reaction to his final surprise was to laugh, a sound he promised himself he would hear at least five times a day from now on. Meg sat obediently to his right. She proudly wore Sarah's mangled gray bonnet. The flowery Burwell chit—he still didn't know her name—had helped him circle the bonnet with a wreath of holly berries to add to the festive occasion.

Everyone seemed to enjoy the addition of the decorated dog, with perhaps, the exception of the vicar, who seemed to worry that Meg would forget all her house training in the middle of the service. She whined softly when he signaled her to stay and went to join Sarah before the minister, but otherwise proved as steady as her sire.

"Dearly beloved," began the vicar.

Although it was the standard form for the beginning of the wedding service, to Ben it seemed to resound with truth. He would stand next to his dearly beloved for the rest of his life. He answered the requisite questions with a strong voice. When Sarah's turn to respond followed, her voice was similarly clear and sure. The only time she looked as if she might weep was when she recognized her mother's ring as he slipped it on her finger.

Then, the ceremony seemed to end more rapidly than any wedding he'd ever attended, and the vicar pronounced them Man and Wife. As if she understood what was said, Meg stated to bark exuberantly. Harold, who'd taken the dog's lead when he surrendered his sister, ineffectually tried to quiet her.

And Sarah laughed again, the sound heating Ben's blood. "Even if she misbehaves, I'm glad you brought Meg," she whispered, then reached over to take the leash and relieve Harold of his duty. "And I'm especially glad you brought Harold." She took a few steps away and hugged her brother. Her actions eliminated the need for Ben to explain the existence of a dog at a wedding, which would have been difficult.

This morning, as he was dashing around putting the wedding plans back into effect, he'd realized that his dogs were part of the equation that had led to his marriage to the one woman he loved. He'd wanted to honor them in some way—and he'd wanted to make Sarah at least smile. Dressing Meg up as an attendant had seemed a way to accomplish both tasks.

His plan had worked, but watching Sarah's delight in her brother's presence made him realize that bringing Harold along might be his most impressive feat. He smiled. He would remind Sarah of his cleverness when they inevitably hit the bumps that every marriage experienced.

"Are you going to linger here while everyone is waiting for the Wedding Breakfast to begin?" Lady Harley appeared at his elbow. Her happy face belied her querulous tone.

"If I can get my beautiful bride away from her brother, we'll be there."

Lady Harley gave him a broad wink. "Oh, I can make that happen."

The older woman walked directly to where Sarah and Harold were in earnest conversation. "Lord Wately," she said, unashamedly interrupting. "I doubt you remember me, since I last saw you when you were only a young boy, but I'm so interested in hearing what you've been doing." Her flow of words didn't stop as she steered him away like a child in leading strings.

Sarah and Ben looked at each other with bemused expressions. "How did she do that?" Ben asked.

To his surprise, Sarah gave him a wink quite similar to the one just bestowed by her former employer. "I have no idea, but it was effective. We seem to be the only people left in the chapel."

A quick glance confirmed this to be true—and Ben didn't waste a second acting on it. Before Sarah could say another word, he gathered her in his arms and lowered his mouth to hers. The kiss she returned was one of hunger and promise. It was what he'd been dreaming of for every frozen mile of the last four days. Well, that kiss and more.

"Do you think they will miss us if we fail to attend the breakfast? I've reserved the best room at the closest inn." He knew it would be very poor form not to show up at their own celebration but...

Sarah's eyes sparkled. "It will take a while to ready the coach, won't it? Probably just enough time for us to put in an appearance and wish everyone a happy Christmas?"

"Sounds perfect to me," Ben said, thinking that Sarah was what was perfect and that this would be his happiest Christmas ever.

After one more kiss, they took Meg into the foyer to find a footman and put their plan into motion. They were ready to begin the new, exciting equation that would be their life.

About Hannah

Hannah's journey to become a writer has been long and circuitous. She always loved words and stories, so, unsurprisingly, when she was growing up, she constantly had her nose in a book. She continued this reading habit throughout school and eventually received a BA and an MA in English from Southern Methodist University. For fifteen years, she taught literature and composition at various high schools and colleges while she followed her subject-to-transfer husband around the country.

After one particularly irritating move, which involved an inept real estate agent, she thought, "I can do this," and embarked on a career in real estate. She quickly discovered more people wanted houses than grammar. It turned out *a lot* more did, and she enjoyed great success as a real estate broker for the next thirty-five years.

But she never lost her love of books, of words, of stories. After one particularly unsatisfying read, she thought, "I can do this," and gave it a try. It was not as easy as she'd anticipated, but she persevered, attending workshops across the country, all the while practicing and reading. She won the Writers of the Future Grand Prize, and this opened a number of doors. She went on to sell over a dozen short stories to the major sci-fi and fantasy magazines.

In 2013. her first historical romance, *Kestrel*, was published. Hannah now has four other books available, including a novella in the original *Christmas Revels*.

Those who visit Hannah at either http://www.facebook.com/HannahMeredithAuthor or http://www.hannahmeredith.com, and who have decent math skills, will notice her picture and the length of her journey don't match. But, as long as there are no mirrors handy, this is what Hannah "thinks" she looks like, and using a half-life picture was easier than losing weight and getting a facelift. This is just further proof that Hannah Meredith lives in her imagination. Please join her there.

Crimson Snow

by

Kate Parker

Chapter One

THE DEEP RED DROPS MADE A TRAIL in the scuffed snow. Jane Merrywether, huddled in a faded cloak, followed them as she walked toward the village. Some poor animal, wounded by a predator or maimed by a wicked trap, had escaped. She pictured it, suffering and alone, and winced.

Except for this track, last night's snowfall lay evenly over the fields and woods. Where earlier flowers had bloomed and grasses had coated the land, now all around her was cozily tucked in beneath winter's blanket.

Then she came to a fence post where the drops had gathered into a bright splash against the still pristine white. She made out boot prints. Good heavens. Not some wounded animal. A person. Someone had stopped here to rest on his way to summon aid.

Jane sped her steps through the cold as she followed the trail, hurrying to the injured person. Was it one of the villagers? Someone from a nearby farm? From the prints, she'd have guessed the boots belonged to a man. It could be someone she knew. And whoever it was, they needed help.

Turning from the wider lane, she followed the trail of blood drops along a footpath into the woods. This wasn't the shortest route to the village and help, unless the injured person was headed for Sir Arnold Grey's home on the edge of the village. Was it one of his staff? She knew them all and had patched up a few in the past several years.

She was nearly running, praying she didn't trip over the body of a friend or neighbor, when the trail appeared to end at the door to a shed. Jane shoved the door open wide to get light inside and waited for her eyes to adjust to the gloom.

"I never thought he'd send a woman to finish me off," a rough baritone said from the direction of one corner.

Jane took a half step back into the sunshine. She didn't recognize the voice. Squaring her thin shoulders, she said, "I've come to help," as she stepped forward into the dimly lit interior. She hoped the injured man couldn't hear the tremble in her voice.

"If the loss of blood doesn't kill me, infection will..." Jane heard the sudden intake of breath and knew the man was in pain, "surely do me in."

Probably a starving soldier, returning to an uncaring England after the war, had been wounded trying to steal food from a farmer not much better off than he. "Let me find a lantern so I can see your wounds. I have experience—"

"No. No light. He'll find me then, and he'll probably kill you as well."

The voice sounded matter-of-fact. Weary. Jane found she didn't fear this man, whoever he was. "Who would kill you? Or me? Who are you?" She went to a shelf by the door and found a lantern and flint. Once she had light, she held up the lantern and searched the area. A pair of sturdy riding boots attached to legs clothed in heavy brown wool protruded from behind a partition.

She took a cautious step forward and peered around the low wall. Half-sprawled amid the straw on the dirt floor was a man with a bloodied nose and lip. His dark eyes were filled with pain. She lowered her gaze to his torso where his hand covered part of his blood-soaked shirt. A slash in the sleeve of his jacket leaked more blood. The light from the weak lantern wouldn't show her more detail.

Faced with the evidence of this savagery, she couldn't find her voice for a moment. "My heavens. What happened?"

"I'm afraid Lord Walbeck has a temper."

Her gaze flew to his face. He was grinning. Grinning and looking like he was about to die. Was he crazy? So many of the troops returning from Napoleon's carnage on the Continent were.

She didn't recognize him, and she thought she knew all of Lord Walbeck's many enemies. She needed to report the stranger's arrival and injuries to someone in authority. But definitely not Lord Walbeck. "Who are you and why are you here?"

"I'm looking for a man named Sir Arnold Grey. Doubt I'll find him now. Until he joins me in the next life."

He seemed to find dying amusing. The stranger was insane. "I'll get his servants and we'll move you to his house."

"I'm not exactly dressed for meeting a baronet."

"You'll freeze if you stay in this shed much longer. Don't go anywhere—"

She was interrupted with a bitter laugh.

Well, it was a stupid thing to say, but she'd never expected to find a bleeding man in a storehouse during the Christmas holiday. "And I'll bring help. What is your name?"

"John Rexford." The two words proudly cracked the cold air. She wondered if the name would mean something to Sir Arnold. It nudged something in the back of her mind. Where had she heard that name before?

She put out the lamp and left the shed, pulling the door shut behind her to limit the wind to only that slicing through the wooden slats. Hurrying down a shortcut, she came to Sir Arnold's brick manor house on the back side of the village. Gasping in cold air, she climbed the front steps and banged on the door.

The butler, Carlyle, opened the door. "Miss Merrywether, you look half-frozen. Warm yourself by the fire while I get Sir Arnold."

"There's no time. Please. There's an injured man in a shed on the edge of Sir Arnold's property. He said he wanted to meet with Sir Arnold. Please send some men with me to bring him here. He'll die otherwise."

"An injured man, miss?" Carlyle never displayed any surprise. Not even now at Jane's words.

"He said he had a run-in with Lord Walbeck. He claims his name is John Rexford."

"Good grief." Carlyle immediately called for two of the largest footmen. At his barked command, they hurriedly pulled on coats, hats, and gloves. Jane led all three men back away from the village to the shed. When they arrived, Carlyle glanced down at the dirty snow, scuffed by Jane's half-boots, and raised his brows. The blood drops had been trampled and mixed with the dirt.

He had to be inside. He couldn't have been faking his injuries, and she couldn't have imagined him. Jane pulled open the door and walked inside. "I've brought help."

There was no reply.

"Quick, light the lantern."

One of the footmen did so and held it up. Jane saw with some relief the man was still there sprawled in the dirt and straw. His eyes were shut, and when she lifted his hand, it was limp.

"Is he dead, miss?" Carlyle asked, staring at the man's face.

She knelt closer and listened. He was still breathing, but shallowly. "No, but he's close to it. We must get him to Sir Arnold's and get him warm."

Carlyle peered closer in the light of the lantern. "Good grief. This is indeed John Rexford." Carlyle then urged the footmen to hurry as he shoved Jane out the door and put out the lantern.

They made a ragged parade, half-carrying, half-dragging the injured man. He was tall and well-muscled and presented a challenge for the footmen that they couldn't quite meet. Rexford, awakened when lifted, tried with little success to walk part of the way and then collapsed. The footmen ended up dragging him backwards, the heels of his well-made riding boots digging two ruts in the snow.

Jane followed with Carlyle, trying not to notice the drops of red in the snow they trod through. It seemed to take forever on the return journey, and she could feel Carlyle's tension as he walked next to her. If Lord Walbeck found them trying to help a man he'd injured, all of them would suffer.

"How do you know him?" she asked.

"Later," the butler told her, scowling as he looked at the unconscious man.

Jane was numb with cold when they were finally in sight of Sir Arnold's. One of the footmen stopped suddenly, causing his partner to stumble under the weight of the injured man and curse.

The first footman motioned toward a horseman approaching Sir Arnold's door. "Lord Walbeck," he whispered.

"Head for the kitchen door. Now. Quickly," Carlyle hissed. Bushes partially shielded the path they followed along lower ground. They all crouched as they hurried toward the back of the house.

The sighs of relief were audible when they entered the back hall. Carlyle gave the kitchen boy and the scullery maid directions to set up a pallet beside the cook stove while the cook's assistant stepped around them to continue turning the roast. The cook was kneading bread, and the smell of dough and spices filled the air. Tomorrow's Christmas feast here would be a jolly one.

"I'll need clean linen, salve, hot water, soap, and whiskey," Jane told the servants as she began to take off her cloak. "And the sewing kit."

"I'll go up and see why Lord Walbeck is here," Carlyle

said.

"I suspect he came to find out if I talked Sir Arnold into coming to Christmas dinner tomorrow. If I don't make an appearance, my guardian will take the house apart looking for me in the guise of being worried for my safety." Jane shivered. It was an excuse he used often. "Whatever I say, agree with it."

"Yes, miss." Carlyle followed her up the stairs. They both paused on the landing when they heard Lord Walbeck's strident voice booming from Sir Arnold's parlor.

Carlyle knocked, and then they both entered the room. A cheery fire burned as Sir Arnold held up a brandy bottle as if offering some to his guest. Lord Walbeck, snow melting off his boots onto the well-scrubbed floor boards, was shouting, "I know perfectly well..." As he spotted Jane, he glared at her. "Where have you been, girl?"

She gave both men a curtsy. "I came over to give Sir Arnold your invitation, but a kitchen lad cut himself with a knife. The staff asked me to see to his care while they summoned Sir Arnold."

When Lord Walbeck opened his mouth, Sir Arnold smoothly broke in before Walbeck could speak. "See, you didn't need to worry about your invitation going astray. Miss Merrywether is here to deliver it."

"I had an unwanted guest today, one I had to send away with a flea in his ear. You haven't met up with the blackguard, have you, Jane? It wouldn't be safe." Walbeck strode over to where Jane stood.

Jane could see it wouldn't be safe by the shape this

unwanted guest was in, but the danger didn't come from the outsider. Her guardian had never worried about her safety. "I didn't see anyone in the lane today."

It was the truth, but she knew Lord Walbeck doubted her words when he held her by the chin and stared into her eyes. She stared back, trying not to show her fear.

"There's no need for that. Not in my house," Sir Arnold said.

Lord Walbeck loosed his hold on Jane with a shove. She stumbled slightly but caught herself and stood proudly erect, wondering how soon her guardian would leave so she could find out what was going on.

"What blackguard is loose in our county, milord? As magistrate, I should be informed of any dangerous persons in the vicinity," Sir Arnold said.

"No one you need to bother yourself with." Lord Walbeck looked over his host with a sniff. "I find it difficult to recall you're anything more than a solicitor. One who once changed the figures on an estate accounting you were responsible for."

"That was a mistake due to a blob of candle wax. I've paid for my mistake." Sir Arnold turned pale, his voice holding equal measures of bravado and begging.

"Still, would anyone trust you as a solicitor or a magistrate if the story got out?" Lord Walbeck smiled with pleasure. "As long as you're coming to dinner tomorrow, Sir Arnold, Jane and I can be on our way."

"I've not finished stitching up the lad," Jane said. "Go ahead, and I'll see you at home later."

"Oh, no. I'll wait." His smile broadened. "And I'll have

some of Sir Arnold's fine brandy while you finish."

"Yes, milord," Jane said with a small curtsy before she turned and left the room. Carlyle stayed behind.

Arriving back in the kitchen, Jane found everything waiting for her, and the man was again conscious. "All right, Mr. Rexford, let's see about patching you up. We'll have to get your coat and shirt off of you."

Focusing on helping a footman remove the man's jacket, Jane wasn't paying attention to her patient until he grabbed her arm with surprising strength. "No."

She looked him in the eye then. "Why ever not?"

"I'd like to meet my maker with some dignity, not showing my body to some wisp of a girl."

"I'm not some wisp of a girl. I've sewn up many a man." That was perhaps an exaggeration. She'd sewn up another kitchen lad's hand and a gardener's leg. But a body was a body, after all. "Let's get these clothes off you before you die of stubbornness."

Rexford knew he'd had plenty of opportunities to die of stubbornness in the past several years. He'd fought in sea battles, been starved and beaten as a prisoner, and plotted and executed a daring escape. Then he'd led his men in making a dangerous crossing of the Mediterranean before traveling through war-torn Europe. In every case, he'd fought against great odds.

Now that things were finally going his way, he didn't want to die.

However, the irony wasn't lost on him. After losing any number of heirs to the Beckingham title, the earldom had come to a man who should have been killed any number of times. To die at the hands of a couple of pig farmers employed by his cousin just as he had returned home in triumph was a fate he never expected.

It was his own fault he'd been caught off guard this morning. He'd expected to see his uncle, the old, grumpy Lord Walbeck who had been awarded his title for butchery during the fight in the American colonies. Rexford had forgotten how much time had passed. Instead, he'd found his cousin, George Rexford, installed as the current Lord Walbeck.

Rexford wondered what had happened to the boy he'd played with in his grandfather's home. Then he remembered lies about broken toys and nasty tricks played on younger children.

He should have expected an attack after Walbeck burned the copy of his royal warrant meant for Sir Arnold and cursed the new Earl of Beckingham from the house for taking the title his cousin saw as rightfully his. The three young thugs who struck him down and stole his horse were no doubt in Walbeck's service.

The stabbing pain in his side jerked him back to the present and he found himself gazing into a beautiful woman's beet red face. The angel taking off his shirt must be a virgin. A married woman would never blush so crimson while removing his clothing. Rexford leaned in and watched the color grow on her cheeks. She was a delight to watch, with her long-lashed brown eyes and shiny brown hair. Pink lips ripe for kissing. Breasts tantalizingly close when she carefully moved his arm.

Never had his physician been as beautiful and lively as this woman. He'd live, if only to have her take off his clothes when he was healed.

"I doubt it'll be stubbornness I'll die of, my sweet, but who knows. You may be right." He chuckled.

The man had bled badly, and Jane was amazed he could still chuckle. The shirt stuck to the wound in his side. Jane poured warmed water on it to loosen the fabric, and the man sucked in his breath as his eyes rolled back in his head.

Thank goodness he was unconscious. That would make sewing him up easier for both of them. She didn't have to worry as much about hurting him, and she could look at his nakedness without blushing. As if he were a farmhand. If he'd been awake, his knowing grin would make working on his firm, muscled body impossible. As it was, she was feeling very warm, and it wasn't from being near the fire.

The cuts had been sliced into his flesh by a sharp blade, so drawing the skin together was easy. Fortunately the injuries weren't too deep, but she was concerned about the stab wound that had slid off his rib cage toward his abdomen. He'd live. Hopefully.

Rubbing against the light hairs on his chest made her fingers want to spread out and touch his uninjured skin. His arm was well-muscled, and she had to struggle against her desire to study those muscles while she sewed the wound taut.

This was no gardener or kitchen lad. She'd never seen so much of a man before, and she'd never seen a figure that looked so much like a warrior. An angel. A prince.

She'd washed the blood from his face and found the injuries there were little more than bruising from a fist. His handsome features would soon go back to turning girls' heads. Including hers if she wasn't careful.

And she always had to be careful around Lord Walbeck.

Her patient awoke from the pain of a last splash of whiskey on the wounds as she began to bind them up. "Can you sit? It would make wrapping your wounds easier."

He winced, but he rose up enough to grab the whiskey bottle from her hand. Taking a long swig, he made it up to a seated position on the pallet.

Then she had a problem getting the linen cloth around his chest. Her arms weren't long enough to reach around him without getting very close. Too close to be proper.

As she quickly leaned in to reach around him the second time, she felt her breasts brush across his chest and then his breath whispered soft on her ear. "I don't bite. Usually."

She jumped back with a gasp, dropping the roll she'd made of the linen strip.

He grinned and handed her the fabric strip lying next to him. "You can come in as close as you like to bandage me. I appreciate your kindness. And so much more."

"Mauk," she called the kitchen boy, "sit behind the man and pass the bandaging back to me." Her cheeks were already hot enough, and her breathing was shaky. She didn't need his making her more flustered.

Mauk did as he was told, and Jane moved with practiced speed to get the man bandaged. She didn't have to worry about hurting him with this last step, and she needed to get away from this intimate contact with him. Lord Walbeck would beat her black and blue if he—

"So this is where you went." Lord Walbeck looked down at them, and Jane wasn't certain if he meant her or the injured man. "Get up, Jane."

"I'll be finished in just a—oh!" she cried as he grabbed her under her arms and jerked her to a standing position. She got her feet under her and stood upright.

"Milord," Sir Arnold said. "Please take care."

"Do you realize you harbor a traitor in your house?" Walbeck sounded pleased. "Are you aiding and abetting? Or are you joining in a conspiracy? The crown will come down hard on you, Sir Arnold, and you'll lose everything you hold dear. If he is John Rexford."

"Won't work, cousin," the injured man said. "I've been recognized by the crown. Rewarded for my service. Thanked by Parliament. And accepted as the new Beckingham. Do you really think any complaints you make to the government will stick? You're just not that important."

"Rexford? You mean you're that John Rexford, the missing heir to the Beckingham title? The one who..." Jane stopped as she realized all eyes were on her. Her knees felt weak, and she reached back to lean on a kitchen table as she absorbed the shock.

John Rexford. The boy her father had said might one day be her husband. The son of her father's childhood friend. The boy she would have met except her mother had died shortly before his intended visit.

It had been snowy that last, happy Christmas, as she had walked between her parents on their way to church. She remembered her mother's belly rounded with promise. Hope that died days later along with her mother and the baby.

Her father wrote letters, and then John Rexford and his father hadn't come. There had been no more visitors, no more traveling. And there'd been no more talk of marriage, to Rexford or anyone else.

John Rexford's voice, now the voice of a man, called her back to the present. A present where the money that had been her inheritance was long gone, a victim of Lord Walbeck's greed. "She may be the only person in these parts who doesn't immediately recognize me. And why should she? Did you think burning a few papers from the crown would destroy my claim, cousin? Not when everyone else knows who I am."

Rexford chuckled, but there was no mirth in his tone. "Even the Farley boys that you had attack me recognized me. They were quick to run when they realized how badly attacking an earl could go against them. They must be in the next county now. Not much help to you anymore. I believe most people will take my side and be glad I'm the new Earl of Beckingham instead of you."

"Not without your warrant from the crown." Lord Walbeck was keeping up his bluster, but Jane could see him backing slowly away from the group.

"I delivered a copy to the magistrate, Sir James Lovell, and another to His Grace, the Duke of Wallopbrook, before I came here. Even though you burned the copy meant for Sir Arnold as the magistrate here, it won't take much to get Lovell and Wallopbrook here to uphold my title. And my rights to my property."

Rexford's voice lost its humorous tone and took on a hard edge. "You thought you were clever, petitioning the crown to declare me dead the moment the heir to the title ahead of me died. But now that I've appeared, I've been confirmed as Beckingham."

"There was no reason to leave the earldom empty on the chance you might return."

"It's amazing how people who are keeping you from a title suddenly die. Did you kill your older brother? Did he meet with a hunting accident like the heir of Grandfather Beckingham's second son?" As Lord Walbeck reddened, the new earl continued. "I see I hit a nerve. He did die of a suspicious accident. Well, I'll be sure to be careful."

They appeared to Jane as two snarling wolves, and to get close to such a fight was dangerous for everyone. Were these cousins like this as children?

Walbeck sneered at the earl. "No one will come until after Twelfth Night. They don't care all that much about who the rightful earl is. And in the meantime, Rexford, with injuries such as yours, anything can happen."

As used as she was to Lord Walbeck, Jane shuddered when she saw the smile that crossed his face.

"Sir Arnold will give me his hospitality." The new Earl Beckingham sounded certain of his welcome.

Jane glanced at Sir Arnold as he swallowed and looked from one man to the other. Two powerful men that he needed to get along with, both as the local magistrate and as a solicitor. Finally, he said, "Of course my hospitality is open to you, my lord."

He'd made his choice and appeared to Jane's eyes to be resigned to whatever happened next. What evidence did her guardian hold concerning Sir Arnold's paperwork error?

"I'll expect you both at my Christmas feast tomorrow. Come along, Jane. We have much to do at home." Lord Walbeck walked toward the stairs, certain Jane would follow.

Jane had never seen Lord Walbeck back away from a fight before. And she knew all too well that he'd just as easily stab any man in the back as in the front. She wished she could stay here, too. She was afraid Lord Walbeck would take out his anger on her when they returned to the manor.

Beckingham and Sir Arnold had a silent conversation with their eyes. Then the earl said, "We'll see you at two tomorrow." To Jane, it looked like he used his last ounce of strength to make his voice carry.

Without turning around, Walbeck said, "I look forward to seeing you then. Come along, Jane."

Jane shot a worried look at Sir Arnold. When he said nothing, she turned and walked toward the stairs to the front hall.

Once upstairs, Sir Arnold lagging behind, Lord Walbeck said, "Outside, Jane. You have a long walk ahead of you."

"I'll loan her a mount from my stable," Sir Arnold said.

"Nonsense." Walbeck's tone was falsely hearty. "Jane

likes to walk. And I'll be right behind her to make sure she doesn't stray from the path."

There was that glee in his voice. He enjoyed giving pain or inflicting fear. He'd be on horseback right behind her. A scary thought on any day, since Jane knew he could run her down whenever he chose. With the snowfall, she might slip and get trod on without any effort on his part or even any intention. Today, facing the loss of his dream of becoming the Earl of Beckingham, he might well act on his threats.

Jane wrapped herself against the cold and walked out Sir Arnold's front door. "We'll see you tomorrow, sir?"

Sir Arnold gave her an encouraging smile and squeezed her hand. "We'll be there. Happy Christmas."

"And to you." She walked down the steps and away before Lord Walbeck could grab her arm. He still had to wait for his mount to be brought around.

She was in the village, talking to the vicar and his sister, when Lord Walbeck reached her. "Come along, Jane," he bellowed.

"I look forward to the service tomorrow," she said, giving the vicar a smile. She hoped she'd live that long. "Coming, milord."

"You're his ward, not a servant," the vicar's sister, Magda, said in a soft voice.

Jane made a rueful face at Magda. Then she moved toward Lord Walbeck without drawing close enough to be struck by his riding crop. As they moved down the street, she said, "Could we ask the vicar and his sister to Christmas dinner after the service?"

"Why?"

"A vicar is always a good ally to have." Jane gave her guardian a knowing smile.

"By gad, you're right. He's the perfect person. Invite them, and then come straight back to the house. There's much to do before tomorrow's dinner." The man sounded smug.

Lord Walbeck rode on, leaving Jane behind. She was no longer in front of his horse, her life in danger. She took a deep breath in relief and turned to rejoin her friends.

Then she thought of the injured man and shivered. What did Lord Walbeck have planned?

Chapter Two

JANE SLIPPED INTO THE MANOR, heart pounding in her chest. She was late. Lord Walbeck would be in the front hall, watching the clock with increasing impatience. Those scenes always led to fearful consequences.

Instead, she discovered Lord Walbeck had locked himself in his study with orders not to be disturbed.

He had said "we" had much work to do at home, but now that they were home, he was in hiding in his office, leaving everyone else to guess what he wanted and do all the work. If only he would disappear into his study and never come out. That would be a glorious Christmas gift.

After she took a deep breath of gratitude for Lord Walbeck's absence, she asked Harper, the butler, "Where is Lady Walbeck?"

"She went for a walk on the grounds."

How odd. Lady Walbeck was an invalid who seldom left her room. What could have driven her outdoors into the snow and cold? "Did she ask for me to accompany her when I returned?"

"No, Miss Jane."

Thank goodness. She was chilled enough as it was. But the lady never took walks unaccompanied. "Who went with her?"

"No one."

How very odd. The world seemed to have turned upside down today. "Do you need my help with anything?"

"You could organize the decorating with the greenery."

As she turned away to bring order to the staff, she said, "The vicar and his sister are coming to Christmas dinner."

"Does his lordship know?"

"Yes. He told me to ask them."

Harper wrinkled his brow. "What is he up to?"

"Sir Arnold and a man called John Rexford are coming to Christmas dinner also. We're to be a large gathering this year." She had never seen Lord Walbeck spend money on a holiday party, or anything, that didn't involve some benefit to himself.

"I could scarcely believe my eyes this morning when I saw Rexford here." Harper appeared overjoyed for a moment, but then looked crestfallen. "Then as soon as Mister Rexford left, he and milord spitting fire at each other in the front hall, his lordship sent for the Farleys."

"Rexford said he met up with the Farleys." She was very willing to share what she'd heard with Harper, but she lowered her voice. Safer to share it only with Harper. The two of them had been allies since she was thrown into Lord Walbeck's household as an unwilling prisoner by her father's death. The butler had made her welcome as her guardian and his wife had not.

"There was a fight, and they left Mr. Rexford

bleeding in the snow. According to him, when they recognized him they took off. With his horse." She shuddered. She'd learned to stay far away from the Farleys. They were the plague of the village and the surrounding countryside. Rude, belligerent, cruel, and vicious. Whenever Lord Walbeck felt someone needed to learn a lesson, he called in the Farleys.

Harper moved closer and murmured, "I was listening in earlier when his lordship received word that Rexford was returning. He wants him stopped at all costs. He needs him dead. And so do the Farleys if they don't want to be jailed."

"The John Rexford I heard about as a child was a younger son of a younger son of the Earl of Beckingham. I can't believe they've gone through all those heirs to get to him."

"They have, Miss Jane. John Rexford is the only surviving child of the old earl's fourth son. What's worse, if he dies, Lord Walbeck, as his cousin and oldest surviving son of the fifth son, inherits the title and all that goes with it."

She nodded. She'd heard rumors about her guardian possibly inheriting the earldom, although Lord Walbeck hadn't answered her questions when she'd asked him. "Where has this man been all these years that Lord Walbeck could put in his claim on the Beckingham title?"

"He joined His Majesty's Navy at the beginning of the war with Napoleon. I remember him riding off so young and proud. He was reportedly lost at sea soon after, but from what I heard listening outside the door to Lord Walbeck and the Farleys," Harper smiled slyly, "Rexford and part of his crew were captured by pirates. He led his men in fighting their way out of imprisonment and back home. The Crown was getting ready to declare him dead when he showed up."

"When Lord Walbeck and John Rexford were arguing at Sir Arnold's, Rexford said he gave copies of his royal warrant to the Duke of Wallopbrook and to Sir James Lovell." Jane glanced around, checking for prying ears. "That must definitely mean he's the new Earl of Beckingham. King and Parliament have confirmed it."

Harper paled. "Which means Lord Walbeck will not be a happy man. Which means we'd better get to work so everything is as milord wants it." He left for the kitchens while Jane went in the other direction to organize the greenery around the manor house.

There was enough pine to do the central staircase and the dining room, but that left the parlors looking decidedly forlorn. "We'll need more evergreen branches to decorate the parlors. Jem and Todd, you need to go out and collect more."

"Yes'm." The two spindly lads, neither more than fourteen years old, eagerly headed to the kitchen to bundle up.

"We need to get this done today. Tomorrow is Christmas, and we'll want to go to the village early for the service," she called after them. She kept her voice low so it wouldn't reach to Lord Walbeck's study.

With the help of two footmen and two maids, she made the front hall and the dining room festive with new cut greenery and ribbon reused from previous years. She sniffed. The spaces now smelled delightfully like the forest.

When she walked into the parlors, she found them stale and musty by comparison. Hopefully, the boys would get enough greenery to mask the unaired stench.

Laden down with evergreen bows and yew branches, the boys returned before Lord Walbeck left his study to discover the task hadn't been finished.

Lady Walbeck followed them in. "I think we've taken every branch with any green we can find in the woods," she said, handing off her cloak, hat, and gloves to Harper. Her cheeks were rosy from the cold and she sounded cheerful.

Cheerful? Jane wondered what had come over the woman. "We'll make it work," she said with more confidence than she felt as she looked at the small, woebegone branches.

Lady Walbeck and Jane's mother had been cousins, but Lady Walbeck was too frail or too disinterested to put up any kind of resistance to the onslaught that was Lord Walbeck's evil nature. Jane quickly decided Lord Walbeck had squeezed the joy and energy out of his wife.

"I know you will, my dear Jane." She pressed a cold hand against Jane's cheek.

"I hope you're not too tired from your walk."

"No," Lady Walbeck said with a pained sigh. "Seeing you always make me feel refreshed."

If she didn't sound so weary, Jane might have believed her words. Giving Lady Walbeck's hand a squeeze, she said, "The vicar and his sister are coming for Christmas dinner, as are Sir Arnold and—a man called Rexford, who I understand is the new Earl of

Beckingham."

"Well, we'll be a jolly party then. I think I'll rest before dinner." Lady Walbeck, looking more skeletal than ever, walked up the stairs with her head held high.

"Yes, milady." Lord Walbeck wanted Jane to act as Lady Walbeck's companion, keeping an eye on everything she did. Lady Walbeck resisted his efforts by ignoring them. Jane wished she could avoid him as well as Lady Walbeck managed.

Perhaps if the lady had been stronger, she could have stopped the worst of Lord Walbeck's sadistic behavior toward Jane. Lady Walbeck loved Jane, she always told her so, but she did nothing about Lord Walbeck's cruelty.

And Lord Walbeck, once he sank his teeth into a target, never let go. Jane could feel those fangs gripping her soul.

As soon as the decorations were finally finished, she rushed upstairs and dressed for dinner. She was in her petticoats when she heard her guardian go downstairs, and she frantically finished dressing. He'd say she was late and that would make for a long and painful dinner.

She reached the dining room to find Lord and Lady Walbeck just being seated.

"Jane," Lord Walbeck snapped, "you're late. You mustn't keep Lady Walbeck waiting."

His wife glanced his way with pursed lips.

"I'm sorry. I must have lost track of time. Have you seen the decorations for tomorrow?" Jane asked.

"Why? Are they any different than any other year?"

"No. I don't believe so," she told him.

"Then why would I look at them?"

"To see if they meet your expectations."

Lord Walbeck looked pointedly at his wife. "I have very low expectations."

Lady Walbeck held his gaze wordlessly.

The footmen, organized by Harper, began serving. Lord Walbeck heaped food on his plate as he said, "I have a surprise for you, Jane. While you were decorating the dining room, I had the vicar, Mr. Miller, in my study. He's asked for your hand in marriage and I've agreed."

"Marry the vicar?" Stunned, Jane automatically took a spoonful of every dish without looking at them. She was a wealthy baronet's daughter, and she was being forced to marry a penniless vicar. A nice man, to be sure, but her heart danced no jigs when he was present.

"I don't want Jane to move away," Lady Walbeck said. "You'll have to keep the vicar on in the pulpit of our church."

"Of course, my dear. I already provide him with his living and his house. Why not his wife as well?" Lord Walbeck smiled at Jane with a malicious glint in his eyes. "What do you say, Jane?"

As bile rose in her throat, Jane leaped up and dashed from the dining room.

This Christmas day, Jane awoke in the dark with a sense of foreboding. There was the new earl. There was the sumptuous feast. And there was her surprise impending marriage.

In short, Lord Walbeck was up to several somethings, and that made him even more dangerous than usual.

Jane lit a candle and went to the kitchen to make up the mulled wine before she'd get in the kitchen staff's way. She was surprised to see a candle already lit by the hob and shocked to see Lady Walbeck pouring a liquid from a pan into a small glass bottle.

"Is there anything I can do for you, milady?"

Lady Walbeck jerked and gasped before she looked at Jane. Then she stoppered the small glass bottle and slipped it in her pocket. She moved the pan to the scullery and added water from a pitcher.

"You startled me, Jane. Could you give the vicar my apologies? I'm going to stay home instead of attending church this morning," Lady Walbeck said. "I slept poorly. I needed a new batch of my pain draught and didn't want to bother Mrs. Ward. But now I'm going to take some and then go to bed so I can face our dinner guests."

No matter how poorly she felt, Lady Walbeck always went to church services. Concerned, Jane said, "Should we cancel the dinner?"

"Never! It's important that we show hospitality on this day of all days, and to the new earl most of all. Will you please take my place this morning? And tell the vicar I welcome him into the family."

"But—"

"You'll be able to stay in the village. We'll be able to visit any time. It's the best that can be hoped for, Jane." Lady Walbeck patted her shoulder.

No. She could hope for so much more. But this was not the time or place to show her independence. "If you're sure you'll be all right this morning?"

"I'm sure. I just need some rest." She looked around her as the sleepy-eyed kitchen maids entered to prepare the roasts and start the baking. "It must be the excitement of Christmas and the lack of my pain draught. I think I might sleep now." She turned away and stopped one of the maids. "Take this pan out into the yard and throw the contents on the ground. That's a good girl."

"Yes, milady." If the kitchen maid was surprised, she masked it well, curtsying and taking the pan in one motion.

"Sleep well, Lady Walbeck."

Jane made a huge batch of mulled wine and placed it in the hot cupboard out of the way of the kitchen staff. She would have plenty of time to make any last minute adjustments to the wine after the church service.

Christmas dawned cold and bright, sunlight reflecting off the snow. Jane shivered as she washed and dressed and then went down to breakfast. She found Lord Walbeck enjoying his toast and tea. She told him what his wife had said about not attending church.

"I'm sure she'll be fine for our dinner party," was his only comment.

Jane and Harper exchanged looks over the teapot. That, at least, was normal. Lord Walbeck never showed concern for his wife's health without a person of importance present.

Soon, all of the inhabitants of the house, except Lady Walbeck, were part of the procession winding its way to the village. They appeared like so many bundles of woolens wrapped against the cold.

Lord Walbeck took the lead on horseback as he

headed toward the church while the rest walked the distance into the village. Jane strolled alongside Harper at the back, making sure no strays decided to avoid the trip and slip back into bed. The walk through the sparkling white countryside cheered her, and she was soon humming Christmas carols.

The cook, Mrs. Ward, older and wider of girth and who seldom set foot outside the house, was soon huffing and puffing at the back of the procession with them. "Where's Her Ladyship? She always rides at the head with…" Mrs. Ward looked around quickly and saw too many ears to her liking, "Lord Walbeck."

"Not feeling well this morning," Jane replied.

"I've got too much to do for Christmas dinner to be marching in the snow, but I'd hate to miss the Christmas service." The cook shook her head. "Poor thing, Lady Walbeck, missing church. The cold must go right through her, thin as she is. Scarcely eats a bite. I fix her treats on the side to spur her appetite, but she just shakes her head. Where's the good in being rich, I ask, if you can't eat food prepared especially for you?"

"I know you do your best, Mrs. Ward," Harper said.

Jane, who thought everything prepared in the house was burned because Lord Walbeck liked it that way, said nothing.

"Have you fixed us any treats for today?" Harper asked.

"Roast meats and fish, puddings, and Jane's hot mulled wine. Just what His Lordship ordered."

"Plenty of sweets, I imagine," Jane said. "I know His Lordship likes his sweets, and it is Christmas."

"Too bad it doesn't sweeten him up," Harper muttered under his breath.

"What's that?" Mrs. Ward asked.

"How are those nephews of yours, the Farley boys?" Jane asked.

As a distraction, this always worked. And this time, Jane really was interested, having seen their handiwork the day before.

"They're such sweet lads. Always doing little services for His Lordship without a word of complaint. Not like some I could mention."

Oh, but I suspect you do mention, raced through Jane's mind. "Have they had the pleasure of serving His Lordship recently?"

"Aye, but you know more about that than me, seeing as how you saved that wicked imposter. And now he'll be eating at His Lordship's table today. I hope he chokes on my roast."

"An imposter?" Harper asked, aghast.

Jane frowned, wondering how Mrs. Ward learned so much about yesterday's events without leaving her kitchen.

"Everyone knows the real John Rexford drowned off the coast of North Africa along with the rest of the crew of his ship," Mrs. Ward told them.

"Apparently not." Harper used his commanding butler voice. "I checked at the tavern—"

"Always a good place to hear the truth," Mrs. Ward scoffed.

"And word has come in by travelers that many of the crew have now returned to England, having been taken hostage by pirates. Although some died in captivity, Lieutenant Rexford of the Royal Navy, now the Earl of Beckingham, found a way in the end for the remaining men to escape. Then they made their way through Italy and the German states. Once the war with Napoleon was over, they were able to cross the channel from the Netherlands to return home. And the men of his crew have all been praising Lieutenant Rexford for saving their lives." Harper finished the story with admiration in his voice.

"My nephews have seen him, and say he's nothing like the John Rexford who joined the navy. Bigger. More muscled. Harder. Bitter as gall. Sneering. And he fights dirty," Mrs. Ward complained.

The Farley's were well acquainted with sneaky combat. Jane decided if Harper's tale from the tavern was true, it explained the changes in the man. Instead of his aristocratic life in England, he'd been held prisoner and had to free himself and his men. She'd liked the man she'd met, found him honest and easy going. Although his body had made her—curious. And over-warm.

They reached the church in time for Jane to enter Lord Walbeck's pew before the processional began. A quick glance over the congregation told her Sir Arnold was in attendance, but John Rexford, the Earl of Beckingham, was absent.

Jane sang the hymns. She stared at the stained glass windows during the long sermon that wandered more than the Three Wise Men. She tried to keep her mind on the prayers. And all the time, she wondered how the vicar felt about their pending nuptials. He'd never given her a hint of any romantic interest in her.

Energy and malice and excitement seemed to shimmer from Lord Walbeck and his hooded eyes as he looked toward the pulpit. He had something planned. Something evil and nasty. And that never boded well for Jane or anyone.

After the service, the servants, knowing they had many chores awaiting them at the house before Lord Walbeck could sit down to his Christmas dinner, hurried away. Jane watched as Lord Walbeck slapped Sir Arnold on the back too hard in the pretense of being jovial. Then he rode off as if he'd forgotten her.

The vicar was busy shaking hands, so Jane sought out Magda. "I didn't know your brother held any affection for me."

Magda gripped her arm. "Only the brotherly kind. Lord Walbeck has ordered him to marry you. The first of the banns will be read on Sunday. He has to do it to keep his living here in the village church. Otherwise, we'll both be out in the snow without a penny to our names."

"So this wasn't his idea?"

Magda looked incredulous. "Goodness, no. He was summoned to the manor house yesterday and told to wed you. Think of something, Jane. This will be a disaster for both of you."

It would. Friendship born of casual conversation would never turn into a happy union. The vicar's mind wandered as much as his sermons. She preferred a practical, active life to the contemplative life the vicar sought. Now she'd have to find a practical solution that would protect Magda and the vicar as well as herself.

"I'll try." Jane walked off, struggling with the idea of this unwanted marriage when she bumped into Sir Arnold. The first thing she could think of was, "Is the patient all right?"

"He's on the mend, but I couldn't see him taxing his strength coming to the service when he has to meet with His Lordship for dinner." Sir Arnold always made "His Lordship" sound ironic. "What's he up to, Miss Merrywether?"

"Lord Walbeck? I wish I knew. Other than forcing Vicar Miller to marry me," slipped out in a bitter grumble.

"Vicar Miller? Why—?" Sir Arnold frowned. "Come back to the house with me and we'll discuss this."

That meant seeing the earl again and being reminded of his fit, firm, adult male body. So unlike the scholarly vicar. Despite the heat on her cheeks, Jane nodded and walked back with Sir Arnold.

"Come check on the earl's wounds while we talk. I don't expect Lord Walbeck will allow you much time before he comes looking for you again," the magistrate said.

The patient lay under thick covers and propped up on fluffy pillows in a fine upstairs bedroom. When Jane walked in, with Sir Arnold following as chaperone, the earl sat up, his broad naked shoulders appearing as the covers slid down.

"Your Lordship, er..." Embarrassment strangled her voice.

"Rexford, please. I grew used to it on board, and afterwards..." He gave her an encouraging smile, knowing she wouldn't understand how a title conveyed so much about a person's status, and nothing at all about the person. He'd left England still a lad and a little jealous of Walbeck. His cousin, then plain George Rexford, who was a couple years older, was more mature, charming when he wanted to be, and less of a gangling youth. Or appeared that way to the child John was.

Looking back, he'd been neither shocked nor surprised when he returned as an adult to learn how the current Lord Walbeck misused his position and mistreated those around him.

The beautiful young woman sounded like his old nanny when she said, "All right. Rexford. I need to look at your wounds and redress them."

"Do you now?" He nearly laughed with joy. Here was a woman who wasn't trying to trap an unattached earl like the girls of the ton nor was she overly deferential in her attitude. Even if she made his wounds burn, he enjoyed her calm, cheerful presence.

"Yes." She sounded quite firm.

"Where are your supplies?"

"Where... Oh. The servants will get them now." Rexford saw the begging look she gave Sir Arnold. Her momentary confusion showed she fancied her patient as much as he did her.

Fortunately for them both, Sir Arnold had anticipated her need. The kitchen boy came in carrying a tray of bandages and ointments.

"Mauk, you will stay and assist," Jane told the boy, completely ignoring Rexford.

The new earl wished she'd pay more attention to

him while the lad nodded his head, wide-eyed.

"Can you sit on the side of the bed?" Jane asked as she finally faced him, glancing into his eyes.

Rexford stared back, noticing her eyes were light brown with flecks of gold. Men would write sonnets to women with eyes like that. Men who hadn't lived by killing those who stood in their way of returning home. But still, he'd do whatever she asked. He moved cautiously to avoid pain, but there didn't seem to be any hope for it. His wounds nearly made him cry out.

She unwrapped his arm wound first, quickly dosed it with whiskey, and began rewrapping the wound. "I'm afraid it will leave a scar."

"To remind me of my lovely nurse," slipped out before he realized he'd spoken the words aloud.

She turned bright red and stared at his arm as she finished the bandaging. "You make fun of my poor healing skills, sir."

"No. I've been too long in the company of jailers and prisoners, warriors and thieves, to speak properly to a young lady. Forgive me. Tell me how you came to be the village nurse."

"Caring for the afflicted should be Lady Walbeck's job, but her poor health left me with the task almost since I came here. Before that, I nursed my father through his final illness."

He watched her with complete trust, something that he'd found hard to come by for the last several years. There was a quality in her that inspired him to allow himself to be completely honest in her presence.

"When did Lord Walbeck tell you your marriage to

the vicar had been arranged?" Sir Arnold said, breaking into Rexford's thoughts.

He nearly came off the bed with a shout. She was magnificent. Too good to waste on a vicar. What was that pig George up to?

Jane sucked in a breath and swallowed before she said, "I found out at dinner last night. Apparently the vicar was informed shortly after Lord Walbeck and I were here yesterday."

"This isn't your idea?" Rexford asked her.

She glanced up and into his eyes. He could see pain leaking out with her tears. "No. Nor the vicar's. He's an acquaintance. That's all."

Rexford realized his arrival must have sparked George's plans. The whole family had known of his father's hope that his son would wed his friend's daughter. "I remember your father saying that, even as a child, you were one of the most capable females he knew. My father said there was no higher praise for a woman or a wife. But when Sir Arnold told me who your father was, he also said you'd not yet wed. Are all the men here stupid, or is this Lord Walbeck's doing?"

Jane's gaze flew to his eyes nearly as fast as her blush deepened. "Lord Walbeck is my guardian, and so far he hasn't deemed any suitor suitable. Or didn't until yesterday, when he found my betrothal somehow useful." She studied his face in silence. "You knew my father?"

"I'd met him. He and my father were friends. They were both good men. I'm sorry they're gone." If they were both still here, George wouldn't be working his evil. He hid his fisted hands in the covers.

She nodded, looking small and sad. Then she drew herself up. "I must do your side now, and I'm afraid it will hurt."

"I've had worse pain."

Again she had to pour warm water on his side to loosen the bandages. When she finally detached the last of the linen from his skin, she said, "There's no sign of infection, and the stitches have held. I'll just put more whiskey on the wound and then bandage you. It won't be anything like what you had to go through yesterday."

When she started, pain shot through him and spots filled his vision. He heard, "Milord! Hold on. Not much more. I'm almost ready to wrap you up again."

He clamped his jaws shut and drew in a sharp breath, fisting his fingers around the sheets. "Just do what you need to do."

Her voice sounded far away when she said, "Do you want to take hold of my arm while I pour more whiskey on your side?"

"Wait." Rexford took the bottle from her grasp, took a couple of gulps, and handed it back as the fire roared down his throat. "Do your worst."

He didn't think she'd take him literally. Fortunately, she moved quickly. He scrunched up his face and shook his head, but he held the scream inside that wanted to slip out.

"Just a little healing ointment, and then we'll wrap you." Jane finished in a hurry, Mauk helping with a serious look on his young face. Only then did she consider touching the patient's warm flesh, feathered with light colored hair, and the heat returned to her cheeks.

"What's this?" Rexford asked, running a finger down the side of her face where her skin burned.

She hopped away from the bed as his touch seared her cheek. "Can you stand? The bed linens need to be changed. They smell like a tavern." Handing Mauk the supplies, she said, "Take those downstairs and send someone up with fresh linens."

"An expensive tavern." He muttered as he rose carefully, leaning on the side of the bed and one of the four posts that held the canopy.

She put an arm around him, avoiding his injuries, and helped him to a chair. Her heart raced as she realized how intimately close she stood to this Apollo. Then she turned to Sir Arnold. "The patient will live and can travel at a gentle pace to my guardian's without reinjuring himself."

She turned back to Rexford. The lump in her throat from her memories didn't let words reach her mouth for a moment. Taking a deep breath she said, "I hadn't heard your name mentioned after my father's death until yesterday. Since then, I've heard about your escape to get home. That takes a kind of bravery and self-sufficiency I can't imagine in either a woman or a man. I'm glad I've finally met you."

He shook his head and brushed the air with one hand, as if dismissing her praise. "Sir Arnold told me you've been the ward of Lord Walbeck for seven years. I think that takes more bravery than I possess."

"Not bravery, my lord. Stubborn determination."

He smiled at her. "I admire determination."

She smiled in return. "I admire bravery." She walked to the door but then stopped. "Keep in mind the cook for this feast is a relative of the Farleys. The men who attacked you on Lord Walbeck's orders."

"Perhaps it would be wiser to stay here. Claim I'm too ill to travel."

"Don't be such a feeble ninny," Jane said, using a smile to take away the sting. "Your presence is needed if we're to figure out what Lord Walbeck has planned. Just be sure to eat from the same dishes as the rest of us and don't wander off alone. We'll keep you safe."

Chapter Three

JANE RETURNED TO THE MANOR HOUSE to find everyone frantically working. Stopping Harper as he rushed past, she asked, "What can I do to help?"

"Milord wants you to make sure the mulled wine is indeed warm and well sweetened. And he said he wants to drink only from his ruby goblet today. The Earl of Beckingham will be served in the emerald cup. He says it will be festive and do the new earl honor, but when did he ever want to do anyone honor?"

"That's a strange arrangement. What does he have planned?" she asked him.

"I have no idea, but whatever it is, I suspect we should stop it," Harper replied.

"If we can."

"Miss Jane, I heard. I'm sorry—"

At that moment, Lord and Lady Walbeck came into the dining room. Everyone quit doing whatever their task was and bobbed a curtsy or a bow to their master and mistress.

"Go on with your work." Lord Walbeck watched them over his wife's shoulder and said, "Do the decorations and the table settings meet with your liking, my sweet?"

"Yes." She raised her eyebrows slightly, faced away from her husband so he couldn't see her surprise.

Harper and Jane exchanged glances. Lord Walbeck never paid attention to his wife.

"Good. Jane," he called in blustery good humor, "heat up the mulled wine. Our guests will be here soon. That's a good girl."

"See what you think of this." Jane gave him a taste of the first serving brought up from the kitchen to see if it met Lady Walbeck's approval. Now that Lord Walbeck drank it, she wished it were poisoned.

He declared it sweet enough and walked off laughing. She scowled as she looked at the parlor maid.

The maid whispered, "I've never heard him laugh before. Have you?"

"Yes," Jane said, shuddering at the image burned in her brain. "What happened next wasn't nice." A vision of the day her father died and Lord Walbeck's immediate invasion, taking everything as spoils, came into her mind. Servants sacked. Jane removed from her home.

The maid looked at her oddly but didn't ask any more questions. She must have heard about the wedding. Jane wondered if she could leave here and never see Lord Walbeck again. There must be a corner of the earl's estate where she could live. Maybe he owned land in a colony far from England. She'd go anywhere to escape this marriage.

The thought made her sad. In the time she'd lived in Lord Walbeck's manor, she'd learned to love the land, the villagers, the staff at his home.

She'd become close friends with the intrepid Magda. If her brother were more like her and less cowering and impractical, she might be willing to go through with the wedding and give up her social standing and inheritance in exchange for leaving Lord Walbeck's grasp. Except, married to the cowardly vicar, she'd never truly escape her guardian.

And if she escaped, Lord Walbeck would punish the vicar.

She went down to the kitchen to check the temperature of the heated wine. Just as she finished her task, one of the maids came in. "The guests are arriving. You're to come to the parlor."

"Arriving already? Oh, dear. Have someone take up the hot wine to take the chill off their journeys." Lady Walbeck would already be greeting the guests and didn't need her help. Jane ran up the back stairs to her room, tidied her hair, and glanced out her bedroom window overlooking the back of the house.

Movement against the snow caught her attention. She pressed her face against the icy windowpane and watched as Lord Walbeck stood with the Farley boys in a huddle, gesturing with his hands. What was he up to? She knew a conspiracy when she saw one.

Whatever had passed between the new earl and the Farleys, it hadn't kept them away long. Lord Walbeck was probably telling them to kill John Rexford next time.

And that couldn't be allowed.

She went down to the parlor to find most of the guests walking around wishing each other "Happy Christmas" or warming their hands by the fire. The footman arrived with pitchers of hot, mulled wine moments after she entered the room.

"Pour the wine, Jane. Let's celebrate Christmas," Lord Walbeck said, entering from another doorway.

Jane poured the first glass into the emerald cup and turned to walk it over to where the new earl stood.

Lady Walbeck took it from her and said, "Thank you, Jane." Then she carried it to the Earl of Beckingham and said, "I hope my lord finds this and all today to your liking."

The earl took the goblet, held it up to all those assembled, and said, "Thank you." He took a sip and said, "This is delicious. Who made it?"

"An old family recipe, my lord," Lord Walbeck said over Jane saying, "I did." And her father's family was the one with the recipe.

Rexford said, "Well done, Miss Merrywether," as he looked at Jane with a smile.

Jane returned the smile until a small noise made her glance toward the furious face of her guardian. She quickly filled the ruby goblet and took it to him, her hands trembling. "My lord, I can't marry the vicar. I beg you. In the spirit of Christmas, release me."

He kept his voice as quiet as hers. "Of course you can marry the vicar. Otherwise your friend will be dismissed and he and his sister thrown into the snow tomorrow. I'll ruin his reputation." His smile was cruel. "Can you live with yourself if you do that, Jane?"

She walked away shaking with anger and fear.

Once the guests began to stroll around the parlors, frequently choosing the one Lord Walbeck wasn't in, Jane walked over to greet her patient. "How are you feeling after your ride here, milord?"

"I don't think I opened any stitches, so I won't embarrass you by making you see my nakedness again too soon," he said in a low voice and then smiled at her.

Heat shot up Jane's face.

"Is that blush because you find me handsome, or because you find me repugnant?" He was still smiling.

Jane wasn't sure what she thought about this man. She found him fascinating, worrisome, and tantalizing. "I find you—dangerous."

"Jane, we're out of mulled wine. Bring some more, girl," Lord Walbeck called out.

She looked up to see Lord Walbeck glaring in her direction. Or perhaps he glowered at the earl. Jane had already made up several huge pots, leaving them covered and warming in the iron cupboard that ran up one side of the fireplace. Lord Walbeck could have quietly asked a footman to bring up another pitcher. She did as she was ordered, her mind still worrying the problem of how she could escape the manor without bringing trouble to her friends.

Jane nodded to a footman. When he returned with a brimming pitcher, she met him in the pantry with the special cups decorated with rubies and emeralds on an ornate silver tray.

She'd just filled them when Lady Walbeck swept up behind her and took the tray. "That must be heavy, milady. I'll carry it for you. Just let me finish this." Jane turned away to wipe the outside of the pitcher.

"No, I'm fine."

When Jane turned back, it was to see Lady Walbeck slip the glass bottle she had filled earlier into a pocket of her gown. "What is that, milady?"

"What is what?"

"In the bottle."

"My pain draught. You saw me make it this morning so I can get through this Christmas dinner without collapsing. Come along, Jane." With a determined expression, Lady Walbeck picked up the tray from the table and disappeared into the hall.

Not waiting for a footman, Jane grabbed the pitcher and followed Lady Walbeck into the parlor. Lord Walbeck was drinking from his cup and Rexford was just receiving his. Handing the pitcher to a surprised footman, Jane picked up the only vessel at hand, a glass cup for an ordinary guest, and walked across the room to Rexford.

"Milord, don't you find this a pretty thing?" she asked, bending down to show him close up. "Your wine may be poisoned," she whispered.

"Aye, it is a pretty thing. The etching is a remarkable design." He set down his goblet and took the cup from her hand. What little color had been in the wounded man's face drained away. "Is it part of a set?"

"It was. Unfortunately, the rest were lost or broken."

"Yet the others I see here look very similar."

"Similar, milord, but they lack the etching of the dove, my family's crest."

He raised his eyebrows and lowered his voice so that the other conversations hid their talk. "The Merrywether crest."

"Yes."

"You've had quite an education for a lady. Are you as accomplished at sewing samplers as you are with wounds?" He sounded impressed.

"The proof will be your good self."

He smiled. "Well, let's not put my good health to any more tests."

Jane curtsied and walked away, leaving him with the glass cup. Then she took the pitcher around and refilled cups, including the glass one that Rexford now held. Taking the empty pitcher, she went downstairs to recheck the temperature of the pots of mulled wine.

When she returned, Lord Walbeck called her for still another cupful of mulled wine. He was joking with the guests, generally at their expense, and laughing uproariously.

If the wine was putting Lord Walbeck in a good mood, it was putting the others in the room on edge. More than one guest walked off, red faced, with Lord Walbeck laughing at their backs. One woman seemed close to throwing her wine in his face until another's hand reached out to stop her. That only made his lordship laugh harder.

Finally, Lady Walbeck signaled that it was time to go in to Christmas dinner. Jane was paired off with the vicar, Mr. Miller, in the march into the dining room.

Everything smelled heavenly. The fragrance of greenery mixed with the aromas of wine, spices, beef, and goose filled the air. The very long table sparkled with china and silver bought by Lord Walbeck with her money. Jane found herself at the middle between the vicar and a man with a good sized farm. She shot a glimpse past what felt like half the village to see Rexford seated between Lady Walbeck and the wife of a solicitor.

Too bad the Walbecks hid her true status. If they proclaimed her Miss Jane Merrywether, daughter of a baronet and a wealthy heiress before Lord Walbeck took control of her money, then she would be seated next to the fascinating earl. Instead, she was sitting between two nice men who held dull but responsible positions in a village. Lord Walbeck's village. He wanted to keep her in her place.

And that had to be the reason for the marriage to the vicar.

Jane kept an eye on the food and drink going around the table and saw no method by which Rexford could be poisoned. Everything was served from communal platters and pitchers. There was no way anyone could poison anyone without sickening others at the same time.

Since the Farleys weren't in the dining room, Rexford was safe from a direct attack during dinner.

"I see you mixed yew with the pine in your decorations in here," the vicar said during the first course. "My mother used yew and holly to decorate for Christmas, never pine. She called pine a lowly plant."

"I thought we only used yew in the parlors. We'd finished decorating in here before we ran out of pine branches and sent the boys out for more." Jane glanced around the room. There was yew in the greenery over the fireplace. It hadn't been there yesterday, had it?

"How unfortunate that you're reduced to using pine." Then the vicar discussed his sermon at almost as much length as the sermon itself.

Was he worried it would be his last in this village?

When Jane spoke to the farmer, he discussed raising crops and animal husbandry and ignored any mention of Christmas, decorations, or national news. She tried to be attentive and put the man at ease. Too late, she remembered the farmer was looking for a replacement wife, his first having been worked to death.

Jane hoped he didn't think she was a candidate.

For this house, it was a merry Christmas feast. The food was rich, and the wine flowed freely. A much more generous table than Lord Walbeck normally set. Jane shot a look at Harper, standing across the table from where she sat and then glanced at all the dishes and pitchers.

He raised his eyebrows in reply.

She was already hot from all the bodies pressed around the table and feeling slightly sick from the unaccustomedly rich food. Setting her fork down, she tried to carry on a conversation with the farmer, but he was busy analyzing their dinner. He was annoyed she didn't know the amount of every ingredient used in every dish.

Jane decided he would be happier eating in the kitchen with Mrs. Ward. They would have more in common.

The vicar whispered to her, "Thank you for going along with Lord Walbeck's orders. The bishop doesn't like me. I'd never get another post, and Magda and I would starve. What else can I do?"

"I don't think I can go through with this."

He grabbed her hand, and she tried to tug it away without success. "Please. You must. I beg of you."

She was aware people were staring at them. "Of course. All will be well."

He let go of her hand, but she could still feel the squeeze in her heart.

Plates were exchanged for clean ones as the next course was brought in. Jane knew the kitchen maids would be frantically scouring these to reuse them for the final course. She'd put little on her plate from the previous courses and with this course, she took practically nothing.

"Jane, you'll waste away to skin and bones," Lord Walbeck called down the table. "Like my wife."

Lady Walbeck shot him a cold stare.

He ignored her. "You need to eat more."

Usually, he told Jane not to be such a glutton. "I'm fine, my lord. I hope you're enjoying this dinner."

"Good food. Good wine. Surrounded by good friends. This is the best of Christmas," he boomed back at her halfway across the room.

"Surely, the birth of our Lord and Savior is the best of Christmas," the vicar said, his voice as meek as Jane always found it when he was forced to disagree with Lord Walbeck.

"I hire you to worry about such things, vicar, not to visit them on me." Lord Walbeck said and laughed uproariously at his own words. "Leave such talk away from those of us who provide your living."

Uncomfortable with his attitude, Jane turned to the vicar and made the first pleasantry that came to her mind. "We've been lucky in our weather this Christmas. Not enough snow and ice to keep people from attending church. You had quite a few in attendance this morning." She suspected she'd said something similar already, but she felt the need to say something reassuring to the vicar.

His sister Magda, across the table from them, glared at Lord Walbeck as if her stare could fire knives at him.

Finally, the meal closed with the puddings and claret. Lord Walbeck looked pleased when Harper presented him with his own small sweet pudding with raisins, brandy, spices, and nuts. Jane had seen Mrs. Ward begin the puddings before Advent, adding more honey and sugar to the small pudding than the recipe called for in the large one.

Jane couldn't imagine how anyone could eat anything that sweet.

Lord Walbeck tasted it and said, "The perfect end to a perfect Christmas. Thank you one and all."

He ate greedily, as usual.

Jane put a spoonful of the larger nut and honey pudding on her plate. Rexford did the same after several others had taken a helping from the larger pudding circulated for the guests. Good. He'd taken her advice to heart.

She found the Christmas pudding smelled better than it tasted, filling her nose with cinnamon while the taste reeked of brandy and overcooked raisins.

Finally, the meal was over. Lord Walbeck had eaten most of his individual pudding. The tablecloth was dirty and everyone was saying they couldn't eat another bite when Lord Walbeck called out, "Magda, pour me another cup of mulled wine. We'll call your service a Christmas gift in exchange for your brother's position as our vicar."

Jane knew how Magda hated the groveling that came with being the dependent sister of the equally dependent vicar of Lord Walbeck's church. Magda gave him a tight-lipped smile with bitterness in her eyes. "This pitcher seems to be empty. Let me refill your cup."

Magda hurried from the room and returned with Lord Walbeck's filled cup just as he led the way into the parlor.

Some of the guests, mostly farmers and their wives, took this chance to leave. Lord Walbeck said, "For those of you who aren't going to enjoy my table and then run away, come into the parlor for entertainment. If you're running away, do so now, but know I will remember." His smile was vicious.

The farmers, who Jane knew had chores to do even on this holy day, gave each other knowing looks and conducted much back slapping with Lord Walbeck before hurrying away.

The first guest implored on to give entertainment was the vicar. He tried to give a dramatic recitation of a poem despite Lord Walbeck issuing orders through part of it. Jane used the noise as cover to crouch next to where Rexford sat and asked, "How are you doing, my lord?"

"Overfed, but not poisoned, I don't think. Thank you for the warning. Where does the threat come from?"

Before she could answer, Lord Walbeck said, "Jane! Come sing a song for us. Now! Come on, girl. Don't keep us waiting."

Glancing at Rexford, she plastered a smile on her face and rose to stand by the pianoforte. "Perhaps you'll join me in singing 'I Saw Three Ships?'"

They were on the second verse when Jane saw Lord Walbeck rise a little unsteadily and hurry out of the room. With a small sigh of gratitude, she continued leading the guests in carols.

Lady Walbeck, she noticed, was enjoying the Christmas songs, and a spirit of Christmas joy, which had been lacking before, began to fill the room. Magda joined Jane at the front, and the pair led the group in a rollicking round song that brought the servants up from the basement to join in. This led to a few of the cleaner tavern ballads sung with enthusiasm.

Finally, the Earl of Beckingham stood and said, "I appreciate the warm welcome you have given me on my first Christmas back in this country after many years. I wish you all the happiest of Christmases. Now, if Lord Walbeck will rejoin us, I can give my host my thanks and make my way back to Sir Arnold's."

Everyone looked around a little apprehensively as if expecting Lord Walbeck to burst into the room and rake them all with his sharp tongue and bruising cane.

Nothing happened.

"Jane, go find Lord Walbeck," Lady Walbeck said.

Jane glanced at Harper, who nodded, and the two of them left the room. The servants slipped away downstairs to their tasks.

Lord Walbeck wasn't passed out in his bed. He wasn't found on any bed, couch, or rug. "This is odd, Miss Jane. Perhaps we should check the barns?"

"It's a bit cold for that, but why not? He must be somewhere."

They put on cloaks and walked to the stables under

clear skies and through the biting air, where the stable boys assured them they hadn't seen their master. One of the lads slipped next to Jane and said, "Tell the new earl to check under his saddle for burrs before he leaves."

"The Farleys have been here?"

The boy nodded wide-eyed.

The cowshed, pigpen, and chicken coop were empty of human habitation.

As they began their trek back to the house, Jane glanced toward the privy. The door was slightly ajar, and something seemed to be spilling out from the inside.

She sucked in her breath and, in response to Harper's questioning look, pointed.

He strode over, Jane on his heels. The stench as they drew close was overpowering. Jane saw Harper swallow before he grabbed the door of the privy and swung it open.

Lord Walbeck pitched slowly forward, landing on his face. Blood and vomit from his mouth stained the snow crimson. His pantaloons were around his unmoving ankles.

Jane gasped and jumped back along with Harper. She could only stare in horror at the gruesome sight.

Lord Walbeck had bullied his last victim.

Chapter Four

JANE HEARD A SCREAM and realized the sound had escaped from her throat. She didn't think it had been loud, but several servants came running, looking about in confusion and alarm.

Harper stood with his back to the corpse in an attempt to block their view. "Get Sir Arnold and the doctor. And go back into the house. You have no need to stand about here gawking." Then he turned to Jane. "Are you all right?"

She took a few deep breaths to slow her racing heart while facing away from the privy to cut down on the smell. She'd feared Lord Walbeck was going to poison Rexford, and instead, Lord Walbeck died. "Are you sure he's dead?" came through chattering teeth.

"Very sure."

Freedom! And then a sense of shame filled Jane's mind. She shouldn't rejoice at another's demise. What kind of a person did that make her? Meanwhile, a little voice inside her kept whispering, "Now you're free."

To silence the thoughts singing hallelujahs in her head, Jane forced herself to focus on practical matters. "Sir Arnold? Then you think there is something—wrong about Lord Walbeck's death?"

Harper looked at her, eyebrows raised. "A healthy but hated man suddenly dies in the presence of his enemies."

"Tell me you had no hand in it. I want to know I can trust you." She was begging, but Harper's innocence was vital to her.

"No, I didn't, Miss Jane. I have an opportunity to kill him every day. I would never do so and imperil my immortal soul."

"Are you going to ask me?"

"No. You're too kind a person to kill. And if this was murder, the person who did it was sneaky enough to catch him out here unawares."

Jane nodded. This death was certainly suspicious. "Then someone will have to ask Sir Arnold to act in his role as magistrate. And tell Lady Walbeck. I suppose I'd better do that. I'll make sure Sir Arnold is on his way out to you."

As it turned out, she didn't have to, because Sir Arnold, accompanied by the Earl of Beckingham and Doctor Fielding, was striding toward her across the snowy lawn before she reached the house. Sir Arnold and the physician nodded to her and kept going. Rexford stopped and said, "Miss Merrywether, are you all right?"

"Yes. I must see to Lady Walbeck. And Sir Arnold must act in his position as magistrate."

"He can't. If Lord Walbeck's was not a natural death, Sir Arnold could be the killer. And I can't do more than see that evidence is preserved for Sir James Lovell as he is the nearest magistrate not in attendance at this dinner." Rexford gave a weak smile. "Lucky man."

Jane looked into his eyes and saw he remembered the same conversation she'd heard the day before concerning disturbing the magistrate's Christmas dinner. Then it had been over the truth of whether he was John Rexford. She patted his arm. "I'm sorry your welcome here has been so terrible."

He gave her hand a friendly squeeze. "Thank you. Walbeck hadn't wanted to see Sir James Lovell in his role of magistrate before Twelfth Night. I suppose he has no choice now. Poor Cousin George."

Lord Walbeck had ordered him attacked, and still Rexford had sympathy over the man's murder. He was kinder than most would be in that position. Jane gripped his hand to acknowledge his compassion. "Lord Walbeck wouldn't want anyone to see him like this. It's not— pretty." She wished she could get what she'd viewed of the befouled, toppled-over figure out of her mind.

"He was strangled?" Rexford asked.

"No. He was violently sick. Perhaps his heart gave out after eating such a big meal. Or, heaven forbid, it might have been poison."

Jane turned to leave, but Rexford grabbed her arm in an imperious gesture that must have been learned in the nursery. "Why did you warn *me* about poison?"

"I saw Lady Walbeck with a small glass bottle. It was a concoction she'd made in the middle of last night. It seemed so unlike her, I was afraid Lord Walbeck had her making something to slip into your food or drink. Since Lord Walbeck didn't want you to claim the title..." She left the rest of the thought unsaid.

"We'd better get that bottle away from her. We can't have anyone else stricken." He made a move to head back to the house.

She grabbed his sleeve. "We don't need to take the bottle. I was wrong. Apparently, she made a batch of her pain medicine. She assures me there is no danger there."

Rexford made a face as if tasting something foul. "The magistrate will have his work cut out for him. I doubt I'm very popular in this area. Showing up at the last moment, taking away the Beckingham title after Walbeck and everyone else thought he'd inherited it."

Jane grinned. "You're very popular compared to Lord Walbeck."

"Why?"

How could she answer that one simple question? "He was a bully, and a cheat, and a liar, and a thief. There are probably a great many of us who aren't sorry to see him gone."

"So he hadn't changed. Am I popular with you, Miss Merrywether?" His gaze focused on her eyes as if her opinion was the only thing that mattered.

Jane held his gaze and spoke with certainty. "Yes, you are. Now if you'll excuse me, milord, I need to see to Lady Walbeck."

He let go of her, gave her a small bow, and walked away to view the remains of Lord Walbeck. Jane watched him for a moment, wishing she had his command and certainty, before dashing in to see to her mistress.

People were standing about the parlor and the front hall and whispering, unwilling to leave until they heard why Sir Arnold, Doctor Fielding, and the earl had been called out of doors after Jane and Harper had left to find Lord Walbeck. They tried to stop Jane when she came in, throwing questions at her, but she kept silent as she headed for Lady Walbeck. The lady sat in the parlor, wringing her hands and answering every query with short, vague words.

Jane knelt down by her. "My lady, I have grievous news." Well, it would be for Lady Walbeck, she thought.

"My husband?"

"Is dead, milady."

Jane heard gasps around her, but Lady Walbeck made not a sound.

"Milady, what can I do for you?" Jane asked in a voice barely above a whisper.

"See to the guests, Jane. I need to lie down." Lady Walbeck rose on shaky legs and made her way across the room. She acknowledged no one as a path opened for her between the guests. Everyone stared as she walked to the stairs and then climbed with painfully slow steps.

Jane moved to the front door and thanked everyone for their condolences, assured them they'd be called if needed, and wished them a happy Christmas. This last seemed odd to her, but she said it anyway.

Magda whispered to her "You're both safe now. No wedding." The vicar clutched her hand with a wistful look as he gave an impersonal vicarly goodbye.

Once everyone was gone and the servants were cleaning up, Jane went upstairs to find Lady Walbeck lying on her bed, still fully dressed. "Milady, would you be more comfortable dressed for sleep?"

"Why? It's daytime, and I do not feel sleepy."

Jane studied her closely. "What was in the glass bottle?"

"I told you. My pain medicine." She pulled a bottle from inside her skirt. "I am in much pain, Jane, and I use a tonic made from herbs to dull it. I made a batch last night because I was running low."

"What's wrong? I want to know if I can do anything to ease your pain. You've never answered my questions and I'm concerned for your health."

The older woman gave her a weak smile. "I've been dying for a long time, or so the doctor tells me. My insides are withering away, and they leave me in agony. Oh, my dear, don't worry," she said, putting a thin hand to Jane's face, "it comes to us all. I don't want you to feel sad."

Jane felt guilty over her callous thoughts about Lord Walbeck's demise. Here was his widow. She at least must mourn him. "Is there anything I can do for you?"

"Have Harper lay his lordship out decently in the cold larder. Let the vicar know that we'll have need of his services. And please see to our guests."

"Is there anyone that you want me to notify? A relative of yours or Lord Walbeck's?"

"I'll write those letters later. After I've had a rest. This has been a most trying day."

"Of course. I'll send up your lady's maid and tell the other servants not to disturb you until you ring." Jane went downstairs and out into the back garden to find Harper there with the doctor, Sir Arnold, and Rexford.

"Excuse me, my lord," she said, curtsying to Rexford. "Harper, her ladyship asks that you see to his lordship being laid out properly in the cold larder and that no one bother her until she rings."

"Two of the footmen have been sent for boards and a sheet to move him in dignity. But there's a small problem, Miss Jane," Harper said. He glanced at Sir Arnold, Rexford, and the doctor for guidance.

"What is it?" She looked from one face to the other, wishing someone would tell her.

"There were yew branches in the dining room, and this looks very much like a case of yew poisoning. He succumbed within a couple of hours of ingestion, with dilated pupils and pale skin," the doctor told her.

Indeed. When she looked down, the first thing she saw was his very white buttocks. She glanced away in horror.

"And there's the cyanotic tint to his face and neck. Another sign," Doctor Fielding continued.

"Then you think..." She didn't want to say it.

"We've sent for Sir James to act as magistrate," Rexford told her. He took her hand and said in a quiet voice, "If this isn't solved, whispers and innuendos will follow me for the rest of my life. People will believe that I am not who I say I am, and I murdered the man who challenged my right to the earldom. I've fought enough since I went to sea. I want to live the rest of my life in peace."

"But surely, my lord, you're above suspicion. We all are."

She would have kept protesting, but Sir Arnold said, "You can't possibly be that naive. No one is above suspicion. Not anyone here today."

"And you can't deny that you warned me against

eating or drinking anything not in common supply," Rexford said. His dark eyes gave her a questioning look. "If he died of yew poisoning, you may well have saved me from being the body here."

"If he were truly poisoned, then I doubt it was a mistake," she said. "He had his mulled wine poured directly into a special cup. And then there was his custom to have his own Christmas pudding every year." Any number of people had handled the mulled wine and the ruby cup. She shuddered. They were all under suspicion now. Especially her.

"Quick, Harper, stop the kitchen staff from eating or throwing away any of the Christmas pudding. Particularly Lord Walbeck's," Rexford ordered.

Harper ran to do his bidding.

She dropped Rexford's hand and ran after the butler, passing the footmen carrying the boards and sheet. Behind her, she heard Rexford say, "You two, take the body up to the cold larder and then come back and clean up the privy. After that heavy dinner, there'll be many wanting to use it. With his body shut away, he can be made more dignified later."

Already he sounded like the man in charge. Then she realized, if he'd rescued his men from pirates and marched them across Europe, he'd become used to stepping in and taking charge of every crisis long before he became an earl.

She reached the kitchen in time to hear Mrs. Ward say, "You'll not tell me what to do with Christmas leftovers, Mr. Harper. As cook, that's my prerogative."

"Mrs. Ward, milord's Christmas pudding may have

been poisoned. You don't want to try it and discover if this is true," Jane said.

"No one ever said my cooking killed anybody." Her eyes blazed as she looked at Jane and Harper.

"Of course not, Mrs. Ward, but anyone could have sneaked into the kitchen, known which pudding would be for the master only, and poisoned it. You wouldn't have noticed a little more liquid poured over it. How could you? You were adding liquid to it all along as part of the recipe."

"That's true." She sounded mollified.

"Where are the remains of his lordship's Christmas pudding?" Harper asked.

Mrs. Ward's look was malicious. "In the slop bucket for the hogs."

Harper looked at Jane. "This will be one Christmas they'll have to do without their treats."

There wasn't much in the barrel. Apparently, the guests and staff had eaten their way through the food before Lord Walbeck was found. Still, she was amazed at how fast Lord Walbeck went from enjoying his Christmas dinner to suffering from poison. Would anyone else's dinner end in death?

"Let's take this to the cold larder. The magistrate will want to examine it for bits of yew," Harper said. He called one of the kitchen lads to do the carrying, and he and Jane followed.

They met Sir Arnold, the doctor, and the new earl outside the building as the two footmen left, looking relieved to be rid of their burden. She told them what was in the barrel, and they nodded agreement. "How long will it take Sir James Lovell to come here to do his duty as magistrate? It's Christmas Day. Won't that affect his arrival?" she asked.

"Because of the circumstances, I suspect he'll come quickly. Probably tomorrow. Lord Walbeck is a large landowner, he was in disagreement with me as the new earl, and we're pretty certain he was poisoned." Rexford gave a grimace of a smile. "It would be hard for a magistrate to do otherwise."

Sir Arnold, Doctor Fielding, and Rexford followed her into the house to leave by the front door.

"My lord," she said, "a stable boy suggested you check under your saddle before leaving. The Farleys were seen putting burrs under it."

He smiled at her. "Thank you, Jane. Once again you've saved my life. I doubt I have it in me to hang on if the horse were to buck." He bent over her hand and kissed the back of it.

When he let her go, she smiled at him and placed her hand over her heart. The tingle that began in her fingers with his kiss traveled the whole way to her toes.

"Does Lady Walbeck require my services?" Doctor Fielding asked.

"She said she didn't want anyone disturbing her until she calls," Jane told him.

"If she wants me, I'll be at home," the doctor said as he left.

Once they were gone, Harper went to oversee preparing Lord Walbeck's body, and Jane went to check on Lady Walbeck.

The new widow still lay on her bed fully clothed, her

eyes shut.

Jane stood quietly in the doorway, not certain if Lady Walbeck was awake or asleep.

The woman's eyes flew open immediately, but nothing else moved. "What is it, Jane?"

"All the guests have left, and Harper is seeing to Lord Walbeck."

"The former Lord Walbeck. The current one is a younger brother. I wonder if he knows. Bad news travels fast."

It would be good news for the new Lord Walbeck, and probably for most of the servants and tenants here. Jane decided to reserve judgment until she found out if Lord Walbeck's death freed her from a guardianship and whether any of her money was left. She doubted his death came in time to save her inheritance, but a tiny voice of hope said *Maybe. There was once a great deal of money. Perhaps he forgot about some of it.*

His death had already come in time to save her from an unwanted marriage. That in itself was a wondrous Christmas gift.

"Do you want me to call the doctor? To give you something to sleep, or to ease your pain?"

"Why? It doesn't matter," the woman said and then turned away from the door.

Jane slipped out of the room, determined to find out how this death affected her guardianship.

An early dusk was already falling over the snowy landscape as Jane walked through the village to Sir Arnold's home. Her knock was quickly answered by his butler. Carlyle hurried her inside out of the cold and brought her to where Sir Arnold was sitting by his fire, sipping a brandy and watching the flames.

"Miss Merrywether," he said, rising and escorting her to a place near the fire. "Would you care for tea?"

"That would be kind." She looked around, her gaze falling on Rexford standing near the window. "I'm surprised you're still awake, my lord. All the activity today on top of your wounds must be wearing you out."

"I'm glad I'm still awake. The cold outside has brought a becoming blush to your cheeks."

Her cold face turned hot immediately. At first he had been a reminder of her childhood, but now it was more. Rexford now brought hope and joy into a room just by entering it. And his presence carried those good feelings into her heart. "I hope I'm not interrupting your evening."

"Not at all. We were discussing places the Farleys may have hidden my horse. He was stolen when they attacked me, and I'd like him back."

"I heard you'd offered a handsome reward for the horse's return. It hasn't helped?"

"Not yet."

"Then they've probably taken it a distance and sold it. You should send word of the reward to every tavern and blacksmith in a day's ride." Jane stopped herself. "I'm sorry. I shouldn't interfere in your business."

He smiled at her. "Don't be sorry. You've given me good advice. Thank you."

Sir Arnold had busied himself with calling for his butler. Once he'd sent Carlyle for tea, he said, "What brings you out in the cold?"

"I need your advice." She sat forward and pressed her hands together. "Advice from both of you. Will my guardianship carry over with Lord Walbeck's titles and lands, or will I gain my freedom with his death?"

"That will depend on the agreement signed by Lord Walbeck and your father. I'm afraid I have no idea what it says," Sir Arnold said.

A flicker of fear sprang to life. "Didn't you write it up for them?"

Sir Arnold looked surprised. "No."

"Lord Walbeck said you did."

"Then he prevaricated. It wouldn't be the first time. I refused to draft the agreement between him and your father. Your father was already dying and I didn't believe the document Lord Walbeck wanted me to create held enough safeguards for you and your money."

Mystified, Jane scowled at the unknown future in front of her. What she'd been told by both Lord and Lady Walbeck was untrue, that her father had signed a guardianship agreement written and approved by Sir Arnold. "Then who wrote it for them?"

"I don't know. There must be a copy in Lord Walbeck's papers," Sir Arnold told her.

"He keeps those in his study. I'll have to look for it." She was about to leave when the tea was brought in, and she settled back into her seat.

"Leave that for his solicitor. Who is he?" Rexford asked.

She looked from one to the other. "I thought it was you, Sir Arnold."

"I wrote his will a few years ago and took care of his

land purchases, but he made clear more than once that I was too independent, as he phrased it, to be his solicitor. Even with his blackmail," he added to himself.

Jane chose to ignore his last words. "I never knew of any other. I will have a look through his study in the morning."

Sir Arnold leaned forward. "If I might make a suggestion, let the Earl of Beckingham and I serve as witnesses to what you find when you search his study. That way no one can say you stole documents or destroyed them."

Suspicions must be rampant already for Sir Arnold to suggest this. Everyone involved in this terrible business would have to protect themselves from accusations and gossip for a long time to come. She nodded her agreement.

A rap at the front door signaled bustle in the hallway and then voices could be heard. A minute later Sir James Lovell entered the study. He was immediately seated and given a glass of brandy.

"A terrible night for travel," Sir Arnold said.

"Under the circumstances, I thought I'd better get here quickly. Tell me all," the magistrate said as he settled deeper into the chair.

They did, with the fire built higher and the tea refreshed.

When they finished, Sir James turned to her. "By your own admission, Lord Walbeck stole from you and was forcing you into an unwanted marriage. And you were spending a great deal of time in the kitchen. I'm sure I can trust you enough not to have to lock you away.

But please, do not leave the village for the next fortnight."

She set down her teacup with a crash. He suspected her.

Rexford nearly jumped to his feet. "She didn't do it."

"I doubt she did," Sir James said smoothly, "but a case can be made against her. Until this business is sorted out, it is better if she remains close at hand."

"I know you didn't do it, Miss Merrywether, and I intend to prove it." Rexford stared into her eyes, willing her to gaze back at him.

His statement brought a look of hope to her frightened, confused expression. "I didn't do it, my lord. I had hoped to ask you to rescue me. Send me to a distant part of your lands. And put in a good word to the bishop to find the vicar a new parish."

"That won't be necessary. Someone has done you a good turn," the magistrate said. "And they may well have ended your guardianship."

Rexford sat down next to her and took her hand. "I'd have done whatever you asked."

"I know. That's why I never would have killed Lord Walbeck. And in such a brutal way." She gave his hand a squeeze. "Someone was very clever to slip the poison into his Christmas dinner. Someone who didn't have the strength or the opportunity to kill him any other way."

What she said made sense. "But why now? What had changed beside your impending marriage?"

She dropped his hand and hung her head. "Nothing. Which means only the vicar, Magda, or I would have killed him. And I'm certain none of us did." She looked into his eyes again. "Please help me prove us innocent."

He gave her a confident smile. She was fearless, and he was very proud of her for her sense and serenity. "Nothing could give me greater pleasure. And if I may, I'll call upon you in the morning to assist with the search of Lord Walbeck's study." He raised her hand to his lips.

When he let it go, she drew her hand to her heart and gave him a smile that shone more brightly than the Bethlehem star.

When Jane returned to the manor house, a maid told her, "Lady Walbeck has been calling for you."

With a sigh, she hurried up stairs and knocked on Lady Walbeck's door before entering.

"There you are. I was afraid you'd abandoned me." The lady was now dressed for bed and under the covers. She was propped up on pillows, looking as white as the bedclothes.

"I went to see Sir Arnold."

She smiled. "And that handsome earl."

"Yes." Jane felt her cheeks heat as she pictured him, undressed now, and in his bed. She almost giggled when she realized that while she pictured him in bed, the covers protected his modesty in her imagination.

"Jane, promise me something."

"What, milady?"

"That you won't leave me. I haven't much longer. Please, don't leave me."

"Where would I go?" A question that hadn't left her mind since the afternoon before.

"Promise me, Jane. It will only be for a little while."

She patted Lady Walbeck's shoulder. "Neither of us appears to have anywhere else to go. But don't worry. Something will work out for both of us."

In a weak voice, the lady said, "But I do worry. I don't want to be left alone. Not at the end."

"I believe the end is a very far distance away."

"Don't treat me like a child, Jane. I know I grow weaker and wearier by the day."

"The new Lord Walbeck, whoever he is, might not want me here and there won't be a thing either of us can do about it."

"I've visited my husband's brother, although it was a few years ago. He's a meek man, prone to do whatever someone tells him. He won't send you away. I won't let him."

It seemed cruel not to agree to the new widow's request, but it was contrary to what Jane wanted for herself. "Let's see what the next few days bring. You may grow tired of my face. The new lord might take a dislike to me. We'll talk again when we know more."

"Promise me, Jane." Her grip on Jane's arm was strong and painful like a hawk's talons.

"My lady, we must wait unt—"

"Promise me, Jane!"

The guardianship agreement would probably leave her stuck here anyway. And it seemed churlish to deny a new widow some solace. "If it will make you rest easy."

"It will."

"All right."

"Say it."

"I promise to stay until the end of my guardianship,"

Jane grumbled.

"No. Stay until the end of my life. I love you, dear Jane."

She felt trapped by the woman's grasp. "I hope to marry long before then."

"But I heard you say you didn't want—" Lady Walbeck waved away her words. "Marriages are sad affairs for the woman. We could be happy living here."

"This is your home, my lady, yours and the new Lord Walbeck's. Not mine." Jane put iron in her tone. "I want a home and a family of my own, and that means marriage."

"But we can be our own little family. You and I."

Shocked, Jane wondered if her disease had attacked Lady Walbeck's brain. "I have horrible memories of this place," slipped out. "And there may be a murderer lurking here. It would be safer if we left." She shook off Lady Walbeck's grip and hurried to the door.

"Oh, no, Jane," Lady Walbeck called after her. "Nothing will hurt you here. I'm quite sure the murderer is finished with his work."

Chapter Five

AFTER BREAKFAST, JOHN REXFORD rode with Sir Arnold and Sir James to the Walbeck mansion, the carriage wheels and horses' hooves making a crunching sound on the frozen gravel. He wished they could travel faster so he could see Jane sooner, but the ice and snow seemed to slow their progress to that of a slug.

She waited in the hallway as Rexford hurried over to her, smiling. She curtsied in response to his bow and then shyly returned his smile as she asked, "How is the patient today?"

The two magistrates appeared to pay no notice when Rexford moved next to Jane and took her hand as he addressed her immediate concern. "Improved enough to help you with the paperwork. Let's go through to the study and find that agreement."

He was relieved when he realized the untidiness of the room didn't mean it had been searched. The room was as Lord Walbeck had left it, with the brandy bottle and one glass on a sideboard, and pastry crumbs scattered on top of papers.

Shaking his head, Rexford grimaced as he realized the amount of work Walbeck had left them. He'd not kept his papers in any sort of order. Even with both of them sorting while Sir Arnold accompanied Sir James on his investigation, Jane and Rexford spent hours organizing deeds, letters, and bills.

"Even in death Cousin George is causing me problems," he grumbled. "Was he this slipshod in everything he did?"

"I'm afraid so," Jane said, rubbing her hands against her arms in the poorly heated room. "And there's still no sign of Lord Walbeck's guardianship agreement with my father."

"Maybe he didn't have one," Rexford said as he scoured a letter from a creditor and tried to figure out why it was with a flyer for a long forgotten horse race. As the room grew quiet, he looked up to find Jane staring at him.

Then she slumped into a chair. "No!"

"What?" Puzzled, he looked at her, wondering what had happened in those years he'd been prevented from coming home.

"Seven years. Seven long years ago, Lord Walbeck swept in after my father died, claimed everything as my guardian, and brought me back here. But he never showed me or anyone the guardianship agreement. He just waved some folded up papers.

"From the looks of these accounts, he spent all my money. He treated me like a servant and beat me for no reason. And now you suggest he might not have had a guardianship agreement with my father? He lied to me? He didn't have the right to anything he stole from me?" Tears poured from her eyes, and she made no effort to stem them.

"How old are you?" Rexford sat down across from her and handed her his handkerchief. Her fingers felt soft against his warrior-rough hands.

She wiped at her tears and breathed deeply in an apparent effort to get herself under control. "Twenty-two. There's—there's supposed to be another three years to go on his guardianship."

"That's absurd." He felt a kinship with Jane after what they'd been through. He couldn't abandon her to more years in this house. "We need to find you a gentlewoman's house to reside in while we straighten this out. Would Miss Miller be suitable?"

Jane gasped. "That explains it." She looked at him with widened eyes as she gripped his hand.

"Explains what?" He could measure her anxiety by the power of her grasp.

"Why Lady Walbeck made me promise last night to stay with her until the end of her life. She says she hasn't much longer."

"Is this true?" he demanded while never taking his eyes from the beauty. He forced his hands not to fist in anger. Walbeck was dead, but his widow might still be taking advantage of Jane.

"Supposedly," she said. "She eats little and spends much time resting."

"Or it's as false as this so-called guardianship. What was going on here while I was away?" He rose and began to pace the room. "We need to confer with Doctor Fielding."

Opening the door, he summoned a footman with a

request for the doctor to come to the manor house immediately.

"I don't trust anyone in this house anymore." He wanted to protect Jane with every ounce of his strength because of her kindness to him as a stranger and her calm fearlessness in circumventing whatever end Walbeck had in mind for him. She was a woman he wanted to get to know better.

"I promised her I'd remain. Three more years, or until the end of her life." Jane looked down and dried her eyes on his handkerchief.

Despite wanting to embrace her, he could think of nothing to comfort her beyond rubbing her shoulder with his hand. He wanted to promise her safety and love, but with a warrior's practicality, the words that passed his lips were, "I fear you'll be the killer's next victim."

She shivered beneath his touch. "You're frightening me."

"I want you to realize you could be in grave danger. The murderer has already struck once." He wanted to get her out of this house today. This minute. Somewhere safe from the killer. And with a chaperone. She deserved a trouble-free future, a happy future, a future he hoped contained him, too.

Jane lifted her head. Lady Walbeck had done next to nothing to make her life easier, and she owed her little loyalty in return. Meanwhile, a murderer was loose, possibly lurking in this house. And Rexford, who'd faced plenty of perils, was afraid for her. "I want to leave. Now that I don't have to marry her brother, I can stay with

Magda Miller." Then she gazed into Rexford's eyes and added, "But is it wrong to leave a dying woman alone?"

He smiled at her. "Not when she tried to coerce you to stay. Those of us who survived to escape the pirates told plenty of lies and broke many a promise to get from North Africa to England. It was the only way to get home. I don't regret any of them."

"But you had to," she told him.

"To survive seven minutes with Walbeck, let alone seven years, you had to be brave. That must have required skirting the truth." She heard the admiration in his tone, melting her fears.

She had been courageous, she realized, and she had the bruises and scars to prove it. No more. With her head held high, she said, "Skirting the truth, yes. Lying, no. May I send my trunk in Sir Arnold's carriage?"

"Of course."

"Then I'll pack quickly." She shook her head. "I haven't much to pack."

"Miss Merrywether, I look forward to getting to know you away from this poisonous house," he said, giving her a deep bow. Showing her the deference no one else had in years.

His smile was different now. He looked less haunted. Happier, perhaps. "I do, too, my lord." Her smile felt joyful for the first time.

"Please call me John and I hope I may call you Jane." Now he looked as if he might laugh from delight.

"Gladly, John." The room suddenly felt as if it were mid-summer outside with a gentle breeze replacing the icy wind slipping through the cracks. She wanted to laugh and sing, but she restrained herself. The time hadn't come. Yet.

She went upstairs and pulled out a single trunk from the box room. Sadly, everything she owned would fit inside. Clothes she hadn't outgrown in the years from child to womanhood. Trinkets she'd saved from her parents.

She'd begun packing before one of the maids came in. "Milady wants you to come to her room now."

"I'll be there in a minute." She was dreading this interview. What if Lady Walbeck truly was dying? Even if the woman had done nothing but use her as an unpaid servant, she was one of God's creatures and should be treated kindly.

She put a few more items in the trunk, the maid watching in wide-eyed realization, and then followed the girl along the hall to Lady Walbeck's room.

Her ladyship was dressed and sitting in a chair, looking thin but with a high color in her cheeks. The remains of a breakfast tray sat on a dresser, the plate empty except for a few crumbs.

"What is all this noise I've heard, Jane?"

Feeling freer than she had in years, Jane replied, "My lady had a good breakfast. Excellent."

"What is going on?" Her voice was more strident.

"I'm packing."

"What?" came out of Lady Walbeck's mouth in a screech.

Jane had to know. "There was never a guardianship agreement, was there?"

"Oh, Jane, you know I can't get along without you."

Guilty knowledge was written on Lady Walbeck's face.

"You knew? You knew and yet you let him beat me and spend my inheritance?" Jane was furious and near to tears as Lady Walbeck's betrayal sank in. She'd always been loyal to her guardian's wife. Until a few minutes ago, she'd believed Lady Walbeck couldn't do anything to make her life better in the face of Lord Walbeck's domination.

But Lady Walbeck had used her as an unpaid companion. Lady Walbeck had known how Jane had been lied to and cheated, and she'd said nothing.

"Jane, I told my husband to be kind to you. I told him how much I relied on you. But I'm weak and tired. I couldn't stop him and his evil ways. What could I do?"

"You could have told me the truth." She turned around and ran back to her room, throwing her possessions into the trunk in a jumble.

Lady Walbeck came in and began to throw them out again onto the bed. "No, Jane. No!"

She put her things back in as fast as the woman pulled them out. "You should have told me the truth."

"This is your home! I'm your mother."

"This has never been my home, and you are not my mother." Jane looked at her in fury. This woman could never compare herself to Jane's mother. She finally saw Lady Walbeck for the cruel, selfish woman she was.

She hadn't expected the slap. She staggered backward, clutching her cheek as tears filled her eyes from the pain.

Lady Walbeck's face turned red as she snapped out her words. "After all I did for you, you ungrateful little brat. I was the only one willing to stop him. Me!" Lady Walbeck ran back to her room and slammed the door.

Jane turned back to her task and quickly finished packing, folding clothes and neatly stacking her possessions in the trunk. At least she wouldn't be bothered by anyone now. To think that Lady Walbeck had the nerve to call herself Jane's mother. And then to strike her face.

She remembered her mother's kindness. Her mother's love. Her mother had been gentle and even-tempered.

When she finished, she went downstairs and asked Harper to send two footmen to her room to bring her trunk down to Sir Arnold's carriage.

After the two young men went upstairs, Harper said, "We'll miss you, Miss Jane, but we know His Lordship and Sir Arnold will take good care of you." The butler gave the men a bow befitting their position.

"I'll miss you, too. The other servants treated me well, but you were the only one in this house who befriended me." She swallowed her tears. "I imagine I'll see you in the village."

"I hope so. Take care of yourself."

They clasped hands for a moment. Then Lady Walbeck's words came back to her. "She said she was the only one willing to stop Lord Walbeck. You don't think—? She said the mixture in the glass bottle was for her pain."

"What glass bottle?" Sir James asked, stepping forward.

"The one I saw her carrying yesterday. The one she filled with a brew she made early in the morning before I began the mulled wine for the Christmas feast," she said.

"I've never known her to make any concoction before. She always said the kitchen was Mrs. Ward's province and she wanted nothing to do with it." Harper turned to Sir James. "Do you want me to check with Mrs. Ward to see if she'd run out of the brew Lady Walbeck took for her pain?"

"I'll go with you." Jane hurried on Harper's heels to the kitchen, the magistrates and Rexford following.

The cook was seeing to a roast on a spit in the fireplace while giving the kitchen maids orders on chopping the vegetables. "Harper? What is this?" she asked, handing over care of the roast to a kitchen maid. "Mind you don't let it burn."

"We wondered if you've been making medicine for Lady Walbeck to help ease her pain," Sir James asked.

"What of it?"

"We found it odd that Lady Walbeck was in this kitchen early Christmas morning making another batch of it herself."

"Who says she was?"

"I saw her myself when I started the mulled wine," Jane told the cook.

"No reason for her to. There are two bottles of it made up on the shelf there," Mrs. Ward said in a brusque tone as she turned her back on them to return to supervising the kitchen. "Besides, she wouldn't know how."

Jane frowned in her confusion. "What?"

Ignoring her, Mrs. Ward leaped forward, grabbing a towel as she shoved the kitchen maid out of the way. "Not like that!"

"She didn't know how to do what?" Jane asked.

"Make up her pain medicine. It's an old recipe passed from one family to another in the village."

"Did she know where you keep her medicine?" Sir James asked.

"Of course. She's no fool, no matter what some think," Mrs. Ward said. "If she needed a new bottle, she'd just send someone to fetch it."

"She's up in her room with that glass bottle and its contents, whatever she cooked down here early Christmas morning," Jane said, feeling her eyes widen.

She rushed up two flights of stairs, Rexford at her side. Sir Arnold, Sir James, and Harper made up the group that reached Lady Walbeck's door as Jane banged on it.

"Lady Walbeck, it's the Earl of Beckingham, here to see how I might assist you at this time," he called out.

A sobbing noise came from within.

Rexford tried the handle. The door was locked.

"We'll have to break it in." He stepped back to put a shoulder to the door.

"Wait! All these locks are the same." Jane ran to her room and brought back her key. "I learned that early in my stay here. I couldn't lock Lord Walbeck and his punishments out, but when I was locked in, I could escape." Swallowing away another bad memory, she opened the door in an instant.

The scene before them was pitiful. Lady Walbeck huddled in a corner, tears streaming down her cheeks. She'd cried so hard that she was gasping between sobs.

"Oh, my lady," Jane said as she moved forward. "You

must be heartbroken."

Lady Walbeck pulled out the glass bottle from her pocket and unstoppered it. "Stay away from me. Stay away—or I'll drink this."

Jane stopped where she was, halfway across the room. "Don't do that. Please don't."

"You know?" Lady Walbeck whispered.

Jane nodded and watched for a chance to take the bottle away from the lady.

"I killed my husband to protect you. And you thank me by rejecting me and moving out of our home. After I've kept you close and protected you as best I could."

Jane heard a sharp intake of breath, and with a glance knew that Rexford understood the deadly consequences of drinking from the vial.

"If you acted to protect your ward, no one will blame you for your husband's death. Please, milady, give me the bottle," he said, moving toward her with his hand slightly forward.

The woman shrank back.

"No one will find fault with you, but we don't want any more accidents, milady. Give me the bottle so we can dispose of it where none will be injured." He made another few steps across the room.

Jane stared at him in wonder. His voice was calm, his movements smooth, and he was gaining on Lady Walbeck without alarming her.

Lady Walbeck turned to her and cried out, "Jane!"

"I'm here, milady. What can I do for you?" She took a tentative step forward, hoping the woman wouldn't drink the potion.

"I'll soon be dead. Don't let them hang me, Jane." The woman began to sob loudly.

Jane pushed past Rexford and reached Lady Walbeck, enfolding her in an embrace while he took the bottle from her hand.

He sighed in relief. "What was in here, milady? It's almost empty now."

"A tea from the yew tree. What I gave Lord Walbeck. The whole bottle."

"Harper, dispose of this safely. In the cold larder, for choice," Rexford said.

Harper took the bottle and the stopper and hurried away.

"Did you put it in his pudding?" Jane asked, holding up the grieving widow so she didn't collapse.

Lady Walbeck nodded. "If he didn't manage an accident first, my husband planned to poison you one day. But when he saw the way the earl looked at you, he knew he had to remove you and any lingering questions about your money this holiday. Before it was too late. Before he had to answer for his theft."

Through her tears, Lady Walbeck continued. "He asked me to make the poison, but realizing I couldn't let him use it on you, I used it on him instead."

"And he stole Miss Merrywether's inheritance?" Sir James asked.

"Yes."

"And you knew?"

"Yes, but..." Jane heard Lady Walbeck gasp. "I couldn't stop him. Not when he decided to do something. I loved her like the daughter I never had."

In that case, she decided, it was better that the Walbecks didn't have children of their own.

Doctor Fielding entered the room and had a hushed conference with Sir Arnold and Sir James. Then he came forward. "What you need, milady, is to rest."

"Jane—"

"Jane is needed downstairs. Doctor, if we could speak after you finish with your patient, I'll be content." Rexford took her by the arm and led her downstairs to the parlor. "Once again, you acted bravely. I'm amazed at your compassion."

"As I am with how well you handled her."

They searched into each other's eyes for a moment before he said, "And now you're free, Jane. You survived."

She burst into tears of relief. He held her, rubbing her back and making small shushing noises. They had treated her like a servant. And her father had been a baronet.

That part of her life was over. Now she was free of Lord Walbeck's false guardianship and the world would learn she hadn't killed the tyrant.

"I'm sorry for all you've gone through. I want to make the future better for you." Rexford embraced her, and when she looked into his eyes, she saw mirrored there the affection she felt for him.

"It's all right, John. You had your own battles to fight to return here. And I'm certain the future will be better for both of us. We deserve it." She ran a hand gently down the side of his face, staring into his eyes. "I want to make your life better, too."

"We're a pair, aren't we, Jane. We've both been

imprisoned. We've both been hurt. We've both learned to live by our wits."

"And now we can both heal. And perhaps help each other learn to live with our freedom."

He rested his hand on the side of her face, rubbing his thumb over her lips. "You can teach me how to treat others with kindness. Gentleness. I've been fighting for so long, I'd forgotten kindness existed until you went out of your way to save me from dying in that shed. And you were so gentle tending to my wounds."

"I'll teach you, if you'll teach me how to face the world without constantly looking over my shoulder. I spent years trapped away in this village with a jailer who constantly watched my every move."

"I think we may be a Christmas gift to each other." He gave her a gentle smile.

Surrounded by the decorations of greenery and ribbon in this room, she saw the Christmas miracle she'd prayed for. "Little did I know those many years ago that the boy my father hoped would one day be mine would turn out to be someone as brave and sensible as you."

"Until Sir Arnold said you were Merrywether's daughter, I had no idea who you were. But then, your father was a fearless man. I'm not surprised his daughter took after him." He ran her knuckles over his lips. "We need to get to know each other better, Jane, if you don't mind. And for more than just the sake of our parents."

She grabbed his hand and clasped it. "For our own sakes. For our future." As the glow of that imagined future warmed her heart, she knew it would come to pass.

About Kate

Kate Parker grew up reading her mother's collection of mystery books by Christie, Sayers, and others. Now she can't write a story without someone being murdered, and everyday items are studied for their lethal potential. It's taken her years to convince her husband she hasn't poisoned dinner; that funny taste is because she can't cook. Her children have grown up to be surprisingly normal, but two of them are developing their own love of literary mayhem, so the term "normal" may have to be revised.

Living in a nineteenth century town has inspired Kate's love of history. Her Victorian Bookshop Mystery series features a single woman in late Victorian London who, besides running a bookshop, is part of an informal detective agency known as the Archivist Society. This society solves cases that have baffled Scotland Yard, allowing the victims and their families to find closure. *The Vanishing Thief, The Counterfeit Lady,* and *The Royal Assassin* are now available online and in bookstores. *The Conspiring Woman* will be out this fall.

Next year will bring a new series featuring a young widow in late thirties London who lands a job as a society reporter for a major newspaper. With Europe on the brink of war, the newspaper publisher finds a second assignment for her, one that can't appear in the paper. The first in the series will be *Deadly Scandal.*

Follow Kate and her deadly examination of history at www.KateParkerbooks.com
and www.Facebook.com/Author.Kate.Parker/.

A Perfectly
Unregimented Christmas

by

Louisa Cornell

Chapter One

December, 1816
Cornwall

A POTATO.

Knocked from his horse, Ben Miserington lay sprawled on the snow-covered drive leading to Pennyworth Hall. He fingered the growing lump on the back of his head and fought not to laugh.

If you want me dead, God, you will have to put a bit more effort into it than that.

Of all the weapons wielded against him since he'd been tossed into the navy at the age of ten and cashed out to join the cavalry at fifteen, a potato masquerading as a snowball at least held the virtue of being unique. Between French sabers and guns on the Peninsula, a well-swung shovel followed by a razor to the throat in the streets of San Sebastian, and an attempted incineration in London, Ben scarcely credited his continued existence at all.

Here he sat, however, and pondered the wisdom of his return to the estate and title he'd inherited from his grandfather—an estate and title it had taken him nearly five years to claim. Somewhere at the end of this tree-lined drive stood his childhood home, the current residence of the only surviving member of his family who had not tried to kill him. Yet.

Once he ceased his meditation on the snow-caked potato, the snow's effect on his new buckskin breeches and more importantly, its icy caress on portions of his anatomy he preferred to keep warm, spurred him to gain his feet and find his horse. Snow, in Ben's experience, was a great deal like a family—cold and beautiful in appearance, a pain in the arse when seated in the middle of it, and deadly if one wallowed in it too long.

He sank his gloved hands into the endless blanket of white that unfurled down the cobblestone drive and pushed himself halfway up only to be bombarded in the arse by two more snow-potatoes in quick succession.

"What the devil!" Ben lurched into a crouched position and did a quick reconnaissance of the yew trees lining the drive between him and the gatehouse. He'd ridden beneath the carved arch only moments ago. No one had stirred inside either of the small square towers that buttressed the arch. A sudden movement atop one of the miniature battlements caught his eye.

A red cap. Dirty yellow hair. Wide blue eyes and a gap-toothed smile. A few more sets of equally wide eyes peered over the mock castle wall and.... *Was that a goat wearing a bonnet?*

Thunk!

Thunk!

A great glob of snow slithered down his back under the collar of Ben's greatcoat. He spun around and with a savage battle cry stretched to his full height. A diminutive figure in a red wool coat scampered into the hedgerow, leaving a victorious trill of boyish laughter behind him.

"Damned well enough of this," Ben muttered. He let loose a high, sharp whistle. His horse, Trafalgar, trotted from around the bend in the drive, dangling, of all things, a fresh carrot from his lips.

Where did the lazy beast find a carrot?

Half a dozen little feet dashed from the gatehouse into the trees behind him. Headed for the village and home, no doubt. Some fathers were about to be visited by the new viscount, make no mistake. Few things annoyed Ben as much as boys without discipline. In all too short a time, they became men without discipline. He'd seen enough of them and the havoc they wreaked to last a lifetime.

"Oh no you don't, you little miscreants." Ben loped toward his horse. "Time to pay the piper. Just you wait— umpf!" He landed face down in the snow. The sudden jolt sent a sharp cannonade into every bone in his battered body. Once he regained the ability to lift his head, he glanced back to see a length of rope drawn ankle-high between the hedgerows on either side of the drive. It had not been there mere moments ago. Clever lads, these.

He staggered halfway to his feet and rested his palms on his knees. Mistake. Murderous shrieks sure to put a company of Scots dragoons to shame issued from the branches of the tallest yew trees. Snow-potatoes came at him from all directions. Ben drew the pistol from his waistband and fired it into the air directly over his head. The screaming ceased.

"What the bloody hell," he roared. Ben spun around

in search of the miscellany of marauders.

Silence. Not a soul in sight, save for his traitorous horse, who ambled up still chewing the unlikely carrot. "Heart of a lion at Waterloo." Ben snatched up the reins and flung himself into the saddle. *Damn!* Only to stand in the stirrups the moment his abused bottom hit the leather. He adjusted his seat to accommodate his latest injury. "And you leave me to fend for myself against a band of children. Come along, you great cowardly lummox."

With one last look around, Ben turned his mount toward the hall. Time enough to go after the local ruffians later. Boys of their ilk usually had a reputation and would be easily identified, especially to the new master of Pennyworth. His desire for justice gave way to his desire for a soft, warm chair for his wounded fundament and a full glass of brandy for his wounded pride.

He held Trafalgar to a slow walk the remainder of the way up the drive. Anticipation of another attack played a part in it, but it wasn't the only reason. In the seven months since he'd returned to England, he'd sought out every single place from his haunted past, like worrying a bad tooth before finally gathering the courage to seek an obliging tooth drawer to yank it out. Those places all appeared smaller now, as he came to them a man of thirty. But not Pennyworth Hall.

The ancient stones loomed in a series of stalwart grey square towers connected by a quartet of newer wings, if one considered two hundred years old new. At the far corner, the one round tower of the original Miserington family keep joined the main hall and housed, if memory served, her ladyship's private parlor. At this very moment, Ben wasn't certain his memory did. Twenty years had passed since he'd last peeked out a carriage window to see this monument to his family's history grow farther and farther away. His memories before that Christmas morning lurked in a broken heap in his mind. Only bits and pieces remained, and he hadn't the need nor the clues required to put them together. Until now.

"My lord?"

Whilst he'd sat and mused over the family pile, the front doors had swung open to reveal servants lined up on both sides of the entrance hall. *Marley.* Standing outside on the portico at the top of the stairs was a grey-haired version of the young butler who had tucked Ben into that carriage all those years ago.

"Is that you, Marley?" Ben swung down and tossed Trafalgar's reins to the groom who had appeared as if by magic at his side. "Take care of him, lad. He's useless, but he's had a long ride."

"Yes, milord."

Ben took the steps two at the time and strode into the entrance hall. "Still here, Marley?" He swept off his greatcoat and handed it to a young footman. His gloves and crop came next.

"Indeed, my lord. Welcome home." Here was a face and voice from his past that evoked no twinge of anger or bewilderment. Only... curiosity.

"Indeed, Marley. Time will tell." With as much grace as he could muster, Ben managed to nod his way through the servants' curtsies and bows. He turned away from the wide, carpeted staircase Marley indicated and started down the White Gallery, which led to the round tower. Twenty years of wandering fled in the face of a house that refused to be forgotten.

"Lord Pennyworth."

Ben stopped midstride. To his left, the portrait of his grandfather as a young man glowered down at him. He glanced over his shoulder at the expectant butler.

"Your bath has been drawn, my lord. Your trunks arrived yesterday morning and your clothes—"

"Lady Pennyworth has seen more than her share of dirt, Marley. And I've waited long enough." He continued down the gallery. "Send in some brandy."

His boots beat a thudded tattoo on the worn Persian carpets covering the stone floors. Once bright blue and gold, the colors had faded to a murky grey and dun. Other inane details swam around in his head. He dug his fingernails into his palms and then flexed his hands open, closed and open again. A footman darted out of the way as Ben reached past him to raise the door latch and march into the dowager viscountess's private lair.

The room had not changed. Murals of Roman ruins and Turkish palaces covered the walls of the round room. Four fireplaces with delicately carved marble mantelpieces kept it warm in spite of two large windows that looked out over the grounds. A pianoforte sat across the way. The furnishings in hues of red and gold forced him to blink, just as they had when he was a child.

"Ben." And then she was there—the Dowager Viscountess Pennyworth. Older, thinner, but no less formidable. She rose from her chair in front of the fire. In a rustle of black bombazine, she crossed the room and flung her arms around him. The scent of violets and lemon drops washed over him. He barely resisted the temptation to reach into her pocket where he swore he heard the crackle of sweet papers. She'd not needed to carry sweets for little boys in a long time.

"Grandmama," he gritted out between clenched teeth. He gave her back an awkward pat.

He'd steeled himself against this moment. He didn't want to feel. *What a fool.* The mind can be made to forget. The heart can be walled behind bricks of ice and rage. But the body is an unfathomable mystery. No power save death can destroy the memories sown into flesh and blood. In this familiar embrace, his body shuddered as a ship when the anchor comes to rest on the sand of home port. God help him.

"My dear boy." She touched his face.

He had no choice but to look down into faded green eyes awash in tears. Her face was the same, only a little more lined. Her hair was completely silver now. Time to put an end to this maudlin farce. "You are trembling, madam." He took her arm and led her back to her place by the fire. "Come warm yourself."

"With joy." She drew a black lace handkerchief from her sleeve and dabbed at her eyes. "I never thought to see this day." She reached up to squeeze his hand. "You are finally home. Fan, where are you girl? Fan?"

"Here, milady." Hardly a girl after nearly thirty years in service. His grandmother's maid had sat so quiet and still Ben failed to see her until she scurried from a chair by the window to her mistress's side.

"Go and lay out my yellow silk dress."

"Milady, it is December, and a cold December too."

"Oh, very well, my yellow wool. Go, girl." She smiled at Ben as the maid hurried off to do her bidding, leaving him alone with his grandmother. "I have worn black since the day we received word you fell at San Sebastian. I swore I would not wear colors again until I saw you here with my own eyes. And here you are."

"Bad pennies do tend to turn up eventually, madam." Ben collapsed into the chair opposite hers. "No matter how far away they are sent."

A soft bark issued from one of the high-backed leather chairs before the fireplace next to the pianoforte. Surely his grandmother didn't still keep those ugly little dogs with the smashed faces.

The great lady stiffened slightly. "You were never a bad penny. Ever." She perused his wet, dirty clothes and the noticeable shadows of his unshaven face. "Although I would have thought they'd teach you to keep a better appearance in the cavalry, especially as an officer. You look like a common ruffian, Pennyworth."

Another snort issued softly from across the room. This time the dowager looked around him and shook her head.

"It is a long ride from London on horseback." Ben spotted the footman who'd slipped in the door bearing a tea tray and more importantly, the bottle of brandy he'd requested. He waved him over, snatched the bottle and glass off the tray, and poured himself a generous portion. Some sort of strangled cough drew his attention to the area near the pianoforte again. Good Lord, she did have a dog and it sounded as if the creature was on its last legs. "And I tend to travel light."

She didn't look up this time but sorted through the offerings on the tea tray and handed him a plate. Ginger biscuits, strawberry tarts, and two miniature mince pies. He wasn't so churlish as to refuse his favorites. With luck they weren't poisoned. His first bite of the mince pie settled it. Poisoned or not, the mince pies at Pennyworth Hall were still the best he'd ever tasted.

"You should have come in the carriage." She raised a cup of tea to her lips. "You are Pennyworth now."

"I prefer not to travel in carriages. They tend to take me places I don't care to go. The last Pennyworth carriage I took carried me off to the navy." He dropped the plate onto the tea table. The ensuing clatter was punctuated by the determined closing of a book from behind a chair before the fireplace next to the pianoforte. Dogs don't read books. Then again, goats didn't wear bonnets.

Ben rose and stalked toward the sound.

"Ebenezer Miserington, I was speaking to you," his grandmother declared. A rustle of fabric indicated she'd risen to follow him.

"Don't call me that." He gripped the back of the leather chair, leaned over it, and came nose to nose with the most striking woman he'd ever seen in his life—soft grey-blue eyes shone from a heart-shaped face framed by a thick halo of braided and pinned sable hair. Not young, but not yet thirty. She blinked, squeaked a word he'd seldom heard a lady use, and promptly swatted at him with a thick, leather-bound book.

Ben caught the book mid-swing and took a step back. "Is there anyone on this estate who doesn't intend to assault me for no good reason?"

The woman erupted from her chair in a wave of grey velvet draped over a very fetching figure. Hands on her hips, she raked him up and down and turned up her blade of a nose. "I had every reason. You startled me." She snatched the book from him and dropped it on the reading table between the chairs. "Who else has assaulted you?"

"Today? A number of vicious urchins, possibly a goat, and a bookish harridan who needs to learn to be quiet if she is intent on success as an assassin. Are there any other women lurking about this room? Startling anyone else might be the death of me." To quash his urge to give the lady a far more lingering once over than she'd given him, Ben gave her his back and returned to the opposite hearth to take up his brandy.

Unfortunately, his grandmother took the lady in question by the hand and led her back to the tea table. "Mrs. Winters, may I present my grandson, Viscount Pennyworth." The two women exchanged a series of looks. Had Wellington allowed his dispatches to be carried between two women who communicated by wordless looks alone, the war would have ended in victory in a fortnight. "Pennyworth, this is Mrs. Winters."

Ben studied them over the rim of his glass of brandy. "And Mr. Winters is?"

"I am a widow, my lord, and a governess by profession." She gave him a suggestion of a curtsey and a grey stare hard enough to break Toledo steel.

His grandmother patted Mrs. Winters's hand. "Belle is my goddaughter. She is between positions at the moment and has been acting as my companion." Another flurry of wordless communication. Lovely.

"I see." He leaned against his chair and took another long draught of brandy. He'd come here for answers, peace, and quiet. Something told him he'd be fortunate to obtain even one of the three. He had, however, succeeded in provoking the viscountess, a useful tool when assessing one's enemies.

"Is it not considered common courtesy to bow when one is introduced to a lady?" Here was the grandmother he knew—no nonsense and elegantly condescending.

Ben straightened, executed a bow, and flopped into his seat. "Your servant, Mrs. Winters."

Something very like "Unlikely," fluttered from Mrs. Winters's very lovely lips. She moved to stand behind the dowager's chair. "Tell me, my lord, you spoke of being assaulted earlier. What manner of attack was it? You appear uninjured."

The two women pinned him with equally pointed expressions of feigned disinterest. He'd been here less than an hour and already new secrets were stacked atop the old. For little to nothing, he'd climb back onto Trafalgar and put Pennyworth Hall and every damned secret it held behind him. Pity was, he couldn't.

"I will certainly show you my injuries, Mrs. Winters, if you wish, but as most of them are to my arse, Lady Pennyworth might object."

"Of all the—"

"Pennyworth. Apologize to Annabelle, this instant."

"My apologies, ma'am. It has been a long day." He shoved out of the chair and started for the door.

"You were not raised to be so rag-mannered, young man."

"I was not raised at all, madam, not past the age of ten. Or don't you remember?"

Thunderous silence was the only reply. Ben fought and lost the urge to look back. Mrs. Winters knelt beside his grandmother's chair and held the cup of tea for the old woman to drink. She took a sip and looked up at him with a wistful smile. Mrs. Winters, however, looked as if she wanted to fling the entire tea tray at him.

"You were always such a sweet boy, Ben. I have missed that little boy with all my heart. What happened to make you so hard?"

He wanted to believe her. But believing her, having faith in anyone but himself, would not give him what he wanted—peace, answers, and the right to feel nothing at all.

Mrs. Winters peered up at him, then quickly turned her grey gaze to the window overlooking the snow-covered grounds.

"San Sebastian, madam. Where after surviving the perils of battle and the chaos of a rabble of soldiers intent on destruction, I was koshed on the head by a shovel-wielding Amazon who mistook my efforts to aid a young lady in distress as something far more sinister. When I awoke, a villain you know rather well crept out of an alley, slit my throat, and delivered me to be buried in a mass grave. It may give you pain to know, the villain in question and the viper who gave birth to him have been shipped off to the West Indies, never to return on threat of arrest and hanging."

An odd expression whisked across his grandmother's face. Had he not known better, he might have believed his speech hurt the old woman. She was Violet Miserington, the Dowager Viscountess Pennyworth. The women in his family did not suffer hurts. They delivered them, wrapped in grace and feigned affection.

"Perhaps you should continue to wear black, my lady," the former governess suggested. If there was a school for governesses, this woman had taken a first in *Refuse to Lose One's Temper No Matter the Provocation.* Taken a first? Hell, she'd taught the class.

"I cannot continue to wear black, Belle," his grandmother said. "My grandson is no longer dead." The fond look she turned on him threatened to take him to his knees. *Where had that come from?*

"That remains to be seen, my lady. The villain's knife failed to take his life, but the Amazon's shovel apparently knocked all sense of propriety and manners out of his rather dense head." Mrs. Winters nodded briefly at the dowager and marched toward the door.

Ben heard something suspiciously like a snort of laughter from the vicinity of his grandmother's chair. He'd be damned if the dowager's completely inappropriate companion had the last word.

"Quitting the field so soon, Mrs. Winters?"

"On the contrary, my lord." She dipped into another shallow curtsey. "I am going in search of a shovel."

Ben stared at the slammed door for some moments

before his grandmother's laughter penetrated the vision of a velvet-clad, grey-eyed Salome handing him his head. Not good. Not good at all. And he had things to discuss with the Dowager Viscountess Pennyworth.

"Before a pair of the Earl of Leistonbury's sturdiest footmen dragged her kicking and screaming onto a boat bound for Port Royal, I asked my mother why she and my brother hated me so."

"Pennyworth, really."

"She informed me the answer was here at Pennyworth Hall, a secret left in your keeping. Would you care to enlighten me?"

Chapter Two

A LADY DOES NOT SLAP A VISCOUNT.

A lady does not kick a viscount's shins, even if his boots are scratched, worn, and badly due a good polish.

A lady does not toss hot tea onto a viscount in spite of his need of a good dunking in a horse trough.

Carpeted galleries made two things impossible. They made it impossible for sensible half-boots to make nearly enough noise no matter how exalted a lady's pique. And they made it impossible for a lady furious enough to spit to know a certain butler traversed the same gallery until he spoke.

"I see you have met his lordship."

Belle jumped in spite of herself. "Marley, must you appear out of nowhere like some solicitous ghost? Or is every man in Pennyworth Hall determined to deprive me of my wits in the same day?"

"I do apologize, my lady." The butler bowed and fell into step beside her. "You were speaking and as I am the only other person in the gallery, I assumed you were speaking to me."

"Was I thinking out loud again?" With the new viscount in the house, she had to curb her tongue. Not one of her strengths, to be sure.

"Not if you did not want to be, my lady. I take it Lady Pennyworth's reunion with her grandson did not go well."

"The man is a rude sneak with the warmth of a Scottish loch and the manners of a herd of sheep."

"A sneak, my lady?"

"He sneaked up behind my chair."

"Lord Pennyworth is rather a large man to be sneaking about a lady's parlor."

"Six foot six if he's an inch." Belle tried to ignore the butler's raised eyebrow. "He moves very quietly for a man of his size."

"Indeed. However, I am still not terribly clear on how or why he—"

"He didn't know I was there." Now she'd done it. She'd have to tell him the whole of it. "I was hiding in one of the late Lord Pennyworth's reading chairs across the room."

"Hiding?" Marley stopped, clasped his hands behind his back, and waited. Expectantly.

"I wanted to take his measure before I met him."

Marley nodded. Slowly. And waited for her to continue, drat the man.

"Lady P wanted to meet him alone, but I... was afraid for her. I had to be certain he wasn't like the other one."

They continued out of the gallery and into the entrance hall. Her boots made a satisfying *clip clip clip* on the stone floor, but her anger had faded. Somewhat. The butler's shoes were silent. Marley could walk across broken glass without making a sound.

"And was he, my lady? Like the other one?" For the first time in a long while, Pennyworth's unshakeable butler looked uncertain. Uncertainty in Marley was akin to absolute terror in any other man.

"He was not. He remained rude and only slightly annoying, even after I nearly swatted him with the complete works of Shakespeare."

"Accidentally?"

"Most decidedly not. After all, he did surprise me."

"Of course." Marley seldom, if ever smiled, but his eyes often did. Belle had to admit the image of Lord Pennyworth's face at the moment of her attempted literary assault merited a smile at least. The man had quick hands for a gentleman. Quick and strong. And as for his face...

"You didn't tell me he looks so much like his brother. Nor did Lady Pennyworth."

"His brother, my lady?"

Belle gave him the look she reserved for rude viscounts, prevaricating boys, and Lady Pennyworth when the dear lady feigned innocence or frailty. It seldom worked on Lady Pennyworth, but it always worked on Marley, poor man.

"Ah, yes, his brother. I take it Lady Pennyworth has told his lordship."

"She has told his lordship precisely nothing, about anyone or anything. She introduced me as Mrs. Winters, her goddaughter and companion."

"Then that is the tale we are to play out, my lady? Fortunately, one of the three is true."

"Apparently so. At least until her ladyship tells us

differently. Which means, you must try and remember I am Mrs. Winters, not my lady."

"I shall endeavor to do so, my... Mrs. Winters."

"As shall I. It will be dashed difficult not to deliver that man the set-down he is certain to earn before this is over."

"We all have our crosses to bear."

"Very amusing, Marley. Actually I rather like being Mrs. Winters. She has far more freedom and is far less civil than—"

"The daughter of a duke?"

"The less said about that the better." Belle often wished she might go the rest of her life without mention of her father.

"As you wish, Mrs. Winters."

They climbed the stairs to the first floor landing. Marley stopped to straighten the lace runner on one of the hall tables. "Pardon my impertinence."

"I do so on a daily basis." Belle teased, but Marley was in implacable earnest. "What is it?" She returned to the butler's side.

Marley squared his shoulders and cleared his throat before he turned to face her. "He wasn't always like this."

"This?"

"In need of a slap, new boots, and a bath." His expression never changed, but his eyes told another story altogether—one of laughter, but also long-remembered sorrow.

"I *was* thinking out loud." Belle blushed and touched her hand to her mouth. The last four years had given her an illusion of peace and freedom. Here in the little world they'd created at Pennyworth Hall, she'd had no need to be anyone other than who she truly was. The arrival of the new viscount changed all that. Men had the most annoying habit of showing up when one least wanted them.

Not that Belle wanted a man. Never. Again. And she wanted this one on his way as quickly as possible. She had a sneaky suspicion she wasn't the only one. Lord Rude and Disreputable had been attacked the moment he entered the estate. And not by village urchins.

"Where are they, Marley?"

"They, Mrs. Winters?"

"Marley." Belle crossed her arms over her chest and fixed the butler with her most *out-with-it* glare.

"As I heard what sounded like the Saracens retaking Jerusalem in the kitchen less than ten minutes past, followed by the thunder of four boys, three dogs, and a goat going up the back stairs, I can only assume *they* are in the nursery wing celebrating their victory with mince pies, marzipan, and God and Cook only knows what else."

"Their victory? You knew."

"His lordship did arrive a bit worse for wear. I suspected." He had the good grace to look chagrined or at least as a chagrined as a stuffy butler with the heart of a small boy could look.

"I can't believe I let Lady Pennyworth talk me into this. It will take a miracle for us to pull this off." Belle blew a lock of hair out of her eyes, picked up her skirts, and started for the back stairs at the end of the corridor.

"Us, Mrs. Winters?"

"You are in this up to your neck, Marley," she tossed

over her shoulder. "Now all I have to do is make certain the rest of our merry band stays hidden and behaves themselves until his lordship leaves."

"We're doomed," the butler muttered.

"I heard that."

Indeed, Belle heard those words every step of the way to Pennyworth's nursery wing. Not every step. She missed a few each time she recalled her first glimpse of Lord Pennyworth's unshaven face, dark eyes, and ridiculously attractive mouth. Attractive, rather until he spoke. She'd learned at an early age to look past how a man looked and to ignore most of what he said. It normally took her no time at all to discover the ilk of a man. Ebenezer Miserington, Viscount Pennyworth, remained a mystery thus far. Belle hated mysteries. Then again, the house she and her charges had called home for the past four years held mysteries up to the rafters. And she was about to add one more.

She stepped around a battalion of tin soldiers strewn down the carpet runners and shook her head at the muddle of coats, hats, and soggy mittens on the wooden settle next to the door which led down the back staircase to the kitchens. A hoot of laughter followed by a crash and more laughter led her to the sitting room at the end of the corridor. How could she tell them after four years living the lives they were born to they must hide once more, must become someone's secret, even if only for a little while? Belle put her hand on the latch, sighed, and opened the door.

Four guilty, grubby faces peered up at her from the

remains of a feast spilled across several plaids spread before the hearth.

"That's torn it, lads. She knows." Frederick swiped his jam-stained mouth with his sleeve and scrambled to his feet. Peter, Martin, and Robert followed suit. At least they remembered some of the manners she'd tried to teach them.

"Your mother always knows," Peter groused. "Her spies are everywhere."

Belle's heart still leapt every time anyone owned her as Frederick's mother. She might ask the boys to keep their secrets until Lord Pennyworth left, but she refused to ask Frederick to lie ever again.

"Indeed they are, Master Cratchitt." Belle retrieved a plate of half-eaten marzipans from the carpet and placed it on a stubby-legged tea table. The brown and white spaniel which had been about to eat it gave her a sniff and removed himself to the settee before the window. "However, I much prefer to hear this daring tale from the four of you."

Ten minutes later, having been regaled with the most ridiculously heroic and noisy account of Lord Pennyworth's welcome to his ancestral home, Belle collapsed into a plump chintz-covered chair before the fire and tried very hard not to laugh. Little wonder the poor man had behaved so rudely.

From what she discerned from the cacophony of four very excited boys, punctuated by much hand-waving, dog-barking, and an occasional goat bleat— Viscount Pennyworth, formerly Colonel Miserington of His Majesty's cavalry and survivor of Waterloo, had been unseated from his horse by a snowball with a potato at its center. What happened after that might well have put a saint in a foul temper. Belle gathered the little bit of indignation she held on Lord Pennyworth's behalf.

"That was very badly done of you, boys." She made a point to gaze into each of their faces in turn. "His lordship is master of this house now."

"We only meant to do some recon… recom… We only meant to take a look at the enemy," nine-year-old Martin declared. "Like Wellington did to Napoleon." Born a dwarf, he'd been shipped off at the age of two to the *school* where she'd found the boys. She had no doubt he and his canine companions had been responsible for the rope across the drive. The spaniel and two hounds lived to serve their diminutive master, and he'd trained them entirely too well.

"Reconnaissance is the word, Martin, dear." Belle retrieved a serviette from an empty plate atop the plaids and motioned the boy to her. Once she'd wiped his face, he climbed into her lap with a grin.

"That's the one, my lady. That's what we were doing."

"Yes, well, reconnaissance means you watch." She put her arm around Martin as the other three settled onto the plaids at her feet. "You don't actually go after him with snowballs."

"Snow-potatoes, my lady," Robert piped up. "You have much better distance if the snowball has a potato in the middle."

"Robbie's the one who knocked him off his horse," Frederick said and patted the younger boy on the back.

"He listened for the horse's bridle and hoof beats."

Belle imagined what his lordship might say should he discover he'd been unhorsed by an eight-year-old blind boy who got around with the aid of a goat with the unlikely name of Mrs. Nelson. The trick was for him never to know—about the boys or anything else. Lady Pennyworth had made it all quite clear when she introduced him to Belle.

"We have to leave." Frederick's remark caught her off guard. Even at ten years of age, her son had an uncanny ability to read people's faces, especially hers. It made her hate what she had to tell them all the more.

"We shouldn't have tripped him." Martin plucked at the ribbon on Belle's sleeve.

"Or hit him with snow-potatoes," Robert added and reached over to pat the goat which seldom left his side.

"It was my idea," Peter confessed. "I'll go, and perhaps he'll let the rest of you stay."

"All or none, right, Mother?" Frederick looked and behaved so much like her brother, Alexander. She hoped they might meet one day, but for now, she had other battles to win.

"No one is going anywhere. I want you all to listen very carefully." She took a deep breath. "Lady Pennyworth and I are going to do a bit more reconnaissance before we tell his lordship about you."

"We could help you," Martin offered.

"You are going to help, but in a different way." She took in their eager, hopeful faces. She and Lady P were doing this to keep the boys safe. They'd planned for every sort of difficulty to come their way. It didn't make it any easier to explain.

"We want you to stay up here in the nursery wing until his lordship has settled in and we find out how long he intends to stay. He has another house in London and a smaller estate in Cheshire. He may go to visit those in a fortnight or so." She sent up a short prayer for him to do so. "You mustn't venture into any other part of the house until we tell you. And you must try and be as quiet as possible."

"Is he like the other one?" Robert asked.

"I don't think so, Robbie, but Lady Pennyworth and I want to be certain. Once we are, we will tell him, and I know he will be pleased to meet all of you."

"What about Christmas?" Peter had been at the *school* the longest. Before he and the other boys had come with her and Frederick to live at Pennyworth, he'd never had a real Christmas.

"Christmas is weeks away, Peter." She pushed his blond curls out of his eyes. He often shied away from any hint of affection. Not today. "Lord Pennyworth may be gone well before that. We'll have this sorted out by then. I promise."

"What about Mrs. Nelson?" Martin asked. "And the dogs?"

"Thomas can take them to the necessary." Frederick stood and put his hand on the back of Belle's chair. "And he can bring us books from the library. Right, Mother?"

"I dare say he will be more than happy to do so." Belle knew Pennyworth's youngest footman to be the boys' staunchest ally. She suspected he'd been cajoled into secreting the potatoes out of the kitchen for this morning's reconnaissance attack. "And Cook will send your very favorite dishes up on trays for every meal. No sitting up straight and making polite conversation at table with Lady Pennyworth and myself."

"Huzzah!" Peter, Robert, and Martin shouted. The dogs barked and even Mrs. Nelson bleated in agreement.

"It will be fine, Mother," Frederick assured her. "We know what to do." He retrieved a book about the Peloponnesian Wars from the mantel, flopped onto the plaids before the fire, and opened it to a page of maps. The others began to describe the maps to Robert. With the inconstant attention of all small boys, they had moved on to something of greater importance than visiting viscounts and dowagers with secrets.

Belle mustered a smile. They did know what to do. Mores the pity. They'd done it before, many times. They'd lived half their young lives invisible. Until she'd found them and brought them here. Now they'd have to be invisible again. At least until she knew who Lord Pennyworth truly was. Perhaps she needed to borrow that book. Battle plans might well come in handy in dealing with a man like the new master of Pennyworth Hall.

She'd changed the rooms. Ben remembered more and more about Pennyworth Hall every moment. His grandfather's chambers—the viscount's chambers—had always been decorated in vicious shades of red and gold. They'd been done over in ivory and blue. Recently. He liked blue. He always had. Had the dowager viscountess remembered?

"When were these rooms made over, Marley?" Ben pulled his banyan more tightly around him and dropped into a vastly comfortable chair before the fire. A hot bath, a shave, and two trays of Cook's food had improved his mood greatly. He still knew nothing of the secret his grandmother kept and even less of her lovely but prickly companion.

"Almost as soon as Captain Delacroix came to tell us you were alive." Marley closed the door behind the footmen who'd come to remove the tub and the remains of Ben's supper.

"He didn't bring his wife, did he?"

The butler closed the heavy blue velvet bed hangings on the far side of the massive mahogany bed. "No, my lord. He came alone and did not stay long. He was anxious to return to his wife and daughter. Did you wish him to bring his wife?"

"Absolutely not. I would fear for my safety had Mrs. Delacroix met Mrs. Winters." At Marley's puzzled expression Ben managed a half-grin. "I would not have wished Mrs. Delacroix to give my grandmother's companion any ideas about the many uses of a shovel."

Marley's eyes widened. "She was the one who—"

"Indeed. I see Delacroix told Lady Pennyworth the whole of it."

"He did not identify the lady by name." The butler busied himself gathering Ben's soiled clothes. He was too well-trained a servant to laugh, so Ben did it for him.

"Mrs. Delacroix and I have made our peace. The estate books look well enough, Marley. Is there anything which needs my immediate attention?" He'd spent the afternoon and most of the evening in his grandfather's study going over estate business and prowling through his grandmother's household accounts. She'd foisted his questions about family secrets off with a sudden attack of faintness. The maid, Fan, had shoo'ed him out of the parlor like a swabbing deckhand. He'd countered by dining in his chambers. Any insult he'd given Cook had been mollified by the second tray of food he'd asked for and devoured. And he needed more time before he faced Lady Pennyworth and the enigmatic Mrs. Winters. Those two were up to something. Of that, he had no doubt.

"There are the plans for Christmas, my lord, but they can wait until you are better settled."

Ben heard a creak and faint scratches from the darkened corner where a bookcase and inlaid chess table stood. *Devil take it.* Some sort of small shadow appeared to move across the floor and disappear under the bed.

"What did you say, Marley?"

"Christmas, my lord. They will want to go over the plans with you, but it can wait."

"It can wait until Judgment. There will be no Christmas here so long as I am master." A metallic clang came from the direction of his dressing room. "Did you hear a bell?"

"No, my lord, I did not." Marley followed Ben's gaze. "I beg your pardon, my lord. Did you say no Christmas?"

"I did, and I will not discuss it further." Ben got up and stalked across the room to throw open his dressing room door. Nothing.

"They will be sorely disappointed, my lord."

"They?" He lifted the bed skirt and checked under

the bed. Now he heard voices from somewhere behind the large Turner seascape hanging between the bookcase and the dressing room door. How hard had that snow-potato hit him?

"Her ladyship and Mrs. Winters."

"Her ladyship and Mrs. Winters what, man? What are you talking about?" Brandy. He needed brandy. There was a full glass on the other side of the bed.

"They will be disappointed not to celebrate Christmas." Marley sounded as if he were talking to a child. Or an idiot adult. Either way Ben intended to end this conversation and go to bed.

"My grandmother and Mrs. Winters, in fact everyone in this house, will need to learn this sooner rather than later, Marley. I lead a very organized and disciplined life. It kept me sane in the navy and kept me alive against the French, the Spanish, and most of my relations. I don't like chaos, and I find sentiment and frivolity a waste of time. Christmas is a frivolous waste of time and money. It is for women and children. I have neither wife nor children. The women in this house may do what they wish in private. I want no part of it."

Ben was tired. It came over him like an itchy horse blanket. He had little experience explaining his decisions. In fact, he hated explaining. He caught sight of himself in the mirror over the mantel. A wild-eyed man with a touch of anger and confusion in his eyes looked back. For a moment, it was as if there were someone else in the mirror, but when he touched the smooth surface, it was his own face looking back.

"It was a mistake for me to come here. I believed this

house was haunted when I was a child. Perhaps I was right." He turned away from the mirror.

"I don't believe houses are haunted, my lord. People are. If you insist on surrounding yourself with ghosts, you will chase the living away." He reached for the glass of brandy on the bedside table.

Ben beat him to it and cradled the glass in his hand as he walked back to the fireplace. "Perhaps that is my intention."

"The road to Hell, Lord Pennyworth." He cleared away the last of Ben's shaving accoutrements and retrieved a silver salver from the blanket chest.

"I've been to Hell, Marley." Ben knocked back the last of the brandy and set the glass on the tray the butler offered. "They called it my childhood. Didn't like it much."

"One wonders then, why you insist on revisiting it."

Twenty years. He'd not seen his grandmother's butler in twenty years, and the man still caught him out as if he were a small boy stealing mince pies and lying about it. *Dammit.* He searched his brandy-fogged mind for the hard-hearted colonel he'd worked so hard to become.

"Doesn't signify, Marley. There will be no celebration of Christmas in this house. Not this year or any other year."

"Very well, my lord." A servant as well-trained as Marley might keep the desire to question the master of the house from his face, from his body, from his voice and his demeanor. Only a saint kept it hidden from his eyes. Marley was no saint. And Ben wanted someone, just one person, to understand.

"You were there, Marley. You know why."

"It was a long time ago."

"It was Christmas Day, and I was ten years old."

"Yes, my lord."

"You were there the night before, and you saw what happened. You know what I did."

"I was there." His answers were so careful. Fulsomely economical. And Ben hadn't the courage to ask what the butler remembered about that Christmas Eve. Ben only remembered it in flashes and what he'd been told. All he remembered clearly was the next morning.

"You knew where they were sending me. You knew I was for the navy, a boy of ten."

"Yes, my lord."

"You gave me mince pies and ginger biscuits. You told me to keep my head down, my mouth shut, and to pay attention."

"Is that all you remember, my lord?"

"I don't know. My memory of that time... before the navy is not clear."

Marley gathered the tangle of cloths from the washstand by the door. He did not turn around.

"My mother said there is a secret in this house. Something she took great pleasure in keeping from me. Do you know anything about that, Marley?"

"Your mother kept a great many things from you, my lord," he said, still facing the door. "This house keeps many secrets, but none of them are mine to tell. Good night, Lord Pennyworth."

"Marley?"

"Yes, my lord?"

"I did what you said. In the navy. It helped."

"I'm glad, my lord." The door *snicked* quietly behind him.

Ben snuffed out the candles and climbed into bed. His body ached from the long journey, but he'd never sleep now. He rolled over and pushed at one of the many officiously useless pillows. It pushed back. It hissed. He pushed it again. It let loose a horrendous yowl.

Several things happened at once. Ben leapt from the bed and let fly every swear word he'd learned, as well as some he'd long forgotten. He fumbled around for a candle and lit it from the banked embers in the hearth. The hissing creature careened off the bed and shot onto the washstand, knocking the basin and pitcher to the floor.

A clanking bell and a witch's brew of voices beat against the wall under the Turner. An annoyance of a memory clicked into place. Ben stalked to the wall and began to push on the wainscoting. One of the panels popped open with a click. A boy of nine or ten years tumbled onto Ben's bare feet. He took one look at Ben, screamed like a banshee, and scarpered out the door into the corridor.

Ben started after him, but was spun around by the escapes of three more boys, some dogs, and a damned goat wearing a nightcap. Once he'd dashed into the corridor, he managed to slip between the motley crew and the back stairs which forced them all to run toward the wide staircase leading to the first floor. They pounded down the thick gold Aubusson with Ben in pursuit.

"Stop, you little—holy hell!" The largest and ugliest

specimen of a cat he had ever seen streaked out of Ben's bedchamber and latched onto his bare leg. Ben grabbed it by the scruff of the neck and dragged it free of his flesh. It blinked at him from its one eye and attempted to bat him with its paws.

"You let go of him, you—" The yellow-haired boy from this morning proceeded to cast dispersions on Ben's mother, not that Ben minded, and on the legitimacy of his birth, which he actually did mind. But that wasn't what made him drop the cat.

Somewhere in the distance, he heard doors slamming and adults running. The boys still shouted. The dogs barked. The goat bleated. It all sounded far away. At the top of the stairs, a boy stood stiff as a board, his eyes glassy, his jaw tight. A boy with Mrs. Winters hair and eyes. He began to shake. Violently.

The vast house, the entire world, shrank down until there was only Ben and this boy, his body wracked with tremors so powerful they caused his eyes to roll back in his head. For a moment, they were one and the same. This boy—the ghost of Ben's worst childhood nightmares come to life.

"Frederick!"

A piercing, feminine scream shot down the corridor behind him. The boy began to tilt backward. Ben ran forward to catch him, lost his footing, and wrapped his body around the child as they both catapulted down the stairs.

Chapter Three

HANDS HELD HIM TO THE BED. Ben fought them. Their voices buzzed and hummed—the words out of reach. He'd had a fit. No. Not him. Someone else. Why were they holding him? He didn't have fits. Not anymore. *Unhand me. Unhand me.*

"Let me go!"

He shot off the pillows and punched in all directions. From the sound of bodies hitting the floor, a few grunts, and one less than polite curse, he'd landed more than one of those blows. The room faded and rushed back to clarity several times. He closed his eyes, drew in a long breath through his nose, and opened his eyes once more. Better.

"Marley, send for the physician at once."

Grandmama. Ben sought a face to put with the voice. White hot pain cudgeled the back of his head. *Damn!* He'd moved too quickly.

"No physician." He touched the tender spot behind his right ear and another at the base of his skull.

"You took a terrible fall, Pennyworth." His grandmother came into the light around his bed. Branches of candles stood sentry on every flat surface within sight. She looked pale and feeble under their insistent illumination. "You've been insensible for nigh on half the hour."

"No physician. Not in this house." His chamber teemed with people. "Marley, send them away. I'm not some cornered beast. I won't attack anyone."

His head hadn't stopped spinning, but it had gone from a ship's wheel in a maelstrom to a hoop spun by a weary child. Devil of it was he saw their faces—his servants. Footmen and maids, Cook and Marley—not afraid. Their feelings were hurt. By what right? He was master of this house—not his grandfather, nor his father, nor his mother. It smacked of his nightmares. This had all happened before, but he hadn't been carried to the viscount's rooms then. He'd been dragged to the nursery and tied to the bed.

The boy. There'd been a boy... having a fit. Other boys too, but only one like him. Only one who suffered his infirmity. They'd fallen down the stairs together.

"Where is he?" Ben pushed himself upright against the thick carved headboard. He winced. His grandmother bustled between the still gawking servants, a thick bolster clutched in each fist. She slapped his hands away and shoved the heretofore useless fripperies behind him—one to comfort his back, the other to cushion his drumming pate. Someone had removed his banyan. Under the layers of crisp, new bedclothes, Ben wore only his smalls and, from what he could see, an assortment of new bruises blooming across his bare chest. A colorful addition to his scars.

"Where is who, my lord?" Marley waved the servants

toward the door.

"You must rest, Pennyworth. We can sort this out in the morning."

"No, Grandmama, we will sort it out tonight. Is he hurt? The boy, is he injured?"

"He is unharmed, my lord." Marley spoke a few words to one of the footmen, who hurried out the door ahead of the others. To another, he motioned to the hearth, and the man set about building up the fire. "You shielded him from harm with your body. Not a scratch on him." Many of the servants nodded in agreement and whispered as they finally left his bedchamber.

Ben spotted a short, round woman with grey hair tucked under a frilly, white cap slowly making her way out of the room. She held a tray laden with a clay pitcher and a matching mug. Steam rose from both in a vaguely familiar cloud of sweetness and spice.

"Mrs. Fezziwig?"

Pennyworth's cherub-faced housekeeper turned quickly for a woman of her size and years. "The very same, my lord. 'Tis sorry I am I wasn't there to greet you when you arrived this morning. I'll just be removing myself now."

"If that is your hot milk and honey tonic, Mrs. F, you'll show me a little mercy and leave it right here." Ben patted the bedside table.

"Clever boy," his grandmother murmured and stepped aside to allow the housekeeper her moment of triumph.

Ben took the mug from the tray and rolled it between his hands. He inhaled the aroma of fresh honey, cinnamon, and a meld of other ingredients. "I remember this," he mused and savored a long draught. It was not as he remembered. It was better. One flavor was missing and the brew was the better for it. What was it?

"And well you should." Mrs. Fezziwig *tsk'ed* and clucked at every old wound and new mark. With martial tenderness she tucked the covers around him, much to his bemusement. "It always helped." She gave the blue bedclothes one last pat and toddled proudly into the corridor to no doubt extol the healing powers of her tonic. The last footman put the guard before the fire, bowed, and closed the door as he withdrew.

Ben studied the butler and the dowager vicountess over the rim of the mug in his hands. "The boy is Mrs. Winters's son."

"He is." His grandmother had begun to mimic Marley. Short answers with only a modicum of information.

"And he suffers from the falling sickness." God he despised those words.

"He does." Lady Pennyworth wasn't going to divulge a syllable more than necessary. Time to cut past the pretty. If he was to be named an arse, he'd be the arse in command.

"Send for Mrs. Winters. I want to assure myself the boy is well." Ben refilled his mug from the pitcher.

"He is perfectly fine, Pennyworth, but he needs his mother."

"Why? I never had mine." His grandmother looked away. "Send for her. I won't keep her long."

"She should be here momentarily, my lord." Now it

was Marley's turn to look away. Ben didn't blame him. Lady Pennyworth delivered looks of betrayal with a rifleman's precision.

"It is late, madam. I suggest you retire. I am in good hands."

"Pennyworth—"

"Good night, my lady." Ben's head ached. His body ached. He'd been home less than a day and his search for one secret had turned into a search for many. His patience spread like too little butter on too much bread. He had just enough endurance to discover one thing about Mrs. Winters. Not enough to deal with his grandmother whilst doing so.

She drew her lips into a solemn line. "As you wish, Pennyworth." Shaky, dry fingers touched the thick scar on his throat. "It will take more than a fall down the stairs to take him away from us, Marley."

"Indeed, my lady."

Ben closed his eyes and continued to sip Mrs. Fezziwig's concoction. Now to deal with Mrs. Winters.

Belle marched down the stairs and entered the third floor corridor without slamming the door. His lordship's summons dragged her away from Frederick. The man's quick thinking and disregard for his own safety, however, had probably saved her son's life. Lord Rude and Annoying Pennyworth had an irritating competence when it came to landing her in a state of confusion.

He'd supposedly sent for her to inquire after Frederick's health. With the boys' invasion of his bedchamber and Frederick's seizure, Lord Pennyworth wanted more than a simple answer as to how her son faired. He'd earned the truth, but the truth occupied many chambers in this house, and she'd given her word to keep some of those chambers closed to him. The boys had remained a secret for less than a day. It did not bode well.

With Christmas on the way, Belle had held not even the smallest hope of keeping them hidden from him. A few more days might have provided a better introduction. Or at least a less injurious one. The viscount's chances of surviving more of the boys' efforts at reconnaissance with all of his limbs intact grew dimmer by the moment. Thank God he'd spent time in the navy and the cavalry. A lesser man would be dead by now.

She tightened the belt of her dressing gown, threw the long braid of her hair over her shoulder, and knocked on the viscount's chamber door.

"Come."

Belle pushed open the door. She'd helped Lady Pennyworth decorate these rooms. In the light of day, the elegant colors and dark woods leant an air of nobility to the bedchamber. The glow of more than a dozen candles gave the room a subtle decadence. Or perhaps it was the broad-shouldered, bare-chested man sitting up in the spacious bed like some Turkish potentate.

"You sent for me, my lord?" She delivered an exaggerated curtsey.

"That will be all, Marley." He addressed the butler, but his dark eyes were fixed on Belle.

"Are you certain, my lord?" The man glanced from

Belle to Lord Pennyworth and back.

Lord Pennyworth handed Marley a mug and pulled the bedclothes over his chest. "Thanks to those bloodthirsty creatures my grandmother calls boys, I am in no condition to ravish Mrs. Winters. She has nothing to fear from me. Unless you have come bearing a shovel, madam?"

"I did not have time to locate one, my lord. Yet." She crossed the room as Marley made his way to the door.

"Well played," the staid retainer murmured as he slipped into the corridor. She did not have to look to know he'd left the door open behind him.

"Little wonder. Hiding four boys such as those from the master of the house must leave you little time to go in search of garden implements." He indicated the chair next to his bed.

"Four boys such as what, my lord?" She stood at his bedside, hands folded at her waist.

"Heathenish, undisciplined, disobedient, and too clever by half." He tilted his head and flinched in pain for his trouble. "What did you think I meant? Sit down, Mrs. Winters. You strike me as capable of raising your hackles, even in a seated position."

She perched on the front of the chair, her spine straight and her hands still clenched tightly together. "They are not as other boys. I am certain you have noticed, even in your short acquaintance with them."

"I hardly call two unprovoked attacks an acquaintance."

"Two, my lord?"

"Too brown, Mrs. Winters. I recognized the guinea-gold haired one from this morning. And the little one must be perpetually cold. He wore the same red coat."

"Martin is a dwarf."

"I have no need of their names." His jaw tightened. His gaze flattened to two black mirrors of endless nothing.

"The blond-haired boy is Peter." She deliberately ignored him. "He is asthmatic. Robert is blind." She watched his expression, intent on discerning his thoughts. Most people made their opinions of such "infirmities" clear in an instant. Lord Pennyworth showed no reaction at all.

"The lad gets on, blind or not."

Why did he stare at her so... boldly? What did he hope to see? "Mrs. Nelson guides him."

"Mrs. Nelson?"

"The goat."

"Of course. Blind, a dwarf, an asthmatic, and your son has the falling sickness." A matter-of-fact recitation with the barest hint of reticence on the last.

"Lady Pennyworth told you."

"That he was your son? No. He looks very like you. His infirmity, I saw for myself."

"It isn't an infirmity. He has seizures. Usually when he is upset or excited. It is nothing. It does not hinder him in any way."

"And what do you do to him? When he has these seizures."

What an odd question.

"There is nothing to do. I see to his comfort until it passes. The other boys are accustomed to looking after him until I can be fetched. It is not a plague. It cannot be passed from one person to another." She did not want to explain. She did not want to defend her child for something not his fault. It simply—

"Mrs. Winters."

Her breath caught. Heat and strength covered her hands, pried them apart. His hand was rough, powerful, and entirely too comforting.

"Your son, he is well? He suffered no harm?" His voice, still hard as iron, worked its way through the gates she'd hung around her fears and defense of her son.

"He was awake by the time the footman, Thomas, carried him to his room. He didn't remember what happened, but the others told him."

"With great relish, no doubt." The promise of a smile creased one corner of his mouth. *Why did his mouth draw her so?* The smile faded the moment she noticed it.

"Indeed. You were made quite the hero." She drew her hands from his. "You saved his life, my lord."

"Purely an act of self-preservation on my part. Between the other boys, the goat, the cat, the dogs, and you, armed with either a shovel or Shakespeare, if anything had happened to him, my punishment was sure to be a horrible death." This time he did smile, but his face was drawn. She'd nearly forgotten how dangerous the fall down those stairs was for him as well.

"Did Mrs. Fezziwig leave some willow bark tea in addition to her milk and honey potion?"

Lord Pennyworth waved toward the mantel. Belle fetched the cup of now cold willow bark tea and held it to his lips. He touched his fingers to the back of hers to steady the cup and watched her as he drained its contents.

"I will leave you to sleep, my lord." She placed the empty cup on the bedside table. He followed her every move. Time to get out of this room. "Thank you again. The boys are all very sorry for their behavior. Good night, my lord." She gave him a sincere curtsey and nearly sprinted for the door.

"Mrs. Winters?"

Drat! "Yes, my lord?"

"Has your son ever attacked anyone?"

Belle turned slowly to face him. "I beg your pardon?"

"In the throes of one of his fits. Has he ever attacked anyone, done them harm?"

"No, my lord. Never." She dared not look away, so curious was the look on his face, so incomprehensible. "Is there anything else, Lord Pennyworth?"

"Yes. I will give you and Lady Pennyworth tonight to concoct whatever story you wish me to believe, but at breakfast tomorrow, I expect to discover how and why those boys are in residence here and how quickly you two ladies intend to get them out of my house." He flung the covers to his waist, rolled onto his side—revealing a long, lean expanse of muscled scarred back—and pulled a pillow beneath his head. "Good night, Mrs. Winters. Close the door behind you."

Chapter Four

NOT IN THEIR ROOMS. Not in the schoolroom or their little parlor. After a sleepless night and the briefest of morning toilets, Belle had hurried down the corridor to see after Frederick and the other boys. That they were well enough to rise, dress, and abandon the safety of the nursery floor allayed her fears. For the moment. Until she remembered how much chaos ensued when these particular boys were left to their own devices. She hurried down the stairs to the first floor.

What are they about now? Lord Pennyworth will have them strung up by their toes if he finds them, horrible man.

"To be precise, Mrs. Winters, he has them washing dishes in the kitchens. He may, however, reserve the right to string them up by their toes later."

"Marley!" Belle clutched the ornate carved balustrade and aimed a daggered look over her shoulder. "Must you sneak up on me? What? He has them where?" She took the last few stairs at an unladylike run and headed toward the back of the house.

"You were speaking, Mrs. Winters." Marley kept his normal, sedate pace and still managed to catch up with Belle before she reached the double doors that led to the kitchens. Doors which the butler now stayed her from entering.

"I intend to speak even more. Let me pass, Marley." Viscount or no, Lord Pennyworth had gone too far.

"I am afraid I cannot, my lady. His lordship asks you to join him and Lady Pennyworth for breakfast as soon as you are up and about."

"He asks?" Belle narrowed her eyes and crossed her arms over her chest. To her surprise, Marley remained unmoved. Dear lord, he'd decamped to the viscount's side, the… the… worm.

"He does. He and her ladyship are in the breakfast parlor." Didn't move an inch.

Belle had no choice. Boyish laughter from the direction of the kitchens made her decision for her. A little dish scrubbing promised little harm to the boys. It might, however, prove hazardous to Lord Rude and Arrogant's health. With a last glare at Marley, she retraced her steps, stopped before the breakfast parlor doors, took a deep breath, and glided serenely into the room.

Only to discover a vaguely familiar scene. Several footmen dashed about in obvious panic. A plate of eggs lay tipped out across the pristine Irish linen tablecloth. Eggs with a large black spot buried in the center of them. A beautiful Limoges coffee cup with a swallow of coffee and a slimy substance mixed in had been tossed onto the carpet. One footman appeared to be emptying the coffee urn out the window. Another ran in with a pitcher of water.

Amidst it all, sat her dear godmother, Lady

Pennyworth, who seemed to be in a great deal of pain were it not for the laughter in her eyes and the handkerchief over her mouth. Belle bit her lip to keep from joining the dowager in peals of laughter. They'd seen this same tactic before, several months prior to the news of Lord Pennyworth's return from the dead. The gentleman in that instance fled the house that morning along with his horror of a mother. Those two were now, according to his lordship, on their way to Port Royal.

At the head of the table, quaffing water directly from the pitcher, her tormenter might well be considering a similar retreat. Their eyes met across the table, and her hopes were dashed. This man did not retreat. He slammed the pitcher down. A footman immediately filled a wine glass with more water and placed it at his master's elbow.

"Out." Lord Pennyworth snapped. "All of you. Out." He followed the footmen's hasty withdrawal with a studied gaze until the last one, having cleaned up the mess, started for the door leading down to the kitchens. "Except you."

The poor man froze.

"Thomas, is it not?"

"Y-yes, my lord."

"Have Mrs. Winters's charges had their breakfast yet?"

"No, my lord. You said not until they finished the dishes to Cook's satisfaction."

"Lord Pennyworth," Belle started toward him. "You have no right—"

The man raised one finger and pointed to the chair

across from his grandmother. "Sit, Mrs. Winters, if you please." He turned back to the footman. "Have Cook send me their breakfast, all of it, and a tankard of Mrs. Fezziwig's best ale."

"You cannot refuse them breakfast, Pennyworth." His grandmother still looked ready to burst into laughter but had recovered some of her normal stern, no-nonsense demeanor.

"If you insist, madam. Thomas, out of deference to her ladyship, they are each to be given one slice of bread with butter and a glass of water for breakfast. Mrs.Winters, do sit down. The toast is unpoisoned, unless my grandmother has powers of which I am unaware. And the bacon is done to perfection." Lord Pennyworth tore a strip off with his teeth and watched her as he chewed.

Thomas hurried around the table to hold her chair. Belle dropped into it. Poor Thomas rushed to the sideboard and filled her plate with mounds of bacon and toast.

"Thank you, Thomas." Belle smiled at the footman only to glare her fury at Lord Pennyworth the minute the footman attempted to escape the room.

"Yes, thank you, Thomas. One more thing." The viscount slathered his toast with strawberry jam.

Thomas stopped, mid-step, a trapped hare in silk knee britches and white stockings. "Yes, my lord?"

"When they have completed their task to Cook's satisfaction, you are to take the boys to the schoolroom until I send Mrs. Winters to them. I don't have a brig. A schoolroom will have to do. If they get into any mischief, it will fall on your head. Understood?"

"Yes, my lord." It might have been her imagination, but Belle thought she heard an agonized *I'm doomed* once the footman was on the other side of the door.

"Where did you acquire them?" The viscount tore off another strip of bacon.

"Acquire what, my lord?" Belle cut her toast into dainty squares. The senior footman backed into the room with a tray laden with platters of eggs, sausages, and Scottish oat cakes—the boys' favorites.

The viscount sat back in his chair, elbows on the arms and fingers steepled beneath his chin, as the footman placed all of the platters and a large tankard of ale before him. The footman scurried out, tray in hand. "I am old enough to know how you acquired your son, Mrs. Winters."

"Pennyworth, please." The dowager refreshed her cup of tea and gave Belle a meaningful look. So, they were still to keep much of the truth from him. Doomed indeed.

"Where did you acquire his diabolical associates and how long have they made their lair at Pennyworth Hall?" He helped himself to the platter of eggs, carefully running his fork through them in an apparent search for more of the pepper with which his last eggs had been dosed. Black pepper was a staple in the boys' mischievous repertoire.

"They came from the Kielder School for the Infirm, my lord." Belle pushed her plate away. "When the school closed, Frederick, the other boys, and I had nowhere to go. Lady Pennyworth graciously took us in four years ago this Christmas."

He swallowed and lowered his cutlery to the table.

"Kielder? In Northumberland?"

"The same." She remembered the bitter cold and the tumble-down manor house where she'd found her son, six years old and determined not to leave his friends. She'd made them all a promise the night they'd stolen down the weed-covered drive and trudged five miles to a coaching inn. They were never going back, and they would never be parted, any of them, ever again. A bold promise for a woman with no money and no desire to drag the only relations she loved into her troubles. Lady Pennyworth had the virtue of being her godmother, not a blood relation, and no one dared question her use of Pennyworth Hall, until the viscount arrived.

"Took a great tenacity of life to survive so desolate a place—yours and theirs." His tone spoke of desolate places of his own. She'd noticed last night—the scars from bullets, sabers and the thin white line across his throat. His color was better this morning, though his jaw and forehead tightened every so often in acknowledgment of the beating his body, especially his head, had taken.

"They have thrived here, my lord. They are good boys. So close to Christmas, one can hardly expect them to leave mischief completely alone." She almost asked if he'd participated in any escapades or high spirits as a boy. What little she knew of his childhood from Lady Pennyworth stopped her.

"All the more reason for me to forbid anything to do with Christmas, Mrs. Winters." He attacked the platter of sausages.

"You cannot forbid Christmas, Pennyworth." His

grandmother shared a horrified look with Belle. "They have been preparing for it for weeks."

"I am the head of this family and master of this house. I may do as I please." He took up another piece of toast. "As I do not intend to celebrate Christmas and it is my fondest wish to have them out of this house as soon as possible, perhaps Mrs. Winters should return the other boys to their families."

"They—" Belle started.

"They have no families, Pennyworth." The dowager tapped her finger on the table. Belle fell silent. "They have nowhere to go. Whatever your feelings about the season, it is not the time to throw children out into the cold. Would you have them sleep in some farmer's stable?"

"I have my reasons for ignoring Christmas, madam, as well you know. And those boys are as close to the Christ child as a Covent Garden doxie is to Mrs. Winters."

"Ebenezer Arthur Aurelius Miserington, I am ashamed of you. Apologize at once." The dowager stood and pushed back her chair in an effort to lord over her grandson.

To Belle's surprise, he rose, dropped his serviette on the table, and bowed to each of them in turn. "I do apologize, ladies. Having my eggs dosed with pepper and my coffee flavored with frogs' eggs tends to make me forget my manners." He settled back into his chair. "You've always been ashamed of me, Grandmama. Why should twenty years make any difference?"

"The children stay, or Mrs. Winters and I will go with them."

Not your best argument. Belle refrained from speaking her thoughts aloud this time. She had to smile, however, when she saw Lord Pennyworth's face. For a brief moment, they knew the camaraderie born of having the same thought at the same time. He might be human after all.

"So long as I do not see or hear even a whisper of Christmas, small boys, or their animal companions, and I am left to occupy my house in peace, they may stay until Twelfth Night. After which, you will make other arrangements."

Mrs. Nelson had more humanity than Viscount Pennyworth. Belle opened her mouth to speak.

Her godmother shook her head. "Thank you, Pennyworth." She walked to the door. "I am certain we can come to some sort of arrangement by then."

"I might be persuaded to allow them to stay longer if you would discuss the secret my mother mentioned." He tossed the offer out with a mild disinterest. Belle refused to look at either of them. It was not her secret to tell. The fact it was hers to keep only made her position more difficult.

His face of sharp angles and hardened features, those fathomless eyes, the overlong dark hair, and the powerful scarred body that had caused her to lose no little sleep last night all told her far more than she cared to know about the adversary she and the dowager viscountess were pitched against. A man with scars was either reckless or dangerous. Reckless men, like her brother, led battles. Dangerous men, like Lord Pennyworth, won wars and conquered everything in their path in doing so.

"Come to me when you and his lordship have finished, dear."

What? Where was the dowager going? Finished what? Belle stared at the closed door and willed her godmother to return.

"Mrs. Winters, would you care for some coffee?" Lord Pennyworth poured himself a cup from the urn which had reappeared on the sideboard whilst she'd stood and gawked at the closed parlor door like an imbecile.

"No, thank you," she said absently." I don't care for frogs' eggs."

An odd sound emanated from the head of the table. He'd chuckled. The man had actually chuckled. Oh dear. What had she said?

"I didn't mean to make light. I mean... What is this?" She picked up two pieces of paper he'd apparently placed next to her plate.

"A schedule and a list of rules, Mrs. Winters." He wandered over to the window which looked over the now dormant rose gardens. The cheery yellow and green decor of the intimate breakfast parlor made him appear all the more intimidating. He leaned his hip on the wide windowsill and crossed one booted leg over the other. Someone, probably Marley, had shined his boots.

Stop looking at his legs and look at this supposed schedule, foolish woman.

Belle glanced up to make certain she had not spoken out loud. She read over the schedule. Then she turned her attention to the rules. She read the schedule once more.

"This is without a doubt the most ridiculous rot I have ever read. These are young boys, Lord Pennyworth, not foot soldiers under some despotic general."

"Colonel, actually. I was Colonel Miserington before my grandfather stuck his spoon in the wall." He placed the now empty cup next to an arrangement of hothouse flowers on the pink marble pedestal next to the window. "The boys lack discipline. A more regimented life will do them good and keep them out of trouble. Their lives will be hard enough, being what they are. You do them no good by coddling them."

"Being what they are?" *A lady does not speak between gritted teeth.* Then again most ladies are not forced to speak with a horse's arse dressed as a gentleman.

"We will not discuss their provenance. Families seldom disown their legitimate children, no matter what their infirmity."

"No, they simply ship them off to the navy." Belle clenched one hand around his ridiculous documents and the other around her skirts to keep from slapping one of them over her mouth.

"Indeed." His smile terrified her and broke her heart.

Did he know how his grandmother wept when she told Belle how they'd sent him away? He thought the other boys bastards. To correct him might cause suspicion. She'd need one of the boys' copy books soon, to keep up with the secrets and lies.

"I came here for peace and quiet, Mrs. Winter. I lead a disciplined, regimented life. I have since I was ten years old. It has kept me alive and more sane than I probably deserve." He indicated the two pages in her hand. "Those are my terms. Are we agreed?"

"And what of Christmas, my lord? Are they to have no part of the holiday?"

"I have not celebrated Christmas in twenty years, Mrs. Winters. Soldiers seldom have much chance on the battlefield."

"This is not a battlefield, my lord. This is your home. And theirs while they remain."

He crossed the room to where she sat. Putting one hand on the table and the other on the back of her chair, he leaned over her. The scent of soap, leather, and cloves made her want to move closer, but she did not dare.

"I have been pelted with snow-covered potatoes, knocked down the stairs, attacked by some unidentified one-eyed creature—"

"Attila. He's a cat."

"By what right does that thing call himself a cat? I have had my breakfast poisoned, my patience tried, and my sanity called into question. What would you call it, if not a battlefield? There will be no Christmas in this house." He blinked. Slowly removed his hands. And took a step back. With a brief nod he turned to go.

"We'll just see about that," Belle muttered.

"Do not go to war with me, madam. I have years of experience and tricks you cannot begin to imagine." He threw open the parlor door and stalked down the corridor, his boots delivering a ringing celebration of his temper.

"So do I, Colonel Miserington. So. Do. I."

Chapter Five

THE WOMAN GAVE NEW MEANING to the word relentless. Everywhere Ben turned, Mrs. Winters and her young henchmen shoved Christmas at him like a matchmaking mama with a spotty, more hair than wit, dowerless daughter. Tied by childish hands, bright red and green ribbons festooned table legs and marble columns. They bedecked every newel at the top and bottom of every flight of stairs. He'd forgotten how many staircases Pennyworth Hall held.

Hand-carved characters meant for some elaborate Nativity showed up on his bedside table, on the desk in his study, and at his place at the table. He had more camels than a Bedouin prince, along with several kings, one who bore a striking resemblance to Prinny. Each time he questioned the two ladies of the house they pled complete ignorance. He'd believe them if they didn't appear more nervous each time one of the carvings appeared. Then there was the singing.

His schedule allowed the boys only two hours outside of the nursery wing—one to be spent in his library and one to be spent out of doors. He'd made certain to schedule his rides on estate business and to visit his tenants for those same two hours. He'd deemed it the perfect arrangement when he'd ignored a blazing headache to pen the pages he'd delivered to Mrs. Winters over a week ago.

Banishment to the nursery wing of the third floor meant nothing to Mrs. Winters's evil denizens. He'd been serenaded at supper every night with Christmas carols shouted out windows. The peace of his sleep had been shattered by a screeching chorus of *I Saw Three Ships* fired down the back staircase accompanied by a thorough-bass of barking dogs, a bleating goat, and what sounded like a cat in its death throes. All before the tweenie had come in to light the morning fires. At this rate, he'd be a raving bedlamite by Twelfth Night.

He'd been prowling the entirety of Pennyworth Hall from its medieval parapets to its ballroom, newly refurbished in the Egyptian style. His mother's idea; he'd tear it out or have it walled up once he found the time. His memory of the first ten years of his life had begun to return. The secret his mother spoke of did not. No hint, no whisper. And even the things he remembered changed and blinked like one of the Trojan War peep show toys he and his brother had played with as children. He had played with Cyril? None of it made any sense at all.

One thing he did recall. The taste missing from Mrs. Fezziwig's potion—laudanum. He'd lived his first few weeks in the navy in agony until the insidious stuff finally released him. Jacob, the old tar charged with his training, had recognized it at once. The man had been the making of Ben. He'd saved his life, made him a decent sailor, watched over him, and in the end encouraged him to cash out and join the cavalry. When news of Jacob's death at Trafalgar reached Ben, he'd stayed drunk for a month. Quite a feat for a boy of eighteen. He'd won a horse at cards at some point during that month. Trafalgar was the name he'd given him, but Ben called him Jacob.

This morning, a carved horse, with an uncanny resemblance to the one currently eating his weight in carrots in the stables, had appeared at Ben's place at the breakfast table. He'd turned it over and over in his hands. And as the memory of the taste of laudanum popped into his head, he glanced up to find Mrs. Winters and his grandmother staring at the carving in a most peculiar fashion. He'd bid them both good morning, left the horse where it sat, and strolled out into the corridor.

"We have to do something. He cannot keep doing this."

Ben suspected he was not the *he* about whom Mrs. Winters spoke. Another mystery for the list. An hour later, he went in search of Mrs. Fezziwig and Cook. He wanted to know by whose authority they'd dosed a ten-year-old with enough opiate to render him senseless and to leave his memory a sieve.

He was halfway down the kitchen stairs when he heard the strains of *While Shepherds Watched* sung in an angelic boy soprano. The music stopped him in his tracks. He lowered himself onto a step and allowed its beauty to fill the stairwell around him. Another voice joined the first, this one distinctly female, rich, and full, but no less heavenly. He recognized this voice. When the singing stopped, a hearty round of boys' *Huzzahs!* stirred Ben from his reverie. He drew his pocket watch from his waistcoat and checked the time.

What were they doing below stairs at this time of day? He wanted to thunder down to the kitchens and scare the devil out of them. He'd established rules for a reason, dammit.

"Give me a turn, Robbie. Cook says we need to stir the pudding and scarper before his lordship catches us."

"You shall each have a good turn, Peter. I am certain his lordship would not want all of the time and work you boys and Cook have put into this year's Christmas pudding to go to waste." It was indeed Mrs. Winters he'd heard singing with one of the boys. For a governess, she cared little for rules.

"He doesn't care. He doesn't want us to have Christmas at all. He's cruel. Like the other one. Not like..."

"Hush, lad," Cook warned. "His lordship is nothing like that one. He has his reasons, though they have little to do with Christmas. Now, who wants to add the currants today?"

Cries of *Me!* and *Oh me, please!* rang out. The door slightly ajar, Ben leaned in to watch. Warm scents of baked bread, strawberry tarts, ginger biscuits, and Christmas pudding wafted into the stairwell. The boys' eyes shone with excitement. More currants landed in their mouths than in the large pudding tied up on the long wooden table. The servants looked on fondly and Cook's laughter boomed throughout the kitchens.

Mrs. Winters moved through the December afternoon's light spilling from the kitchen windows to hug one boy here, to brush another's hair from his eyes there. Her son, his name was Frederick, Ben remembered. The boy gazed up at her and smiled at something she said. She pulled him to her with one arm whilst steadying the little dwarf boy on a stool with the other.

They had no families, no home. Their past had not been kind. Mrs. Winters spoke of it with such sadness it provoked an irrational anger in him. The boys' future was uncertain at best. They had no reason to celebrate the birth of a child adored by all the world. Unwanted, they'd been exiled to a part of England known to kill strong men with its harshness, let alone frail children like these.

With a zealot's devotion, Ben had avoided joy and hope born of nothing but an age old promise. He saw no profit in it, nothing to gain but pain and the hurtful memories of a Christmas past. Mrs. Winters had made these boys terribly foolish. And Ben hadn't the strength to look away.

"Enough now, my dears." She wiped her hands on the pinafore she'd donned over a wine red wool dress. "It is a bit early according to his lordship's schedule."

Decidedly uncomplimentary mutterings about said schedule ensued.

"If you can do so quietly, I dare say you can make it to the stables without disturbing Lord Pennyworth. Caps and coats, boys. Caps and coats." Mrs. Winters moved out of Ben's sight. In a few moments, the door to the kitchen garden slammed and then silence.

"Be back in the nursery in an hour." elicited chuckles from the servants and Cook. Mrs. Winters stepped back where Ben could see her. "Thank you all for keeping our little secret."

Amidst the round of responses, bows and curtseys Ben heard something very like *my lady*. A mistake perhaps. His grandmother had made it clear her goddaughter was not of the nobility. Lady or not, she strode purposefully toward the door to the stairwell. Incomprehensibly, Ben loped up the stairs and waited at the door to the first floor.

"Mrs. Winters." He inclined his head. "What are you about this afternoon? Poisoning my supper, perhaps?"

She jumped slightly but recovered to glance back down the stairs before she met his gaze. "There is no amusement in trying to poison someone who is always on his guard." She started down the corridor. "Rumor has it you have Marley taste your food now."

"Nonsense. I try it on that thing you insist on calling a cat." He clasped his hands behind his back and slowed his steps to match hers.

"I must warn you I have it on the best authority Attila is immune to poison."

He liked her. She was bright, bold, completely uncensored, and devious to a fault when it came to keeping secrets.

"Where are you going, Mrs. Winters?"

"I am going to discuss the menus with Lady Pennyworth." She gave him a long, sideways glance. "You should join us."

"No, thank you. I have other matters to attend." He bowed and stepped toward his study.

"You should not have let her believe you dead for so long."

"I beg your pardon, but it is none of your affair." This

was not a subject he wished to discuss. The look on her face said she knew it.

"Three years, my lord. You let her believe you'd been taken from her for three years." She moved in front of him, so close her wine colored skirts brushed his boots. "How could you be so cruel?"

"I was taken from her twenty years ago. She did little to look for me then. I hardly thought she'd miss me."

"You left her alone at the mercy of your heartless brother and his vile mother."

"You didn't find Cyril handsome and gentlemanly? How sad for him." He'd managed to get through months and weeks without saying his brother's name aloud. Mrs. Winters made him say and do things he'd sworn never to do again.

"He's a monster. I know what he did to you. And what she did. Lady Pennyworth had nothing to do with any of it. You should have come home." She gripped his forearm and shook it.

"Why would I?" He snapped in spite of himself.

"What on earth do you mean?" Her incredulity surprised him.

"There was no one to cry over my grave. Why not stay dead?"

"Your grandmother cried. Every night from the moment they brought the news. I was here when the letter came. She cried and prayed for you every night."

He looked down at her hand on his arm. How did one tell a woman with this sort of strength of the weakness that made a man want to stay dead?

"My family never gave me a moment's indication

they gave a damn about me, Mrs. Winters, not in twenty years. Three Spanish grave robbers showed me more kindness than I ever received from my relations."

"Those men may have pulled you from that grave, but I have no doubt it was her prayers that brought you home safe and sound."

Ben laughed. "Prayers. I've little use for those, Mrs. Winters. You cannot spend nor eat them."

"I've little use for God myself, my lord. He has not been kind to those I love. But not even God is so foolish as to ignore your grandmother's prayers."

They stared at each other. A door slammed down the corridor. A maid, broom and bucket in hand, backed out of the library, took one look at them, and fled into a drawing room.

Ben shook his head. "Then God is far wiser than I have ever credited Him and, if it is true, He has my gratitude."

"And your grandmother?" Those blue-grey eyes demanded, gave no quarter or mercy.

He cleared his throat. "Has what little devotion I have left, meager as it is. Good afternoon, Mrs. Winters."

Belle snatched the folded missive off the salver and crumpled it into a ball. Marley looked from the salver to her closed hand and back. Lady P *harumpfed* and picked up a carved sheep from the tea table.

"Where did you find this one, Marley?" She placed it next to an equally well executed shepherd.

"In his lordship's dressing room, my lady."

"Did he see it?"

"No, my lady. Not this time."

Belle set about preparing her tea, the ball of paper still in her hand. "According to Thomas, he found the one left in his chair in the library. A king, I believe. A very good likeness of Wellington."

"Mrs. Winters?"

"Yes, Marley?"

"Are you going to read his lordship's message?"

Belle put down her teacup and uncrumpled the paper. The words scrawled across it stoked the temper she'd held for the last three days to a raging inferno. She stood up so abruptly she nearly upended the tea table. "He has forbidden them the library. Of all the clod-pated, addle-brained, churlish, selfish things to do."

"Marley, do stop her."

Belle had crossed the room and had her hand on the parlor door latch before she knew it. The butler gently pushed the door to and escorted Belle back to her chair across from the dowager. She gave him a fulminating glare but plopped into the chair and picked up her tea. "Two weeks of this nonsense, Godmama. Two weeks, and for the last three days, he has done nothing but send out edicts from his throne room, denied the boys every sort of amusement, and terrorized the servants."

"His throne room?" Lady P looked to Marley for clarification.

"The study, my lady. His lordship spends his days and much of his nights in his study." He turned to Belle. "He has not terrorized all of the servants, my lady."

"I am Mrs. Winters, Marley. Do try to remember. At least until my godmother tells us otherwise. And we all know not even the devil himself can terrorize you. The Four Horsemen of the Apocalypse might ride up the drive and you'd send for grooms to take their horses and ask Mrs. Fezziwig to make up their rooms."

"Only if his lordship ordered me to do so." The butler refilled her cup.

"I am certain your master is on intimate terms with the devil and the Four Horsemen." Belle turned to her godmother. "What are we to do? The carvings continue to appear. Lord Pennyworth shows no sign of leaving. According to the footmen and the maids, he is going through every piece of paper in the study. His treatment of the boys becomes more cruel and unreasonable every day."

"Indeed, Mrs. Winters. One wonders what occurred three days ago to inspire such behavior." Why couldn't her godmother have a stupid, oblivious butler like other ladies?

"I haven't the faintest idea." Belle nearly burned her throat raw gulping down her tea. Her conversation with the viscount in regards to his grandmother had obviously set him on this irritating path. In all her twenty-six years, she'd never learned to hold her tongue. It had landed her in a great deal of trouble, but never so much as now.

"It is not my place to ask," Marley began.

When had it ever stopped him?

"Do you ever intend to tell him, my lady?"

Belle and Marley waited for Lady Pennyworth to answer.

The dowager's expression grew wistful. She pushed the biscuits and tarts around on her plate. When she finally spoke, they had to strain to hear her.

"He will never forgive me. After all that was done to him, all he has suffered, how can I add even one thing more?"

"You've told me how his father and grandfather sent him away. I know what Cyril and his mother tried to do to him. They are all gone now. He cannot blame you for their perfidy."

"They sent him away to die, Belle, dear. And I did nothing to stop them. I did nothing to stop any of it until my husband and son were in their graves."

"But surely he will understand his brother—"

"They sent Ben away to die. He had the falling sickness and they sent him off to the navy to die."

Belle lowered her cup. She missed the table. Had Marley not been quick, the cup might well have shattered in spite of the thick carpets spread over the stone floors.

She'd been privy to so many of the Miserington family secrets. She thought she knew the worst of them. Perhaps she did, but she'd never expected this.

"He *had* the sickness? I don't understand. Is there a cure?" Her questions made no sense to her. Some part of her mind still tried to sort out who this viscount was and how this colored his treatment of the boys, especially Frederick.

"I do not know," Marley replied as he draped a shawl around Lady Pennyworth's shoulders. "His lordship told me he has not had an attack since he was sixteen. It simply stopped."

"Little wonder he does not want the children here," Belle mused. "The look on his face when he saw

Frederick that night. He looked as if he'd seen a ghost."

"And so he did, a ghost from a Christmas long past. He had such a spell before my husband's guests on Christmas Eve. He was your Frederick's age. They sent him away the next morning. Now you understand why he is so difficult, my dear." Lady Pennyworth patted her hand. "He will tire of country living soon enough. He will go back to London, and everything will return to the way it was."

Marley and Belle exchanged a look of dubious agreement. Whatever the butler intended to say next was cut off by a frantic knock at the parlor door.

"Mr. Marley. Mr. Marley, please come quick."

"Fan?" The dowager, Belle, and the butler rushed to the door.

Her ladyship's maid fanned herself and gulped a breath. "I walked by his lordship's study and I heard a terrible crash. One of the maids took him his supper. I heard a scream. And shouting." She covered her mouth with her hands.

"Oh for goodness sake, hush, girl. Marley, will you see to it?"

"What if he has attacked her?" Fan whispered, all the while darting haunted looks down the corridor. "Like before?"

Enough. Belle had had enough. She stormed down the corridor toward his lordship's private lair—the master's study. "I will put an end to this nonsense once and for all."

"Do take care, Belle, dear," the dowager called after her.

"He won't hurt her, my lady."
"It isn't her I'm worried for, Marley."

Chapter Six

'TWAS NO CHRISTMAS ANGEL who stormed into his study without so much as a knock on the door. Had Ben known, he'd have berated some poor unsuspecting maid for bringing his supper late long before now. Doing so had delivered a very different Mrs. Winters from the one he'd met hiding in his grandmother's parlor. This woman came clothed in elegant grey silk and furious beauty. She looked ready to murder him. And for one night with a woman capable of such passion and loyalty, Ben might well hand her the knife.

"Would you like to explain yourself, sirrah?" If a glare had the power to kill, he'd be laid out in the ballroom in his best clothes surrounded by flowers five minutes past. She took in the papers and ledgers strewn across desk, chairs, and carpets and turned up her nose.

"I am not accustomed to explaining myself, Mrs. Winters." He leaned back in the worn leather chair and crossed his boots on the expansive oak desk.

"You frightened poor Jane to death." She stalked across the room and planted her hands on the front of his desk. "And for what?"

"Who is Jane?" He loved to bait her. Somewhere in

the back of his mind, a bugle called retreat. He folded his hands across his stomach.

"The maid who just dropped your supper." She waved in the direction of his abandoned supper tray on the floor across the way. "And ran from this room as if the devil himself were after her. Are the people who live and work in this house so unimportant to you that you cannot remember a single name other than your own?"

"I remember your name, Mrs. Winters. Annabelle." Her little gasp sent a lance of heat up his spine. Waking up after a long sleep was painful. Doing so at the merest breath of this woman was dangerous as hell.

"I have not given you permission to address me so, Lord Pennyworth." She removed her hands from the desk and drew herself into a straight grey line.

"I have not given you permission to come marching into my private study over some timid little maid's tears." He sat up and drew a stack of blue bound ledger books in front of him. "I cannot abide timid maids. I am not an ogre."

"By whose definition?" she muttered.

"You and everyone in this house have been warned. I lead a strictly ordered life. I expect my rules to be obeyed and at the minimum, I expect my meals to be delivered on time. I cannot abide tardiness."

"You have made that perfectly clear, my lord." When she looked at him like this, he wanted to know what she saw. She asked questions with her eyes. She expected something from him, and he despised the idea he was not the man to deliver it.

"If you will excuse me, Mrs. Winters." He had to get

her out of this room.

"I will not, my lord." For the first time, he saw uncertainty in her face.

"What do you want, madam? As you can see, I am occupied." He opened one of the ledgers. Damned thing was upside down.

She reached across the desk and righted the ledger. "I can see that. I should never have discussed your grandmother with you. I am sincerely sorry I did, as it has set the entire house at sixes and sevens."

Too late to surrender and too tired to fight his way out. God save him from intelligent women. "It does not signify. I assure you I have forgotten our conversation completely."

She skewered him with one of those merciless governess looks. That monstrosity of a cat chose this moment to prowl from behind a bookcase, a large, dead rat in his jaws. He suddenly had a great deal of sympathy for the rat.

"Too brown, my lord. You have been like a bear with a sore paw these last three days. You have turned the boys into prisoners and the servants into foxes at the sound of a hound."

"A bear and a hound? Quite an accomplishment for one man in so short a time."

"Not at all, my lord. Both are beasts."

Ben's fists clenched. His muscles pulled as bowstrings on a new bow. He'd practiced every day of his life to shed his concern for the opinion of others. She had no right.

He pushed out of his chair.

She took a step back.

Something in his chest squeezed.

"You berated me for staying away, Mrs. Winters, but I am here now. I have devoted twenty years of my life, some of it not by choice, to defending king and country." He rounded the desk and came to stand in front of her. She did not move. "I slept and fought and bled in mud, in rain, in cold so you and my grandmother and my servants and those boys could sleep soundly in their beds. I came home for peace, quiet, and order. Is that too much to ask?"

Grey-blue mirrors, sheened by tears turned up to meet his. "No, my lord." She touched her fingers to his chest. He did not breathe. Hoisted on his own petard.

No. No. No.

Ben stepped back.

Her hand fell to her side.

He pulled his handkerchief from his pocket and offered it to her. "No need for all that, Mrs. Winters. I cannot abide maudlin sentimentality, as well you know."

Well, that set the spark to the tinder. She snatched the handkerchief from him, spun on her heel, and marched to the door.

Ben made a strategic move behind his desk and sat for good measure. Manners be damned.

She turned back. "Is there anything else you cannot abide, my lord?" If this woman was someone's poor relation, he'd eat the damned dead rat. She spoke like a duchess and moved like a courtesan. Fortunately, he'd sat down before she saw what her fury had wrought. Decorum dictated he stand as she left the room. Good manners didn't wash when accompanied by a cockstand, unless English decorum had changed a great deal in the twenty or so years he'd been away.

Ben turned his bleary gaze on the tatty accumulation of fur, claws, and nasty disposition she called a cat.

"If you cannot abide him, you will have to negotiate with Attila, my lord. He has been in residence here far longer than either of us."

"I do not negotiate with cats."

"It's just as well." She stalked back to his desk, picked up the blue ledgers, and stepped over the carnage of the dropped supper tray. "Attila doesn't negotiate."

The cat in question ripped the head off the dead rat and began to devour it. The former governess had the audacity to smile.

"And as you cannot abide timid maids, you will have to clean up in here and light the fires yourself."

The tempting aroma of roast beef, boiled potatoes, and venison stew wafted up from the plates smashed on the well-worn Persian carpet at his feet.

"And my supper, Mrs. Winters?"

She glanced at his ruined meal. "Is getting cold. Good night, my lord." She swept from his study in a shush of grey silk skirts and the scent of gardenias and lemons, punctuated by a none-too-subtle slam of the door.

Ben rested his head in his hands and groaned.

The cat made a gravelly feline comment.

"Stubble it, Attila, or I'll have that rat for my supper."

What in God's name had possessed him to say such things to her?

❖ ❖ ❖

What in God's name had possessed her to say such things to him?

Belle had not slept two minutes together without the memory of her confrontation with Lord Pennyworth creeping into her dreams. She'd called him a beast. She'd wounded him with her words, though he was far too stubborn and proud to admit it. Part of her understood his desire for peace and solitude. Part of her wept for the years he'd survived, the years that made him think solitude was the only peace he deserved.

The heat and leashed anger she'd discovered when she touched his chest did not bear contemplating. Well, it did, but not whilst she was going in search of four young boys who had eluded the harried footman charged with their keeping.

"It is rather cold outside, Mrs. Winters." Marley stood at the front door, her heavy green cape in his hands.

She shook her head and allowed him to help her into it. "Was I wool-gathering again?"

"Not if you did not want to be."

"Dear, Marley. What would we do without you?"

"Perish the thought," he said solemnly.

"Where are they, Marley?" She pulled on her gloves.

"They?" He opened the door and bowed.

"Marley. If you do not tell me, I shall put you to delivering his lordship's meal trays." She bit her lip to keep from laughing at his horrified expression, only a little feigned.

"You might try the stables. It is my understanding the space between the tack room and Trafalgar's stall is top of the trees for shooting marbles."

"The proximity to a battle-proved cavalry horse does not hurt."

"Indeed."

Belle shoved her hands into the pockets of her cape and followed the path from the front of Pennyworth Hall, along the sleeping, snow-blanketed lawns to the stables. The grooms and gardeners took turns keeping it clear. Cornwall was a cold, barren place in the winter. Unforgiving winds invaded from the sea and often filled the silence with howls and grumblings.

She and the boys had made their home here, and they loved it. Lord Pennyworth had traveled all over the world and had every reason to turn his back on Cornwall. Yet, he'd come home. Perhaps the secret his mother taunted him with gave him reason. There was more to it than that.

What was she doing? She'd spent most of the night thinking about Colonel Ben Miserington. His reasons for returning to Pennyworth were his own. She longed to know how he'd managed to survive in the navy with the same sickness her son so hated and feared. Had the shame associated with the falling sickness hardened him to the point he could never allow anyone to express even a moment's compassion for him? She didn't want that for Frederick.

She'd stolen her own child from a horrible place. She'd made herself and the boys disappear, denied her heritage and cut herself off—even from the brother and sisters who loved her. She'd done it for Frederick. She'd do it again. No one had done anything for Pennyworth's new master.

Stop it, Belle. His troubles are none of your affair. You have enough men in your life who need you.

"Good one, Martin. You'll never match that one, guv'." Peter's voice drifted out of the barely open stable door.

Belle slipped inside and waved at the young groom brushing down one of the carriage horses. She followed the sounds of good-natured ribbing and marbles clacking to the block of stalls at the back of Pennyworth's large, well-appointed stable. She rounded the corner and immediately ducked into an empty stall.

He was here.

She upended an empty feed bucket and stepped onto it to peek over the stall door.

On his knees, at the edge of a circle surrounded by Frederick, Peter, Martin, Robbie and the two youngest stable boys, Lord Rude and Arrogant studied the colorful glass orbs in play. His even white teeth bit one corner of his lip. Belle's stomach did a little funny dance.

What was he doing here? Playing marbles? With the boys?

Lord Pennyworth lined up his shot.

Thwack!

A bright blue marble shot out of the ring.

A round of groans and jeers ensued.

"She makes you give her a marble every time you swear?" Lord Pennyworth sat back to make room for someone else to shoot.

"Every time," Robbie said.

"She keeps them in an old portmanteau in her

room." This from Frederick.

Thwack!

"That's one of yours, your lordship." Martin patted Robbie on the back.

"How does he do that?" Lord Pennyworth asked.

"I think Mrs. Nelson helps him," Peter teased.

"I don't know which is worse—defeated by a blind boy or defeated by a goat." The viscount eyed Mrs. Nelson's flower-bedecked bonnet dubiously and shook Robbie's hand.

Robbie's grin melted Belle's heart. It did not, however, put her suspicions to rest. There had to be a reason the man was spending time with boys he'd exiled to one floor of the house.

"Do you know any good swear words, your lordship?"

Trust Peter to ask such a question.

"I do, but I won't be sharing them with you ruffians. I dare say you have an impressive list of your own if it takes a portmanteau to hold your penance. How long has she been collecting marbles from you?"

As she'd taught them, Robbie ignored the viscount's prying question, but then, to Belle's horror, the boy rattled off the list of words she'd informed them no gentleman said.

Lord Pennyworth let loose a long, low whistle. "Now that is a list. Where did you start this list?"

How dare he! He was using the boys to glean information about their pasts.

"Some of those are new. We learnt them from Lady P," Martin informed him.

Ben—when had she started to think of him as Ben?—choked with laughter. "Probably the same ones I learned from her." He suddenly looked startled, as if he'd remembered something long forgotten.

"Lady P says you fought at Waterloo. Did you?" Peter asked.

"I did."

"She says you are the bravest man she knows," Frederick added in quiet earnest.

"Her ladyship speaks a great deal of nonsense." He stood and strolled over to scratch his horse between the eyes.

"I like her," Robbie said. "She lets us ride her ponies. And she always has sweets."

"Lemon drops." Lord Pennyworth turned around.

Belle ducked down out of sight. She heard booted footsteps draw closer.

"In her pockets." He leaned over the stall door. "Good afternoon, Mrs. Winters. What is your mission today—spying or assassination?"

How dare he. "I might ask you the same thing. Ouch!" She rubbed her head. She'd hit something when she popped up to confront him.

Oh dear.

Lord Pennyworth stood clutching his nose. And swearing.

Chapter Seven

BELLE HANDED HIM THE HANDKERCHIEF she'd taken from him last night. She refrained from asking him if a little maudlin sentimentality might be in order. The two stable boys had scooped up their marbles and disappeared into another wing of Pennyworth's massive equine accommodations. The one farthest from their bleeding master, no doubt. Her four boys stood in awe-struck silence as Lord Pennyworth blistered the air with a muffled litany of ungentlemanly invective.

"That's torn it, guv'. You've lost all your marbles to her now." Not the most helpful thing Peter might have said.

To his credit, the viscount stopped swearing and gave Belle a brief bow before he leaned his head back and pinched the bridge of his nose. "Bweg pwadon, Mwissus Winters."

The boys broke into gales of laughter. Mrs. Nelson bleated in agreement.

Belle shushed them and retrieved the bucket from the empty stall. "Run out and fetch some snow for his lordship's nose. It will slow the bleeding."

They dashed out in a tumble of stumbling feet and

high-spirited shouts. Their return was equally noisy and produced enough snow to pelt an entire regiment with snowballs. She packed a small amount into a ball and stood on her toes to apply it to his nose over the handkerchief. He lowered his head. Enough to meet her gaze with those unreadable dark eyes.

"Hold it there for a moment, my lord. It should ease the pain as well."

"Will it?" He trapped her fingers between the snow and his hand.

She cleared her throat and drew her fingers away. Thank goodness Thomas chose that moment to hurry around the corner in search of his charges.

"M-my lord, I do apologize." The footman looked ready to faint dead away.

Lord Pennyworth soaked the handkerchief with a handful of snow and wiped the remaining blood from his face. "Not your fault, Thomas. Is it, boys?"

Four young faces fell. Much mumbling and dirt kicking ensued.

"You owe Thomas an apology." Belle was pleased to hear four heart-felt apologies.

"Gather your things. Then back to the house with you," Lord Pennyworth ordered.

They immediately collected their marbles and donned their caps. With a quick bow to the viscount and then to Belle, they each snatched a carrot from a nearby bin and paid homage to Trafalgar who devoured their tribute in short order. As they filed out behind Thomas, Frederick stopped to hand the viscount a faded velvet bag.

"Your marbles, my lord."

"Best give them to your mother. A gentleman always pays his debts." He gave Belle one of his rare smiles. "And his penance."

Frederick grinned and handed the bag to Belle before he loped off to join his friends.

"Shall we?" Lord Pennyworth offered her his arm, and they strolled past Trafalgar, who stuck his head over the stall in search of more offerings. "You've had enough, you old beggar." He still paused to scratch the bay's white muzzle.

He led Belle through the stables a different way than the one she'd traveled in search of the boys. They came out to the path along the ash grove which eventually meandered through the apple orchard before it reached the back terrace of the house.

"How is your nose?" she finally asked. She'd walked on the arm of a number of men. Never with one of such strength and such silence. The wind picked up. It was a cold December day. Her side next to his simmered with heat. The longer they walked, the more that heat seeped into the rest of her body.

"I will survive, Mrs. Winters. It will take more than a drawn cork to kill me."

"Especially a cork drawn by a woman."

He covered her gloved hand with his. "By a woman's hard head. Yes."

She laughed. "I suppose it would make for a most ignoble monument in the churchyard."

"Planning my funeral already, Mrs. Winters?" He looked down at her with that enigmatic expression she was learning to read as humor.

"I do believe in being prepared, my lord. Life is often full of unpleasant surprises."

"I should think a woman with such a fondness for Christmas would love surprises."

He stopped to watch a hawk fling itself into the sky from a tall ash tree just ahead of them. Once the bird soared out of sight, Lord Pennyworth still lifted his face, eyes closed, into the feeble Cornwall sun.

"I was surprised to hear you apologized to Jane, my lord."

He continued their journey beneath the snow draped trees. "Nothing happens in Pennyworth Hall without your knowledge, does it?"

"And you gave her a watch to pin to her pinafore." It pleased her to see him made uncomfortable by her compliments. She did not want to think why.

"It will ensure my meals arrive on time. A small price to pay." His mouth curved into a wicked grin. "It belonged to my mother. I found it when searching her rooms."

"Would it enrage her to know you gave it to a servant?"

"Undoubtedly." He stopped to remove a branch which had fallen across the path. "The maid, Jane, refused to take it unless I provided the other maids with watches. Strange girl." This time he did not have to offer his arm. Belle simply took it.

"And did you say you would?"

"Had no choice. She did not want the other maids to feel slighted."

"We are a family here, Lord Pennyworth. We look

out for each other. Does that surprise you?"

The snow crunched beneath their feet. The bare limbs of the apple trees clattered their resistance to the December wind's efforts to break them. Belle slid a little on an icy spot. She had only to tighten her grip on his arm to steady herself. A light snow began to fall.

"I should think, Mrs. Winters," he finally said, "you make a family wherever you go."

She made no reply. They'd wandered into dangerous territory. He knew nothing of her family nor of the boys' families. Their lives depended on his not knowing. Her suspicions about his joining the boys for a game of marbles returned. He'd asked them questions, any of which might lead to his discovering their secrets—her secrets.

"How did you come to be in the stables with the boys, my lord?"

"A better question might be, how did they come to be in there shooting marbles with my stable boys?" He used his boot to clear a ridge of snow and ice from the path.

"I have no idea." Two could play at this game.

"They have been sneaking out to the stables about this time every day for weeks now."

Belle sighed. "They are supposed to be translating Caesar's *Commentaries*."

"And are the assignments completed?"

"Every day. I don't understand."

"They are doing the assignments the night before. The number of candles burned in the nursery has increased."

She stopped so quickly he had to step back to avoid dragging her. "Are you always so..."

"Meticulous?" He brushed snowflakes from her hair. His hand brushed down her arm to cup her elbow through her cape. "Obsessive?" He tugged his glove off with his teeth. With great care for a man with such powerful hands, he brushed the snow from her face.

"Attentive to details," she said once she finally found her voice. Such a confusing, fascinating man. Confusing made him a man. Fascinating made him a peril.

"It has kept me alive. I don't like surprises."

"Everyone likes surprises." She needed to run, swiftly and with no care for grace or propriety.

"Have you ever awakened in a large grave filled with the bodies of your comrades?"

"Of course not."

"I don't like surprises." He cradled her hands between his and blew his warm breath over her gloves.

"I would not consider something so horrible a surprise, but a shock."

"Is there a difference?" He pulled her close, her hands trapped between their bodies.

"Certainly." She gazed into his eyes and had the sensation of waking up and falling asleep in a lightless room all at once. "A shock is unpleasant. A surprise is usually quite nice. Not that you would ever be remotely acquainted with nice."

Belle closed her eyes. Why had she said that?

A rich rumble of laughter breathed across her lips. His hands locked behind her back. "Tell me, Mrs. Winters." He touched his lips to hers. "Is this a surprise?"

He kissed a snowflake from her bottom lip. "Or a shock?"

His mouth brushed hers with a militant tenderness. Her fascination with his lips had cause now. Merciless, his kiss held winter at bay, held tomorrow and trouble and fear and all reason captive behind barricades of heat, passion, and a gentle persuasion she'd never seen in this man.

Belle ran her hands beneath his jacket and up the landscape of his embroidered waistcoat to savor the warmth of the bare skin above his crumpled neck cloth. He groaned at her touch. His right hand caressed and held the back of her head. Pins and braids fell with the snow. And then the true conquest began. He pulled her against the muscled wall of his chest and thighs. His tongue begged, demanded and invaded her mouth. She moaned at the bone-melting fever into which she fell and answered him with demands of her own.

"Belle." His voice a hoarse whisper, he traced her face with kisses—her closed eyes, her cheeks, her nose, her jaw, and the tender spot at the side of her neck. Like the hawk soaring from an ash tree into an endless sky, her heart flew. "My Annabelle."

His?

Oh no. What had she done?

Belle pushed against his chest.

He did not release her but rested his forehead, eyes closed, on hers. "I won't apologize. Not for a single breath of it."

"There is no need, my lord. I am equally to blame." She gulped a breath. Her body shook, and she prayed he would believe it was the cold. One by one, she tucked every sensation he'd stirred into the secret recesses of her mind. Every woman had a place she kept the few precious memories life had afforded her. Belle's place was now filled with the last few moments.

He opened his eyes. Then opened his hands, still fisted against her back. Belle stepped away. She shook out her cloak and patted her disheveled hair. She took a step down the path toward the house. Lord Pennyworth—Ben grabbed her arm.

"We should be getting back. They will wonder—"

"To hell with what they will wonder. What is it, *Mrs. Winters*? What secrets are you keeping from me? Who are you, Annabelle?"

For the first time, she could read every unspoken word in those stark features. She'd allowed herself to grow weary. Comfort and a place to let someone else be strong was a powerful lure. To not take what he offered broke her heart.

"I am a woman who knows the price of kisses, my lord. And it is a price I cannot afford." She walked toward the terrace she saw dimly through the snow and whatever else blurred her vision. "Stop questioning the boys," she said without turning around. "It is unfair and beneath you, Lord Pennyworth."

In that moment, so was she.

Ben sealed the last of the letters he'd written and hefted them in the palm of his hand. The boys had given him far more information than Annabelle Winters ever suspected. He'd spent last night in a torment of erotic dreams and had awakened countless times to a guilt he didn't understand. He wanted to help her. At least, that is what he told himself.

Something about those boys being banished by their families made him intent on making it right. Once more, she made him do things he'd never done before, and it niggled at the back of his mind that perhaps she was right to keep her secrets. Pity his abhorrence of secrets, especially those kept from him in his own house, forced him to do what he now contemplated. Like a fool, however, he'd give her one more chance.

He'd not seen her since he'd kissed her in the apple orchard in the snow. She'd taken her meals with the boys. Ben had eschewed his trays in the study to sit at the head of the ridiculously long dining table in the first floor dining room with his grandmother. The conversation had been sparse at best.

He'd sent for Mrs. Winters to join him in the library. The smaller, more intimate confines of his study provided too great a temptation. One word from her, one look, and his newly awakened desire would have him pinning her to the Jacobean paneled walls with no intention of ever letting her go.

He dropped the letters onto the library escritoire and paced to the windows that overlooked the terrace. He stared at the snow-covered landscape much as he had yesterday when she walked away. Their kiss had so shaken him he'd been unable to follow. Had he tried. he'd probably still be collapsed onto the icy path like some head-clubbed beast. Once he finally returned to the house, she had gone to ground in the nursery wing, and her last words to him became clear. As did the actions he must take.

"My lord?"

Ben turned to find Marley at the library doors. "Yes, Marley?"

"Mrs. Winters to see you, my lord."

She'd had the butler announce her? Not a good beginning at all. "Send her in, Marley."

As he walked to a pair of comfortable chairs before the fire, Ben heard a creak and rustling in the area of the globes and maps tables. Murderous damned cat ridded the house of vermin, but at the most inopportune times and places.

"You wished to see me, Lord Pennyworth?" Mrs. Winters, dressed in black today, stood just inside the library. Close enough to make a hasty retreat into the corridor. Apparently, he was the ogre today.

"Yes, Mrs. Winters." He indicated one of the fireside chairs. "Please, be seated."

"Please?" A faint smiled creased her lips. *Do not look at her lips.* "I am impressed." She perched on the edge of the seat, a dove poised for flight.

"Dining alone with Grandmama has forced me to dust off my manners, ragged though they may be." He sat down and stretched his legs before the fire, one booted foot over the other.

"I am certain she appreciates the effort." She folded her hands in her lap and looked at him, all prim and decidedly disinterested expectation. "I have a great deal to do, my lord. What is it you wish to discuss with me?"

"No polite conversation?" Irritation pricked at his skin like a bad nettle rash. "Straight to the point then. You lied to me, Mrs. Winters."

"I beg your pardon? When have I ever lied to you?"

"You let me believe those boys were someone's discarded by-blows." He watched the shock and then a tenacious anger take over her face.

"I never said a word either way. What you chose to believe is none of my affair. And those boys are none of yours."

"On the contrary, you have been hiding them away from society in my house for these last four years. How much are you being paid to keep their well-born families' secrets out of sight, Mrs. Winters?"

"How dare you." She shot to her feet.

"Sit down, Mrs. Winters, if you care for those boys at all." He thought she might refuse. Once she settled back into her chair, he continued. "Whether you are paid or not, you do them a great disservice. No one knows better than I the damage done by the knowledge your family sees you as something shameful, to be hidden away and forgotten."

Her face softened. "I understand your concern, my lord." She tapped a finger on the arm of her chair. "You had no right to pretend interest in them to pry into their lives."

"Their families should be made to care for them. It is unfair to ask you to sacrifice your life to accommodate some noble's vanity."

"It is no sacrifice, my lord. I love them. Their families do not. They are safe with me. Protected from society's scorn."

"And when they are grown, what then?"

"What do you mean?"

"Who will protect them then, Mrs. Winters? My life was hard, but I learned to deal with derision and insults early on. It has served me well. Isolating them in the far reaches of Cornwall with a family of women and well-trained servants will not help them. Had I spent more time with my family, I might have avoided trusting them enough to allow them the proximity to nearly murder me. There is an enlightening virtue in knowing exactly how people see you."

This time when she stood, he did not stop her. He'd watched her so often when she did not see. Annabelle Winters was a woman who needed to move to think. Pathetically, he loved to see her storm across the Persian carpet in clipped angry steps.

"You believe being forced to live with a family that despises their very existence is better than being with people who love and care for them?"

"It is better than allowing their families to get away with discarding them like rubbish. Their parents should take responsibility for them. Blood should mean something."

"Blood means nothing at all. Sometimes being exiled from one's family is the safest place for a child to be."

"The voice of experience, Mrs. Winters?"

She stopped in her journey from library table to bookcase and back. "What?"

"Why are you here, Annabelle? You are a beautiful young woman, widow or not. You could have your pick of men."

"I've had my pick, Lord Pennyworth. I did not choose

well, and I thank God every day Frederick no longer has to suffer for my choice."

"So you stay hidden away for your son's sake?" The library had been a mistake. She looked small and alone in the middle of so large a room. He wanted her to reveal something, anything, to help him understand.

"Just because your family cast you aside doesn't mean everyone's life is a Greek tragedy, my lord. I do what I do because I want to, not because I have no choice."

She was lying, and she was the one person from whom, for some mad reason, he wanted honesty.

"Why did your family cast you aside? Youthful indiscretion? Accident of birth? Who are you, Mrs. Winters?"

"You are talking nonsense. I won't listen to this." She marched toward the doors.

"A woman doesn't spend years of her life coddling another's cast-offs unless she's been cast aside herself."

Tell me, Belle.

Trust me.

I'll make them pay.

She stood with her back to him, hand on the door latch. "This conversation is at an end."

"They deserve the right to make their families accept them. You are allowed to be a coward. You have no right to make those boys cowards as well."

"Coward?" Had the room not been so quiet, he would not have heard her. She turned, eyes ablaze, and did not stop until he had no choice but to stand to meet her. "Coward?"

He raised his hands to place on her shoulders. She slapped them away. "I do not doubt your courage, Belle. Merely your faith in it, faith enough to put it to the test. For those boys. For yourself. For us."

"You may be the brave cavalry officer, but you have no right to choose what battles the rest of us must fight."

"You won't find your courage until you do fight. And neither will the boys. Let me help you." He brushed his fingers down her cheek. "I want to help you."

"Courage isn't always about facing death, my lord. Sometimes it is about facing life. Knowing you will rise to a day of misery, or abuse, or being ignored, or having tiny bits of yourself torn away by the cruel words of others." Her voice broke. "Knowing it because every single day is the same and has been as long as you can remember. Knowing it and getting out of bed anyway. A dull sort of courage in your eyes, perhaps, but courage nonetheless."

She choked back a sob. He opened his mouth to speak. No words came. The sight of her tears rendered him speechless. Her balled fists struck his chest. Once. Twice. He offered no defense. She ran from the room. The fire popped and hissed in the quiet. Ben stumbled back into his chair. A dull thud drew his attention to the rug beneath an old backgammon table. He picked up the carved figure he'd found on his bedside table this morning. Inexplicably, he'd brought it to the library with him. An exquisitely carved angel with a too familiar face stared back at him.

Someone coughed.

"You can come out now." Ben placed the angel on the table.

The boy with the yellow hair scooted out from under a maps table and brushed himself off.

"You're the asthmatic. I heard you wheezing."

"And you're the arse of a viscount." The boy climbed into the chair abandoned by Mrs. Winters and propped his feet on a horsehair ottoman. "You did a right job of it, guv'. Bolloxed it up good and proper."

"That's *Lord Arse* to you. Don't say bolloxed." Ben held his hand out for the marble the boy offered him.

"I could use the other word. Lady P says to use the most descriptive word when you swear."

"She did, did she?"

The boy nodded solemnly.

"What other word?"

The disheveled cherub with the golden curls let loose a particularly foul descriptive.

Ben repeated it and handed the marble back to him. "I did indeed." He traced the face of the carved angel. "Your work?"

For once, he'd managed to stun one of the little imps to silence. For a minute or two.

"Not mine Where'd you find it, guv'?"

"Doesn't matter. Off with you now. And no more eavesdropping."

He hopped out of the chair and strolled for the doors. *Peter.* The boy's name was Peter.

"Peter?"

"Yes, guv'?"

"Who is she?"

The boy shrugged. Ben knew the gesture well. In this boy's face, he saw his own after life had taught him just how little he mattered. "Who do you want her to be, guv'?"

Chapter Eight

FOUR DAYS BEFORE CHRISTMAS and not even the presence of the boys in their best clothes brought an ounce of cheer to the dinner table. The clink of china, crystal, and silverware gave pale imitation to the robust Christmas carols of scarcely a week past. Belle and Lady Pennyworth exchanged furtive glances of concern.

Thomas had informed her the boys did spend time in the stables every afternoon, but his lordship had not returned. In fact, few in the house had seen Lord Pennyworth since he'd summoned her to the library. When he ate, he sent for a tray from the kitchens. More often, he sent to the cellars for brandy. He divided his time between the study and the billiards room during the day. Most nights, he wandered the house, searching rooms seldom used anymore.

Belle came by this information honestly. She asked with no care as to what the servants made of her inquiries. She'd turned his accusations over and over in her mind. When the man barged into idiot territory, he did so with a flourish. When he was right, his words ran through her head like an old song sung over and over without mercy.

She watched Martin surreptitiously push his peas off his plate onto the floor. His chair teetered slightly as three dogs with less finicky tastes disposed of them with military efficiency.

Military.

Had the years of regimentation made Lord Pennyworth so hard and certain of himself? Would the boys suffer as he had, knowing their families saw them as damaged? Had she done them a disservice in sheltering them from the cruelty they would eventually face? She'd allowed her husband to send Frederick away *for his own good*, to save him from society's scorn. Four years later, when her husband died, she knew the truth. He'd sent their two-year-old son away to save himself the shame of having fathered an imperfect child. Had she saved Frederick and the others only to hide them away in a gentler manner than the one in which she'd found them?

Damn Ben Miserington. He'd planted seeds of doubt which had grown into an entire garden in a matter of days. Worse, he'd offered to help her. He said the word *us* as if it meant something.

"Belle, dear, did you hear that?"

She looked at her godmother and blinked. Everyone at the table appeared to be waiting for her to respond.

Boom!

Boom!

Belle nearly jumped out of her skin.

"What's that noise?"

"Gunfire. Peter, elbows off the table." Belle chased an errant potato around her plate with her fork. Difficult to do when one's hands shook as if palsied.

Boom!

"Should we send someone to put a stop to it?"

"He's the master of the house, Godmama. He may do as he pleases." An unladylike gulp of wine did not steady her hands, to say nothing of the pounding of her heart.

Boom!

Lady Pennyworth leaned across the table. "What if he's shot someone?" she whispered.

"There would be screaming."

"Belle, really. What if he's shot himself?"

"There would be swearing."

"Suicide is a sin," Robbie declared with a piety an archbishop would be hard-pressed to muster.

"Yes, dear, but it generally requires only one shot." Belle placed her serviette on the table and stood. "Even he cannot be so poor a marksman."

The boys scrambled out of their chairs.

"Thank you, gentlemen. Return to your seats and enjoy your pudding. It's treacle tarts this evening." She left the dowager to sort out the excited speculations of four young boys as to the source and reasons for the gunfire. She had an excellent idea as to both.

She climbed the stairs to the second floor. Marley met her on the landing.

"Are you certain about this, my lady?" The butler nearly ran to keep up with her. "He's in his cups and not to be trifled with, I fear."

"I would hope he isn't about this sober, Marley. He has upset his grandmother, excited the boys, and frightened the servants. I am not to be trifled with either."

"To be sure." He stopped in front of the billiards room doors. "It's quiet now. Perhaps it should be left until morning."

"Not if he's reloading. Let me pass, Marley." She reached around him for the door latch.

"I cannot think what reason he would have to do something this foolish." Marley slowly raised an inquiring eyebrow.

"Me. Now step aside and clear the corridors."

The room was dark save for the billiards table. A number of branches of candles had been placed around it. On the far end of the table, a collection of carved beasts, shepherds, kings, and angels had been set up as targets. As had several of the boys' elaborate Christmas ribbons. Atop the black and gold Italian marble mantlepiece, only the Christ-child, an angel, and the manger had been spared. Apparently some things even a drunk cavalry officer held sacred.

He might have saved himself the trouble. He hadn't hit a single thing. Belle allowed her eyes a moment to adjust to the darkness away from the billiards table. Oh dear. Sprawled in a chair that listed badly to one side, Lord Pennyworth downed the dregs of a glass of brandy and grinned at her.

"Come to dis-sharm me, Misshush Winters?" He hoisted himself out of the chair, gun still in hand, and bowed. Then sat to keep from falling on his face. Dressed in buckskins and boots, with his shirt open at the neck and only half tucked in, he looked utterly disreputable. And utterly desirable. Belle despaired of her sex ever having sense when it came to handsome, half-dressed men.

As he was behaving like a spoilt child, she'd treat him like one. Didn't make him less desirable, but it helped her to manhandle him to his feet without kissing him. Just.

"On your feet, Colonel." She grabbed his free hand and pulled him out of the chair. He swayed a bit and then stood still. "Give me the gun."

"Can't. Might have need of it. People keep hitting me."

"I have to agree with you there, my lord." She reached for the firearm. For a drunk, he proved quite agile. "Shot at, carved with sabers, koshed with a shovel, throat slit and buried alive, trapped in a burning house. You're either the hero of one of Mrs. Radcliffe's novels or the most irritating man alive."

"Irritating?" He did foxed and indignant rather well. And looked entirely too handsome doing so.

"Practically everyone who knows you has tried to kill you."

"Precshisly."

"Nonetheless, I will have the weapon now, Lord Pennyworth.

"Don't think ssho. You'll sshoot me."

"Nonsense. This is a new dress. I'd hate to get blood on it." She draped his arm around her shoulders and half-dragged him into the corridor.

"Very practical of you." He waved the gun at Marley and the two footmen who stood at the bottom of the staircase that led to the third floor. "You can go now. Misshush Winters is taking me to bed."

"Mrs. Winters is taking you to your chambers, you great looby. You will be sleeping alone."

"Sshame that."

They started up the stairs. Marley and the footmen followed at a safe distance. He slid more heavily onto her shoulders with each step. For a man who led a regimented life, when he lost control, he did it bang up to the mark, as the boys might say. Thank God they did not see their hero behaving in such a manner.

"You're quite pretty, you know." He took three tries to land the last step, all the while waving a possibly loaded pistol in her general direction.

"So I have been told, my lord." Belle pointed him toward his bedchamber. The quick turn disoriented him enough for her to wrest the pistol from him. He didn't appear to notice and continued to stagger down the corridor.

He stopped in the middle of the Persian carpet runner and looked back at her. "Sss'not good."

"On that we are in complete agreement, my lord." She handed the gun off to one of the footmen, who scurried down the staircase as if the hounds of hell were on his heels. Once she caught up to her cup-shot charge, he threw his arm back across her shoulders and leaned into her with a completely improbable grin.

"No. You don't undershtand."

"I seldom understand sot drunks, my lord. I find myself completely unwilling to try. In you go." Belle threw open his chamber door and somehow managed to maneuver him into a seated position on the edge of his bed. Two shoves against the linen-clad rock wall he called a chest and he lay flat on his back. For a moment.

"Sss'not good." He sat up and braced his hands on the lush blue counterpane. "You're the most intellishent woman I've ever met."

"I see." Belle pushed him back down. "Do stop trying to sit up." She'd put riotous children to bed with far less trouble. Of course, one flex of her hand against his shoulder told her Ben Miserington was no child.

"Pretty and intellishent sssnot good." He locked his dark eyes, clear now—haunted, hunting—on her face.

"If… " She swallowed. Hard. "If I were more intelligent, I would not have stormed into a room occupied by an armed drunk with an unreasonable vendetta against Christmas decorations."

"Sshnot. Good." He raised his hand and let his fingers brush a delicate adagio across her cheek.

"For whom?" Belle's heart ceased to beat. She really should breathe, but she'd forgotten how.

"Me. Very dangsherous for me." He sank back across the bed. His hand rested on top of hers.

Belle turned her hand and allowed his palm to rest in hers. Two long scars crossed the back his hand—saber cuts, perhaps. Even at rest, the muscles and sinews exuded strength and spoke of a life more at war than at peace. The viscount was not the only one in danger.

She slid his hand onto the bedclothes and set about removing his boots. It took two tries to heft his legs onto the bed. Once she had, she tugged the sides of the counterpane over him and tucked a pillow beneath his head. A stack of sealed letters stood propped against the lamp a servant had lit on the bedside table. Belle shoved them into her pocket to give to Marley to post. If Lord Pennyworth flailed about in his sleep, he'd have the entire house on fire.

On foolish impulse, she brushed his long, dark hair off his face. Without his neck cloth, the white line across his throat stood out against the golden tan of his skin. Belle touched her forefinger to it and flinched. The cut had been meant to kill. The pain must have been excruciating. To know it came at his brother's hand must have hurt far more. She knew the agony of betrayal at the hands of a loved one. And in lying to him and keeping his family's secrets, Belle betrayed him too.

Not that he loved her.

She certainly did not love him.

Oh dear. Time to go.

Belle took a step away from the bed.

"Are you a ghost?" His hand outstretched, Lord Pennyworth looked at her through half-closed eyes.

"All my life, my lord. Sometimes being a ghost is all the protection life affords." Unable to resist, she placed her hand in his.

He pulled her closer, kissed her hand, and drew it over his heart. "Ghosts here. I see them." He sat up, eyes open, but not awake. "I need to take you away. The ghosts. Not safe. I'll keep you safe."

Belle sat on the side of the bed and gently pushed him back onto the pillows. "I know you will. Sleep now. You need to sleep. I'll stay and keep watch." She slipped her hand inside the open neck of his shirt.

"Can't sleep. Ghosts come when I sleep. Keep them away from you. Not safe."

"I'm with you." She stretched out on the bed beside him and rested her head on his shoulder. "I am safe."

As she sank into the comfort of sleep, she knew of all the things she'd said to him this was the most true. And the most frightening.

Ben awoke to a throbbing headache and the smell of gunpowder. He opened his eyes and discovered the only thing worse than the summer sun reflected off a Spanish pampas was the December sun glinting off snow-covered lawns in Cornwall. Who the devil had thrown his drapes open?

He pushed his way out of bed and nearly tripped on the counterpane as it slid to the floor. The effort to retrieve it caused his stomach to lurch. As he threw the counterpane back atop the other bedclothes, an air of gardenias and lemons wafted from its folds. *Mrs. Winters? In his room? In his bed?* The previous evening's events rushed into his memory like the tide. Ben groaned. He'd made a complete cake of himself last night. Mrs. Winters had put him to bed, after she took his pistol away from him. Several selections from the boys' swear words list came to mind.

The servants had built up the fire, and the water in his wash basin was still warm. He splashed his face and debated pouring the entire pitcher over his head. He started toward his dressing room when he saw the panel beneath the Turner painting slightly ajar. Once he pushed it fully opened, he heard the echo of voices down the passageway.

His grandfather had been of the opinion servants,

children, and even wives should remain invisible until needed. The house was a maze of hidden passages and staircases. Ben retrieved a candle from the branch on the mantel, lit it, and stepped into the cold, dark space behind his chamber wall. He remembered this. Chasing through these secret tunnels at play with his brother. Again the idea of playing with Cyril was out of place. Perhaps his younger brother had not always hated him. No, that wasn't right.

He followed the voices and came to a staircase. It led to one of two parts of the house—the servants' quarters or the attics. Had Mrs. Winters gone up through the attics to avoid being seen leaving his room this morning? Why had she stayed? The voices grew louder and more distinct. He eased up the stairs and down a brief narrow corridor to the place he saw an open door and a great deal of light. He slid along the wall until he reached the door jamb. God help him if Mrs. Winters had a volume of Shakespeare with her.

"I didn't mean to frighten you." The voice was childish, petulant, and most definitely that of a grown man. *What the devil?*

"I know, dear. I wasn't expecting to see you in his lordship's room. Have you gone there before?" Mrs. Winters was in this attic room with a man he didn't know. Either Ben was going mad or his entire household was.

"I try to keep an eye on him, Mrs. Winters, but he's clever as a Covent Garden pickpocket. There isn't a lock as can keep him behind it, is there, lad?" What was Mrs. Fezziwig doing up here?

"I want to play with the boys. I want to see Grandmama. I want him to go away. He shot my shepherds."

"He'll go away soon, and then it will all be like it was. I promise." Did Mrs. Winters know something Ben didn't? He had no intention of going away. What was she up to and who was this man?

"Why do I have to hide? Frederick said he's not like the other one. I didn't do anything wrong. This is my house. Grandmama said."

The other one?

Grandmama said?

"They sent him away. I was bad, and they sent him away." The childish voice grew louder and more insistent. There was a crash, as if a chair had fallen backwards. "He hates me, just like the other one."

All of those broken pieces of the past began to come together. Ben leaned against the wall and closed his eyes, willing himself to remember.

"He's not like the other one. He came back. Why do I have to hide? I don't understand." Broken sobs. A crash of wood against stone walls.

He'd heard these sounds before as a child. There had been shouting. People running. Not today. Then. He'd run toward the noise, but his father had stopped him. Someone was there, just out of reach, calling his name.

Her voice, Belle's voice, cut through the noise and memories. "Tim, darling, please. Please stop. I'll make it right. I'll find a way to make it right."

Tim.

Ben stepped into the room. A wooden elephant lay

broken against a wall painted bright yellow. Shelf after shelf lined the chamber—full of an incredible array of beautifully carved figures. A tester bed with cheery red bedclothes stood against one wall. It all faded to nothing.

Belle, her face wreathed in shock and guilt, looked up from her seat in a battered rocking chair. In this moment, hers was not the face Ben wanted to see. The face he sought lifted, tearstained, from her lap.

His brow.

His nose.

His chin.

His hair.

His body, only a little less muscled.

The eyes were his too, as they'd been when he was a boy.

No ghost had invaded his chambers or disappeared around corners or up staircases. Here was the secret his mother took such pride in keeping from him.

The man at Belle's feet smiled at him—the innocent, simple smile of a child. "Good morning, Ben."

"My lord, I—"

Ben held up a hand to Mrs. Fezziwig and turned his gaze, made dim by fury, on the woman who'd stayed with him last night to keep the ghosts at bay.

"Mrs. Winters, why is my twin brother locked away in the attic like the family lunatic?"

Chapter Nine

HE'D FORGOTTEN. How could he have forgotten a brother with whom he'd shared everything? All the memories of playing in this house, in the fields and forests—he'd never been allowed near Cyril. It had been Tim, always Tim.

"Tim, dear, sit down. He won't hurt us. Your brother is simply upset." Mrs. Winters cajoled his twin into a chair before the fire in their grandmother's parlor.

"I am not upset, Mrs. Winters. I am furious." Ben folded his arms across his chest, fists tucked in to keep from hitting something. "I know why our mother lied and kept us apart. She was a pernicious bitch. She ordered the servants to dose me with laudanum to the point I forgot my own brother. What possible reason could you two women have for keeping her secrets?"

Tim looked anxiously from Mrs. Winters to Ben and back. "He's shouting again. Grandmama, why is he shouting? Did I do something wrong?"

Lady Pennyworth reached across to pat Tim's hand. "Of course not, dear. Your brother doesn't know how to speak without shouting. He's very glad to see you. Aren't you, Pennyworth?"

"Of course I am. I would have been glad to see him when I first arrived. I would have been glad to see him any time in the last twenty years. What sort of women toss their children aside or lock them away simply because they aren't perfect?" Without realizing it, he'd begun to pace—from the door to the windows, from the far fireplace to the piano.

What had been done to Ben had been heartless enough. Now the veil over his memory had lifted, he remembered Tim as he was then. It was easy to remember, for in Tim's mind, time passed only slowly. He'd always been a little different, more apt to stare off into space. The boy had been trapped in the man, which made his imprisonment all the more cruel.

"Is there any answer you ladies can give me for what was done to us, for what you continued to do even after I returned from the dead?"

"Stop shouting at my mother." Frederick stood in the parlor door, his hands curled into small fists. The rest of his warrior band—boys, dogs, and goat—crowded into the doorway behind him. Where was the damned cat?

"I don't like you." Tim dumped the chair backwards as he stood. "You're like the other one. He shouted at Grandmama and made her cry."

Ben looked to Mrs. Winters. "The other one?"

"Cyril. He came here and demanded to know where Tim was hidden. Lady Pennyworth wouldn't tell him."

Ben almost felt guilty at the reproving glare she sent him. Almost. The first woman he'd trusted, the first woman who'd held his interest and met him measure for measure, and she'd proved to be as perfidious as the rest.

He'd come here to feel nothing and now a thousand emotions roiled through him, threatening to break his control into pieces.

"Boys, I want you to take Tim upstairs with you." Mrs. Winters led Tim to the door and ushered them all into the corridor. "Marley, please ask Cook to send up something special for the boys. I'll come up and speak with you soon. Lord Pennyworth, Lady P, and I will sort this out, and everything will be fine as five-pence by morning."

After several protestations and a hushed conversation, the corridor grew quiet. Mrs. Winters stepped back into the parlor and closed the door behind her.

"Now. Lord Pennyworth." She stalked across the room toward him. "You want to know what sort of women toss their children aside when they aren't perfect?" She poked him in the chest. "I'll tell you what sort."

"Belle, dear," his grandmother pleaded. "You don't have to do this."

"The sort of women who do what was done to you, and your brother, and my son, and those other boys are the ones who have no choice. We give birth to our children, but they are not ours. They are the property of our husbands, and when our husbands die, they are the property of whatever *men* our husbands saw fit to name as guardians." Her eyes brimmed with tears. "They take our children from us and ship them off to some ungodly place out of their sight because their pride far outweighs their love for anything other than themselves."

"I don't understand." He did. Somewhere inside he did, but he wanted her to stop. He didn't want to know the rest. It hurt her to speak of it, and, God help him, he wanted to die rather than see her hurt.

"I stole my son, and Tim, and the other boys from the school at Kielder. Your grandmother hired a Bow Street runner the day your grandfather died. Women don't have power over our children, my lord. We are forced to steal back what our positions in life take from us and with enough money, you can find and steal back anything… or anyone."

His fierce Boadicea swayed on her feet. Ben placed his hands on her shoulders. She raised her fists to rest on his chest, too tired to beat him. He steered her toward the chair Tim had thrown over, righted it, and pushed her gently to sit. Grandmama gave her a handkerchief.

"When your grandfather died, he named the same man Tim's guardian as had been named as Frederick's guardian," Grandmama explained. "The Duke of Wharram."

"The Duke of Wharram?" Ben's memory stirred. "He's the man I attacked. He's the reason father sent me away."

"You attacked the Duke of Wharram?" Belle appeared inordinately pleased with him, a brief madness, no doubt.

"No, Ben. You didn't."

"He laughed at me." Ben tried to walk away. His grandmother clasped his hand. "I had a fit during my parents' Christmas Eve party. Father was horrified. Mother was furious. And the duke laughed at me. I remember he laughed at me. They told me—"

"They told you how you crept into his bed chamber and beat him with a riding crop. It wasn't you, Ben."

Ben sat on the arm of Grandmama's chair. "It was Tim. Tim beat him for laughing at me. And my mother's nasty footman, the one who always teased me?"

"Tim pushed him down the stairs." His grandmother was a frightening woman when she smiled just so.

"And peppered his eggs to the point he almost choked to death?" Ben's heart thumped as if he'd stood on top of the parapets about to fall.

"I wondered where the boys learned that trick." Belle had the oddest expression on her face. "Tim beat Wharram with a riding crop. How utterly perfect."

"Now, Belle," Grandmama warned.

"What is so amusing?" A lightness came over him. He wanted to be angry. He wanted to hurt someone. He wanted to be free of twenty years of torment.

"The Duke of Wharram is my father."

These women, these duplicitous, magnificent women... What?

"What did you say?" Men were simply shuttlecocks in a game of battledore where Belle and Grandmama were concerned. What other surprises did they hold in store for him?

'That may have been a bit much for him, Belle, dear. He has had quite a day. I must say he has handled it all admirably."

"The Duke of Wharram is what?" He'd found a twin brother he'd forgotten. Discovered he was not the violent monster his family painted him. And now the woman he might possibly... care for, if she'd ever stop lying to him, was the daughter of the Duke of Wharram. Which made her—

"The Duke of Wharram is my father. I'm not Mrs. Winters. I was born Lady Annabelle Chastleton. Two weeks after my fifteenth birthday, I became Lady St. Charles."

"Fifteen? Good God."

"God had little to do with it, my lord, and even less to do with my late husband."

"Chastleton? That means your brother is the Marquess of Winterbourne."

"The very same. Are you well, my lord?" Belle stood and touched her palm to his forehead. "You don't look well."

"I don't look well?" He stepped back, turned around, and then faced the two ladies once more. "It is a wonder I am not a raving lunatic." He threw his hands up. "Why didn't you tell me all of this the day I arrived? Do you have any idea what I have been going through since I was knocked off my horse in my own drive?"

"Your grandmother and I have not done well with the men in our lives." Belle settled back into her chair. "They have lied to us, taken our children, and caused us to do things no lady should have to do."

"Like steal children from a school." Ben studied their faces—one older and somehow less severe than he remembered, and one young, but with a terrible knowledge of what it was to be powerless. "Is a magistrate going to turn up at our door to arrest you, *my lady*?"

"Only if word of the children's whereabouts turns up in London. The master of the school was told to dispose of them. When they disappeared, he told the man who gave him the order he had done as commanded." Belle made it sound so simple.

Ben's stomach fell. He'd written letters. A number of letters seeking information about the boys and their governess. What had he done?

It suddenly struck him. "How was he to dispose of them?"

"I don't think it's necessary for you to know. Belle stole them away in the dead of night, and no one is the wiser."

Ben turned his inquiry toward the thief in question.

"My father is a very vindictive man, Lord Pennyworth. I told the boys they were to be sent to the navy." She rose, every inch the proud queen he'd named her. "They were to be sent to a particular brothel in London, one that caters to a class of men even more diabolical than my father."

His blood slowed in his veins. He stared at her in disbelief. In spite of his best efforts he imagined those boys, imagined his brother with the mind of a child, imprisoned in such a place. He had known evil men in his life. His brother, Cyril, came to mind. He had seen depravity first hand in the streets of San Sebastian. What sort of man sent children, one of them his own grandson, to a hell such as that to suffer a lingering, degrading destruction and death?

"My lord?" A soft hand touched his face. "Ben?"

Belle.

Here was a woman who defied such a man. She had risked her reputation, her freedom, and any possibility of a life in society with, perhaps, a decent man in the future, not for her son alone, but for three other boys. And for his brother, who had been failed by every one of his relations save one.

"Grandmama. Belle. I don't… " He shook his head. Words were so damned useless sometimes. "I can't… "

"Oh, hush, boy," Grandmama chided. "You'll have me weeping like some missish watering pot."

"Can't have that, can we?" He bent down and kissed her cheek.

A brief knock on the door and Marley stepped into the parlor. "A minor crisis, Mrs. Winters."

"That's Lady St. Charles, Marley," Ben corrected him.

"About time," the butler muttered.

"The crisis, Marley?"

"Ah, yes, my lady. I do beg your pardon. The boys have worked themselves into a state as to what is going on down here, where you will all go should Lord Pennyworth throw you into the hedgerows, and exactly how a certain wooden shepherd can be situated in the Nativity display as he has apparently been shot in the arm. There are some tears, and you know how Master Tim can take a turn."

"Oh dear. Let me go to them." Belle picked up her skirts and hurried into the corridor.

"I'd like to go." Ben caught up with her at the bottom of the stairs. "I want to apologize." *Damn!* Why was that such a difficult word to say? "I'd like to go with you, if I may."

❖ ❖ ❖

"You are master of the house, my lord," she teased. "You may do as you please."

"I am master of nothing." He'd never spoken so softly, so gently. "Not where you are concerned. Belle."

She stepped onto the first step and reached back for his hand. They walked in silence up to the nursery wing. As they drew close to the boys' parlor door, they heard sniffling and Tim's voice questioning over and over again as he always did when he had worked himself into a state. Ben stopped short of the door.

"Perhaps I should wait until morning. They might do better with you alone."

"You braved French cannons and murderous relations, but not five small boys?"

"Five?"

"Very well, four small boys and one large boy." She squeezed both of his hands. How difficult it must be for him. They were twins, together since before they were born. One had been forced to become a man too soon. One would always be a child. "You do understand, he will only ever be a boy in a man's body."

"He is my brother. And he is here, safe thanks to you and Grandmama. I don't care about the rest."

"Then you will be fine." She tugged him forward and pushed him into the parlor. And tried not to laugh at the apprehension on his face, matched only by that on the faces of the boys and Tim. Even Mrs. Nelson appeared nervous.

"Have you come to shout at us now?" Peter asked, ever ready to defend his friends.

"According to Grandmama, I don't know any other way to speak."

Tim edged his way in front of Peter. "Grandmama said you were glad to see me."

"And so I am, Tim. Very glad."

"Then why did you shout? Shouting isn't nice. I'm not supposed to shout."

Four little boys and a goat nodded in agreement. Poor Ben. Perhaps she should intervene.

He lowered himself into a chair by the fire. "I learned to shout in the navy, and in the cavalry, I was an officer. I had to shout to get my troops' attention." The boys and Tim moved a little closer. "I shouldn't have shouted at you. And I most definitely should not have shouted at Grandmama and Lady St. Charles. A gentleman does not shout at ladies."

Frederick's eyes widened. Robbie, Martin, and Peter looked to Belle. She smiled in reassurance.

Robbie tugged at Tim's shirt. "Lord Pennyworth fought at Waterloo."

"He did?" Tim dropped to the hearth rug and sat cross-legged. The other boys followed suit.

Ben glanced up at Belle, his expression half confused and half relieved. She settled onto the settee with the spaniel. The two hounds collapsed at her feet.

"I did. I rode that great lummox of a horse out in the stables. I like the carving you made of him very much, Tim."

"You didn't shoot that one."

"No, I didn't."

"Did people shoot at you at Waterloo?" Martin asked.

"They certainly did."

"It takes a great deal of courage to charge at someone who is shooting at you, doesn't it, Lord Pennyworth? To face death like that?" This question came from Frederick.

Ben's eyes met Belle's. "Courage isn't always about facing death. Sometimes it is about facing life. Which makes you lads some of the bravest men I know."

The conversation continued until the boys began to nod off, too tired to hold up their heads but unwilling to give up the chance to talk of battles and heroes like Wellington and Nelson. Belle took them off to bed whilst Ben followed Tim up to his attic room. He had tried to get Tim to take one of the large guest chambers or even one of the nursery bedchambers. Tim preferred his cozy haven under the eaves.

Once she'd tucked the boys in, Belle quietly climbed the stairs to Tim's room. She peeked in the door to find Tim under the bedclothes in his large tester bed with Ben seated on the side of it.

"I like my room." Tim pointed up at the large panes of glass fitted into his ceiling. "I can see the stars and the moon. It's never dark. I don't like the dark."

"You will never have to be in the dark again, Tim. I promise."

"We're brothers."

"That's right."

"I'm glad."

"So am I."

"I was mad, you know. I hurt people. They sent you away. Because of me." Tim picked at a loose thread on his counterpane. "I'm sorry."

"You were protecting me. All of these years, you were alone. All these years we missed. Brothers should be together. I'm the one who is sorry, Tim."

"But we will be together every day now, won't we, Ben?"

"Yes, we will. For the rest of our lives."

"That's fine then." Tim rearranged his pillow and pulled the covers over his shoulder. Good night, Ben."

Belle stepped back, her eyes blurred with tears.

"Good night, Tim." Ben's voice broke.

He stumbled out and fell against the faded silk wall-covering of the passageway. A great gasp wracked his body. He did not see her. She touched his arm, murmured his name. Slowly, he raised his head. She saw no tears there, only the agonized burn of great loss. His hands clenched against his thighs. Belle cupped his face with her hands and touched her lips to his. He pulled her to him with such force her feet left the floor.

He kissed her. Took the benediction she offered. Poured every hurt, every lost person and moment into her with each soul-sharing brush of his lips. When there was no breath left in her body, she broke away and took his hand. She led him through the dark passageways to his chamber.

The fire had been lit. A branch of candles stood on the mantle-piece, another on the tallboy across the room. The bed was turned down. A supper tray, a cold collation of meat and cheese and bread, sat on the table before the hearthside chair. He ignored it all, gathered her in his arms, and kissed her again. With tender touches, he turned her bones to nothing. His tongue caressed her lips with seductive flicks and strokes. She opened to him, let him inside. He groaned, and her body shook with the power of it.

She shoved his jacket off his shoulders, pulled it from him, and dropped it to the floor. Her fingers made quick work of his neck cloth and pulled his shirt from his buckskins. Their lips parted only long enough for him to pull it over his head. He tossed it away and snatched her back into his arms. Belle scarcely had time to breathe or think, only to wonder at the passion and tenderness she found in a man she'd thought to have none.

Her hands memorized every line, every sinew, and every scar of his chest and back. He trembled at her touch, and she gloried in it. Married four years to a man she thought she loved and never had she needed to caress and learn a body before the one beneath her fingertips right now.

"Belle," he gasped. Breathing hard, he rested his forehead against hers. When he opened his eyes, the desire she saw nearly struck her knees from under her. His hands moved to the buttons at the front of her gown, paused. She reached between them and started at the bottom. He loosed the ones at the top. Their hands met in the middle. He pushed the sides of the bodice apart and swept the sleeves down her arms.

His lips wandered across her face—to her nose, her cheeks, her chin, and down the column of her throat. He nipped the line of her collarbone, and a shiver careened down her body to shimmer between her legs. His fingers found the laces of her stays. All the while he plucked and tugged at them, his mouth worked at every inch of exposed skin until Belle wanted to scream.

The stays loosened, then fell away. He pushed her gown down her body and followed it to the floor. Kneeling, he pressed kisses to the underside of her breasts over the thin lawn of her chemise. Belle moaned, and he breathed softly across her stomach. He removed her shoes and kissed and licked the soft flesh of her knees. He nipped the inside of one thigh even as one hand gathered the hem of her chemise and raised it ever so slowly up, up, until she felt the hot blast of his breath on the place already made warm and damp by the mere promise of his touch.

Shock gave way to blinding pleasure when he kissed her there and then licked and flicked and tortured. Tremors shook her body to the point she thought she might break. He held her up, his tanned and scarred hands wrapped around her thighs to force her to the will of his wicked tongue.

She couldn't breathe.

It went on and on, an agony, a sort she never wanted to end.

He showed no mercy, gave no quarter. He demanded complete surrender.

In a blinding flash of pleasure and flame, Belle threw her head back and cried out his name.

Her body still quivered as wave after wave of heavenly sensations washed over her. He swept her chemise over her head, dropped it, and lifted her into his arms. The luxurious touch of the velvet counterpane caressed her back and her bare bottom as he placed her on the bed. She barely had the strength to turn her head to watch him shed the rest of his clothes.

He was magnificent. The lines of a well-muscled body used to days in the saddle meshed with battle scars that only made him more desirable, more the man she now knew she loved. Belle raised her arms. He prowled onto the bed on his hands and knees and covered her, so slowly she had time to savor each place their flesh met and melded.

She raised her knees to cradle his hips and pulsed against him. Her already tender flesh met the thick, hard length she craved. Ben bent his head and put his lips to her breast. He drew her nipple into his mouth, sucked and tugged and then bit down. She moaned and continued to raise her hips in an ageless demand for more.

Ben released her breast with a gasp. He looked into her eyes, held her there with his. Slowly, every vein, every part of him brushed her nether lips and the already throbbing place at the top her sex with a torture she thought might kill her. Until finally, at long last, he was completely inside her.

He let loose a long, dark moan and lowered his head to take her mouth with a merciless, all-consuming kiss. She pressed her feet into the mattress, lifting her body into his. It was all the request she needed to make. He withdrew and stroked back inside of her, once, twice, and then the rhythm of their matched desire took over.

She dug her fingers into his back as they came together over and over. He filled her, stretched her, loved her until there was no Ben, no Belle—only one body in search of the absolution only total surrender could give. She had the sensation of flying. Free. She had no memory of such a freedom, such pleasure, such ignorance of any other time or place as she did in Ben's arms.

"Belle," he panted. "Belle."

"I'm here," she gasped. "Oh, Ben. Oh!"

With a shout, he emptied himself into her. Still he thrust. His eyes burned into hers, demanded, and her body answered, back bowed, hands clutching the counterpane, she flew apart into a thousand pieces of fire and light.

She did not know how long they lay there until their breath slowed and he finally rolled to one side. He studied her with those dark eyes, not flat now, but aglow with a heat that both frightened and captured her.

"Belle, I... "

She touched her fingers to his lips. "We will talk about it tomorrow. Tonight, I only want you."

He kissed her fingers and bent his head into her caress. With a few tugs, he moved the bedclothes from beneath them and drew her into his arms. As the covers settled over them, she watched him. He lay on his side, one arm beneath her and the other across her waist. He said not a word, merely stared at her as if she might disappear until exhaustion and sleep closed his eyes. She snuggled into his embrace and pressed her palm over his heart.

Their clothes lay scattered across the rich blue Aubusson, a testament to their passion and to his complete loss of control. The letters she'd intended to give to Marley had fallen from her pocket. Fortunately, they fell closer to the bed than to the fire. Her languid-weighed eyes made out two of the addresses. A thought tried in vain to work its way into her head. Ben murmured her name and pulled her closer. Tomorrow. She'd think about it tomorrow. Tonight, they'd come a long journey. For the first time in her life, Belle wanted to let go of her fear and take a road she'd never traveled to a place where Ben Miserington might know the promise of Christmas and she might know what it meant to be free. Tonight she would love.

Chapter Ten

"WHERE ARE THEY, MARLEY?" Ben stood in the empty nursery parlor and marveled at the skill with which silence cut him more efficiently than any saber ever could. He'd asked a question to which he already had the answer. A desperate man will do so in the hope, however slight, of redemption. Christmas Eve might offer such to the entire world. It had never been a good day for Ben.

"They, my lord?" The butler retrieved a little red coat from the floor, folded it, and placed it on the settee before the window.

Martin will be cold without his coat.

Ben handed Marley the letters he'd found opened and scattered on his bedroom floor at dawn. The man took only moments to read the contents and to discover what Ben had done. No doubt, Belle had taken even less time to see his betrayal and to do the one thing she always did when a man proved himself unworthy of her.

Love proved far more painful than hate. Hate only pretended to keep a man warm. Love warmed a man to his very soul. And left a man cold beyond reason when it walked away.

"I don't know, my lord." Marley had to say the words twice for Ben to hear them.

"Marley."

He shoved the letters into Ben's hand. "She and the boys are quite accomplished when it comes to disappearing without a sound, Lord Pennyworth. They have had a great deal of practice." The butler gave a curt nod and walked out of the room.

"I wanted to find their families." Ben stepped into the doorway after him. "I wanted to force their families to recognize them and accept them." How stupidly noble it sounded when spoken out loud. "I wanted to know who she was."

Marley turned to face him. "Well, that certainly worked out well for you, my lord, didn't it? You were fortunate to survive your family's recognition."

"She should have talked to me. She should have trusted me. I thought... Never mind what I thought. I was obviously wrong." He allowed the pain to roll over him, through him. After the pain would come nothing. And Ben was prepared to deal with nothing. He'd done so all his life.

"Families are not always about blood, my lord. You cannot make someone do the right thing if the right thing is not in them, not even for the sake of blood. And if you'll forgive me for saying so, you always knew who she was. If you didn't, you're a damned fool. Go after her."

"That isn't what she wants."

"When has that ever stopped you, my lord?"

For the first time in fifteen years, Ben didn't know

what to do. He'd never feared storms at sea, or cannon fire, or even men intent on death and destruction. He'd never known acceptance, save with men with whom he'd gone into battle. Until he met a duke's daughter masquerading as a governess and four heroes masquerading as little boys.

He wandered the corridors in search of answers, in search of peace. He found only ghosts.

Frederick in the throes of a seizure at the top of the stairs.

Martin and Belle singing whilst the boys stirred the Christmas pudding.

An empty bed, an empty nursery, an empty house.

Twenty years a warrior, with no thought of home or family, no thought of anything past the next battle. Now, with no more battles to fight, the rest of his years stretched out before him, and Ben finally knew fear.

"Pennyworth."

He looked up to find himself standing in the door to his grandmother's parlor. One look at her face told him she knew. He walked to the windows that looked out over the lawns. A light snow was falling.

"Your grandfather was an arse to pack you off so young."

Ben looked over his shoulder at her.

"He was an arse about a great many things." She set about preparing a cup of tea.

"A trait I seem to have inherited."

"I should never have allowed him to send you away, Ebenezer." She held the cup out to him and smiled.

"My father had a hand in it." He walked back to the

hearth and took the cup of tea she offered. "And you may call me Miserington or Pennyworth or Ben. Not. Ebenezer."

"My son was an idiot."

"For naming me Ebenezer?"

"For nearly every breath he took after the age of twenty."

Ben smiled in spite of himself. "An arse for a grandfather and an idiot for father. Where does that leave me?"

She moved a plate piled high with ginger biscuits across the tea table. Her hand trembled. The Viscountess Pennyworth had remained fixed at a certain age in his mind. When had she grown old?

"It leaves you too stubborn and too clever to die." She folded her hands in her lap and leveled him with the gaze of his childhood memories. "There are worse things, my boy, than death. You and I know that better than anyone."

"I betrayed her, Grandmama. Unintentionally, but with a full measure of my own foolish arrogance. She doesn't trust me, and rightly so." He put the teacup down and tried to walk away. Her frail fingers touched the back of his hand.

"You have such a wealth of love to give, Ben. Will you hoard it away for fear it will be wasted?"

"My love isn't worth much. And hers would be wasted on me."

"Love is never wasted. Even if you never see a moment's profit in it. Even if it takes you thirty years to find it. Love isn't for the one who receives it, my dear boy.

It is for the one who gives it."

Ben watched the snow fall onto the endless blanket of white before his ancestral home. The house was quiet. Too damned quiet. He'd come here in search of peace and answers. Now he had both, and it wasn't enough. Not nearly enough.

"Marley!" he roared.

The door popped open and the butler fell into the room, followed closely by the footman Thomas, and Cook. Ben turned a suspicious eye on his grandmother. She raised an eyebrow in perfect imitation of Marley.

"Thomas, I need the best carriage and my horse readied at once."

"Yes, my lord." The footman sprinted out the door.

"Cook, I need a basket of food. The boys will be hungry. Be quick about it."

She smiled, nodded, and waddled away.

"Marley."

"Yes, my lord?"

"Stop looking so smug. Where is my brother?"

"Upstairs with Mrs. Fezziwig. He is quite upset."

"I know how he feels." Ben marched to the escritoire in the corner and scribbled a brief list onto a piece of paper. He slapped it into the butler's hand and headed for the door. "Take care of this. Tim can help. Tell him I asked for his help. We'll be back by nightfall."

"Of course, my lord." The man grinned. He actually grinned, the old devil.

"Pennyworth?"

Ben returned to his grandmother, squeezed her hands, and kissed her cheek. "Thank you, Grandmama.

For everything."

He and Marley marched down the gallery into the entrance hall. A footman handed him his gloves and greatcoat. Ben jerked on the gloves and threw on the coat as he stepped onto the front portico. In moments, the carriage rounded the corner. A groom led Trafalgar to the bottom of the steps. The maid, Jane, hurried to the back of the carriage and secured a large basket beneath the rumble.

"Thomas, why are there dogs and a goat in that carriage?"

"Begging your pardon, my lord, but as we don't know which way they went..."

"Brilliant, man." Ben swung onto Trafalgar's back. "If this works, I'm making you under-butler to Marley. God help you."

"Yes, my lord!" Thomas climbed onto the carriage box next to the coachman.

"My lord, about this list," Marley started, clutching the paper in his hand.

"What about it?" Ben turned Trafalgar toward the front gate.

"This last, sir. Have you actually asked her ladyship?"

"No. But when has that ever stopped me?"

Belle had never been so weary in her life. They'd caught the mail coach in the village and traveled as far as St. Germans. After a few hours wait in the public room of the Horse and Crown, the boys had stopped crying, which didn't make matters better, only worse. Crowded into the public coach to Boscastle now, they'd refused her offer of bread and cheese. They stared out the windows, hollow-eyed, much as they had the day before they arrived at Pennyworth Hall four years ago. They did not speak, which gave Belle entirely too much time to think.

She smiled bitterly at herself. What a fool she'd been. She'd only meant to slip from Ben's bed long enough to add some wood to the fire. An instinct born of a lifetime of dealing with duplicitous men had led her to pick up and open those letters. He'd written to the most devout gossips in London, women and men who knew everything about everyone. What he wrote indicated the correspondence had been going on for weeks. He'd not received any specific information, but the details he'd provided insured someone would recognize her or one of the boys eventually. She had no choice but to flee.

He'd changed. She'd seen it. Or so she thought. Perhaps she simply recognized a fellow creature—one whose trust was so badly broken it would never be whole again. He was a man who despised secrets, and he had good reason. Secrets had nearly destroyed him. Her secrets kept her safe. Last night, she'd forgotten what it was to keep something back. She'd allowed herself to be who she truly was, and the price proved almost more than she could bear.

In spite of everything, she loved Ben Miserington, and God help her, she feared she always would. She'd risked the boys' safety for the love of a man who had lost the ability to give himself completely. Belle knew what that was like—the loneliness, the endless nights, and empty days save for the moments she spent with her boys.

"Why do we have to go, Mama? It is Christmas Eve. I don't understand."

"I know, Frederick, but we have no choice. This is the only way I know to look after you and keep you safe. We will have Christmas when we arrive in Devon."

"Lord Pennyworth needs a bit of looking after. Who will look after him, my lady?" For a boy who had never known love, Peter Cratchitt had a great deal to give.

Peter was right. Ben needed someone to look after him. Belle had chosen the boys. It was not always an easy choice, but it was the only one she'd ever considered. Ben cared for her, but it wasn't enough. And she'd decided a long time ago never to settle for anything less than everything her heart desired. Which made for a lonely bed if one didn't count four boys and a mangy one-eyed cat in a basket.

"Mischief." Martin threw himself across the plump matron seated next to him and nearly fell out the window.

"Martin, no!" Belle grabbed the back of his trousers and pulled him into her lap. The matron frowned and muttered something nasty under her breath.

"It's Mischief. I hear him barking," Martin protested.

"Sweeting, we left the dogs and Mrs. Nelson at Pennyworth. We'll send for them as soon as we're settled." Parting the boys from their boon companions had been heart-wrenching. She'd had to lock the animals in a stall in the stables to keep them from following after them.

The coach slowed. The other passengers shifted in their seats, eyes wide and bags clutched tight. The boys, however, poked their heads out the windows to see what was the matter. The baying of two hounds, matched with the sharp yips of a spaniel drew close. The sound of horses coming up behind them sent their traveling companions into a panic.

"Highwaymen!" The matron clutched her reticule to her bosom, terrified.

"Highwaymen usually aren't accompanied by dogs," Belle observed. She pulled Frederick away from the window and took a look. "Or their personal carriage. What is he doing here?" She fell back into her seat and closed her eyes.

The coach came to a halt. The barking and baying turned deafening and was accompanied by scratching at the coach's door. A goat bleated.

"Mrs. Nelson," Robbie cried and tried to crawl out the window.

"Woman, have you no control over these unfortunates?" A severe-looking vicar blinked at Belle through spectacles knocked askew by Robbie's enthusiastic attempt to leave the coach. "Where is their poor father?"

"Right here." The coach door opened to reveal a dirty, disheveled viscount wearing a rakish grin and covered in snow. "A poor father indeed, but I intend to do better. And they aren't unfortunates." Ben looked at each of the boys in turn. "They're my sons."

"Lord Pennyworth, what are you doing?" Belle's question was drowned out by the sound of four noisy boys leaping from the coach into a swarm of ecstatic dogs and a bleating goat.

"Fetching you home." He grabbed her hands and attempted to pull her from the coach. "I was warned not to return without you."

"By whom?" Her ridiculous, fickle heart leapt at the strength in his hands and the banked heat in his eyes.

"The entire household." He climbed half into the coach, wrapped his arms around her and swept her out onto the road. "Tim is inconsolable. And so am I."

"What's this all about?" the coachman demanded from atop his box.

"Looks like a runaway wife to me." One of the passengers riding atop the coach offered.

"She had cause." Ben tightened his arms around her. "I am an idiot, Belle. Please forgive me."

"She needs a good thrashing," the old matron suggested. "The very idea. Leaving your husband and dragging his children away, crippled and all."

"My children are not crippled, madam. They are better men than I could ever hope to be." He pulled a thick brocade ribbon from his waistcoat pocket. A gold medallion hung from it. "They are strong and brave like their mother. She left because I forgot to give her a Christmas gift."

He draped the ribbon around her neck. "Wellington gave me this for bravery." He kissed her—a sweet, tender, lingering kiss. "For courage, my Annabelle, when mine failed me. I should have trusted you. Come back with me. I'll kill any man who tries to take these boys from us. Please, Belle. Don't leave me."

The boys watched her, their faces alive with excitement, merriment, and hope.

"You don't fight fair, Ben Miserington." She stood on her toes and kissed him hard.

When he finally pulled away, he laughed. "I fight to win."

She picked up the medal hanging from the ribbon. "This will not be easy, Ben. We both—"

He touched a gloved finger to her chin and tilted her head up to gaze into her eyes. "We will learn together, Belle. I don't know what the days ahead may bring. I only know I don't want to live a single one without the woman I love. Marry me."

"Wellington?" She turned the medal over in her hand.

"Don't swoon because it was touched by the great man, please. My fragile pride will perish altogether if you do." Never had he looked more handsome, more desirable, or more like her every secret wish come true.

"To hell with Wellington. It was awarded to the man I love. The bravest man I know if you're going to marry me and take on this rabble." This time when he kissed her, it was to the boys' hearty huzzah's and a chorus of barks and bleats.

"If I am the bravest man you know, you keep rather sad company, my lady." He swept her into his arms and marched back toward his carriage. "But I'll not let you go to seek out better. Come along, lads. Let's go home."

Epilogue

BELLE'S WEDDING TO BEN MISERINGTON was everything her first wedding was not. It was conducted in her godmother's parlor on Christmas Day. The house had been hung from top to bottom with an entire forest of ribbons, greenery, and mistletoe by the servants of the house—under the direction of Tim and his loyal assistant, Marley. In attendance were four boys in their very best clothes, three dogs who slept through the entire event, and a goat wearing a very fetching Christmas bonnet. Marley escorted Belle to her bridegroom's side. Tim stood up with his brother. Mrs. Fezziwig and Cook wept copious tears, as did all of the maids and some of the footmen.

The vicar declared it to be the most unusual wedding he'd ever officiated. But the mince pies served at the wedding breakfast were delicious. And he greatly admired the table as it was decorated with a beautifully carved Nativity featuring a large cast of characters, including a shepherd with a bad arm and Wellington, Prinny, and Lord Nelson as the three kings.

The untimely arrival of Belle's brother, Alexander Chastleton, Marquess of Winterbourne, caused quite a stir when he caught his former comrade-in-arms kissing Belle under the mistletoe in the library. He punched Belle's new husband in the nose. After which a hidden door in the paneling crashed open and he was set upon by four boys, some dogs, a goat, and a hellish creature the former Colonel Miserington, now Viscount Pennyworth, had the audacity to call a cat. All the while, a man who looked exactly like the viscount was held back by the Dowager Viscountess Pennyworth, who kept him from pounding Belle's dear brother into the carpet.

In the middle of the fray, Marley announced the arrival of Captain and Mrs. Christian Delacroix and the Earl and Countess of Leistonbury, who took one look at the scene and began to laugh. They continued to laugh even after Belle put two fingers in her mouth and produced a whistle a London dockside worker would be proud to call his own, which promptly ended the dustup on the library's newly cleaned Persian rug.

"Mary was worried you might be sitting here brooding through Christmas in this big house all alone," Captain Delacroix declared as Marley handed out glasses of champagne.

"I want to know how you ended up married to my sister after all of England thought you dead for three years." Winterbourne threw back one glass of champagne and snatched another from the tray. "How's the nose?"

"Fine. Your sister drew my cork not a fortnight ago. She hits harder than you do." Ben put his arm around Belle and bussed her cheek.

"After last Christmas, Leistonbury felt certain you would provide us with a calm, orderly holiday, Lord

Pennyworth. He said you were the most regimented officer to ever sit a horse." Belle liked Lord Leistonbury's wife, Elizabeth, the moment the lady picked Martin up and set him on Ben's desk to keep him out of the scuffle.

"I love you dearly, Leistonbury, but I am so glad you were wrong," Mary Delacroix declared.

"Mary thought you were a bit stuffy, Colonel. She thought your life needed a little chaos." Delacroix, his sleeping one-year-old daughter in his arms, gazed at his wife and winked.

"As long as it isn't delivered at the end of a shovel," Ben replied, to which everyone laughed.

"A toast." The Earl of Leistonbury lifted his glass, his arm around his wife. "To the bride and groom, may all of your Christmases be as magical as this one."

"We must gather like this every Christmas," Countess Leistonbury suggested.

"God help us, everyone," Winterbourne declared.

The room erupted into a merry cacophony of friends and family, a music designed to put ghosts and bad memories to rest.

"Shall we have such a Christmas every year, husband?" Belle wrapped her arms around Ben and tilted her face up for his kiss.

"I hope so, my love." He kissed her and rested his forehead on hers with a sigh. "I certainly hope so."

And they did.

About Louisa

Louisa Cornell read her first historical romance novel, Jane Austen's *Pride and Prejudice*, at the age of nine. This inspired her to spend the next three years writing the most horrible historical romance novel ever created. Fortunately, it has yet to see the light of day. As Louisa spent those three years living in a little English village in Suffolk (thanks to her father's Air Force career), it is no surprise she developed a lifelong love of all things British, especially British history and Regency-set romance novels. (And Earl Grey tea!)

During those same three years, Louisa's vocal talent was discovered. Her study of music began at the London College of Music and continued once she returned to the States. After four music degrees and a year of study at the Mozarteum in Salzburg, Austria, Louisa was fortunate enough to embark on a singing career in opera houses in Germany, Austria, and most of Eastern Europe. As a traveling diva, Louisa discovered playing a role costumed in lingerie in March can be a chilling experience, and in most Romanian B&B's hot water is strictly a matter of opinion.

Now retired from an active career in opera, Louisa

has returned to her first love— writing Regency-set historical romance. Her publishing debut, *A PERFECTLY DREADFUL CHRISTMAS* (from the anthology *Christmas Revels*,) won the 2015 Holt Medallion for Best Romance Novella.

Two time Golden Heart finalist, three time Daphne du Maurier winner, and three time Royal Ascot winner, Louisa lives in LA (Lower Alabama) with a Chihuahua so grouchy he has been banned from six veterinary clinics, several perfectly amiable small dogs, one large goofy dog named Duke, and a cat who terminates vermin with extreme prejudice.

You can learn more about Louisa and her future publication plans at : www.louisacornell.com and https://www.facebook.com/RegencyWriterLouisaCornell or follow her on Twitter @LouisaCornell.